Deborah Carr, *USA Today*-bestselling author of *The Poppy Field*, lives on the island of Jersey in the Channel Islands with her husband and three rescue dogs.

Her Mrs Boots series is inspired by another Jersey woman, Florence Boot, the woman behind the Boots (Walgreens Boots Alliance) empire. Her debut First World War romance, *Broken Faces*, was runner-up in the 2012 Good Housekeeping Novel Writing Competition and *Good Housekeeping* magazine described her as 'one to watch'.

Keep up to date with Deborah's books by subscribing to her newsletter: deborahcarr.org/newsletter.

www.deborahcarr.org

twitter.com/DebsCarr
facebook.com/DeborahCarrAuthor
instagram.com/ofbooksandbeaches
pinterest.com/deborahcarr
bookbub.com/profile/deborah-carr

## Also by Deborah Carr

**The Mrs Boots Series**

*Mrs Boots*

*Mrs Boots of Pelham Street*

*Mrs Boots Goes to War*

**Standalones**

*The Poppy Field*

*An Island at War*

*The Beekeeper's War*

# THE POPPY SISTERS

DEBORAH CARR

One More Chapter
a division of HarperCollins*Publishers* Ltd
1 London Bridge Street
London SE1 9GF
www.harpercollins.co.uk
HarperCollins*Publishers*
Macken House, 39/40 Mayor Street Upper,
Dublin 1, D01 C9W8, Ireland

This paperback edition 2023
1
First published in Great Britain in ebook format
by HarperCollins*Publishers* 2023
Copyright © Deborah Carr 2023
Deborah Carr asserts the moral right to be identified
as the author of this work

A catalogue record of this book is available from the British Library

ISBN: 978-0-00-853461-5

Printed and bound in the UK using 100% Renewable Electricity
by CPI Group (UK) Ltd

*To my father, Adrian Troy.*
*I remember hearing many stories from his time as an evacuee in the
Second World War, and although this book is set during the Great
War I believe that listening to those stories sparked off my fascination
about ordinary people and how they coped with the extraordinary in
times of war.*

# ONE

## Phoebe

OCTOBER 1916

### Stationary (Base) Hospital in Étaples, France

Phoebe heard a commotion coming from somewhere outside and, leaving her food, ran to see if she might be of any help. She stopped in her tracks when she saw the dishevelled group of soldiers, some carrying others.

'What's happened?' Doctor Parslow called as he joined her, closely followed by Doctor Marshall, Hetty and several orderlies and nurses.

'Trouble at the Bull Ring,' one of them replied, clearly distressed by his friend's head injury and what he had witnessed.

Phoebe had heard of the infamous training grounds in the sand dunes nearby. Soldiers she had treated claimed being at the front was preferable to being in the army base camp. Phoebe had thought it exaggeration but now she wasn't so sure.

'I want you two to help take this man through to admissions,' Doctor Parslow said, pointing to two orderlies.

'Nurse Robertson, kindly take this gentleman ...' he hesitated, staring past Phoebe as he thought, '... and the others who are uninjured for something to eat and drink.'

'Yes, Doctor Parslow.'

She waited for the injured men to be taken away and then motioned for those waiting behind. 'Please follow me this way.'

The weary-looking group followed her to the canteen. Phoebe got them each a cup of tea and something to eat then sat with them, curious to know what had happened.

'How did those men get hurt?' she asked.

There was a mumbling and several of the soldiers spoke at once, until one of them raised his hand and the others went quiet, allowing him to speak. 'Trouble broke out on Sunday.'

'That was three days ago, mate.'

The man, a sandy-haired private who Phoebe assumed could be no older than twenty-five, closed his eyes and shook his head. 'Was it? So much has happened, I've struggled to keep track of time.'

She supposed they were also probably suffering from shock.

'Sorry,' he said. 'I was telling you what happened, wasn't I?'

'It's fine. You don't have to if you'd rather not.'

'No, I want to. People should know.' He took a mouthful of his tea and swallowed. 'It's a terrible place and yesterday there was an altercation with one of the New Zealanders. He was arrested.'

Phoebe was horrified. 'Arrested? What for?'

'Apparently he tried to bypass the military police pickets at the bridges,' he explained, his eyes wide. 'They were there to stop access to Le Touquet.'

Another of the soldiers continued. 'It's common knowledge that men visiting the township walked across the mouth of the river when it was low tide. I think, though, that in this chap's case the tide had come in and so he used the bridge and was caught by one of the Red Caps.'

'Then he was locked in a cell.'

'It was disgusting,' one of the other soldiers added. 'Uncalled for but typical of that place.'

'What happened after that?' she prompted.

'A crowd amassed and we were all pretty irate by then. They did let him go but there was too much bad feeling by that time.'

'It's not the first terrible thing that has happened,' the other soldier interjected.

'Nah,' another chipped in. 'It was just what lit the flame and set us all off.'

The original private gave them both withering looks and they sat back and focused on their tea and the bowls of soup and bread in front of them. 'Then we heard shooting.'

Phoebe gasped, horrified.

'I heard that a corporal was killed,' the private said. 'I think a local woman was injured too but I heard she was going to be all right.'

'How, then, were the men you brought in hurt?'

The private and his companions exchanged glances, seemingly deciding whether or not to tell her. 'We marched through the town today and ...' he thought for a moment, '... there was a riot.'

'A riot?'

He nodded. 'It sounds bad but tension has been building since Sunday and it sort of happened.'

'Your friends were hurt in the rioting then, I imagine?'

He shook his head. 'No, they brought in cavalry and machine-gun squadrons, and we knew we had run out of any chance to keep going without a lot of us being killed. Everyone began to disperse and we brought those blokes here to be treated.'

'Nurse Richardson, we need dressing!' Matron called from the doorway, and Phoebe said a quick farewell to the soldiers and rushed back to her post.

Why hadn't she given herself more time to grieve, she wondered for the hundredth time since signing up for British Red Cross voluntary aid detachments training that summer. What made her think she was in the right state of mind to focus on anything, having just lost both her parents and her brother Charlie in a Zeppelin attack?

Phoebe felt her lack of steeliness keenly and hated that she wasn't as good at the job as she had imagined she would be. She should have taken time to consider that her sister Celia was better at being a nurse because she had been qualified for a few years already and it was all she'd ever wanted to do. Whereas Phoebe had been happy working as a kindergarten teacher until the devastation of her brother and parents' deaths had made her react drastically and change her job to train as a VAD. She had thought it might ease her sense of loss to help care for men worse off than herself near the front line. It hadn't.

She pushed aside thoughts of her family that she missed so deeply and hurried to deliver the fresh dressing to Matron, unable to take her eyes from the gruesome sight in front of her.

It had been six weeks since her arrival and despite her best efforts, Phoebe was finding it difficult not to regret her hasty decision to come to France. What had she been thinking? If only she could have followed Celia to Jersey where she was now working in that prisoner-of-war camp. Then she would at least have been able to speak to someone about their shared loss. She had misjudged what life here at the base hospital would entail and had even contemplated putting in for a transfer to a hospital back in London. She had never been a quitter though, and so she was going to do her best to stick to this work and try to get used to what was expected of her.

The traumatised soldier cried out in pain as Matron and the nurse in front of Phoebe attempted to redress his badly damaged ankle.

'Don't just stand there gawping, Nurse,' Matron snapped. 'Make yourself useful and help prepare the new patients for surgery.'

'Yes, Matron.' She glanced around her at the bustling ward where a new influx of patients had arrived earlier that morning and spotted a nurse frantically waving for her to join her at a patient's bedside. 'Coming.' She ran over, gritting her teeth when she saw the state of the young man lying on the bloodied bed, his eyes wide with fear as he turned his gaze towards her.

The nurse grabbed Phoebe's wrist and pulled her hand to the soldier's blood-soaked leg. 'Keep the pressure there while I fetch the doctor,' she instructed, running off without waiting for any reply.

Phoebe did as she was told and, recalling her training when they had explained that the patients would take their lead from the nursing staff, forced her expression into one of confidence and calm. If she didn't seem panicked by what was happening, she knew the patient would be less likely to become distressed by his condition.

'Will I die?' he asked, eyes wide.

'We're going to look after you,' she said, having no idea

whether or not he might survive but aware that she needed to calm him as soon as possible. 'The doctor will be here soon.'

'He will?'

She gave him a shaky smile. 'As soon as he can be.' She softened her voice. 'Lie back, if you can. You're in the best place you can be right now.'

'Nurse is correct,' Matron said, giving Phoebe a satisfied look as she stepped over to join them. 'You need to calm yourself and trust us to look after you.'

'Yes, Matron,' he mumbled, squeezing his eyes shut before collapsing back onto the bed, unconscious.

'What are you doing here, Nurse?' Matron asked, taking a fresh dressing and indicating for Phoebe to remove the bloodied one quickly, before replacing it with the new one.

'Waiting for the nurse to fetch one of the doctors, Matron. She told me to keep pressure on his leg wound.'

'Right, then you keep doing that.'

Phoebe willed the doctor to come to the bed. If he didn't hurry up and do something, the soldier was going to bleed to death.

---

'I heard you had a bad one today,' Hetty said as they lay on their beds that evening in the newly built hut they shared with other VADs. 'Poor chap didn't stand much of a chance, so I'm told.'

Phoebe shook her head miserably and gazed at her hands. She could still feel the stickiness from his wound on her palms, despite having washed her hands many times during the day. 'I've no idea how he survived as long as he did. One of the nurses told me that they thought a piece of shrapnel might have moved in his leg when he was lowered to the bed and pierced an artery.' She brushed away a tear. 'Do you ever think that we're fighting a losing battle here?'

She stared at her petite, pretty, blonde friend and was once again grateful for her presence. Phoebe had taken to her instantly. There was something about the girl that made Phoebe smile, and she thought it was probably to do with their new roommate's cheerful countenance.

'It does sometimes feel like we're trying to stop an incoming tide,' Hetty said thoughtfully, keeping her voice down so as not to disturb any of the other women resting on nearby beds. 'But we are making a difference, and even though not all of the men survive, we're helping others to, and that surely is worth staying here for.'

Phoebe contemplated her colleague's words. Hetty was right. Then again, she usually was about most things. 'Thanks, Hetty. I sometimes feel like I don't know enough to even be here.'

'You're not the only one.' Hetty sighed. 'I heard two of the doctors chatting the other day when I passed their hut, and they were saying how no training could have prepared them for what they're dealing with, day in and day out here. I think we're all just going to have to try to keep on doing our very best for as long as it takes.'

Phoebe agreed. 'I'm glad I'm here with you,' she admitted. 'You're always a comfort to me, do you know that?'

Hetty's face lit up. 'As you are to me, Phoebe. We'll be fine, mark my words. This is all still very new to us, don't forget. Anyway,' Hetty continued, 'I've heard a rumour that they're bringing in more nurses in the next day or so. We certainly need them.'

'What, VADs like us or trained nurses?' Phoebe hoped it would be more trained nurses.

'No idea, but whatever training they've had, they'll at least be more hands to help do the work that we've all been coping with these past few weeks. That can only be a good thing, don't you think?' Hetty asked.

'Definitely.' Phoebe pictured the field where their dormitory sheds were housed. 'Where do you think they'll sleep?'

Hetty's cheery smile faded. 'Ahh, I hadn't thought of that.'

'Right, I'm going to be late to my shift if I don't hurry off.'

'True, and Matron wants to speak to me.' Hetty grimaced.

'What do you think she's summonsed you about?'

'I've no idea.' Hetty sighed. 'But if we don't hurry, one of those things will be a reprimand about me being late because I was chatting with my colleague.' Hetty widened her eyes and they both moved swiftly towards the door.

---

Phoebe left Hetty outside Matron's office, giving her a reassuring smile. 'Good luck. I'll probably see you on one of the wards later.'

Before Phoebe could say anything further Matron called her name. 'Nurse Robertson.'

'Yes, Matron, I'm here.'

'Accompany this patient to the ward and clean him up, ready for the doctor's inspection.'

Phoebe acknowledged the orderly who was finishing unloading the patient out of the back of an ambulance. 'This way,' she said, seeing the mud-caked body of the soldier lying unconscious on the stretcher and wondering how she was supposed to clean him properly with just a sponge and a bowl of warm water.

The orderly followed her into the admittance area and lifted the patient onto a bed before returning to the ambulance.

Phoebe looked at the unconscious patient and wondered what had happened to him, as it wasn't clear where he had been injured. She pulled a screen around his bed and hurried to fill a bowl with water and grab some dressings, sponges and dry cloths. She then began unbuttoning his uniform and slowly peeling off his heavy, filthy clothes. It was disgusting work and soon her hands were caked in mud. It looked as if he had been wounded on his side as he wore a bloodied bandage just below his muscular torso, near his waist. There was another around his thigh.

Once she had finally stripped him of his mud-caked uniform, she covered the lower half of his body with a cloth and began cleaning him from the head downwards. It took a lot of water to shift all the muck from his face, torso, hands and arms, but she finally finished with his upper half. Taking a deep breath, she moved the towel and began cleaning around his private region, relieved that he was still unconscious and oblivious to what she was doing. Finishing as quickly as possible, she moved on to his legs, and before long she was satisfied that his entire body was as clean as she could possibly make it.

Phoebe saw one of the other VADs collecting the discarded uniforms and realised she hadn't emptied the soldier's belongings from his. She delved into his pockets and pulled out a few coins, a comb, a notepad, two pencils and a penknife, and laid them on top of the small table by his bed before dropping the uniform onto the floor.

Having washed her hands yet again, Phoebe asked another

VAD for help changing the bedding so that he was lying on clean, dry sheets, then manoeuvred the soldier into the pyjamas she had taken from the store cupboard at the back of the room. She was leaning forward to tie the pyjama bottoms when the soldier gasped and pushed her away.

'What the hell are you doing?'

Phoebe frowned. 'My duty, soldier. What do you think?'

She stared at him, surprised to see how dark his brown eyes were and noting mortification register on his face.

'You washed me?' he whispered. 'All of me?'

She realised that he was in shock. 'Yes, I did.'

He looked down at the flannel pyjama bottoms and grabbed both ties, wincing in pain at the sudden movement.

'Here,' she offered, 'let me.'

'No.' He sounded indignant at the thought. 'I can tie my own trousers, thank you, Nurse.'

When he cried out and fell back against the sheets, Phoebe took the opportunity of him being distracted and tied them herself. Covering him with a sheet to make him feel more comfortable, she took a folded blanket, shook it out and covered him with that too.

'I assure you I've seen it all before, if that's what you're worried about,' she said, hoping to reassure him.

'It is what I'm worried about,' he said, frowning at her before closing his eyes. 'You might have seen other men in my state, but this is my first time waking to find a strange woman has seen me naked.'

Phoebe stared into his chestnut-brown eyes and saw that they were flecked with gold and framed with long black lashes. What was wrong with her? This wasn't the first time she had washed a man's naked body and probably not the hundredth either, but this was the first time she felt embarrassed for a soldier to discover that she had done so.

'I understand,' she said, her voice gentle. 'I'm sorry. I didn't mean to shock you, um...' She went to find the document that had been delivered with him, to learn his name.

Suddenly a look of panic crossed his face. 'My notepad. I had a pad in my uniform. Where is it?'

She was surprised he wasn't as bothered about the level of his injuries as he seemed to be about a notepad, but she had enough experience as a VAD to know that many patients reacted in ways she wouldn't expect. Wanting to keep him calm, she reached out and picked up the pad, holding it in front of him. 'I put it here next to you. And two pencils, as well as everything else that was in your uniform.'

His shoulders relaxed and he took the pad from her, resting it against his chest with a sigh. 'Thank you, Nurse. I'm Captain Archie Bailey,' he said sheepishly in his northern accent. 'I'm sorry for making a fuss. I hope you'll excuse me this once.'

Her heart gave a tug. How could she not forgive him?

She took a steadying breath and clasped her hands together to try to at least look as if she was in control of the situation. 'I do, Captain Bailey. I will allow you to snap at me this one time only.' She reached for a second pillow and, taking him by the shoulders, urged him to sit forward, and plumped up the pillows so that he was sitting more comfortably and better supported.

'Now, if you'll wait quietly, the doctor will be in to see you shortly.'

'Nurse?'

'Yes?' She tried not to sound impatient and wasn't sure if it was because he had snapped at her, or due to her unexpected reaction to him when she'd looked into his eyes.

He reached out and took her hand in his, his touch making her flinch, but she didn't pull her hand away. 'I am grateful for what you've done for me,' he said, his voice weary. 'You don't know how much of a relief it is to be clean, wearing freshly laundered clothes and to be lying on a bed instead of making do in a muddy trench.'

He stared at her and for some reason she wasn't able to tear her eyes from his. After a few seconds she found her power of speech and slowly withdrew her hand from his. 'There's no need to be grateful, Captain,' she said. 'All I ask is that you mind your manners and allow me to do my work.'

She didn't miss the confusion in his eyes as she turned from him and wished she didn't feel the need to push him away. Her attraction to him was disconcerting, though, and she had no idea how to deal with it. Anyway, she thought as she took his filthy discarded clothes and dressings to the laundry to be boiled clean, she was here to look after these wounded soldiers, not seek a husband.

# TWO

## Celia

OCTOBER 1916

### Les Blanches Banques Prisoner-of-War Camp, Jersey

Celia watched her colleague handing a pile of disgusting-looking washing to an orderly and waited for Elsie to notice her. They weren't close but as two of the trained nurses working at the camp, they were often in each other's company.

'I'm not sure I'll ever get used to working here with that lot,' Elsie grumbled.

Celia wasn't surprised Elsie was upset. Ever since the women had been sent to work at the camp from the general hospital where they had worked briefly together the previous year, Elsie had shown her distaste for the German patients. 'When I trained as a nurse no one mentioned I would be forced to look after German soldiers.'

'I understand how you feel,' Celia admitted.

'I know you do,' Elsie said nodding. 'We've both lost family to these bastards.'

Celia cringed. 'We have, but we need to remember what we were told before being sent here, Elsie.'

13

'What? That they're wounded soldiers and need our care?'

'Yes, exactly that,' Celia snapped, unable to help herself. She couldn't imagine getting used to working in this place either, but both of them had little choice but to act professionally and do their level best in the circumstances. 'I would also rather be working in the General, but I'm here now. It's war time and we all have to do what we're told.'

'Don't you think it's beyond the pale?'

Celia sighed. 'Yes, if I'm honest with you, I do. But whether we like it or not, they are our patients and we are duty bound to care for them, so we can't allow ourselves to think of them simply as the enemy.'

Elsie folded her arms across her chest. 'I can't look at each one I have to nurse without wondering if he pulled the trigger that killed my brother.'

Celia rested a hand on Elsie's shoulder. 'I know. I have trouble not asking if they might have been flying on the Zeppelin that dropped the bomb that landed on my parents' home the night they and my brother died.'

Celia's grief still caught her off guard months later. As painful as it had been to lose her parents, she struggled most to come to terms with her brother Charlie being killed while he had been home on leave. Supposedly safe. The irony of him being in more danger while off duty haunted her.

Thank heavens her sister Phoebe had been staying with a friend that evening and survived, or she would have no one left.

Elsie frowned. 'Are you all right?'

Celia nodded. 'I will be. Look, Elsie,' she said, hoping to pacify the girl. 'We've all lost people we love and I'm sure these soldiers in the camp have as well.' Determined to avoid Elsie's scowl, Celia looked over towards the back of the sheds that made up the ward. 'We have a choice of constantly blaming these men for what happened to us, or treating them as the patients they are. I know which choice I've made,' she said, wondering if saying it enough would make her feelings come into line with what was expected of her. 'And if you don't want to get into trouble, I suggest you do the same.'

'Fine. If I have no choice, then I suppose I shall have to do as I'm told. But I won't like it.'

'I'm sure you won't,' Celia said, noticing the newest sister enter the ward. 'But I know your professionalism will make you do the best you can for them.' She lowered her voice. 'Sister O'Brien has just arrived, so we'd better get a move on.'

'Fine.'

'Girls, that's enough chat,' Sister O'Brien said, turning to them when she reached the ward door. 'Remember, you are expected to leave outside the ward any reservations or hostile feelings you may have towards the men.'

Celia and Elsie swapped confused glances. Had Sister overheard them chatting?'

'Do you hear me?'

'Yes, Sister,' they said in unison.

'Good. I expect the best from those working under me and will not stand for anything other than complete professionalism. Is that clear?'

'Yes, Sister.'

'Good. Now, follow me.'

Celia took a deep breath, unsure what to expect when she walked inside the ward. They were just men, she reminded herself as she closed the door behind them and waited for Sister to speak.

'*Guten tag*,' Sister began, speaking to the men.

Celia and Elsie swapped astonished glances. Celia wasn't

sure why she was so shocked to hear the new Sister speaking in German, as it made perfect sense that Matron would appoint someone who was fluent in their language to be in charge of the ward, but she couldn't help wondering where the woman had learnt to speak the language in the first place.

'At least she'll know what they're saying behind our backs,' whispered Elsie.

'That's true.' But Celia felt little comforted by the thought that Sister O'Brien had the sense to let the men know that they would be understood, by her at least.

She realised Sister O'Brien had finished speaking and was addressing her. 'Nurse Robertson?'

'Er, yes, Sister O'Brien?'

The sister narrowed her eyes briefly. 'I want you to go and change the dressing on Oberleutnant Hoffman over there. You will find that he speaks a little English, so you should be fine conversing with him.'

Celia nodded. 'Yes, Sister O'Brien.'

'Nurse Baker, you see to Hauptmann Meyer on the bed nearest the window. He also speaks a little English. Wachemeister Schmidt does not and so communication might be a little difficult at times. I shall see to him now, but any problems, come and fetch me if I'm not here, understand?'

'Yes, Sister O'Brien.'

Celia braced herself for what was to come, and before she had time to think further, stepped forward and made her way over to the oberleutnant's bedside. She wondered how Phoebe was getting on. It was still strange to think that her sister had left teaching children to train as a VAD, especially as Phoebe had always been a little squeamish and it was difficult to imagine her dealing with a bloodied patient.

She arrived at the patient's bedside. 'Good afternoon,

Oberleutnant, um…' She tried not to panic as she attempted to recall his name.

'It's Oberleutnant Hoffman,' the soldier said. 'Otto Hoffman.'

Celia knew she should look him in the eye when she spoke to him but couldn't quite bring herself to. *This man could have killed my family,* she thought, but quickly pushed the notion away. She couldn't think like that if she was to do her job properly.

'I, er, will need to check your dressing and change it,' she said, wishing she could force herself to speak louder, but her nervousness was threatening to take her voice from her completely.

'Thank you, Nurse,' he said, his voice clipped but not as harsh as she had imagined it would be.

Celia looked up then, straight into his eyes. They were almost aquamarine, she thought, stunned for a moment by a strong pull of attraction to the soldier as she stared into his vivid blue eyes. Repulsed by the strength of his appeal to her, Celia cleared her throat and looked away. What was she thinking? He was an enemy soldier.

Fetching a dressing from the small cupboard across from the doorway, Celia took a moment to gather herself.

'You're well, Nurse?' Sister asked at her shoulder.

Shocked to have her in such close proximity, Celia wondered how quietly the woman must have walked, not to have alerted her to her presence. 'Yes, Sister O'Brien.'

'Good. Then kindly do your duty.'

Clearly the new sister was intending to watch her nurses very carefully, she realised. Celia took hold of a kidney bowl, a fresh dressing, some cotton wool and saline solution, and returned to the patient.

Placing everything onto a small table near to his bed, she quickly read his notes. 'You have a bullet wound to your right calf and also on the right of your chest, is that correct?' She looked at his wounded leg hanging in a sling contraption above his bed. It looked very uncomfortable.

'It is, Nurse.'

She pulled back the sheet and blanket covering his torso and undid the buttons of his pyjama jacket, opening the right side. His chest was surprisingly smooth, unlike most of the British patients she had seen so far. He also had a slight tan, and she wondered where he might have been able to make the most of what little sun there had been in the past few months.

She untied the bandage around his broad chest and then carefully began to peel away the dressing a couple of inches below his collarbone. He clamped his teeth together and sucked in his breath, alerting her to the pain she was causing him.

'Sorry. I'll try to be gentler,' she said, aware that her hands were shaking. She glanced up, hoping Sister O'Brien hadn't noticed what she'd done. 'I'll attempt to soak the dressing off.'

'That would be kind, thank you.'

As she worked on the stubborn dressing, Celia couldn't help thinking how odd it was that the previous year she had arrived in Jersey, excited to be in the place where her family had brought her on summer holidays, then working in the General Hospital in St Helier as a newly qualified nurse. Now she was attending an enemy soldier, whether she liked it or not. It was disconcerting and a little surreal.

The dressing looked as if she had freed it enough to try and peel it back further from the dried blood that had glued it to the oberleutnant's wound. 'I hope this isn't too painful,' she said, surprised that she meant it.

What had happened to the woman who had decided all Germans were equally guilty for causing her parents' and brother's deaths? She glanced up into his face, taken aback to find him staring at her. She looked away, angry with herself for giving in to her curiosity.

The dressing finally came free, revealing the red wound that had been caused by an Allied bullet. Celia knew that only earlier that day she would have expected to be pleased to see such damage to an enemy soldier. Yet already, after working with this patient for just a few minutes, for the first time she was beginning to see them simply as men rather than the enemy.

'I'll give it a bit of a clean,' she said, looking up at him again and finding it a little awkward that her face was so close to his. Maybe it would have been better to start working on his calf first, before dealing with this wound?

She washed the wound slowly and carefully, aware that the biggest dread for the doctors and nursing staff was infection. She had no idea what had happened to this man or where he had been caught, and most of all she had no wish for her lack of attention to result in an infection of tetanus or gangrene.

'There,' she said, satisfied she had done a good job. 'I'll dress it now for you, and then we can look at doing the same with your calf.'

'Thank you.'

She glanced up at him. 'I'm only doing my duty, Oberleutnant.' She knew she should probably be a little friendlier and she would have been, if he was an Allied soldier. These men, though, needed to be kept at a distance.

# THREE

## Phoebe
___

'This stew is tastier than I imagined it might be,' Phoebe said before taking a mouthful of the warm concoction, which consisted mostly of boiled root vegetables. It was better than nothing and at least they had a slice of bread to go with it this evening. She smiled at Hetty as her friend placed her bowl on the table opposite her and sat down.

'How did it go today?' Phoebe asked. She wasn't sure if she was envious or not that Hetty had been asked to assist the theatre nurse during surgeries.

Hetty stifled a yawn. 'Not as bad as I had anticipated.'

'No?'

Hetty shook her head. 'No, thankfully.' She lowered her voice and waved for Phoebe to lean in closer to her. 'Sister Evans speaks fluent German.' She looked over her shoulder before adding, 'What do you think of that then?'

'Maybe she spent time in Germany before the war,' Phoebe said. 'I've heard that many people liked to travel there and some likely went as exchange students. But how do you know Sister Evans speaks German?' She mouthed the word 'German' so as not to alert anyone who might be able to overhear their conversation.

'One of the operations was on a German prisoner and I heard her speaking to him,' Hetty whispered. 'He was brought in sometime after dawn this morning and had tried to kill himself.' She shuddered. 'He must have been terrified about what might happen to him here.'

Phoebe hated to think that someone was frightened enough to cause themselves injury.

'Did you see him when he was conscious?'

Hetty nodded. 'He was only a boy,' she said sadly. 'He looked petrified, but we were in the theatre at that point, and I'm unsure whether he was more terrified by how heavily he was bleeding, the fact that he was about to be operated on by a British surgeon, or that he was in a British hospital at all.'

Phoebe thought of being in the boy's situation and could only imagine his fear. 'This war has a lot to answer for.'

'I agree.' Hetty indicated her food with her fork. 'I think we should eat this while it's warm. It's only going to become less tasty as it goes cold.'

She had a point. They sat in silence, eating the rest of their meal, and Phoebe tried to block out the chatter and noise of the other staff as they caught up with their friends. Her shoulders ached, as did her back and feet. She really should be used to this work now, she decided. Her mind drifted to the captain and to his handsome face and dark-brown eyes that reminded her of the deep pools she used to stare into in the shady pond in the wood near her childhood home.

'Phoebe.'

She realised she was staring into her half-empty bowl and that Hetty was addressing her. 'What is it?'

'You were miles away,' Hetty said, a suspicious tone to her

voice. 'Has something happened that you want to tell me about?'

'Sorry? Um, no.' She shook her head. 'It's nothing,' she fibbed, not wanting to share her thoughts about Captain Bailey. 'I'm just a little tired, nothing more.'

'I'm not certain I believe you,' Hetty said, staring at her thoughtfully for a few seconds. 'But I know what you mean about being tired. I don't know what's more painful at the moment: my head, my feet, or my poor lower back.'

'I feel that way too,' Phoebe agreed. 'I think we should finish up here and go to bed as soon as we can this evening. Who knows what we'll have to face tomorrow?'

'I'd rather not think about that right now,' Hetty said, focusing on her food once again. 'I feel sorry for the new VADs. I saw some arriving earlier and they looked terrified. I'm not sure they expected to come somewhere so busy.'

Phoebe recalled how she had felt arriving almost two months ago at this hectic place. 'I know that I felt like turning around and going straight home five minutes after my arrival.' Her mind drifted back to the captain. It was his first day at the hospital too, although he was seeing things from the opposite side to her and Hetty. She hoped he was settling in. But what was she doing, thinking about this man all the time? She shook her head to dispel all thoughts of him and ate the last mouthful of the stew.

'Do you mind if I make my way back to the dorm before you?' she said, pretending to yawn.

'Don't be silly.' Hetty smiled. 'I'll see you there soon.'

Phoebe left the canteen and realised it was raining slightly. She folded her arms and concentrated on not slipping on the wet boardwalk. A loud crack of thunder made her jump. *That was close*, she thought, relieved she wasn't as terrified of thunderstorms as she had been as a little girl. That was one outcome of this war, at least; it was now more unnerving hearing distant canon fire than seeing forks of lightning shoot through the sky.

The rain fell harder and she realised she was outside Ward III. She decided to escape the worst of the rain in the ward and wait for it to subside. She closed the door just as thunder rumbled loudly and a flash of lightning lit up the miserable October sky.

'Nasty night,' one of the VADs said as she hurried past, carrying a blood-soaked dressing.

Phoebe wondered if she should at least offer to help while she was in the ward. She turned to see where the nurse was coming from, realising for the first time that she was in the same ward where the captain was situated. Her stomach twisted in anxious dread. *Please don't let him be the one who was bleeding so heavily.*

She automatically looked in his direction and saw he was watching her as he rested on his pillow, his head on his arm. He smiled and Phoebe instinctively smiled back.

'What are you doing getting in the way here, Nurse?' Sister Taylor asked, scowling. 'You're not on duty, are you?'

Phoebe shook her head. 'No, Sister.' She could sense the captain's gaze on her and tried to ignore it, not wishing to antagonise the sister further. 'I'm sorry, I stepped inside from the rain. It's torrential out there.'

'You're dripping on my clean floor, Nurse. I suggest you get a move on and find your way to wherever you're supposed to be, and leave what little room we have left in here to those attempting to perform their duties.'

'Yes, Sister. Sorry, Sister.'

Without a moment's hesitation she turned and left the

ward, wincing as the driving rain hit her and soaked her almost instantly. She had no option but to run and hope she didn't slip over.

'Hey! Watch where you're going.'

Phoebe leapt out of the way of the oncoming doctor, slipping on the muddied wood.

Doctor Marshall grabbed her arm. 'Steady on.' He almost slipped over himself and Phoebe, mortified to have caused such a scene, grimaced.

'I'm sorry, Doctor, I was…'

'Trying to get out of the rain. Yes, I can see that.' His eyes went to his hand on her arm and he let go. 'On your way, Nurse. No harm done.'

'Thank you, Doctor Marshall,' Phoebe said before doing as he had instructed and hurrying on again.

She ran into the dormitory and was about to slam the door behind her when someone stopped it from closing. Phoebe smiled when she saw it was Hetty. 'I didn't see you there.'

'I think that much is obvious.' Hetty wrinkled her nose, holding out her dripping hands. 'I decided to follow you after all,' she explained.

'I think we need to get into some dry clothes before we catch our death.'

'Good idea.'

Phoebe led the way to the other end of the room where their beds lay and grabbed her towel, hurriedly drying her wavy auburn hair. 'I hope we don't have an entire winter of this weather to look forward to,' she grumbled, walking over to stand near the small iron burner giving out a meagre heat that you needed to be standing within a few feet of to feel any benefit.

'I saw Doctor Marshall say something to you,' Hetty whispered. 'What happened?'

Phoebe told her, her cheeks reddening, feeling embarrassed about her clumsiness.

'That's a shame, I thought it was something a little more friendly than that.'

'He's an important man. Why on earth would he look at a volunteer? Let alone during a storm when he's in a rush to get somewhere.'

'I was only teasing.' Hetty shook her head. 'You shouldn't take things so seriously.'

Phoebe knew Hetty was right and opened her mouth to speak, but all thoughts of what she intended to say vanished as the front door burst open and a sodden woman stepped inside. She didn't recognise her and presumed she must be one of the new intake of VADs.

'Grab a towel and come and dry yourself off a bit over here where it's warmest,' Phoebe said, seeing rivulets of water cascading from the woman's coat onto the wooden floor. 'When we're changed, I'll make us all a cuppa.'

'Thank you,' the girl said, going to one of the bedside cupboards and taking out a towel. 'My name is Aggie. I'm new here.'

———

Twenty minutes later Phoebe sat on her bed facing Aggie and Hetty as they sipped their cups of tea on Hetty's bed.

'It's good to be dry again,' Phoebe said, running her hands through her damp hair. 'I hate this weather. I don't mind when it's windy or raining, but both together is too much.'

'I'm used to wild weather, as I'm from near Exmoor,' Hetty

said before taking a sip of her drink. 'For some reason, though, I assumed that the weather here would be much nicer. Sunny, even.'

'You did?' Aggie asked.

'Well, we're in France, after all, aren't we?' Hetty sighed. 'This is northern France, though, and from what I've seen, it's not too different to back home in Britain. More's the pity.'

'It's a shame.' Aggie sighed. 'Mind you, we'll probably be happy for it not to be too hot when summer does eventually get here.'

'We'll have to wait and see if that is the case.' Phoebe smiled at their new friend. 'Tell us how your first day went, Aggie.'

The girl crossed one slim leg over the other. 'It was busy.' She laughed. 'I think the thing that surprised me the most was the sheer number of different injuries that can be caused by shrapnel,' she said, her voice quieter as she stared into space. 'I've no idea how some of them survive what happens to them.'

Phoebe was still astounded by the same thought.

'How were your days?' Aggie asked them.

Phoebe listened as Hetty described her day in vague terms. Usually she went into detail about a soldier, his state and what she had done for him, but this time she kept details to a minimum, and Phoebe couldn't help being suspicious as to why that might be.

'And how about you, Phoebe?' Hetty asked, sipping her drink again.

Phoebe told her about the men she had helped with and how tired she felt, but didn't mention the captain. Her eyes shifted from Aggie to Hetty. Maybe Hetty, too, had a patient that she had connected with more than usual?

At least the patients they attended to were Allied soldiers. She thought of Celia in Jersey nursing German prisoners of war, and just for a moment wondered if these kinds of connections were happening there, too. But no, her sister could never fall for a German soldier. She wasn't that disloyal.

# FOUR

## Celia

NOVEMBER 1916

Celia was busily scrubbing floorboards and grumbling to herself when one of the patients screamed something in German. Not realising that she was the only medical member of staff in the hut, she took no notice for a few seconds, expecting the sister to deal with it.

'Nurse?' She heard panic in the man's voice and looked up. For a moment Celia couldn't work out what was happening. Then she realised that Hauptmann Meyer, in the bed next to Oberleutnant Hoffman, was in a terrible state. He had only arrived at the camp a few days before and was struggling to come to terms with the loss of one of his legs. She looked around frantically as she rose to her feet. Where the hell had the other nurses gone?

She hurried over to the patient. 'It's all right, Hauptmann Meyer, try to calm down.' His eyes were wide with terror and he was grabbing hold of the amputated end of his leg, screaming something at her. 'Please try to relax,' she said, wishing she had learnt more German.

'He is asking where his leg is,' the oberleutnant said,

throwing back his sheets and trying to climb out of his bed, then wincing in pain when he moved too quickly.

'You mustn't get up,' she shouted, flinging her arm in his direction to try and stop him doing anything that would damage his fragile wounds. 'Please, you must stay in bed.' In the moment that she was distracted, the panic-stricken hauptmann's hand connected with the side of her face, almost knocking Celia off her feet.

Oberleutnant Hoffman ignored her orders and got out of bed. 'You need help.'

'No!' she shouted, seeing him remove his leg from the sling. 'You mustn't do that.'

The hauptmann grabbed her by the hair and pulled her towards him, screaming in her face, but then Oberleutnant Hoffman hobbled over to her side and grabbed the hysterical patient's arms and helped restrain him, talking to him calmly.

Celia had no idea what Oberleutnant Hoffman was saying but he seemed to be getting through to the patient. She was terrified that he had done damage to his already badly injured leg by helping her, but was secretly relieved that he had.

'What are you doing?' Celia asked when Oberleutnant Hoffman then began inspecting the patient's leg.

'I need to tell him that he will be all right,' he said, his voice strangely calm. 'He must be sedated, and soon, if he's not to hurt himself,' he added. 'Leave now and fetch a doctor.'

'Surely he can't have forgotten he has lost his leg?' she asked, confused.

'He's delirious, Nurse.' He seemed surprised that she hadn't worked that out, and Celia felt put in her place. 'I believe he has an infection.'

She stared at him in stunned silence. 'I hope not.'

'He needs the surgeon to look at him.'

'I'm not allowed to leave you alone,' she said, unsure what to do.

'You have no choice, Nurse,' he said, pointing to the door.

Celia shook her head. She couldn't do anything without this other patient's help, but to leave was to go against the rules. 'No, I can't leave you here without anyone to watch you.'

'Nurse, I can only restrain him for a limited time. He needs a doctor immediately.'

'You don't know that,' she argued.

'I do.'

Celia frowned at him. 'I'm sure you might think that you do,' she began.

'Nurse, listen to me.' She could see the patient was now struggling against him again and the oberleutnant was looking pale, as if he might pass out soon.

'I am a doctor.' He shook his head in frustration. 'Or at least, I *was* a doctor. I know what I am dealing with here and he needs proper medical attention. He is in a lot of pain and I will not be able to hold him much longer.'

He was a doctor? She had no idea if he was lying to her or not, but she had little choice but to run for help. 'Hang on,' she said, running out of the ward only to be confronted by Sister O'Brien.

'Where do you think you're going, Nurse Robertson? How dare you leave your post.'

'Sister, I had no choice. Hauptmann Meyer is in a terrible state. I think his leg might be infected. I'm going to fetch the doctor.'

'Wait a minute.' Sister opened the door and went inside the ward. She had barely spent any time at his bedside when she turned to Celia, her face ashen. 'Never mind the doctor. Fetch a

30

couple of orderlies instead. I'll give him something to sedate him, but we need to get this man to the operating room.'

'Yes, Sister.' As she ran towards the canteen, Celia heard the sister shouting at someone else to tell the doctor to prepare for surgery. 'I need two orderlies,' Celia shouted from the door of the canteen, furious when a couple of them laughed and then made a rude comment. Refusing to be intimidated by their immaturity, she glared at them, her heart racing. 'What's wrong with you?' she snapped. 'You're mocking me when there's a patient who's running out of time.'

'Come along, chaps,' one said, amusement vanishing from his expression. He stood and moved towards her.

'Fine,' the oldest one grumbled, looking shame-faced as he went to follow his colleague.

Celia stepped back to let them pass. 'You know where to go. I'll go and warn the doctor that you're on your way with the patient.' Without waiting for them to reply, she ran out of the canteen.

Celia reached the theatre, relieved to see Doctor Burton gowning up. He looked surprised to see her bursting into his space.

'I'm so sorry, Doctor, but there's a patient, an amputee who I believe was operated on just before being sent here. Sister believes his leg is infected and is having him sent to you.'

His surprised expression vanished.

'He's delirious,' Celia explained, hearing the oberleutnant's voice in her head. She saw Doctor Burton narrow his eyes as he noticed her bruised cheek. Celia's teeth were chattering as she spoke, and she clamped them together for a couple of seconds, willing her jaws to relax so that she didn't sound as if she was cold.

'It's fine. Take a breath and tell me everything that's

happened.' As she did, another nurse came in and handed him a fresh mask and gloves.

They both looked up as footsteps and voices could be heard outside. 'In here,' the doctor shouted.

Celia moved out of the way to make space for the orderlies carrying the stretcher.

'Thank you,' Doctor Burton said. 'Nurse, I suggest you go and make yourself a cup of tea. You've clearly had a bit of a shock.'

She realised he was addressing her. 'Yes, Doctor.' She looked briefly at the now unconscious patient before following the orderlies out of the theatre. He might have been fighting for the enemy but he looked a similar age to her brother when he had been killed.

She went to pass the orderlies when they stopped to light cigarettes. 'Thank you for helping.'

'Don't thank us, Miss,' the taller one said. 'We should have assisted you as soon as you asked.'

'Yeah, we should have.' The youngest of the two looked a little sheepish. 'We didn't notice you'd been hurt, at first.'

Celia left them to their cigarettes and returned to the ward. She needed to check there was nothing else Sister needed her to do. And, she realised, she felt the need to check that Oberleutnant Hoffman hadn't been too disturbed by the incident. She doubted he would be if he was in fact a trained doctor. He must be, she mused as she walked back to the hospital ward. He'd seemed more in control than she had been, hadn't he?

Celia entered the ward and saw that the oberleutnant was now back in bed, his leg in the sling and the colour in his face slightly better. Sister looked up from where she was checking his wound and looked her up and down. 'I know you've had an upsetting time,' she said. 'But that isn't any reason to allow yourself to look anything less than professional, Nurse Robertson.'

Celia's hands went to her hair, and she realised her veil was crooked and her hair unkempt. 'Sorry, Sister, I hadn't realised.'

'You have a cut on your face.' Sister moved closer to inspect Celia's cheek. 'Clean it with iodine and then get back to work. It's little more than a scratch, but you'll probably have a bruise for a few days.'

Celia stifled a groan. 'Yes, Sister.'

She tidied herself up and returned to her work, relieved to see the sister was busy speaking to another nurse.

'You did a good job.'

She heard the German accent and looked up at the oberleutnant. Celia wiped her forehead with the back of her right hand, realising she hadn't had a chance yet to have that cup of tea.

'Are you really a doctor, Oberleutnant Hoffman?' she asked.

'I am.' He sighed. 'Would you please call me Otto when the sister is not around?'

She wasn't sure she should do something like that. 'I beg your pardon?'

'Do you not think you can, Nurse?'

'I'm unsure whether I should,' she said honestly. 'We're not supposed to fraternise with...'

'The enemy?'

'I was going to say Germans,' she admitted, unsure whether that sounded any better.

'I might fight for the German Army.' He gave her an amused grin. 'But I am not German. I'm from Austria.'

'That's irrelevant, really. I'm not supposed to fraternise

with any patients,' she corrected him, and saw the sadness that crossed his face. How difficult it must be for these men to not only be patients in a hospital far away from their homes, but to also be hated by everyone treating them. He couldn't help where he was from, any more than she could. Would it really be all that harmful to call him by his first name when they wouldn't be overheard by one of the senior staff? It would certainly be easier than using his rank and last name. She decided to try to be a little more friendly. After all, he had rescued her from a dangerous situation. 'Otto. That's an unusual name.'

'Not really. I was named after my uncle.' He smiled at her. 'May I be so bold as to ask your name?'

She contemplated refusing, then felt ridiculous. What harm could it do? 'My name is Celia.'

'Celia.' He said it as if it was a name he recognised. 'That is a beautiful name.'

She wondered if he had ever known another person with the same name, but didn't like to be nosy. 'How do you speak such fluent English?'

'I studied at Oxford for one year,' he said. 'I made good friends there…' His voice trailed off and she realised that his reminiscences were making him sad. 'It is hard to imagine that my friends from that time are now on the opposing side of this terrible war.'

'It must be,' she said, deciding to change the subject slightly. 'Do you miss being a doctor?'

'I do.' He nodded. 'Very much.'

He reached out and touched her cut cheek lightly. 'I'm sorry he caught you like that,' he said, frowning. 'Does it hurt much?'

She shrugged. 'It aches a little, especially since I had to put iodine on it, but it's fine.' She felt her legs starting to ache and knew she must get back to work before the sister returned to the ward. 'I think you probably saved Hauptmann Meyer's life with your quick thinking.'

'I hope he does survive. I have not spoken to him much but I do not relish the thought that my small band of brothers might diminish.'

Thinking of the orderlies she had asked for help earlier and their clear disdain for these German patients, she could understand why. 'I'd better finish this cleaning,' she said, not wishing to get into an awkward conversation.

# FIVE

## Phoebe

DECEMBER 1916

'Doctor Marshall wants to raise the spirits of the medical staff, and especially the patients, by putting on a show.' Phoebe listened in rising excitement as Matron told them the doctor's ideas for Christmas. It cheered her to think that they would be celebrating the coming festivities in some way, other than a few bits of holly and red tissue paper. 'He insists that everyone take part in some way, even if it's a group song, a poem, or a small piece from a play.' She looked at each of them before asking, 'Any questions?'

Phoebe was used to taking part in the annual festivities at the church hall back home, and tried to decide what she would most enjoy doing as her part of the entertainment.

'Yes, Matron,' Phoebe said, raising her right hand slightly.

'Go on.'

'Who will be in charge of organising everything, do you know?'

Matron's face softened for a second before she smiled. 'Are you offering your services for the role, Nurse Robertson?'

'No.' She heard tittering coming from a couple of the nurses behind her and turned to glare at them. 'I was just wondering who to speak to about what each of us should do.' Her voice trailed off as she watched Matron's expression change, and realised she had walked into a trap. *Damn*, Phoebe thought, furious with herself for being so enthusiastic in speaking first. Now she had drawn attention to herself.

'I nominate you as the co-ordinator for the event,' Matron said. 'Anyone else who would like to offer their services, please do so after you leave here. I estimate that Nurse Robertson will need at least two, or maybe three of you to help with the preparations and planning.' She scanned the room once more and this time, Phoebe noticed, Matron left her gaze on each one of them for long enough to make them fidget guiltily when they didn't speak up.

'I'll help, Matron,' Aggie said.

'And so will I,' Hetty shouted, giving Phoebe a friendly smile.

'Thank you, both,' Phoebe said, relieved to have their support. Encouraged, she turned to face the rest of her colleagues, looking at each one in turn.

'I'll do it,' a clipped voice said, and though Phoebe's mood dipped, she fixed a smile on her face and turned to the owner of the voice, Verity Lansdown. Phoebe knew who the girl was and had worked several shifts with her but had quickly tired of Verity's over-confidence and superior attitude. Phoebe had managed to avoid spending time with Verity out of work hours up until now and didn't fancy having to listen to the woman's chatter off duty.

'Well done, Nurse Lansdown,' Matron said, clapping her hands together. 'Good. I expect the performance to be on Christmas Day. The pastor will give his service on Christmas morning and visit each ward, for those patients unable to leave their beds. They will then be given luncheon and will be ready for some entertainment afterwards. Say, around two o'clock.'

She gave Phoebe a satisfied nod. 'I expect you to put together an enjoyable display, but if you do not have enough people offering to take part, I would like you to let me know and I will chivvy them along. I will leave you to persuade the patients – well, those who are able – to do something too. But don't push them too hard. We are mostly putting this on to cheer them up.'

'Yes, Matron,' Phoebe said, amused by Matron's use of the word 'we' when as far as she could tell, Matron would be doing very little at all. She had no idea where to start arranging something like this, having only ever taken part in local events near her family home in England.

Matron waved them all away and the dismissed VADs filed out of her office.

'Well done, Phoebe,' several of the other volunteers said, each looking relieved that they hadn't been the one singled out.

'Don't look so worried,' Aggie said, coming to her side. 'You're not alone doing this, don't forget.'

'No,' Hetty agreed. 'We're here to help you.'

'As am I,' Verity said, giving a girlish giggle that immediately drove Phoebe to suspect that planning the event would be hindered by Verity's involvement rather than helped.

'Thank you all,' Phoebe said, deciding to give Verity the benefit of the doubt for the time being. 'I appreciate you joining me in this.'

Aggie linked arms with her and Hetty moved to her other side and did the same.

'We should all give some thought to how we're going to go about this,' Aggie suggested. 'I'm sure that once we have some sort of idea about what we each need to do, it'll then feel less intimidating.'

'I agree. I'm going to have to do it after my shift, though,' Phoebe said, realising she was going to be late if she didn't get a move on. 'I'll catch up with you all later.'

Phoebe hurried to the ward, happy to be inside, out of the damp cold. Summer couldn't come quickly enough, she decided, relieved to step into the relatively warm hut.

'Where would you like me to start, Sister?' she asked when she saw the older woman watching her arrival from the other side of the room.

'You can check each of the patients have filled water jugs by their beds, and then come and help me with one or two of them when you've done that.'

Phoebe filled a large enamel jug from the canteen and carried it carefully back to the ward, warily looking where she was walking in an attempt not to slip on the muddy walkway. She worked around the ward from bed to bed, keeping her voice cheerful when she spoke to each of the patients, even as she was hit with a sudden longing for the comfort of her family. She had naïvely thought that her grief might lessen as time passed, but for some reason it seemed to come in waves, with the worst hitting her when she least expected it. Was that the same for everyone, she wondered?

She heard an almost imperceptible groan and focused her attention on pouring water for a young, badly injured soldier who seemed to be dreaming. She watched him for a moment, unsure whether to wake him, then, recalling how her mother insisted that sleep was the best medicine, left him to rest. Most patients were pleasant, although a couple saddened her as they fought to survive their life-changing injuries, like this particular man.

'You're looking extra thoughtful today, Nurse Robertson,' Captain Bailey said, lowering his pencil and closing his notepad. 'Something troubling you?'

'I'm fine, thank you, Captain,' she said automatically. She was impressed by his perceptiveness, but it wasn't the done thing to become too familiar with the patients, and sharing her thoughts was something she knew she should not do.

'Were you drawing something?' she asked, intrigued to know why the pad was so important to him.

'I love to sketch,' he admitted. 'I always feel calmer when I have a notepad and pencil to hand.' He studied her. 'Anyway, don't change the subject. I have a feeling you're not really fine,' he said, keeping his voice low and narrowing his eyes. 'They do say a problem shared is a problem…' He frowned.

'Halved,' she said, ending the quotation for him as she picked up his glass and poured water into it. Her mother had loved to use that quote. Phoebe's heart tightened. Would she ever come to terms with not being at home the night her family had died? She pushed away the thought, aware that there was nothing she could have done to help and she was only tormenting herself.

She realised she was still holding the captain's glass and went to place it back on the small cabinet next to his bed. She sensed him smiling at her and realised she had been tricked. Phoebe raised her eyes to meet his, which were twinkling in amusement. 'You think you're very clever, don't you?' she asked, unable to stop herself smiling.

'I wouldn't have to resort to trickery if you told me what was bothering you, though, would I?'

'Nothing is bothering me,' she insisted, glancing over her shoulder to check she wasn't being watched by the sister.

'Have it your own way,' he said. 'You looked so sad just

then,' he said quietly. 'I know we don't really know each other, but I have two siblings and know from experience that it helps to share concerns with someone else.'

Phoebe thought of Celia and missed her even more than usual. 'I have a sister, too,' she confided.

'Does she work here?'

Phoebe shook her head, wishing Celia was nearby. 'Unfortunately not.'

'Aww, well,' he said, his voice gentle, 'if you change your mind and want to unburden yourself, then I promise I'm a good listener.'

'I should be the one looking after you,' she said. 'Not the other way around.'

'You would be helping me, though,' he argued, a twinkle in his dark eyes.

Her senses reacted in a way that surprised her. Was it attraction to him that gave her that strange feeling? 'Whatever do you mean?'

'I would be delighted to have something else to think about in this place.'

'I see,' she said.

'And who knows,' he continued. 'I might even be able to help in some way.'

Phoebe was unexpectedly comforted by his offer and found she wanted to help him in return. She hated to think of him being bored, and wondered if maybe he might be able to offer some practical help for the show. 'Fine.'

'What's fine?' He pushed himself further up his pillow and winced.

'Here, let me help you.' She took hold of him and, helping him lean forward, puffed up his pillows so he could sit up. 'Better?'

'Much. Thank you.' He smiled at her. 'You were saying?'

'Oh, yes. Four of us VADs have been tasked with arranging a show for the patients and staff on Christmas Day. I'm supposed to be the one in charge of arranging it.'

He frowned. 'You don't look very happy about it.'

'That's because I've never done anything like this before and have no idea where to begin finding acts.' She sighed. 'Or deciding what those acts might be.'

'That's easy.'

Thrown by his flippant and unexpected reply, Phoebe shook her head. 'And how do you figure that?'

'I can help you come up with ideas.' His face lit up, but she couldn't understand why he appeared so enamoured at the thought of helping her.

'Have you ever planned a show before?' she asked, relieved to have something to take her mind off missing her family.

He reached for his glass and took a mouthful of water. Swallowing, he smiled. 'For all you know, I could be an entertainer.'

Phoebe couldn't contain her surprise. 'Are you?'

He laughed and shook his head, replacing the glass on the cabinet. 'Sorry, no. But I have had some experience arranging events, and have taken part in enough of them.'

Phoebe wasn't sure what he might be alluding to. 'In what capacity?'

He motioned for her to move a little closer to him, and after checking that Sister wasn't anywhere nearby, she did. 'I've helped build theatre sets,' he whispered. 'I'd happily help build a simple set that you could use at the back of your show.'

'You're a builder?'

'Architect.' When she gave him a confused look, he explained. 'My cousin is an actress and found me a job at one of the theatres where she worked during one of my school summer holidays. I learnt a lot there and thoroughly enjoyed myself.'

Phoebe gave his suggestion some thought but had to dismiss it. 'Captain, Sister would have a fit if she thought I was encouraging one of her patients to do something that might cause a delay in his recovery. Thanks all the same, though. I appreciate your offer.'

He looked downcast and Phoebe immediately felt guilty for rebuffing his offer to help. 'I'm sure we'll think of something that you can do, though. I'll let you know when I think of it.' She heard footsteps and, seeing that it was Sister, she grimaced. 'I'd better get on before I'm in trouble.'

'May I ask you something?'

Phoebe nodded. 'Of course.'

'I was wondering if you always wanted to be a nurse?'

It was an odd question, she thought, but then he had just told her what he did for a living, so what was the harm in answering him? 'I was a kindergarten teacher. But after most of my family were killed in a bombing raid, I found I couldn't bear to stay in the area without them.' She heard his sharp intake of breath and wished she had thought to keep her family loss to herself. 'So I applied to train as a VAD and was thrilled to be sent away from England and come here to France.'

'Good grief. Are you all right?'

Was she? Not really. But she could hardly tell him that. 'Most of the time,' she admitted. 'Now, I really ought to be running along.'

'Right you are, Nurse Robertson. And thank you. You've given me something to think about while I'm lying here. I'll come up with a plan for you, don't you worry.'

'Thank you.'

---

Phoebe worked the rest of her shift, unable to shake Archie from her thoughts. He really was a very handsome man, she decided, her heart giving a flutter each time she pictured his cheeky expression and the way his eyes seemed to bore deep into her soul whenever he looked at her.

Desperate to share her feelings with someone, she could hardly wait until the end of her shift, when she determined to write to her sister and share her unexpected feelings for this patient:

*Dearest Celia,*

*I hope this letter finds you well and that you are not being too badly treated by the prisoners under your care. I'm slowly getting used to dealing with the gore that one comes across at a hospital and although I am shocked most days by some of the injuries, I'm proud to say that I believe I hide my shock very well, at least in front of the patients.*

*Which leads me to tell you about one particular patient we have here now. His name is Captain Archie Bailey and he is the handsomest man I've ever seen. Maybe you won't think so, but there's something about him that stirs my very soul, and each time I catch his eye my breath seems to vanish for a few seconds. I think he might like me too. Oh, Celia, I wish you could meet him and tell me what you think. He is funny and kind, and I hope that I'm able to see him again when all of this is over.*

*I fear that since our shared losses, life can't possibly return to anything we recognise as normal, but meeting Archie has reminded* me that there is still some happiness to be enjoyed in the world, and for that I'm grateful. I hope you're not too shocked and also that you are coping with all that's happened to us.

Please write back as soon as you can so that I know you are fit and well.

With affection, your sister,

Phoebe x

# SIX

## Celia

C elia frowned and, crumpling up her sister's letter, threw it down onto her bed. What was Phoebe thinking? Did her sister have no self-discipline? How was she going to keep her role as a VAD if she was going to lose her heart to the first handsome soldier to smile at her?

She knew she must write back immediately. She checked the clock and noticed she had a mere five minutes in which to write her thoughts, scrambled as they were.

*Dearest Phoebe,*

*I am well and happy enough working here at the camp. It is very different to the General Hospital in that we only deal with German prisoners, and I admit that I miss looking after local women and children on a daily basis. That said, this place is very well run and most of the prisoners are decent men who have been conscripted into fighting a war that, like the British soldiers, they probably would choose not to take part in if they had the choice.*

*I must keep this letter brief in order to post it before my next* shift, because I want to reply to you as soon as possible. To say I was shocked by your letter is an understatement. Do you not understand how unprofessionally you are behaving? You might not be a qualified nurse, Phoebe, but you still hold a position of trust and therefore have a duty of care towards your patients. Finding those patients attractive should be the last thing on your mind, and I cannot stress strongly enough how disappointed I am to hear that you are behaving so flippantly.

I'm sorry to be harsh towards you, dear Phoebe, but you really need to think about your behaviour before you end up in serious trouble and lose your job at the base hospital.

I really must press on and do send you my love, but please take note of what I've said and be careful.

Your affectionate sister,

Celia x

# SEVEN

## Phoebe

P hoebe read through her sister's reply for the third time, unable to stop shaking with anger. How could Celia have replied to her so harshly? She had clearly been mistaken in thinking that Celia was the person she could confide in about her feelings, and had no intention of putting herself in the same predicament again. She would take care not to share her deepest thoughts or feelings with her sister in the future.

That evening, as Phoebe, Aggie, Hetty and Verity sat at a corner table in the canteen making plans, Phoebe studied her notepad and ran through the list of the points each of them had made.

'The first thing we need to do, then, is make a poster to go on the noticeboard in here.' It was the one room everyone visited at some point in the day. 'Hopefully they'll give our suggestions some thought as they're eating their meals or taking a break, and sign up.'

'Sign up?' Hetty asked.

'Yes,' Aggie interjected. 'We'll pin a sheet of paper next to the poster for them to sign their names if they want to be involved.'

'We can have columns,' Hetty said, excitement in her voice. 'One for their name, one for what they intend doing, and a final one so that we know what song they'll be singing, or poem they'll be reciting and so on.'

'Good idea,' Phoebe said. 'We don't need several people giving different renditions of the same song, do we?'

They laughed.

'Oh, I know,' Verity shrieked in her babyish voice. 'How about we make suggestions on the piece of paper?'

Phoebe wasn't sure what she meant. 'Like what?'

'Well, we could come up with ideas for the show, you know, songs we think will cheer people up, poems that will brighten people's Christmas Day, that sort of thing. Then we can list them onto the paper and the first person to sign their name against it performs it.'

Phoebe gave Verity's suggestion some thought.

'We don't have to stick to just those suggestions,' added Verity. 'People could add their own, but it would be to ensure we have certain acts in the show that we know will entertain people.'

Phoebe nodded. 'That's a very good idea, Verity. Don't you think so, girls?'

'I like it.' Aggie smiled at Verity. 'Well done.'

'Yes, so do I. I'm always lost for ideas when I'm put on the spot,' Hetty said. 'Now all we need to do is come up with some of the acts we would like people to perform.'

Phoebe tapped her lower lip with her pencil, trying to think.

By the time they had finished their supper they had a half-way decent list that included magic tricks with cards, and jokes – although they all agreed that they would need to hear the jokes prior to the show, to ensure they weren't too risqué or potentially offensive to some of the less worldly patients or staff.

'We could end with something like "Pack Up Your Troubles" and "Keep the Home Fires Burning",' Hetty suggested.

'You don't think that maybe they should come somewhere in the middle of the show?' Aggie replied.

Phoebe agreed. They wanted to end the show on a cheerful note, or something Christmassy, rather than singing songs that might make the patients, and even the staff, feel homesick.

'And we mustn't forget to include a range of Christmas carols,' Phoebe said, alarmed that she had not thought to write this idea down earlier. 'I think they are what we should end the evening singing. They will remind us all that although this is not the Christmas any of us would choose, it is still the festive season and we should celebrate it in the best and most positive way we can.'

'I agree. Life is so turbulent most of the time right now,' Verity said. 'We need to help lift everyone's spirits as much as we can, and this is the perfect way to do it.' She grinned at them. 'And we definitely need to sing carols.'

Phoebe began writing down some ideas for the carols she found particularly uplifting, and as she sat trying to come up with an extra one, her parents sprang to her mind. She pictured them sitting how they always used to, in their sunny living room reading quietly before retiring to bed. The fire would be keeping them warm and they would be finishing cups of cocoa before going upstairs. *They would have enjoyed putting up their Christmas decorations too by now,* she thought as a wave of grief hit her. It had been such a difficult year.

'What's the matter?' Aggie asked quietly. 'You look ever so down.'

'You do a bit.' Hetty frowned. 'You've not received bad news, have you?'

Aggie rested a hand on Phoebe's. 'You haven't, have you?'

'No, nothing like that. I … I was just thinking about my parents.' She studied her trembling hands. 'I'm sorry. I know everyone has gone through their own heartache this year. I try to keep myself occupied so that I don't have so much time to wallow, but sometimes…'

'You're allowed to grieve, Phoebe,' Hetty said quietly. 'You've had a terrible time of it, and there's nothing wrong in allowing yourself time to think about those you've loved and lost.'

Phoebe gave her a grateful smile for her understanding. 'Thank you.'

'Hetty mentioned that you had lost them in a Zeppelin attack,' Aggie said. 'I'm so sorry.'

Phoebe looked at the glum faces sitting at the table and shook her head. 'I think I'm frightened to give in to my grief,' she admitted, aware for the first time that it was what had been holding her back.

Hetty stared at her for a moment before speaking. 'I think I understand what you mean.'

'I just worry that if I start to cry about them, I might never be able to stop. So many people must be doing the same as me.' She sighed deeply. Then, seeing how sad her friends seemed, she shook her head. 'So much for lifting people's moods. All I've done is make you all miserable.'

'No you haven't.' Hetty patted Phoebe's hand. 'We simply

became serious for a little while. It's only natural, being away from home and especially at this time of year. We need to focus on something more cheerful.'

'Like what?' Verity asked.

'Like what Christmas carols we're going to ask our acts to sing, and …' she grinned, displaying her dimples, '… who we assume might have the best voices among the patients.'

# EIGHT

## Celia

'I'm sorry, I know it's painful, Oberleutnant Hoffman,' Sister O'Brien said. 'But I'll be as quick as possible. We'll soon have you settled down again and then you may continue reading your book.'

'Thank you, Sister.' His voice was tight and Celia wished she could comfort him.

Otto caught her eye and she couldn't miss the pain he was struggling to hide as Sister worked on the wound that was being purposefully kept open in an effort to help save his leg.

She realised she needed to try to take his mind off what was being done. Not easy when the man was a doctor and seemed intent on watching Sister's hands at work.

'It will soon be Christmas,' she said, giving Sister a worried look when the older woman's head snapped in her direction, before she seemed to recognise what Celia was trying to do and focused back on Otto's wound.

'I wonder if it will snow,' she continued.

His politeness finally won over his pain and he winced. 'Snow?'

*Was that a hint of amusement?* Celia wondered. Encouraged, she continued. 'Yes. Is snow common in winter where you come from?'

He winced before gathering himself and replying, 'I am from a village near Innsbruck. We have snow every winter.'

'In Austria?'

'Yes. Where do you come from?'

Sister looked at him. 'I don't think it's appropriate to ask personal details of my nurses,' she snapped.

'My apologies, Sister O'Brien.' He groaned loudly then, and seeing him gripping the sheet tightly, Celia placed her hand over his.

'Sorry, Oberleutnant,' Sister said, continuing with her work.

'It is fine, Sister.'

Clearly it wasn't, but Celia admired his bravery. His skin had taken on a grey pallor due to the pain he was battling, and she wished Sister would hurry and finish what she was doing.

Sister stood. 'I will be back shortly,' she said before marching out of the ward.

His deep-blue eyes gazed into Celia's and she felt an almost magnetic pull to him. 'Where are you from?' he asked again.

'I'm from a village north of London.'

'Village.' He said the word quietly almost to himself. 'It is a pleasant place to live, yes?'

'It is.' She pushed away the image of her parents' wrecked home and the damage to the church and rectory. She now knew her home had been one of several places targeted by the Zeppelin as it made its way to London that dreadful night.

He smiled, before it vanished when he winced.

'I remember your English pubs with affection. I visited many when I lived in England.'

Celia grinned. 'I imagine you probably did.'

'Tell me about your pub, please.'

'We have a few, but there's one especially lovely one near my home.' She pictured the small, white-painted building with its disproportionately large inglenook fireplace and low-beamed ceiling. 'There aren't many tables, but the fire keeps the place cosy, and there are a few nooks where people can find a little privacy for quieter conversations. The landlord has a black Labrador who is always ready to welcome any hikers who pass the place and want to drop in for a pint. There's also a large garden that opens onto the river that runs by our village.'

'It sounds very beautiful.'

'It is,' she said, missing her home even more than usual.

'I should like to visit it someday. After this war ends.'

'You should.' She hoped that he did survive the war and, without thinking, glanced at the wound on his leg.

Sister returned with another bottle of antiseptic liquid and Otto flinched as she resumed cleaning his wound. Finally, a few minutes later she finished. 'You may now dress around the leg, Nurse. Take extra care.'

'It is doing well, my leg?' he asked Sister, and Celia knew he must have been thinking about the hauptmann and his leg.

'There's no sign of infection,' Sister replied with a satisfied nod. 'That's a good start.'

Celia's shoulders relaxed and she realised how tense she had been. 'You see?' she said. 'You might just get to The Dog and Duck after all.'

Sister shot her a look of disgust. 'Nurse Robertson, that is enough. Kindly remember where you are. Tidy up here and then press on with your duties elsewhere.'

'Yes, Sister.'

'It is all right,' Otto said quietly once Sister was out of earshot. 'She has gone now.'

'Thank you.' She didn't dare turn to check, trusting him to tell her the truth. She straightened his sheets and helped him sit, plumping up his pillows before collecting the kidney bowl with the old dressings.

'The Dog and The Duck is the name of your pub?'

'Yes,' she said smiling. 'It's The Dog and Duck, no second "The".'

'I understand.' He nodded. 'You will join me there for a drink, maybe? After the war?'

Celia was so taken aback by his unexpected question that she didn't have a chance to stop herself from showing her surprise.

His eyebrows knitted together. 'You are shocked?' She saw panic register on his face. 'I am sorry. I have offended you. I am aware that I am a prisoner in your country and should never ask such a thing of a young lady.'

'I, well … I was surprised, that's all. You haven't offended me, Oberleutnant.'

'I am pleased to hear you say so.' He kept his attention on his leg. 'But please, call me Otto when we speak. I find it …' he hesitated, '… I find it strange to be in a hospital and referred to by my rank, and not as *Doktor*.' He looked down at his hands, turning them to study his palms and fingers.

'I'm sure you do.' She wondered if she should do as he asked and call him by his first name, or if it might seem too familiar and lead to awkward situations. What if he became too familiar with her? She had little experience dealing with men from her own country, let alone one from a different country altogether, and one who was on the other side of the war, at that.

He gave her a questioning look. 'You will do that for me?'

'Nurse Robertson,' Sister shouted. 'Why are you still standing near to Oberleutnant Hoffman? Have you not finished yet?'

Celia pulled an anguished expression before turning to Sister and grabbing the kidney bowl. 'I'm finished now, Sister.'

'Nurse,' Otto said quietly as she went to walk away.

Her breath caught in her throat and her stomach clenched, making her tense when his hand rested on hers. 'Yes?'

'Do you think there will be snow here?' She looked down at his hand on hers and he immediately withdrew it. 'I am sorry. I forgot myself.'

'I don't know about the snow,' Celia said once he had removed his hand. 'I hope we have snow. It will give the camp much-needed decoration.'

As she hurried away from Otto's bedside, Celia thought back to his invitation to join him at The Dog and Duck. She couldn't help imagining what it might be like to spend time with the handsome blond doctor in the cosy little pub. What would they talk about? She supposed that after what they had both witnessed, there would be enough common ground between them. Then again, would they want to forget everything they had endured while here? Possibly.

She had felt the same way as Elsie once, but now she had spent time with these prisoners, it was clear to Celia that most of them hated what they had been expected to do to their fellow man in the name of war. They might be the enemy, but most of them had been conscripted and had little choice but to fight for their country. Some, like Otto, had given up careers they had loved, having spent years training to qualify. She might be nervous around them, but that was probably just due to most of her experience being on a female surgical ward at the General Hospital.

---

That night Celia got into bed but had to give up on sleep after almost an hour spent staring at the ceiling. She couldn't force thoughts of Otto from her mind. He seemed such a pleasant man, not at all like the officers she had imagined she would be nursing, and he had put his health at risk coming to her aid when Hauptmann Meyer was attacking her. She pictured Otto's handsome face and piercing blue eyes. Even as unwell as he was, there was something about him Celia couldn't help feeling attracted to. Damn it. This wouldn't do. What was she thinking? And after all that she had said to her sister too, following Phoebe's admission that she liked one of the patients she was looking after.

Maybe she should request a transfer away from the camp to somewhere back home in England? She would be just as busy but less likely to be treating a German officer, decreasing the chance of her being attracted to such an unsuitable man. A much safer option indeed.

But the truth was, she had no home. Not anymore. She didn't even have Phoebe, as she had been sent to work in France. Maybe she should ask for a transfer to France? But Celia wasn't sure if being closer to Phoebe would be a comfort to her sister as she grieved, or merely a painful reminder of the family she had lost. And how could she hope to help her sister feel better when she herself felt so lost?

She would write a letter to Phoebe in the morning, she decided. Celia lay back on her pillow and tried to work out what she might say. She wanted to share her grief for their lost parents and brother, and tell Phoebe how much she missed being able to give her a hug.

Celia thought of Otto and how she wished she could share her confused thoughts about him with her sister. But sharing all that wouldn't bring comfort to Phoebe, would it? Especially after she had reacted so badly to Phoebe's letter about the injured soldier she had feelings for. She punched her pillow and turned on her side. She doubted she would fall asleep any time soon, but she needed to try, at least.

# NINE

## Phoebe

'I assure you, Nurse Robertson, I am more than capable of building a simple backdrop for the Christmas show.'

Phoebe rested her clenched hands on her hips and gritted her teeth. He really was the most impossible man, if also one of the most attractive. Her sister's words came to her when she smiled at him, but still irritated with Celia for not even trying to understand, Phoebe pushed them away. She liked Archie and she had seen only too clearly while at this hospital how short some lives could be. Phoebe had no intention of letting her miserable sister take away any chance of happiness she might possibly have with Archie, however brief.

'Captain Bailey, if you do not do as you're told and stay in your bed, then you leave me no option but to report you to Sister Taylor.' Phoebe had to concentrate on not letting the amusement she was truly feeling show. 'You are supposed to be resting.'

He sat back on his bed and folded his arms, grimacing in pain when the quick movement snagged at his wound on the side of his torso.

All amusement vanished and Phoebe rushed forward to check he was all right. 'Please, take things a little easier. You might be healing well, but you don't want to pull the wound and risk tearing it open, now do you?'

He shook his head, his face ashen. 'That was ruddy stupid of me.' He groaned and she helped him back into bed.

Feeling sorry for him, and aware that to have come from battle and be expected to lie still for most of the day must be nothing less than torment after a few weeks, especially when the patient was feeling much better, she knew she needed to relent and involve him in some way. But how? Phoebe gave it some thought as she arranged his pillows in an effort to make him as comfortable as possible.

'I know!' she said, surprising him by her unexpected exclamation.

'What?' He gave her a hopeful smile. 'You've changed your mind?' He grabbed the edge of his cover and went to throw it back.

Phoebe caught his hand and stilled it. 'No, I haven't.' She saw his face fall. 'But I do have an idea that might keep you busy for a few more days, to help your side heal just a little bit more. Once it's slightly better, I'll ask Sister if you can be allowed out of your bed for a period of time to come and help.'

His face softened. 'Go on, then. What's this idea of yours?'

'You said you're an architect and if I recall correctly, you did offer to help design the backdrop.'

'That's right, I did, didn't I?'

'Maybe you didn't really want to.'

'I do want to,' he said, the expression on his face kind. 'I want to help you.'

She was thrown by the look in his eyes for a few seconds. Could he be as attracted to her as she was to him, she wondered. 'Um, either way, if I bring you a pad and pencils, will you design something? Then once that's done, I can take it to Matron and we can find a couple of orderlies to start collecting whatever we need to make it, and you can instruct them about how best to build the backdrop. What do you think?' She didn't really need to ask, because he was already smiling and looking much happier than he had done seconds before.

'I think you're very perceptive, clever ... and very pretty,' he said, whispering and quickly looking about him, '... and a very kind lady, Nurse Robertson,' he added, taking her hand in his.

Phoebe's stomach flipped at his touch. She told herself not to be so silly. She was supposed to be acting in a professional manner and not like some love-sick schoolgirl, though she couldn't help relishing every second that his hand was wrapped around hers. It was a strong, comforting hand and when she looked up from where his fingers were on hers, their eyes locked. Phoebe couldn't mistake the look in his eyes this time. She gasped and covered her mouth with her free hand.

'I'm glad you feel the same way,' he murmured.

What was it about him that made her feel so deeply for him? Was it the fact that anything could happen at any moment to take him away from here?

Phoebe tried to steady her breath. She couldn't let Sister see them this way. 'No, this isn't right.'

'But you do feel something for me, I can see it in your eyes.'

She swallowed to try and speak. 'I'm here to care for you.'

'And you do that well.' He let go of her hand and she instantly missed his touch. 'I'm sorry. I was wrong to put you in that position. Please forgive me.'

She folded her arms protectively across her chest. 'There is nothing to forgive. You are right, I do feel the same way as I assume you do for me.'

'You do?'

She raised a finger to her lips. 'Shush, you must keep your voice down. I would be sent home in an instant if Sister suspected anything was happening between the two of us, and I can't face going home, not yet anyway.'

He frowned. 'I'm sorry, I should be more thoughtful.' He smiled. 'But I want you to know how happy you've made me.'

'I'm ... um ... pleased,' she said, unsure how exactly to respond. 'Now I must move on and do some work.'

'I know.' He leaned forward slightly when she bent to pick up the pencil she had dropped. 'Will you tell me your first name? I promise not to use it if anyone is within earshot.'

Phoebe thought it only fair, since she knew his name from his records. 'All right then. It's Phoebe.'

'Phoebe,' he whispered. 'Such a beautiful name and a perfect one for you.'

She was glad he thought so. 'Thank you.'

'As you know, my name is Archie.' He pulled a face. 'Archibald, after my father, but thankfully my family call me Archie to differentiate between the two of us.'

'I think it's a lovely name,' she said. 'Now I really must be going. Would you like me to try and find you a fresh notepad and some pencils?'

'No, thank you. I have my own here. I'll have a think while I'm waiting and try to come up with something suitable for the event.'

Phoebe moved on to the next patient and helped him change, as he'd suffered a misfortune with a glass of water spilling down his pyjama top. The whole time she was aware of Archie lying in the next bed and wondered what he was thinking about.

However tiring it had been planning the show during her off-shift hours, Phoebe had a new spark of enthusiasm, knowing that Archie would now be part of the preparations.

The door to the ward opened and two orderlies rushed inside, followed by a concerned-looking Matron. Phoebe recognised that expression, as there was never a day when they didn't have new patients arriving at the hospital, despite the Somme Offensive having finally been brought to a conclusion the previous month. She sighed heavily.

'We were wrong to presume that there would be fewer casualties after November,' she said to Hetty, who had come to help rearrange the ward yet again, to find what little space they could to fit in yet more beds.

'We were,' Hetty said as she pulled a pillowcase onto one of the pillows on the next bed. 'I'd never heard of trench foot before coming here, and some of the cases I've seen this past week alone have been enough to turn my stomach.'

Phoebe tried to force away from her mind the terrible swellings and nephritis she hadn't imagined possible before coming to work at the hospital. 'It's the low temperatures and the dreadful weather that's not helping,' she said. 'That, and the meagre nutrition these poor men are expected to survive on.'

'And having permanently wet feet. Ergh.' Hetty shuddered. 'It's no wonder they're making their way here in droves.'

For once, Phoebe was glad that Archie was still not well enough to even be considered for returning to the Front. At least here he was safe ... well, as safe as any of them were, with the air bombardments they were experiencing of late. 'We'd better get a move on, so the first ones can be brought in here and made comfortable.'

After finishing preparing the ward, they went to welcome the new arrivals, Phoebe carrying a large tray holding mugs of strong, sweet tea and biscuits. She looked at the rows of men waiting for attention and sadness swept through her. The exhausted, filthy soldiers mostly sat in subdued silence, their hollow eyes staring at no particular sight as the orderlies did their best to pull off their boots. Boots so caked in mud that the nurses were not expected to try and remove them, because they simply would not have the strength. Phoebe tensed each time she saw a foot being withdrawn. She had seen many toes falling off when that happened due to the terrible trench foot, and it never got easier to witness.

Giving herself a mental shake, she made her way from one man to the next, handing out a mug and a biscuit and giving each of them a smile, trying her best to let them know that they were now somewhere where they could expect to be cleaned, looked after, and where their weary bodies and troubled minds could hopefully find some relief from all that they had been facing.

Several of the soldiers had deep, painful-sounding coughs and Phoebe recognised the bronchitis that had begun to plague many of the new arrivals. She hoped she didn't succumb to it, especially now that several of the nursing staff and one doctor had already done so. It wasn't surprising, she thought; they were all exhausted and struggling to find the strength to fit more into their routine each day.

'Good morning...' She tried to read the man's rank on his arm but his uniform was so filthy that it was almost impossible. 'Captain?' These poor men needed to be stripped of their soaking uniforms as soon as possible if they weren't to catch their death.

'That's right, Nurse.' He smiled, displaying a row of chipped and mostly rotten teeth. He took the tea from her hand and cupped it between his fingers gratefully before breathing in the smell. 'This will perk me up a bit,' he said, as if he had suffered no more than a mere inconvenience.

She lowered the tray slightly so that he could see the tin of biscuits better. 'Take a biscuit too,' she said. 'They're not too bad, and I'm sure you haven't eaten in a while.'

'Not anything worth eating, Nurse.' He gave a tired laugh. 'I can't tell you how good it is to be here, out of the rain.'

She smiled. 'I'm glad. Don't worry, we'll have you cleaned up and in a warm bed in no time.'

His face brightened. 'You're an angel,' he said. 'The lot of you ladies are. Thank you.'

Phoebe had to swallow her tears at his kind words as she moved on to the next man. These men had been through a living hell and were sitting here shivering, exhausted and battle weary, and still found it in themselves to thank her for a cup of tea and a biscuit. And she had thought herself tired.

---

She and the other women had planned to meet up to go through their progress for the concert arrangements, but by seven o'clock they were all still helping to assess the new influx of patients.

'I don't know why we don't simply cancel the concert,' Verity said.

Verity had been sent from her usual ward to help settle the new patients, and Phoebe noticed the strain on her colleague's face, certain it hadn't been there the previous day. Or maybe it had been and she was simply too wrapped up in her own tiredness and worries to have noticed. The thought made her feel guilty.

Her thoughts were interrupted by nearby coughing, and Phoebe turned to look for the person responsible, as they sounded as if they were struggling to catch their breath. Noticing a young soldier who looked to be little more than seventeen and with barely any weight on his body to lose, she went to help him. His eyes were large and panic-filled and she suspected that helping him to relax slightly would be the most beneficial thing she should do first.

'Let me help you sit up,' she said, keeping her voice calm as she took him by the top of one arm and gently pulled him forward, indicating for Verity to grab a spare pillow and bring it to her to place behind his back.

'Please bring a bowl of hot water, a towel and some coal tar,' she asked after thanking Verity.

Several minutes later, Phoebe was sitting on a chair next to the private who was holding the bowl of steaming liquid on his lap and was bent over it, a towel over his head to keep the steam to a maximum.

'That's it,' Phoebe soothed. 'Breathe in slow, deep breaths and try to relax.'

Twenty minutes later she took away the bowl and slowly lowered the young man to lean back against his pillows. 'Is that better?'

He nodded and held his handkerchief up to his mouth. 'Yes, thank you.'

'Bronchitis is not very pleasant but I think we should try that again tomorrow, as it will help.'

He coughed again but the redness in his face dissipated

slightly. 'I've 'ad this comin' on for a couple o' weeks. It's wrung me out, it 'as.'

'I'm not surprised,' Phoebe said. 'But you're in the best place here,' she added. 'You need to make the most of the rest and let us take care of you.'

He smiled for the first time, and she was reminded that he might be a soldier, but he was still little more than a boy, and so similar to how her brother Charlie had once been that her heart hitched in pain.

'You're very kind, Nurse.'

'Try to get some sleep, if you can.'

'I don't recall the last time I 'ad a proper night's sleep,' he said, his voice muffled behind his handkerchief.

'Well, we'll have to make sure you get your fair share while you're here then, won't we?'

As she turned, she spotted Archie watching her. He gave her a smile and after checking to see where Sister was, Phoebe grabbed a jug of water and went over to him on the pretext of filling his glass.

She poured the water and returned his smile. 'How are you feeling today, Captain?'

'Sister says my wounds are improving slowly but steadily, and I can't ask for more than that.'

'That's good news.' She was happy to hear he was making progress but knew that with every improvement, Archie was one step closer to being discharged, and if his calf healed as well as Doctor Marshall hoped, then he would be returned to the Front rather than home to Blighty. It seemed wrong to hope that men didn't completely recover, but it also meant that they might return to the safety of mainland Britain and their homes and loved ones – and that, as far as she was concerned, was the best option, especially for him.

# TEN

# Celia

'Good morning, Nurse,' Otto said, smiling at her as she entered the ward.

'Good morning,' she said, walking up to his bedside. Surely there was no harm in being friendly, she decided, aware that Sister was attending to a patient on the other side of the small ward. She greeted the other patients as she passed them. 'Did you sleep well, Otto?' she asked quietly. It was odd addressing him by his first name. She caught his smile from the corner of her eye and, embarrassed, focused on straightening his bedding. 'How's your leg today?'

'It doesn't look pleasant,' Otto said, grimacing as she touched the side of the wound lightly.

'The treatment seems to be doing the job, though,' she said before remembering he was a qualified doctor and perfectly able to see that for himself.

'I do not like it but as long as this keeps any infection away, I will suffer it.'

'You're doing very well.' Celia knew what he was going through was viciously painful and was relieved he understood the reasons behind Doctor Burton's decision to put him through this. 'It will be worth it when your leg has healed.'

'I agree, although…' His smile faltered and she wondered what might be wrong.

'Is something the matter? Can I do anything for you?'

'No, thank you. I have some pain, but it is only to be expected.' He frowned. 'I had a nightmare. It has made me a little out of sorts.'

'I'll be back in a minute and then you can tell me all about it,' she said, knowing how nightmares could upset her entire day when they were truly realistic.

She went to check on the other patients then returned to Otto's bedside with warm soapy water, a facecloth, towel, toothbrush and toothpaste to wash him.

She helped him sit and remove his pyjama jacket. Glancing over her shoulder and seeing that Sister was busily making notes, she asked quietly, 'What was it about, your nightmare?'

'I dreamt of my brother.'

He hadn't mentioned having a brother before. Celia was glad that he had now so that she could find out a little more about Otto's life before the war back in Austria. 'Is he older or younger than you?'

'Younger by two years.'

She placed his toothbrush in the toothpaste powder and then, dampening it, handed it to him with a glass of water and watched him clean his teeth. It was strange to think how intimate it was acceptable to be with a man you barely knew when you were a nurse. She realised that she already knew every inch of Otto's body, probably even more than her mother had ever seen of her father's.

When he handed back the used toothbrush and glass of water, Celia placed them on the side table. 'And why do you think you were dreaming about him?' she asked as she wrung out the flannel and handed it to him.

He washed his face thoroughly before returning it to her and taking the towel to dry his skin. 'I think it was because you mentioned you had a sister. Are you close?'

'Very.' Celia smiled, grateful to have someone left in her life that she loved deeply.

'My brother and I are also.'

She didn't wish to pry but supposed he wouldn't mind her asking him further questions, especially if he was wanting to share his nightmare with her. 'Is he at home in Austria?'

He shook his head. 'No, unfortunately not. He enlisted before I did and was captured last year.'

'That's terrible,' Celia said immediately, wondering where the camp might be, as surely it was a British one. Maybe Otto's brother was being held somewhere in France?

'I do not know where he is being kept.' He sighed miserably.

'Poor man, I hope he's being well treated.'

'I pray each day that he is. My brother isn't as robust as I and was prone to sickness when he was a child.'

Celia could tell Otto was more anxious about his brother's predicament than he was letting on.

'He is a gentle soul. He didn't wait to be conscripted and only joined the German Army because he thought our father would be impressed and think him more of a man.'

'Really?'

'I believe that to be so.' He took the soapy flannel from her and began washing himself. 'I worry for him and how he will cope with being incarcerated for ...' he gave a shuddering sigh, '... for the years he will be there. It troubles me greatly to think of him on foreign soil and not knowing whether he will survive.'

Celia wasn't surprised. She tried to imagine how she might feel if her brother was being held in a prisoner-of-war camp in Europe somewhere. 'At least he's still alive,' she said, wanting to cheer him up. 'And presumably safer than he would be at the Front.'

He stared at her and then handed back the flannel and took the towel from her hand, their skin touching as he did so. Her stomach contracted and their eyes met. She saw his perfect lips move but for a second couldn't hear what he was saying as she fought the pull to press her mouth against his in a kiss. Celia gasped at her shocking instincts.

'You are all right?' he asked, concerned.

Celia could feel the heat in her cheeks, so looked away and wrung out the flannel, desperate to compose herself before turning back to him. 'I, um, had a thought, that's all,' she said, hoping he hadn't noticed the look on her face as he was speaking. 'What was it you said?'

'That you are kind to say this to me. I had not thought of Karl's situation in this way. You are right. If they are treating him well, and I hope that they are, then he is probably better to be there than to be fighting.' He shook his head. 'I could never imagine my sweet brother using a gun and having to try to kill another man.'

Celia couldn't imagine Otto fighting either. 'It must have been troubling for you to have to do it too.'

'You mean to try to kill another man?'

'Yes.' She hoped she wasn't overstepping the line of familiarity by broaching the subject.

'Because I am a doctor, or because I am, I believe, a decent human being?'

'Both, I suppose. Mostly, though, because you are a doctor and have sworn the Hippocratic Oath.'

'It was never something I imagined myself having to do. But I think that most of the men being forced to take up arms on both sides of the war probably feel the same way.'

She supposed he was right. 'Yes. I know my brother Charlie found it alarming.'

He smiled. 'You have a brother? He is a soldier?'

She cleared her throat, wishing she hadn't mentioned Charlie. Now she would have to concentrate on keeping a check on her emotions. Sister would not be impressed to find one of her nurses in tears at a patient's bedside.

'He *was* a soldier,' she explained, her voice cracking with emotion. 'He died last year.'

Otto reached out and took her hand in his. 'I'm so sorry, Celia,' he said, his voice gentle. 'No one should have to lose someone they love because of others' choices.'

She stared at his hands holding hers, comforted by his warm skin cocooning hers like a soothing balm on her heart. 'Thank you,' she whispered. She looked into his bright-blue eyes and her heart flipped over. She wished they lived at any other time in history. She couldn't miss the love emanating from his gaze and didn't care that her feelings likely shone straight back at him.

They gazed at each other in silence for a few seconds, each lost in thought. Celia wondered if Otto was thinking the same thing as her and hoped that there would be a time in the future when they could discover if their affection for each other was real, or brought about because of him stepping up to help her, and her nursing him when he was at his lowest ebb.

Doctor Burton arrived then, interrupting the moment, and Celia watched as he removed the dressing from Otto's muscular chest to check his wound. 'This is doing well, I'm pleased to say,' he said. 'Nurse, all this will need is a fresh dressing.'

'Yes, Doctor,' she replied, happy to know that Otto was doing well.

She then waited anxiously as the doctor inspected Otto's calf. She knew Otto was desperate to be able to get up and move around more, and hoped that Doctor Burton might have some cheering news for him.

'What do you think, Doctor?' Otto said when Burton had finished.

'I'm very pleased with your progress, Oberleutnant Hoffman. There is still no sign of infection and your leg is now starting to heal well.' He smiled at Celia. 'You have the dedicated attention of these wonderful nurses to thank for your continued recovery.'

'I do, Doctor.' Otto smiled at her and Celia felt heat rise in her cheeks. 'I am very grateful to them all.' He turned his attention back to the doctor, who was about to leave his bedside. 'Excuse me, Doctor.'

'Yes, Oberleutnant?'

'Do you believe my leg may soon be closed up? I'm finding it difficult not being able to get up each day, and wondered if I might be allowed to walk about soon?'

Celia couldn't miss the concerned expression that flitted across the doctor's face. 'We are at that stage where I can close the wound. Probably tomorrow. You'll have less pain then and will be able to move freely once it has had a bit of time for the incision to heal.'

'Thank you, Doctor.'

The doctor patted Otto's shoulder. 'We'll soon have you outside taking exercise with your comrades, don't you worry.'

Celia gave Otto a sympathetic smile as she followed the doctor to the next patient's bedside. She could see Otto was putting on a brave face and wondered how badly he was hurting inside. He must desperately have wished he was in a German hospital closer to home.

# ELEVEN

## Phoebe

With Christmas fast approaching Phoebe was determined to finalise everything for the show. As more injured men were brought to the hospital the strictness of what the VADs were allowed to undertake softened slightly and Phoebe liked the feeling of being able to do more than simply clean away filthy uniforms and bandages.

She was looking forward to the Christmas show and decided to check the list on the noticeboard and saw that there were almost enough acts to make the event entertaining enough, so she unpinned it and took it with her to the table where she was meeting Aggie, Verity and Hetty.

She placed the list and notepad down on the table and began jotting down the names of the nurses, VADs, orderlies and, she noticed with delight, one of the doctors, who had volunteered their time, and what they intended doing for their performance.

'Gosh,' Hetty said, her large eyes wide at the long list. 'We've done well, don't you think?'

'Yes,' Phoebe said, relieved that the medical staff had come up trumps and that she could hold her head high as the main organiser. 'Matron can't be disappointed with this lot.'

Verity leaned over the list. 'By the looks of things there's quite a mixture too. Singers, some poems...' She grimaced. 'I hope it's cheerful poetry though, I'm tired of all the dismal war poets.'

'I think most of them sum up how the soldiers must be feeling,' Aggie argued. 'I know it puts into words some of my thoughts, and I'm only a VAD.'

'There's nothing "only" about what we do, Aggie,' Verity scowled.

'Sorry, you're quite right. I didn't mean it that way.'

'I'm very happy with this lot,' Phoebe said, trying to change the subject back to the show before her friends fell out. 'Now we need to work out an order so that everyone's interest is kept piqued throughout. We don't want too many poems following on from each other, and the liveliest songs should, I believe, be in the middle and at the end.'

'I agree,' Aggie said. 'Have you found someone to play the piano in accompaniment yet?'

Phoebe knew she had forgotten something and hoped that this was it. 'Not yet.'

'Maybe we'll need a couple of them,' Hetty suggested. 'In case they become tired. It might be a long evening.'

'That's a good point.' Phoebe made a note to sign up two pianists. She thought of Archie's offer and, looking from one of her friends to the other, she tried to judge their reaction to what she was about to suggest. Aware that she had no idea what they might think, she decided to just say it. 'I'm going to ask one of the patients to design the backdrop,' she said, focusing her attention on her notepad rather than looking them in the eye.

'Is that really necessary?' Verity asked, a mocking tone to her voice.

She raised her gaze to Verity's. 'I think it will add some professionalism to the event, don't you agree?' She looked to Aggie and then Hetty for support.

She saw a hint of confusion flash across Hetty's face and knew her friend suspected there was a reason behind her determination. Well, Phoebe decided, she would answer any questions Hetty might have when the time came.

'Hetty?'

'Er, oh, yes. I think it's a grand idea.'

'So do I,' Aggie said, nodding enthusiastically.

Verity harrumphed. 'If you all think so, then I suppose we should do it.' She narrowed her eyes slightly. 'Do you have someone in mind to ask?'

Phoebe hoped her cheeks weren't as warm as she suspected they might be. She had never been a good liar. 'Maybe.' She decided to leave it at that. 'I've been waiting for the patient's injury to heal a little bit more before mentioning anything. I'll let you know more tomorrow, now that I know we're all in agreement.'

She made a note to ask about the backdrop to give herself time to calm slightly and hide her excitement. It was going to be wonderful to spend time alone with Archie away from the ward.

It was lovely to have something to look forward to, as today would have been her brother's birthday and the first one without him was proving difficult. Phoebe had struggled all morning to keep a check on her emotions as they threatened to overwhelm her. How could Charlie be dead? He was only twenty-four, with his entire life ahead of him. His future had vanished. She swallowed the lump in her throat, suddenly desperate to get away from her colleagues for some time alone where she could regain control over her emotions. She checked the clock, relieved that she only had a few minutes to cope through until her shift ended.

---

As soon as she had the chance, she put her head down and, without speaking to any of the other VADs, left the ward and hurried away, stopping only to consider where to go. She couldn't return to the dorm because she knew for certain that she would never have any peace there. So, instead she headed down the side of the building and began walking across the field behind it where many bell tents had been erected for the staff.

She thought she felt a spot of rain and put out her hand. Looking up, Phoebe saw heavy, steel-grey clouds that threatened stormy weather. She knew she shouldn't be outside when that broke, but she kept walking, struggling to contain her upset and unsure what she was looking for, or if she should just turn around and go back to the dormitory after all. So what if she cried in front of anyone else? No, she thought. She couldn't do that.

Finally Phoebe came across what looked to be an unused tent. One flap was tied open and the other flapping in the wind. She stepped forward and cautiously peered inside, surprised to find that apart from an unmade bed and a rickety-looking desk with a plain kitchen chair, there was little else in it. Strange, she thought, with the cramming in of medical staff and patients, that this small tent lay uninhabited. Maybe the previous occupant had left and it was waiting for the next one to arrive.

She looked behind her to check that she wasn't being watched by anyone and, not seeing another soul nearby, Phoebe went inside. She untied the open tent flap and let it drop closed. Then, pulling out the seat, she sat at the desk, dropped her head on her arms and let her heart break all over again as her grief for her family washed over her.

Phoebe sobbed until there were few tears left, at least for now. She knew there would be more occasions – birthdays, anniversaries – when she would feel as wretched as she did today. She took her handkerchief from her skirt pocket and blew her nose.

'Who are you and what are you doing in here?'

She gasped and looked up to find that one of the doctors had walked in. Shocked to be discovered in the tent and horrified that someone had witnessed her torrent of tears, Phoebe wiped her eyes with the backs of her fingers and took a deep breath, desperately trying to gather herself. She stood to leave but wavered as she stepped forward.

'Hey, steady on,' the doctor said, taking her arm and leading her back to the chair. 'Sit there and take a moment.' His voice sounded gentler this time and she could tell that she had shocked him by being there as much as his arrival had surprised her.

'I … I'm terribly s-sorry,' she said, blowing her nose once more and blinking away further tears to try and see who she was addressing. She hadn't seen him before but he had kind, hazel eyes and wavy, sandy hair. 'I'll go.'

'No, you won't,' he said firmly. 'I suppose you came here for somewhere solitary to think.'

'Something like that,' she said. 'I didn't know this was anyone's tent, otherwise I would never have presumed to enter.'

He shook his head. 'It's no trouble.' He smiled at her. 'In fact, you weren't actually intruding, because until a couple of minutes ago this wasn't my tent either. I've just arrived at the hospital.'

'I see.' She was surprised and relieved. 'That does make me feel a little better.'

'Good. I'm glad.' He smiled at her and proffered his hand for her to shake. 'I'm Doctor Sutherland. Geoffrey.'

She took his hand and shook it. It was firm and cold and, she realised with surprise, oddly comforting. There was something about him that made her feel safe. 'I'm Nurse Phoebe Robertson.' She wiped away another tear that tickled her cheek with its dampness. 'I'm sorry again for being here when I'm sure you were hoping for a little peace.'

'Don't be, Nurse Robertson. Or may I call you Phoebe when we're not on duty?'

She blinked away her surprise. 'Yes, of course.'

'That was rather forward of me, wasn't it?' He shook his head. 'I must apologise. I'm a little rusty at expected social niceties. I've been living in the country far too long with my sister and seem to have forgotten how to behave.'

He gave her a friendly smile and Phoebe thought how relaxed she felt in his company. It was a comforting feeling and rather like the familiarity she felt when some of her brother's friends used to come and visit them at home.

Geoffrey narrowed his eyes slightly. 'I have a feeling we're going to become good friends.'

Happy at the notion, Phoebe smiled. 'I think so too.'

'I'm glad.' His smile vanished then and was replaced by a look of concern. 'Now that we've established that we're to be friends, do you think you might want to confide in me about why you were so upset?' When she hesitated, he hurriedly added, 'Not if you don't want to, of course. I only want you to know you have someone to share things with, should you feel the need. I don't wish to pry.'

She wanted to tell him about her family but knew it would only bring on fresh sobbing. 'Thank you, but I shan't, if you don't mind. But it's kind of you for caring enough to ask.'

'Not at all.' He thought for a moment. 'Do you have siblings?'

She was grateful for him trying to change the subject, but wished he had chosen a different one. Reasoning that he could have also suffered some family loss, Phoebe took a deep breath, determined to remain calm.

'Yes, one,' she replied. 'Celia. She's a nurse working in the prisoner-of-war camp in Jersey.'

His eyebrows rose. 'I didn't realise there was one there.'

'Nor did I until my sister told me.' She was feeling a little better now, she realised.

'Your sister, is she older or younger than you?' he asked.

'She's younger but only by ten months. We're quite alike in looks and are more often than not taken for twins. Celia is a trained nurse, unlike me. She's also a little more serious about life than I am, and more cautious.'

'Yes, well, that's sisters for you!' he laughed. 'Mine worries that I think too deeply and miss out on the fun side of life.'

'And do you?' she asked, intrigued. 'Miss out on fun, I mean?' He didn't seem to her as if he missed out on any opportunities. Hadn't he been welcoming to her, despite his shock at finding her in his tent? That was surely an instinctive reaction rather than a deeply considered one.

'I have done.' He sighed and Phoebe wondered whether it might have been a matter of the heart that he had been too slow to react to, or something else entirely. 'But I am to change that. This is a new start for me. My first time away from England, in fact.'

'Gosh, it's mine too.' They seemed to be kindred spirits in several ways and his honesty only helped reassure her that they were to be good friends. Thinking of Hetty and aware that her friend might wonder where she had disappeared to, Phoebe stood. 'I really ought to be getting along.'

'Please don't leave. Not just yet.' He seemed to hesitate before pointing towards the tent flap. 'It's pouring out there now and you'll only get soaked.'

She heard the heavy rapping of the rain on the canvas all around them and looked up. 'It does sound rather heavy.' She was sorely tempted to stay in the dry tent with Geoffrey but the thought of being discovered there worried her. She also didn't fancy having to explain where she had been all this time to Hetty and Aggie. 'However, if I don't go back to my dormitory now my friends might worry and come looking for me.'

He seemed to consider her words. 'Yes, I imagine it would be better for you not to be found here alone with me.'

She gazed down at her feet, embarrassed now to find herself in such an awkward position. 'But thank you for being kind enough to allow me to stay for as long as you did.' She looked him in the eye as a troubling thought occurred to her. 'You will keep this, er, meeting between the two of us, I assume?'

He moved back to let her pass. 'Naturally. I might be a little lax in my manners but I would never wish to compromise a lady's integrity. Or mine.' He gave her a friendly smile. 'I wish I had an umbrella to offer you.' He lifted the canvas flap and held it back for her. 'Take care, Nurse Robertson. I hope to see you around the hospital over the coming days.'

She smiled shyly at him. 'Good luck settling in, Doctor Sutherland.'

'Thank you, and I hope you're feeling a little better now.'

'I am,' she assured him, realising that though she did not feel much better, she was at least more in control of her emotions, and that was a relief.

She folded her arms across her chest and held onto the sides of her cloak as she braced herself to step outside. Flinching under the heavy rain, Phoebe made a run for it, hoping she wouldn't slip as she hurried in the direction of her dormitory. She was grateful no one else seemed interested in where she might be coming from or going to, as everyone was intent on getting to where they were headed to get out of the rain, so they took no notice of her. It would be ruinous for anyone to know that she had spent time alone with the doctor in his billet.

However, she did hope she would be able to spend time chatting with Doctor Sutherland again. He seemed such a kind and decent chap and she missed having someone to confide in. She wished more than anything Celia was nearby. How was her sister coping with the run-up to their first Christmas without their parents? Was she doing better than her? Phoebe doubted it. Maybe the best thing for both of them was to keep as busy as possible. After all, what good would they be to each other if all they did was cry on each other's shoulders? It wasn't as if either of them could bring the rest of their family back to them.

She paused under the small overhang outside the door of the dorm, pinched her cheeks to bring a little colour into them and shook off the worst of the rain from her sodden cloak before opening the door and stepping inside.

# TWELVE

## Celia

---

Otto groaned and Celia saw he was slowly regaining consciousness. It would be a relief for him and the nursing staff that the wound on his leg had now been closed. He had been in such pain with the treatment but she knew that it would all be worth it, as it meant Doctor Burton had managed to save his leg from the damage the shrapnel had done and the threat of infection.

She pulled a chair to his bedside and sat, glad that she was by herself in the ward now that Sister and other nurses were elsewhere. Celia glanced at the door and around the room to double check that she was the only member of staff in the ward, and that the other patients were either asleep or busily reading. She took Otto's hand in hers.

'Otto?'

He murmured something but didn't open his eyes.

'Otto, it's Celia,' she soothed. 'You've had your operation and Doctor Burton said it went very well.'

His eyelids flickered a few times before slowly opening. He

85

gazed at her and she wasn't sure he was fully awake, so went to say something further but stopped when he began to speak.

'Celia.' His voice was soft. He smiled then closed his eyes again. '*Mein Schatz.*'

Celia's breath caught in her throat. She had picked up enough German to understand he was calling her his darling, or something similar. The tone of his voice was loving and she wondered for a moment if he knew she was the one sitting with him or if he was thinking she was someone else.

'Otto,' she said again, this time in a more professional tone, so as to not confuse the semi-conscious man. 'It's Nurse Robertson.'

His eyes opened once more and this time he appeared to be more conscious. 'Celia. It is you.' He swallowed. 'I think I might have said something inappropriate.'

Not wishing him to be alarmed, Celia shook her head. 'No, you didn't.'

He didn't seem convinced. 'I didn't tell you I loved you?'

'No,' she said smiling. 'You called me your darling.' As soon as the words left her lips, she saw his face light up. Damn. He had caught her out. Why hadn't she pretended to be offended, instead of repeating what he had called her as if it was no matter at all? Fool. 'I'll make you a drink,' she said, getting to her feet and letting go of his hand.

Otto reached out for her. 'Please, don't go. Not yet.'

Flustered and not sure what to do for the best, Celia tried to withdraw her hand from his. 'This is wrong, Otto.'

'I know.'

'Then you must stop. You're putting me in a difficult position.' Was it guilt that she reciprocated his feelings, or fear of being found out that was worrying her most? She wasn't sure.

He let go of her hand, embarrassed. 'May I ask you a question before you go?'

How could she say no? 'Of course you may.'

He went to say something but stopped. He thought for a moment, staring down at his hands before looking up into her eyes. 'I was hoping you might feel something for me.'

She stared at him, surprised that he would ask her something so openly. He had meant every word he said, she realised, seeing the depth of emotion in his eyes. 'You really do, er, like me?'

He swallowed. 'More than that.' His voice was barely above a whisper and held all the emotion she felt swirling around in her heart.

'Oh.'

He looked troubled. 'I am sorry,' he said, shaking his head and pulling his hand back. 'I did not mean to unnerve you. I should not have spoken. I spoke out of turn. I...' He took a deep breath. 'I shall blame the anaesthetic for me speaking out of turn.' He smiled and she saw that he was trying to cover for his unexpected openness with her.

'Hush,' Celia said, wanting to stop his humiliation. She had hurt him with her silence. 'Don't be sorry,' she said quietly as she rested her hand on his arm. 'I'm a little taken aback, but only because your words were unexpected.'

'You are not offended?'

She shook her head.

'Then dare I believe you might have feelings also?' He rested his hand on his chest, his eyes wide in disbelief. 'For me?'

For such a strong, athletic man he seemed strangely vulnerable. She felt compelled to take him in her arms and comfort him, but knew she could never do such a thing. 'I suppose I do.' She could barely believe the words she was hearing coming from her lips.

He stared at her silently.

'We must not dwell on how we feel, though,' she said, thinking of how Elsie would react should she ever discover Celia had formed an attachment to one of their German patients. 'This is war time and we are on opposite sides, whether we like it or not.'

'We are.' He looked deflated. 'But one day this war will be over. We will find a way to be together then, maybe?'

Celia realised that she liked the idea but knew she mustn't encourage him. She didn't have it in her heart to hurt him by rejecting him, though. 'Maybe, Otto. One day.'

# THIRTEEN

# Phoebe

'Like this, you mean?' Archie smiled at Phoebe over his right shoulder as he began playing a fun ditty on the piano. She had mentioned that morning that she was looking for two people to play and was delighted when Archie told her that he wanted to be one of her pianists for the show.

Phoebe marched over to him, draped the tinsel around his neck and placed her hands on her hips as she stood next to the piano.

'No, Captain, that's not what I meant at all.' She feigned anger, aware that her amusement was obvious. 'You've been given special permission by Doctor Marshall to play the first half of the scores for the show, but only ...' she gave him a fierce look, '... notice that I'm saying *only* if you behave yourself.'

Archie sighed dramatically. 'You're such a tyrant, Nurse Robertson. I'm sure Matron wouldn't give me such a hard time.'

'Matron certainly would if you were misbehaving,' Matron

announced, making Phoebe jump and wonder how much the older woman had witnessed.

'Oops,' Archie said, giving Matron a charming smile. 'Caught out. I promise to behave from now on.'

Matron rolled her eyes heavenward and smiled at Phoebe, clearly charmed by Archie. 'You have my full permission to send him back to the ward at the first sign of him forgetting this promise, Nurse Robertson.'

Relieved Matron was amused rather than annoyed by what she had walked into, Phoebe smiled gratefully. 'I will do, Matron. Thank you.'

Matron looked at the makeshift stage at the back of the canteen and nodded. 'Yes, this is beginning to look very festive. Well done, Nurse. You and your team have done an impressive job here and I look forward to watching the show.'

'Thank you, Matron. I'm delighted you're happy with what we've done so far.' She watched the woman leave and felt much more confident about how the different acts might be received.

'I had intended asking you to design a backdrop,' Phoebe admitted.

'I'm happy to do it,' Archie said with a shrug. 'But I'm not sure of the best way to go about it.'

She smiled.

'What?'

'You're a natural designer, aren't you?'

'What do you mean? I'm an architect.'

'Yes, but you design houses. I'd barely mentioned the backdrop and already you were planning how to do it.'

'Can you tell I've been missing my job?'

She nodded. 'Yes. It must be difficult being stuck here when you would normally be drawing up plans for buildings.'

He stared at her for a while before answering. 'It would have been far harder if you hadn't been working here.'

Phoebe's heart fluttered with excitement. 'You really think so?'

Archie smiled. 'I wouldn't say so if I didn't.' He gave her a look that made her stomach give a little flip. 'I've enjoyed spending time here with you today. It's why I volunteered to be one of your pianists when you mentioned it in the ward earlier.' He gave her a pondering look. 'Was our ward the first one you came to with your request?'

'Yes. Why?' she asked guiltily. Had he worked out what her intentions had been?

'Were you hoping I'd offer?'

'I don't know,' she fibbed. Then seeing the disbelief and amusement on his face, she nodded. 'Fine. Yes, I was. Happy now?'

'Very.'

Embarrassed, Phoebe concentrated on sorting through the box of tatty tinsel.

'She's right, you know,' Archie said, interrupting her thoughts.

'Who? Matron?'

'Yes.'

'About what?' Phoebe rested one hand on the top of the piano and stared into his beautiful eyes, then without thinking lowered her gaze to his lips.

'That you've done an excellent job,' he said, his voice barely more than a whisper.

She heard him speaking but was unable to tear her eyes from his. She watched his hand reaching up to her face, barely able to quell the excitement that he might be about to kiss her.

His hand moved behind her head and she closed her eyes as he slowly pulled her head down towards him.

'Oh, Archie,' she whispered, scarcely able to breathe.

'I've wanted to do this for so long,' he murmured just before his lips met hers in a kiss.

Phoebe pushed her fingers into his hair as she held him tightly against her, relishing his mouth on hers. She had been kissed before but never anything like Archie was kissing her now. Her entire body seemed consumed by the sensations his lips on hers were causing.

He broke away and smiled at her.

Had that kiss only lasted a few seconds? Or was it minutes?

'You kissed me back.' He looked stunned, delighted.

'I did.' She liked that she had surprised him with her passion.

He stared at her and Phoebe couldn't miss the attraction and desire emanating from his eyes.

They didn't speak for a moment. Phoebe could barely think.

'I was angry at first, not to be sent straight home to England,' Archie said eventually, resting his hand on her cheek. 'But coming here to be treated meant that I met you and I'll always be grateful for that. When I look at you, I feel like nothing else matters.'

She opened her mouth, aware that she should say something in reply. Maybe tell him that their emotions were probably heightened because of the war, the uncertainty of their futures and everything they had already both suffered, but she closed it again when she couldn't find words to do her feelings justice.

'This is wrong,' she said, remembering her place. 'You're one of the patients and I work here. We can't do this.'

'No,' he said, going to stand, then wincing in pain and cursing under his breath.

'Don't try to get up so quickly,' she said, crouching in front of him so that he wouldn't try standing again. 'You mustn't exert yourself. You still need crutches to stand, don't forget.'

He reached out his free hand and slipped it behind her head, pulling her gently towards him once again. Phoebe hardly dared to breathe.

'I don't care about the rules. This is our lives, Phoebe. You won't always be a VAD and I certainly have no intention of being a soldier once this terrible war ends,' he whispered, staring into her eyes as their lips met once more.

They kissed for a few seconds, then Archie pulled back slightly, staring at her. 'I've imagined doing that ever since the very first time I saw you.'

'The very first time?' she teased, surprised.

'Almost.' He moved forward and kissed her again, this time with more intensity.

Phoebe sighed as the pleasure of their kiss transported her. She slipped her arms around his neck, not wanting the sensations that coursed through her heart and body to end.

Someone gave a delicate cough and Phoebe immediately pulled away from Archie and rose to her feet. She spun round and relief flooded through her. It was only Hetty.

'Thank heavens it's you.'

Why was she scowling at them? 'I'm sorry,' Phoebe said, desperately attempting to rescue the moment. 'I know I shouldn't be, um...'

'Kissing a patient?' Hetty snapped, frowning. 'No, you shouldn't. Imagine what would have happened if Matron had walked in on you?'

'You're right,' Phoebe said, ashamed to have forgotten her duties so easily. 'I'm sorry.'

'Don't apologise to me,' Hetty said. 'I'm not the one who'll send you away from here. I understand how emotions are heightened at times like these, but you must be more careful.'

'I will be,' Phoebe promised. 'Thank you.'

Before Phoebe had a chance to say anything further, Hetty raised her hand. 'I was on my way to another ward when I passed the door and saw you. I'd better get going again before I'm in trouble.'

Hetty rushed out of the room.

'Do you think she'll tell anyone?' Archie asked.

Phoebe shook her head. 'No, she was just concerned for me, that's all.'

He frowned. 'Please don't let what happened change things between us.'

She didn't want it to but had to decide whether this attraction between them was worth risking everything she had worked so hard towards. The thought that she could lose her job made Phoebe realise that she had come to love her work. When had she come to think this way?

'Phoebe? Are you all right?'

She snapped out of her reverie and stared at him for a moment, still taken aback by her revelation. 'I'm well,' she finally answered, 'but I think we're going to have to take a step back from whatever this is.' She hated to see the hurt in his eyes. 'It's the only sensible thing to do, Archie.'

He opened his mouth to speak, then closed it again. 'You're right,' he said, disappointing her. She wasn't sure why. Maybe because she had hoped he might at least try to persuade her otherwise. 'I'm being selfish and that's not gentlemanly.'

'This was wrong ... but I don't want this to end. I know I'm taking chances with my work, but I've never felt this way before about anyone.' There, she'd said it.

He closed his eyes briefly and smiled. 'Maybe we should get to know each other a little better and take things very slowly. Then you can at least tell your colleague that we've become friends and know each other well enough to be able to take risks with our future.'

She thought about what he'd said and nodded. Hetty would likely be calmer if she knew Phoebe wasn't being reckless, and it was far better than having to agree to end things with Archie.

'We could start by telling each other more about ourselves. Shall I begin?'

'Yes, that would be lovely,' she said, fascinated to find out about his personal life 'But before we do, I'd like to kiss you again.'

His mouth fell open but he quickly recovered himself. 'Then don't let me stop you.'

Phoebe laughed and moved towards him, kissing him hard on the lips, delighted when Archie reacted instantly by taking her in his arms.

Satisfied, she let go of him and moved slightly away. 'You were saying?' she teased.

He raised his eyebrows and shook his head. 'Er, I'm from a pretty village in Yorkshire called Sandsend.'

'Sandsend?' She smiled at him for a moment, trying to think whether she had heard of the place before. 'I don't know it. What's it like?'

His eyes had a faraway look in them as he thought about his home. 'It's small and very pretty and only a few miles up the coast from Whitby.'

'It sounds delightful.'

'It is,' he said dreamily. 'I was very lucky growing up there with the beaches and coast right on our doorstep.' He smiled at her. 'How about you? Where's home for you?'

She thought about her home village and how it no longer felt like home for her and Celia since the Zeppelin attack in July that year had changed their family dynamic forever. 'It used to be a village a few miles north of Greater London.'

'Why don't you think of it as home? Was it because of that bombing raid you told me about?'

'Yes. Little of the house was left after the bomb exploded on it.'

'My poor, sweet Phoebe,' he said, looking devastated for her. 'I hate to think of you suffering such terrible loss.'

She loved him for being upset on her behalf. 'Thank you. Sometimes I think I'm doing well and then a wave of grief knocks me sideways. I'm grateful to still have my sister Celia.' She realised she wasn't being honest with him. 'I'd rather she was closer, but I'm not sure how much I'd be able to help her just yet.' She shrugged. 'Celia and I aren't the only ones to have suffered, though, are we? We can only do our best and keep going.'

'I think you're doing very well,' he said. He stared deep into her eyes. 'After this is all over, I'd like you to think of my home as yours too. And Celia, if needs be.'

'Your home?'

'Yes, my parents died one after the other three years ago now. I have a twin brother and a sister, but she's married and lives in London with her husband and three children.'

'Who's looking after your house while you're away?'

'I bought my brother and sister's shares of our parents' home but my brother stays there when he's on leave. The rest of the time the house is cared for by Mrs Dunwoody, who lives in the same lane. She's my housekeeper.'

'Oh, right.' He seemed so organised. 'Do you miss it? Your house, I mean?'

'Often. My office is there. I miss that room most of all, I think. The house isn't very big but it has a decent-sized back garden with an ancient, gnarled apple tree taking up a large part of one of the back corners.' He gave her a lazy smile. 'I can't wait to take you there and show it to you.'

'Neither can I,' she admitted, trying to picture the pretty place.

'Nurse Robertson!'

'Gosh, that's Matron's voice. I must run.'

# FOURTEEN

## Celia

C elia listened to Elsie grumbling about the prisoners yet again. She was tempted to snap at the nasty woman but didn't dare antagonise her, in case Elsie began to watch her and Otto more closely and catch an unguarded look passing between them.

It made her worry about how everyone would look at her and Otto if they did end up being together whenever this war ended. The unfairness of their situation infuriated her. What if the war didn't end, or continued for years? What would they do then?

If only she had someone to confide in. Phoebe had always been her confidante but Celia could hardly write to her admitting what was happening between her and Otto, especially given how harsh she'd been when Phoebe had confessed her own feelings for a patient. She sighed, realising she felt further away from her sister than ever. If only they could spend a few hours together to catch up with each other, share their thoughts about their family, comfort one another. She missed Phoebe so deeply, now more than ever.

'Celia? What's happened?' Elsie asked, her voice filled with concern. 'Are you all right?'

Celia took a steadying breath. 'Yes,' she lied. 'I'm fine.'

'What utter tosh.' Elsie frowned at her. 'Something's happened and I'm not leaving you here until you tell me what it is.'

'Why do you care all of a sudden?' Celia asked without thinking.

Elsie's thick eyebrows rose in shock at her reaction. 'We are colleagues, Celia,' Elsie said quietly.

'I can't tell you,' Celia murmured, aware that Elsie was one of the last people she could ever confide in. But it was clear her colleague had no intention of letting this go. She needed to tell her something to satisfy her. 'Fine.' Celia sighed. 'I was overcome thinking about my parents and brother.'

'Really?'

'Yes.' She realised she had said it more sharply than she had intended but Elsie's nosiness had annoyed her. 'I'll get on then,' she said, not wishing to spend any longer with Elsie in case she began questioning her about something else.

She sensed Otto watching from his bed further along the room but was determined not to catch his eye. Celia had no intention of giving Elsie any chance of suspecting that their feelings had changed from nurse and patient to two people who had formed an attraction towards each other.

It frightened her to find herself in this position. She had imagined that she might fall in love and marry at some point in her life, but having been focused on her nursing for the past few years, was happy not to rush into anything. Now, not only had she developed feelings for one of her patients, she'd also fallen for someone she struggled to imagine a future with because their countries were at war with one another.

## FIFTEEN

## Phoebe

Phoebe was laughing at a ditty Archie was singing as he played a tune on the piano near the back of the room, when she heard the distant sound of a plane engine.

He sang on for a couple of bars before noticing something was wrong. 'What is it?'

Phoebe listened. 'A plane.' She cringed. 'I think it's coming this way.'

'Are you sure?'

A bomb whistled downwards and Phoebe, aware he couldn't move quickly enough to safety, ran to Archie's side. She reached him just as it detonated somewhere in the hospital grounds, flinging her into his arms, the weight of her body against his toppling him from the piano stool and onto the floor. She didn't have time to worry whether she had hurt him before the windows exploded. There was a stunned silence before people began screaming and someone shouted orders.

'That's one way to show a man you're interested in him,' Archie teased, a mischievous glint in his blue eyes.

'How can you joke at a time like this?' she asked, grateful to him for his strange humour. At least she knew he was unhurt. She pushed her hands onto the floor and went to stand.

'Not yet you don't,' he said, and she realised he had his arms around her back.

'I have to get up and check that you're fine,' she said, happy to stay exactly where she was but concerned in case someone saw her lying on him.

'The best way for you to comfort me is to stay right where you are.' He lowered his voice. 'Just for a moment. Who knows when we'll have another minute in private?'

'You mean when you'll have me lying on top of you like this,' she said, surprised to hear herself speaking in such a blatant way. He had a point though. She glanced around, seeing that the piano was blocking anyone's view of them from the door and an upturned table hid them from the other side of the canteen, where staff had been working moments earlier.

He moved slightly so that she was lying next to him in his arms. She liked the feeling very much.

'Just for a short while then,' she said, unable to help smiling. Hearing another plane and remembering where she was and what was going on around her, Phoebe stiffened. What was she thinking? 'Sorry, I must help you up.'

'I'm quite happy here though,' he insisted.

'Yes, but I need to get you somewhere safe.'

'Under the piano?'

'All right, but then I need to go and see if I can help anyone else,' she reminded him. 'You're not the only patient I care about.'

He smiled at her and, taking her face in his hands, pulled her gently towards him and kissed her.

Phoebe knew she must go and went to move away, but as his kiss deepened, she couldn't help herself and returned his kisses. Sensations she had never experienced before flowed through her. Was this what it was like to want a man? Truly want him? She groaned as his hands held her tightly against him, the movement answering any questions she had about his feelings for her.

'Hello?' a voice shouted. 'Is everyone all right in here?'

Horrified to think that someone had heard her groan and presume someone was hurt, Phoebe pushed away from him and began to stand. 'I think so,' she said, pulling a face at Archie when he grinned at her.

'Jolly good.'

As the footsteps receded Phoebe went to take his hands. 'I must help you up,' she said. 'Unless you're hurt, but somehow I doubt that you are.'

'Get down!' He pulled her down to him as another plane flew over and dropped another bomb. 'Bloody Boche. Who bombs a hospital?'

His hand rested on the side of her head, holding her protectively to his chest. It was odd that despite hearing the engines of yet another plane nearing, Phoebe felt safer in his arms in this moment than she imagined she might do anywhere else. She wrapped her arms around him, feeling his heart pounding rapidly against her cheek, not wanting the moment to end too soon.

'Are you all right, my love?' Archie asked quietly as the planes finally receded. 'This will all be over shortly.'

'I know,' she said, wondering when they might ever find themselves in each other's arms again. How sad was it that they had to be caught in a bombing raid for her to be this close to the man she was falling in love with? Then again, if she hadn't come to France and to this place filled with chaos and heartache, she might never have met him.

'I'm supposed to be the one caring for you,' she said, tilting her head up and kissing his jaw. 'Not the other way around.'

He looked down at her and kissed her forehead. 'I will always protect you.' He frowned. 'At least I always hope to be able to.'

'Don't talk like that,' she said, her heart aching to think that one day he would be recovered enough to leave her. 'Let's just enjoy the time we have together right now.'

'You're so sensible,' he said, kissing her again. 'I wish we weren't here and that our lives were different.'

'So do I,' she said miserably. 'You never know, though. One day this might all be over and we'll be lying like this in a cornfield somewhere on a sunny day.'

'Or on the lawn of our own home.' His voice was far away and Phoebe knew he was picturing the scene.

'I like that idea.'

Hearing voices and footsteps running past the canteen, Phoebe realised their time alone was over. For now. 'We need to get up,' she said, thinking of her friends and praying silently that Hetty, Aggie and Verity had been unharmed by the bombing.

'Not yet.'

'We must,' she said, not daring to be caught lying in his arms. Aware that he would need to sit as soon as he got to his feet, she let go of him, stood and righted the piano stool, then reaching out for him, helped him up.

He did as she asked, wincing as he rose to his feet and grabbing the piano stool quickly.

'That's better.'

'Good.'

'It isn't really,' he teased. 'But I suppose it'll have to do.'

'Behave yourself, Captain, otherwise I'll report you to Matron.'

'You wouldn't dare!' He grinned. Pressing his lips together thoughtfully, he shook his head. 'Maybe you would.'

'I would if I thought it was in your best interests.' Phoebe heard the rest of the staff calling orders. 'I must go and see what I can do to help the others. I'll come back as soon as I can.'

## SIXTEEN

## Celia

Celia gasped when the siren blared out its alarm. She heard footsteps running and now one of the doctors hurrying in her direction.

'What's happened?' she asked, looking up to the sky, terrified in case they were being warned of an impending Zeppelin attack.

'An escape attempt,' the doctor said, frowning. 'This isn't the first time, I gather, but it seems that this time they might have made it to the other side of the electric fencing.' He shook his head. 'Where they think they're going to on an island completely surrounded by the sea I've no idea, but I suppose they feel the need to try.'

'Do we know yet how many? And how they managed it?'

'Three, I believe. Dug a tunnel, which in my mind is stupidly dangerous when you think that this camp is built on a base of sand.'

Celia couldn't help but feel sorry for the prisoners who had more than likely wasted their time digging their tunnel. 'I imagine they'll be back here soon,' she said, hoping none were hurt during their escape. The forty-four beds in the hospital were already almost at full capacity and she had hoped to have some time relaxing over the Christmas period.

She thought of Otto and hoped that he hadn't been silly enough to be one of the escapees. His leg still had a long way to go before it was fully healed and she doubted he would be able to crawl through a tunnel, let alone walk quickly enough to get away and hide once on the other side of the fence. All the same, she wanted to check that he was still in the hospital where he should be.

She reached the ward and opened the door, looking directly at his bed to check he was there and still safe. He was.

His eyes were wide and he cried out when he saw her. Thank heavens she had thought to come here. He looked bewildered.

'Why is a siren sounding?'

Another two of the patients shouted something to her in German. She could see they were all a little panicked and she understood why. Most of them weren't well enough to get to safety if the place was bombed and they were hoping for some reassurance.

'It's fine,' she said, raising her hands. 'A few prisoners have escaped.'

One of the men cheered and Celia sent him a quelling look. 'They will be caught soon and brought back here.'

'How do you know this? Maybe they will remain free?' Otto asked quietly.

Celia shrugged. 'Only if they have a boat hidden away somewhere,' she said. 'That's the only way they're going to get away from the island.' She sighed. 'Anyway, here is probably the safest place to be right now, I imagine. You're fed well, have decent accommodation and once your leg is healed, you'll be able to join the others outside in games of rounders and football.'

He gave her a sad smile. 'I have no love for sport,' he said. 'Books are what give me the most pleasure. Or at least they were … until I was sent here.' Celia could see his attraction for her in his gaze.

Looking away, she glanced over to the other men in their beds, grateful that none of them seemed interested in anything she and Otto were discussing.

'Celia,' Otto whispered.

'Is something the matter?' she asked, wondering if his wound hurt.

'Nothing is wrong,' he said, his voice quiet. 'I am always feeling well when you are near to me.' He took the tips of her fingers in his. 'I do resent that we are unable to show our true feelings to each other though, to be together.'

'What are you doing?' she whispered, snatching her hand from his touch. 'Don't you know how dangerous this could be for me if anyone was to catch us? Catch me?'

His gaze fell from hers. 'I am sorry. I only meant to let you know how much I care for you.'

Guilt coursed through Celia, replacing her fear of discovery. 'No, I'm sorry. I didn't mean to snap, but you're putting me in a terrible position.'

'I do not wish to cause you harm, Celia,' he said. 'But I have never felt like I do about you for anyone before. It is making me forget myself.'

His thumb grazed lightly over the back of her fingers and the look in his eyes softened. 'I thought you felt as deeply for me. Is that not the case?'

She bit her lower lip to stop from blurting out her true feelings. 'I am your nurse, Otto. I must remember that and not allow myself to give in to my feelings for you, whatever they may be.'

'I understand.' He gave her fingers a gentle tug and she moved slightly closer to him, her heart racing. 'But I am determined to show you that my feelings for you are real and that there is a future for us.'

She could see he meant everything he was saying despite how impossible it might seem for them to even consider being together. 'How?'

'I do not know yet, but I will think of something.'

She smiled at him, sensing that if anyone could make it happen, this decent, powerfully built man would be the one to do it. She rested her free hand on top of his. 'Then I'll hold you to that.' When he frowned in confusion, she added, 'I expect you will find a way to make it happen. When the war is over and we are no longer classed as enemies.' Forgetting herself for a moment, she lifted his hand and kissed the skin on the back of it.

'Celia!'

Hearing Elsie's startled voice, Celia dropped Otto's hand as if it had stung her and spun on her heels to face her. Elsie's mouth hung open in shock as she stared at Celia, and several other patients were also now staring at her and Otto, wondering what they had missed. At least Sister wasn't there, she thought, relieved. She glanced down at Otto, unable to miss the horror in his eyes at being discovered.

'I'm so sorry,' Celia whispered. 'I must go to her and try to explain my actions.'

'Is there anything to explain?' he asked before closing his eyes and shaking his head slowly. 'Please, take no notice of me. I do not know what I am saying. Go to the nurse and tell her that I am not a bad man.'

'You are the best of men,' she whispered, wishing she didn't have to leave him.

'Go, my love. I will still be here when you are finished.' He smiled at his feeble joke but the smile didn't reach his eyes.

Why did Elsie, of all people, have to walk in at that particular moment?

'I can't leave the ward right now,' Celia said quietly to her colleague.

'But I want to speak to you. Now.'

Celia hated the sense of dread filling her chest. 'I know you do, but as I said, I'm unable to leave here until Sister Evans returns, and that could be some time yet.'

Maybe Elsie would calm down slightly if she was unable to confront her for several more hours, Celia thought hopefully. She doubted it.

When Elsie didn't speak Celia realised she needed to act fast. Find some way to placate the nasty woman before things got out of hand. Celia took Elsie's arm and led her to the doorway, keeping their backs to the patients and her voice low. 'I know you think you saw something terrible…'

'I did see something terrible, Celia,' Elsie snapped. 'I saw a fellow British nurse kissing an enemy soldier, that's what I saw.'

## SEVENTEEN

## Phoebe

P hoebe forced her trembling legs to keep moving as she ran towards the voices calling for help.

As she struggled to contain her emotions, her mind went to Archie. She cared for him so much, but who knew how long the war would continue? She felt trapped in the surreal world that was happening all around her. How different things were today from two and a half years ago, before the war began.

Phoebe slipped on a lump of mud on the wooden planks and reached out to grab something to stop herself falling over. As her hand came in contact with a rough piece of wood on the corner of a window, the pain tore through her palm and, just as she expected to hit the ground, two strong hands caught her under her arms.

'Steady on,' a deep voice she recognised bellowed as he slowly lifted her to her feet. 'That was close.'

Phoebe turned to face her saviour. 'Doctor Sutherland.'

'You remembered.'

She wasn't sure why he would think she might forget it after the two of them had spent time alone together in his tent.

He had been so kind then and she wasn't surprised that he was the one who had stopped her falling now.

'You saved me from making a spectacle of myself.' She tried to picture how she must have looked, almost falling, and frowned. 'Well, maybe not, but you did stop me from landing in an unladylike heap in the mud, so thank you.'

He gave her a dazzling smile. 'I can't imagine you being anything other than a lady, Nurse Robertson.'

She was surprised how pleased she was to hear his compliment. 'Thank you. Again.'

His eyes moved from hers and she felt him take her by the wrist. 'You're hurt.' His expression hardened. 'How did that happen? Did someone…?'

'Oh, no. No one has done anything at all,' she hastily corrected him. 'I must have cut myself when I reached out to save myself from slipping over.'

'Then you must come with me and I'll clean it.'

Embarrassed to be such a nuisance, she shook her head and attempted to pull her wrist from his hold. 'No. Please. I'm sure you have other people who need your help more than I do right now.'

He shook his head. 'Thankfully, there don't seem to be many casualties and the other surgeons are already setting up in the theatres.'

'Thank heavens for small mercies,' she said quietly. Then seeing his questioning look, added, 'I'm quite fine and perfectly capable of dressing it myself.'

He cocked his head to one side. 'And are you able to stitch the wound yourself too?'

'You think I need stitches?' She grimaced and looked at her bloodied hand. 'I've never had stitches before.'

'There's no reason to fear them now,' he said, soothing her

with his tone. 'I promise.' He smiled. 'Anyway, I only said you might need them. You might not, of course, but I will only be able to tell if I clean this wound up first and have a look. Now, enough chatter, you're coming with me.'

Phoebe did as he ordered and accompanied him to a surgical tent.

'I'm afraid you can't use that one,' a sister said, stopping them from going inside. 'Doctor Marshall is performing an operation and I doubt he'll be finished for a time yet.' She indicated a row of smaller tents. 'You might find one of those free, though.' She studied Phoebe's face and then looked down to her wrist, still being held by the doctor.

'Possible stitches required,' he explained.

Satisfied, the sister nodded. 'Will you need me to send a nurse to assist?'

'No, thank you. I'm sure Nurse Robertson can assist me, if necessary. Isn't that so, Nurse?'

Phoebe liked the idea of passing instruments to him as he worked on patients but wasn't looking forward to doing so as he repaired her own injury. 'Yes, of course, Doctor Sutherland.'

'Right then, let's go and get this hand of yours sorted.'

Once inside one of the tents, Phoebe watched as Doctor Sutherland gently cleaned the cut, trying her best not to flinch whenever it stung.

'I'm sorry,' he said. 'I know it hurts but we need to be certain it's completely clean.'

'I know, Doctor,' she said, smiling as his gaze reached hers.

'Of course you do. I forgot you're a nurse.'

'I'm only a VAD,' she corrected him. 'But I hope to train as a Registered Nurse one day. I admire all that they do and want so much to learn all that I can about nursing.'

'Ah yes. I seem to recall that your sister is a nurse, isn't she?' He smiled.

She winced at the thought of Celia and wished she knew how her sister was doing.

'Did I hurt you?'

'Sorry?'

'You flinched.'

She shook her head. 'No. No, I'm fine.'

He worked silently before speaking again. 'Something is wrong though, isn't it?'

She caught his eye and seeing that he appeared genuinely concerned, Phoebe knew she needed to give him some sort of answer.

'I'm worried about my sister, that's all. After the bombing here I can't help wondering how she's getting along in Jersey. She's the only family I have left now,' she said, aware that her voice was tightening at the increase in emotion.

'I'm sorry about that,' he said. 'You're close then, I take it?'

'We're very close, ordinarily.'

He gave her a comforting smile. 'These are not ordinary times though, are they?'

'I suppose not.' If only he knew quite how strange these times were for her.

'I'm sure you'll be together again at some point,' he said, holding up her hand to inspect her palm more thoroughly. 'Try not to let it worry you too much. It's exhausting enough just dealing with all that we face day in and day out.'

He wrapped her hand in a bandage. 'This doesn't need stitches, but you will need to take things easy for a couple of weeks. Maybe you could be sent home for a break.' He studied her face. 'It might do you good to get away from here for a while. Completely away.'

If only she had a home to return to.

'Is something the matter?' he asked, frowning. 'I thought you might be happy for a chance to return home to your family for Christmas?'

Phoebe shook her head. 'My home was bombed earlier this year. Unfortunately my mother, father and brother were sleeping there at the time. This will be the first Christmas I don't celebrate with any of my family,' she said, misery washing over her.

He pinned the final piece of the bandage into place. 'There,' he said, looking thoughtful. 'All done.'

Phoebe went to stand.

'No, please wait. I've had an idea.'

*About what?*

'I have a sister. She lives in Cornwall and I'm sure she would be happy for you to stay with her for a few days.'

Why would he offer for her to stay with his family?

He smiled. 'I can see that you're confused by my offer. Don't be. My sister was widowed last year and I worry that without me living nearby, she's lonely.'

'Wouldn't your sister think it odd for you to send someone you barely know to stay with her?'

He shrugged. 'She won't be surprised at all.' He laughed. 'She's always telling me off for inviting waifs and strays home.'

'I'm a waif then?' she asked, amused but also a bit taken aback.

His face fell. 'Heavens, no. Not at all.'

'A stray then?'

He shook his head. 'No. Of course you're not. I didn't mean that at all. I was merely...'

Phoebe could see he was horrified to think she had taken

his offer the wrong way, and wanting to reassure him, rested her good hand on his arm and smiled. 'I'm teasing you.'

'You are?'

'Yes. It was wrong of me and I'm sorry.'

He frowned but she could see amusement return to his hazel eyes. 'That was very mean of you, Nurse Robertson.'

'Phoebe, please. I think that if we're close enough friends for you to invite me to stay with your sister, then you can surely address me less formally.' He nodded his agreement. 'Now, why don't you tell me exactly where it is that your sister lives so that I might know more about this place you're intent on sending me to?'

'It's a small village on the Lizard Peninsula called Pennwalloe. There are a few shops and pubs and the locals are peaceful and friendly, I'm sure you'd enjoy it there.'

'Is it where you come from then?'

'It is. I love it there and always feel rested when I've spent time in Pennwalloe. Do you think you might take me up on the offer?'

Why not? What harm could it do to go and stay with a widowed woman for a couple of weeks? It wasn't as if she had anywhere else to go while she was unable to work.

'Yes,' she said, agreeing before her nerves got the better of her and she changed her mind. 'Why not?'

'Thank you. I shall write to my sister today and ask if she minds.'

'That's very kind of you. I appreciate your thoughtfulness.' She thought of her work and her mood dipped. 'But what about my work here?'

'I'll inform Matron and she can make the necessary arrangements to find you passage home.'

---

*What about Archie, though?* she thought as she left the tent to return to her dormitory. She hated the thought of not seeing him for a couple of weeks. And what about the show? How could she simply leave now, just a couple days before it was due to go ahead, after all her hard work? She reached the dorm and had only just sat on her bed when Verity popped her head in the door and called out to her.

'Phoebe, Matron is asking for you.'

'She is?' Surely it was too soon for the doctor to have spoken to her?

'Yes. She's been looking for you and wants you to go to her office immediately.'

Groaning as she stood, Phoebe winced as her hand ached. She felt exhausted and was glad she hadn't had a chance to take off her cloak. It would have been much more of an effort to make her way to Matron's office if she had begun to relax.

---

'I am reliably informed that you will be incapable of carrying out your duties for a few weeks, and therefore I would like you to be one of the nurses accompanying a group of patients who are to be sent back to England.'

Phoebe realised that Doctor Sutherland had wasted no time speaking to Matron about her.

'Of course, Matron.'

'Here is a list of the patients' names. I want you to go to Ward 3. As you will no longer be able to do much physically, you are to accompany the other nurses and assist where you can.' She screwed the lid onto her fountain pen before looking up at Phoebe. 'Any questions?'

'Yes. I was wondering when we leave the hospital?'

'First thing in the morning. There's no time to waste, as their beds are desperately needed. I'll expect you back here in ten days.' She took a sheet of paper and looked down at it. 'That will be all.'

'Matron?' Phoebe said, aware that she had to try and make some sort of arrangement for the show. 'If I leave now, then who will continue making the final preparations for the show?'

'I'm sure that your small team will be fine without you, Nurse Robertson. Surely you've already finalised most of what was needed by now?'

Phoebe thought through what was still left to do. 'Yes, I suppose so.'

'Then leave it with me and I'll speak to them about it.'

Relieved, Phoebe nodded. 'Thank you, Matron.'

Phoebe left the office and stopped a few paces away to read the list of names in her hand. She was barely able to contain her delight at seeing Archie's name on it. She would be travelling back to England with him! The thought made her smile as she walked towards the ward to tell the sister in charge who would be leaving the following day. Then it occurred to her that once they had reached England, she would be moving on to Cornwall to stay with Doctor Sutherland's sister while Archie was to be sent to an auxiliary hospital.

It was unfortunate but at least they would have a couple of days travelling together.

She handed the list to the sister in Ward 3 and as she waited for her to work through it and make notes, Archie caught her eye. When Sister finished and called over another couple of nurses, Phoebe made the most of the opportunity and went over to his bedside.

'You've hurt your hand,' he said, looking concerned.

'It's only a flesh wound. I slipped on some mud and went to grab hold of something to steady myself, cutting my hand in the process. Clumsy of me.'

'I'm glad you're all right.'

She smiled at him, desperate to tell him their news. 'I am.' She checked Sister wasn't looking and pretended to straighten his bedclothes so she could lean a little lower. 'I have news that affects us both,' she said. 'We'll be travelling together back to England tomorrow. Isn't that wonderful?'

'And then what?'

'I'm going to stay with a friend in Cornwall,' she explained. 'Then I'll be returning here once my hand has healed. I've been given ten days' leave.'

'But we'll be going our separate ways when we arrive in England and I'll be stuck in another hospital somewhere.' Archie gave her a pleading look. 'I can't bear to think that you'll be so far away from me.'

'Neither can I,' she admitted. 'But at least we will have some time together on the journey. It could be worse,' she added when he still looked sad. 'I could be leaving and you might have been sent away while I was gone. Then we wouldn't even have had the chance to say goodbye.'

She heard Sister's voice in the background. 'I must go now, but I'll see you in the morning. Try to get a good night's sleep. This weather has been stormy for the past few days and I can't imagine our crossing to England is going to be at all smooth.'

'I will,' he said. 'And Phoebe?'

'Yes?'

'Thanks for telling me. I'm grateful that we'll have this time together.'

'So am I.'

## EIGHTEEN

## Celia

'I wasn't kissing him,' Celia argued, her stomach churning in fear. She knew she was twisting Elsie's words to try and wriggle out of the compromising position.

'Don't lie to me. You might not have been kissing his mouth but you were certainly showing blatant acts of affection.' Elsie glared at her. 'There is no excuse for what I witnessed. I'm appalled and … yes, I have to admit it, I'm sickened by what you've done.'

Celia moved back to distance herself from Elsie's venom. The woman's cruel words felt like a slap on her face. 'How can you be so mean-spirited?'

'You dare to call me names?' Elsie's eyes pierced Celia's and she almost had to close hers to block out the fury emanating from them. 'Do you know what will happen to you if people around here discover what's going on between you and that …' she pointed in Otto's direction and lowered her voice, '… that man? Do you?' she asked, almost spitting out her words in disgust. 'For pity's sake Celia, have you lost your mind?'

'I wasn't kissing him,' Celia protested again, hoping that if she argued with Elsie about it enough the woman might think she had imagined what she saw and begin to doubt herself.

'I know what I saw.'

'Fine. I forgot myself. I was trying to comfort a man in pain and I simply didn't think.'

Elsie narrowed her eyes, unsure. 'He did seem surprised, I'll give you that.'

Celia stared at her hopefully, then seeing Elsie's expression return to disgust, saw that she wasn't going to get away with it that easily. 'You're looking at me as though you hate me,' Celia whispered, her voice catching. She didn't see Elsie as a friend and could even admit to herself that she didn't really like the woman, but no one had ever shown such distaste for her before. 'I've done nothing wrong,' she fibbed, hoping Elsie might believe her. 'Truly I haven't.'

Elsie took a slow, deep breath, looked over at Otto once more and then back at Celia. 'If you don't know that what you've been doing is wrong, Celia, then you know nothing. You should be ashamed to wear that uniform. I'm ashamed of you.' Celia flinched and for a second saw Elsie's stare soften minutely. 'I'm sorry,' Elsie added, 'but I am. I think it best if I leave now before I say something I might regret.'

At the word 'regret' Celia thought back to her unfeeling response to her sister's admission about her feelings towards one of the patients at the base hospital. *At least he was a British soldier*, Celia thought guiltily, once again wishing she could take back that letter she had sent Phoebe and rewrite it.

Elsie reached out and, taking Celia's shoulder, pushed her sideways away from the door so that she could pass.

'Elsie,' Celia called, unsure what she was going to say next but hoping to think of something to stop the woman leaving and reporting her. But before Elsie replied Sister appeared in front of her.

'What are you doing here, Nurse Baker?' she snapped.

'I, er, I came to see if Nurse Robertson needed any help,' Elsie explained. 'After the siren sounded.'

Had Elsie come to the ward hoping to catch her and Otto together, Celia wondered. She wouldn't have put it past her.

'That's understandable, but now you've seen she's coping perfectly well, I believe your assistance is better used elsewhere.' Sister Evans moved to the side to let Elsie leave.

Elsie walked away without a glance back and Celia felt her heart drop. She knew instinctively that making an enemy out of Elsie Baker was a dangerous thing to do.

# NINETEEN

## Phoebe

P hoebe knew she had a few minutes before 'lights out' and decided that now was the best time to let her friends know she would be leaving the hospital for a couple of weeks. She needed to resolve her argument with Hetty and still felt guilty having to leave them just before the show, but reasoned that most of the planning had already been completed.

'Hetty,' she said, waiting for her friend to close the novel she was reading.

'Is everything all right?' Hetty asked, her eyes wide as she set the book onto the small cabinet between their beds.

'I'm sorry if I annoyed you earlier.'

'You didn't.' Hetty pushed herself to sit upright. Phoebe gave her a doubtful look. 'Well, maybe a little. But it was only because I worry for you, Phoebe. Our behaviour has to be seen to be exemplary, otherwise they will replace us with some other VADs.'

'I know. And I'm sorry for being so thoughtless.'

Hetty shook her head and Phoebe saw that her friend had forgiven her any indiscretion. 'It's fine.'

'Has something happened?' Aggie asked, looking worried as she joined them.

Phoebe told them quickly about slipping over. 'I'm fine, but I'll be unable to work until it's healed, especially as we're dealing with mucky uniforms and so many infectious wounds.'

'Will you be going home to your family then?' Aggie asked innocently.

Phoebe realised that she hadn't thought to share her story with her friend. She took a steadying breath. 'I don't have any family left in England,' she explained.

'Oh, I hadn't realised,' Aggie said, frowning. 'You have a sister in Jersey though, don't you?'

'I do, but I can't stay with her. She lives and works at the prisoner-of-war camp.'

'What will you do?' Hetty asked. 'I could write to my mother if you'd like. I'm sure she would be happy to welcome you.'

Phoebe shook her head. 'That's very kind of you, but it's not necessary.'

'You're going to stay here then?' Hetty asked.

Phoebe shook her head. 'No. Doctor Sutherland has offered me somewhere to stay—'

'Doctor Sutherland?' Hetty interrupted. She looked upset and Phoebe couldn't understand why for a moment, then suspected that she might have feelings for the surgeon.

'It's not what you think,' Phoebe corrected her. 'I met him when he first came here and we simply became friendly. Nothing more than that. He mended my wound and, knowing I don't have a home to go to, he said his sister would be happy for me to stay with her in Cornwall over Christmas.'

'Christmas?' Verity asked, joining the conversation. 'You're leaving before Christmas?'

'I'm leaving in the morning,' Phoebe explained. 'I'll be travelling to England with some of the patients who are being repatriated to auxiliary hospitals to recuperate.'

'Don't you think it odd that a man you barely know offers for you to go and stay with his family?' Verity asked. 'And over Christmas? Because that sounds very odd to me.'

It hadn't seemed strange to Phoebe at all. But now she thought of it, doubts niggled. Was she doing the right thing going to stay with a complete stranger? Should she have refused the offer?

'There's nothing strange about it at all,' Hetty snapped. 'He's a doctor here, so he's hardly a stranger.'

Phoebe gave her friend a grateful smile. 'Thanks, Hetty.'

Verity glared at her. 'I've never come across him.'

'Well, I have,' Hetty said. 'And I think he's very kind to offer for Phoebe to go and stay with his sister.'

'So do I,' Aggie agreed.

'Thanks, girls. It'll make a nice change after all that's happened recently.'

'Why?' Verity asked, intrigued. 'What else has happened to you, then?'

Phoebe glowered at her, getting irritated with her. 'I meant the bombing raid.'

'For pity's sake, Verity,' Aggie grumbled. 'Can't you be pleased for Phoebe that her Christmas won't be completely ruined?'

Verity sighed loudly and pointedly ignored Aggie. 'So we really have to put the show on without you?'

Phoebe couldn't miss the accusatory tone in the woman's

voice. 'I wish I could be here for it, but I can't stay if I'm not contributing. I'm sure you three will be fine.'

'Of course we will,' Hetty said, giving her a reassuring smile. 'Everything is organised now anyway, isn't it?'

Phoebe was going to say that it was, when she remembered that Archie had agreed to be one of the pianists accompanying the acts. 'Mostly.'

'What's that supposed to mean?' Verity snapped, giving the others a 'Hah-I-told-you-so' look.

'You're going to need to find one more pianist. Apart from that, though, I think everything is settled.'

Verity groaned but before Phoebe could say anything, the VAD said something surprising. 'Ignore me, I'm being a misery.' It was the first thing Verity had said that Phoebe could agree with. 'I'm nervous about doing the show without you and a little envious that I'm not going to see my family over Christmas.'

Phoebe's feelings for the VAD softened. 'I understand. The three of you know what to do though, so you won't even know I'm gone. And as for Christmas, I understand how you must feel, and I'm sorry.'

Hetty leaned forward and hugged Phoebe. 'I am sorry you won't be here for the show but we'll do our best to make sure all your hard work doesn't go to waste.'

'We will,' Aggie agreed.

'Lights out, everyone,' Sister called as she entered the large dormitory and plunged the room into darkness before anyone had much of a chance to lie down.

'Hetty?' Phoebe asked, wanting to settle a nagging thought that had occurred to her.

'Yes?' Hetty whispered.

'Do you have feelings for Geoffrey?'

There was a brief silence before Hetty answered. 'Geoffrey?'

'Yes, Doctor Sutherland.' Phoebe already guessed the answer by her friend's evasive reply. 'It's fine. I think I already know.'

'Don't tell anyone, will you?'

'You know I won't.'

'Thank you. We've only spoken a few times and I don't think he suspects how I feel about him yet.'

Phoebe smiled to herself.

'I'll write to you while I'm away, if you wish?'

'That would be lovely,' Hetty said. 'Maybe you could send us a postcard of the town where you're staying.'

'Maybe.' Phoebe tried to imagine what the place would be like. The thought of Cornwall made her a little nervous but as she listened to the rain battering on the wooden roof of their hut, Phoebe began to look forward to some time away from the noise and mud. It would be fun to have a break from the hospital and sharing a room with so many other women. The only thing she was dreading was bidding farewell to Archie when they reached Victoria Station in London.

## TWENTY

## Celia

C elia couldn't shift the feeling of being watched all the time and hated that Elsie had been the one who saw her and Otto together. She had been expecting to hear from Matron, or at least be called to speak to Sister, but so far nothing had been said. It was odd, Celia thought, for Elsie to make such a point about her disgust for her and Otto, and then not follow it through by reporting her. What was she up to? Whatever it was, her unexpected silence was making Celia anxious, so she decided to speak to Otto about it. She would have to ensure that Elsie was kept busy elsewhere while she did so, though, because she didn't want to give her any further ammunition to use.

Her opportunity to speak to Otto came sooner than she had expected, when Elsie was sent with one of the other nurses to assist the doctor carrying out check-ups on the escaped prisoners who had now been caught. As soon as Celia was certain they had left, she went to the ward.

'What do you think she's up to?' she asked him after sharing her concerns about Elsie. 'I can't work it out.'

He checked no one was watching them, then reached out and rested his hand on her forearm. 'You are trembling.' It was a statement rather than a question. 'It is not cold in here, so it must be because you are frightened.'

Celia hated to worry him, but he had already seen through her bravado, so there was little point in denying it. 'I'm probably being silly,' she said, certain that she wasn't, but wanting to play down her concerns so that he didn't overreact and do something that might make matters worse for them both. 'I only mention this to you because I can't work out what she's playing at.'

'Playing at?'

'What her intentions are for me. It's making me uneasy. I expected her to report me by now.'

'She is enjoying having power over you. She is a cruel woman.'

He was right. It was as simple as that.

'I'm not sure what to do about it, though.'

He sighed. 'I'm unsure whether there is anything you can do. I would wait. Bide your time. She will show her intentions to you soon enough.' His reassuring smile calmed her slightly. 'You are strong, Celia. Try not to let this woman upset you.'

'I won't,' she said, feeling a little stronger. She saw movement from the corner of her eye and went over to the window. 'It's snowing,' Celia exclaimed. She knew snow might lift the sullen mood in the half-empty ward. 'I wonder if it'll stick.'

It did, and the following morning Celia was grateful for her ankle boots as she had to traipse from the nurses' quarters to the wards through a few inches of snow. She stopped halfway to the hospital and looked around. Everything was white and even the sea looked wintery somehow. There was a quietness about the place, most of the sound being muffled by the thick blanket of snow covering the area. She wondered what this place had looked like before the camp had been built. Would it still look like this fifty years from now? She hoped not.

Celia liked this time of day best of all. The sun was finally up and soon the days would begin to get longer and the nights shorter. She couldn't wait for that to happen.

It occurred to her that if someone had told her about living and working at a POW camp, she would have assumed it would be very frightening. The men hadn't given her cause for worry though, she mused. In fact, the only time she had felt fear so far had been when Elsie had issued her veiled threats. Celia groaned, aware that there was little she could do about Elsie until her colleague showed her hand.

For now, she would continue carrying out her duties to the best of her abilities, while being careful not to let anyone else catch her being too attentive to Otto. Maybe if she kept her focus and worked hard, then her seniors might not believe Elsie's tales. The thought cheered her.

'Yes,' Celia said to herself. 'That's what I'll do.' It wasn't much of a plan but it was better than nothing and it gave her back a small semblance of power over her situation. She recalled one of her mother's sayings: *You can't help what someone does to you but you do have control over your reactions.* Her mother had always been a wise woman, Celia thought, as a pang of grief swept through her.

## TWENTY-ONE

## Phoebe

The train journey to the docks took far longer than the few hours Phoebe had imagined, but at least she was able to spend that extra time with Archie, as she'd volunteered to keep an eye on the men who, like Archie, were mostly strong enough to walk. And with the nursing staff being kept busy, Phoebe and Archie had managed a few stolen moments alone.

'I wish you were coming with me to work at the new hospital,' he said quietly when they found themselves alone in a carriage with only other sleeping patients. 'I'm dreading being stuck in a ward without being able to look forward to your beautiful, smiling face coming in each day.' He gave her a wistful sigh. 'You really have made my stay in France such a different experience to what it could have been. It was so much more …' he struggled to find the words, 'I don't want to say "enjoyable", because it was hardly that.'

'I'm glad I made a difference.' Phoebe grinned.

He reached for her and rested his fingers on her chin. 'When I first arrived there, I thought my life as I knew it was over. I had lost my two closest pals, who had joined up after I persuaded them to. We were neighbours and went to school together.'

Phoebe watched his face as he reminisced. 'I hadn't realised,' she said. 'Why didn't you mention your friends to me before?'

He looked at her, his dark eyes seeming brighter in his sadness. 'I couldn't speak about them before without needing to cry,' he admitted quietly. 'And I didn't want you to see me being weak.'

'I could never think of you as weak, Archie. You're one of the strongest men I know.'

'How can you say that? You've only ever known me as a patient.'

'Maybe,' she said, wanting him to see himself as she saw him. 'But don't forget that I know how you face pain. I've seen you having to endure operations and procedures during your recovery. I've witnessed your reaction when the hospital was bombed and we were so near to the blast. You're a brave man, Archie, and I won't hear anyone, especially you, say otherwise.' He went to argue, but she continued speaking. 'And if you're going to say that men shouldn't cry, then I'll have to disagree with that. It's a release of emotion that we all have a right to. In particular, all you men who've faced the horrors of war and coped with months of operations after being wounded. You've earned the right to react as you see fit. If you need to cry, then cry. I certainly won't think any less of you.'

He squeezed her hand. 'You are an amazing woman, Phoebe Robertson. Do you know that?'

She leaned forward and, checking that the other patients were still asleep, kissed him. 'I know that I love you and that

I'm going to miss you terribly when I return to France, and you're not there each day.'

He raised her hands to his lips and then slipped a hand behind her head and gently brought her head to his so that his lips could meet hers again. 'You'll at least be busy,' he said afterwards. 'Whereas I'll have little to do but think about you and try to imagine what you're doing.'

'You'll know exactly what I'm doing.' She grinned. 'I'll be washing out bedpans, changing soiled linen and dressings. Just the usual, I imagine.'

'Will you write to me?'

She gazed at him and her heart contracted to see the hope in his face. She hated to make him unhappy but knew that there were rules she must abide by while she worked as a VAD. 'You know we're not allowed to form attachments to patients, Archie. I can try to find a way, but I'm not sure quite how just yet.'

'Then I'll think of something,' he promised. 'There's nothing stopping you from writing to me from your friend's home in Cornwall though, is there?'

She thought about it. 'I suppose if I write to you as someone else, then that should be fine. No one will be able to trace it back to me.'

His mouth drew back in a wide, happy smile. 'That sounds perfect.' He grinned at her. 'Any idea what name you'll use?'

'Why?' she asked, amused; then a thought occurred to her. 'Do you have other women who'll be sending you letters from Cornwall?'

He laughed and she covered his mouth to quieten him when one of the other patients stirred. 'Sorry.'

Phoebe shook her head. 'Well, do you?'

'You know I don't. I'm merely intrigued to know what name I'll be receiving correspondence from.'

Phoebe gave his question some thought. 'My second name is Medina, after my maternal grandmother, so I suppose I could use that, and her maiden name was Glenn. I doubt anyone could find out the connection to me,' she said thoughtfully. 'Yes, I'll sign my letters off as "Miss Medina Glenn".'

He beamed at her. 'Perfect.' He kissed his fingers and placed them on her lips. 'It's a pleasure to meet you, Miss Medina Glenn. I look forward to receiving your letters.'

'I look forward to the freedom of being able to send them to you.' She really did. It would be an added bonus to staying in Cornwall. 'I'm also looking forward to being able to act like any other couple who are kept apart from one another. It's a shame it'll only be for ten days, though.'

'It is.' He looked glum but then cheered slightly. 'We're not going to allow ourselves to be sad. We're lucky to have this trip together and the next ten days corresponding. I'm going to make the most of it.'

'I will too.' She would, Phoebe decided. She was also going to spend the time trying to work out how they could continue to keep in touch once her holiday was over and she was back at the hospital. There had to be a way for them to manage it, surely.

———

The boat trip was delayed for a few hours but the stormy weather abated slightly once they departed from France.

'Eugh, if this is better weather,' Phoebe said, holding a bag in front of her in case her seasickness worsened, 'then I hate to think how it was for the poor souls who came over from England earlier today.'

Archie stroked her back. 'It is rather rough.'

She would have laughed at his understatement if she hadn't feared vomiting when she did so. 'How are you doing so well?'

'I grew up going out in my father's boat,' he said.

'Your father had a boat?' She knew he grew up in a seaside village but for some reason hadn't thought that his family might have a boat.

'Yes. He used to love going out fishing and would take me and my sister with him when the weather was fine. When I was older and my sister had found other pursuits, he took me out even more often, and I loved it when a storm brewed and the sea got a bit rougher.'

She couldn't imagine choosing to be out in rough waters. 'And you weren't frightened?'

'Not at all,' he said, gazing out to sea as if recalling those special times. 'I found it exhilarating.' He turned to her. 'I think I expected to find the same rush of excitement when I enlisted.' He laughed but it was a hollow, haunted sound that saddened Phoebe. She went to speak but he took her wrist. 'Come along.'

'Where?'

'Out on deck.'

Was he mad? 'No, it's too stormy out there. We'll get washed away.'

'We won't, I promise you. It's sheltered at the back.' He gave her wrist a gentle tug and Phoebe stood and waited for him to do the same. 'You'll feel much better in the fresh air.'

She doubted she would but felt too nauseous to argue, and was at the point of being willing to try anything, just to overcome her seasickness.

As they left their seats and made their way to the back of the boat, Phoebe had to keep grabbing hold of seats and anything she could reach to stop herself falling over. 'I really don't think this is a good idea,' she said through waves of nausea.

'It is,' he insisted, grabbing her to stop her from falling and almost toppling over himself. 'Blast, I keep forgetting I only have one good leg.'

'Please be careful,' she groaned. 'I'll be in for it if you arrive in England worse than when you left the hospital.'

'I'm fine.' He took her hand. 'Now, come with me, we're nearly there.'

They stepped outside and the gust of freezing air that slammed into Phoebe's face took her breath away. 'Gosh, it's so cold out here,' she cried as sea spray dampened her face. 'Are you sure we wouldn't be better off back inside where it's at least dry?'

He shook his head. 'Not yet.'

She realised he was staring at her with an expectant look on his face. 'What is it?'

'I was wondering if you still felt as unwell.'

Phoebe realised she didn't. She laughed despite the cold and wet. 'No, actually. I feel much better.'

'Happy to remain out here for a bit longer then?'

'Yes.' Finally able to think of something other than her stomach, she recalled him saying how he had expected to feel exhilarated by warfare. 'We all expected something different to how it really is in France,' she said. 'I know I certainly did.' She tucked her scarf under the lapels of her coat. 'It's probably a good thing, though.'

'In what way?'

'I suppose most of us wouldn't have joined up if we had

known exactly what to expect.' She pushed her hands deep into her pockets to try and warm them. 'Some would have because it's the patriotic thing to do, but I'm not so sure I would have been as determined to come to France if I'd known how mucky the job of a VAD really was.'

He leaned on the railing and stared at her. 'What did you expect?'

She gave his question some thought. 'I'm not really certain. I suppose I imagined something that would keep my mind too busy to miss my family. Maybe I expected the work to be a little more glamorous.' She smiled. 'I thought I would be part of a sisterhood of heroines helping rescue our men from the horrors of war.'

'And you don't think that's what you've been doing?'

'No.'

'I think it's exactly what you VADs and nurses do.'

'What, washing mud off men and running back and forth to the laundry, carrying heaps of bloodied bandages and soiled linen?' She winced. 'Hardly the stuff of Florence Nightingale.'

He pushed his free hand into her pocket and took her hand in his. The intimate action warmed her soul and reminded her that she was not as alone as she had felt for so long.

Archie gave her hand a gentle squeeze. 'What you do is give hope to men who had all but given up. Your kind words and gentle touch and care slowly work through the layers of our pain and wounds, our guilt for surviving when our friends haven't, and reassure us that there are still some things that are orderly and trustworthy. It's the greatest gift, or at least it was to me.'

His thoughtful words touched her deeply and Phoebe couldn't think what to say.

'I hope I haven't embarrassed you by saying that?' he asked, looking uncertain.

She shook her head. 'Not at all. I'd just never thought about what I did in that way. I've always admired the doctors and nurses, and I suppose I felt inadequate, thinking that all I was doing was clearing up mess for the most part.'

'You shouldn't. We are all cogs in the war machine, with none of us less important or vital than the others.'

She wasn't sure he was completely right about that but didn't wish to argue. It was lovely to hear him saying such kind things about her and the other VADs, and it made her proud that she was at least trying to do her best. 'Thank you,' she said eventually.

Phoebe turned to look at the wake stretching out behind the boat that was taking them further with each second from France and the fighting. For the first time since their journey began Phoebe started to relax. No having to worry about being strafed or bombed. No need to sleep with an ear cocked in case of an emergency. No need to wash her hands a hundred times a day to clean away the blood and muck from her skin. No Archie.

Her mood dipped and she turned her hand in her pocket and gripped his tightly. 'I'm going to miss you so much,' she said, her lips near to his ear.

He gave her hand a squeeze as he turned to kiss her. 'I will miss you too, my sweet girl. But I will at least have the comfort of knowing that you will be safe in Cornwall. The sea air will be good for you.'

'I'm looking forward to it,' she admitted. 'Although I'm a little wary about meeting Doctor Sutherland's sister. What if she doesn't like me? What if she resents him inviting me to stay with her?'

'I can't imagine anyone resenting you. She'll probably end up being a firm friend after your stay there.'

'I like that idea. I do hope we will get along well.'

'I'm sure you will. And if not, then you're only there for a short period of time.'

Several heavy drops of rain landed on Phoebe's forehead, making her flinch.

'We should go inside now, if we don't wish to be soaked,' Archie suggested.

She laughed as they unsteadily left their hold on the railing and stumbled back to the door and inside the boat. 'Phew, that was a little hairy.'

She rested her back against the wall, grabbing onto a door frame. Archie stumbled as the boat dipped to one side and Phoebe wrapped her free arm around his waist to steady him.

'That was close,' he said, holding onto her. The boat then tipped the other way, forcing Archie's body against hers. 'Oof, sorry.'

'Don't apologise,' she said, leaning forward so her lips met his. 'You can lean against me any time.'

'Lean? Or press against you?' he asked with a mischievous glint in his eyes.

Phoebe laughed. 'Both.'

'How are we ever going to survive being apart?' he asked, quietly kissing her again.

'I've no idea.'

---

As the hours passed and the time neared for them to part, Phoebe found the thought of watching Archie go more and more painful to contemplate.

'We'll be at Victoria Station soon,' she said miserably as they sat in the silent train carriage, the other occupants lost in an exhausted sleep. 'I can't bear not to see you, Archie.'

'I know, my sweet. I'm dreading having to say goodbye to you, but I'm trying to find comfort in knowing that you will be resting at the coast with the good doctor's sister. It will do you good.' He looked at her and smiled and Phoebe's heart beat a little faster as she looked into his dark eyes. 'I know that we will see each other again.'

'We have to. I can't bear the thought of not seeing you.'

'I promise you haven't seen the last of Archie Bailey yet.' He grinned before quickly kissing her on the tip of her nose. 'We have an awful lot of living to do together yet, my sweet Phoebe.'

They sat holding hands behind a newspaper that Archie was pretending to read, exchanging the occasional kiss when it was safe to do so and relishing every stolen second together.

Phoebe felt the train slow. Two of the other men stirred. 'We're nearly there,' she said, only just managing to hold in a sob.

She felt Archie's fingers give hers a gentle squeeze and he bent behind his paper to give her one last kiss. 'You make the most of your rest in Cornwall, Nurse Robertson, you hear me?'

She forced a watery smile. 'I'll do my best.'

The train drew to a halt and the doors began opening. 'Write to me and I'll find you.'

'Promise?' she asked.

'Always.'

# TWENTY-TWO

## Celia

C elia finished changing the dressing on Otto's leg and realised that the sound interrupting her concentration was coming from outside.

'What on earth is going on out there?' she grumbled as she tidied up the old dressing and dropped it into a bowl for disposal.

'It sounds to me as if someone is having fun,' Otto said, sitting up higher in his bed and peering outside.

'It must be the snow,' another of the patients shouted, pointing to the window. 'Look and tell us what is happening please, Nurse Robertson.'

Happy to do as he asked, Celia crossed the room and gazed at the scene playing out in the recreation area. She laughed and covered her mouth with surprise. 'They're having a snowball fight.'

The men cheered.

'I wish I was out there with them,' a patient said.

'So do I,' Otto agreed. 'When do you think I may join them, Nurse?'

Celia felt sorry for Otto, being cooped up inside the ward when he would much rather be having fun with the other soldiers. 'The doctor said it wouldn't be too long now,' she reminded him. 'Maybe another week.'

'The snow will have melted by then, though.' He gave her an appealing look. 'Do you not think you might help me to put on a coat so that I may go to watch them for a short while?'

Celia instinctively went to say no, then reasoned that it would probably do him more good than harm, at least mentally.

'All right,' she said, hoping she wasn't making a mistake by agreeing. 'But I will have to clear it with Sister first.' The last thing she wanted to do now was to find herself in even more trouble.

The men groaned, making Celia smile. 'Would you rather I got into trouble?'

'No,' Otto said. 'We would hate for that to happen. We will wait while you speak to Sister for us.'

She smiled at him, grateful for his understanding and support. 'I'll be as quick as I can.'

She called for another nurse to watch over the men while she went to Sister's office, returning less than five minutes later with her blessing.

'Sister said that we can accompany you outside but you'll need to sit on chairs by the door.' When there was a chorus of groans, she added, 'It's either that or stay inside.'

Another round of comments filled her ears and Celia raised her hand to quieten them. 'Let's not waste any time. I'm only allowed to keep you out there for half an hour at the most.'

It didn't take long to put the men's coats and hats on, and Celia carried several chairs and set them down outside the front door of the hospital so that they could watch their colleagues playing. They were a little way away from them but she reasoned that at least this way the patients wouldn't get caught by a stray snowball and get wet.

'There you go,' she said when Otto and four other patients were seated. 'I'll be right back. I'm just fetching some blankets for your legs. We don't want you all catching chills now, do we? Not when you're all doing so well with your recovery.'

Once all the men were catered for, Celia and two of the other nurses stood by the doorway to keep an eye on them. She enjoyed watching them smiling and laughing, passing comments to the other prisoners and calling out to each other as snowballs were flung between two opposing teams.

She glanced back at Otto, delighted to see colour in his face. He looked happier than she had ever seen him before and Celia was glad she had asked Sister O'Brien about bringing the men outside. This would do them far more good than any medicine.

Her gaze strayed from the snowball fight to the electric barbed-wire fencing. It was ten feet high and surrounded the entire camp. How difficult must it be for them to deal with being trapped on enemy soil? Though they were well catered for with entertainment, better food than most of the locals, and warm beds at night, they were still being kept in here against their will as prisoners of war, and none of them knew how long they would be here or how long the war would last.

It had been over two years now since it had begun and it could last another two years, for all she knew. She hoped it wouldn't, though. For all the excitement of the snowball fight, many of these men struggled to cope with being behind the barbed-wire fencing day in and day out. There was no other life for them to watch from this dip in the bay, with the sand dunes rising high above them at the back and lower ones blocking their immediate view of the sea ahead. There was no connection to anyone's usual reality, not even hers. No wonder some of them struggled.

Celia wondered if she would ever return to the island after the war. She hoped so. She would love to come here and see this place as the holiday destination she had known as a child when her parents had brought her, Charlie and Phoebe to stay in a little guest house while they visited family friends. She sighed. Could she dare to hope that life would ever return to normal?

'What are you thinking?'

Celia's stomach clenched at the sound of Elsie's voice so near to her. She tensed and, reminding herself that she was not going to let Elsie frighten her if she could help it, she made a concerted effort to appear relaxed.

'I was thinking how odd it was to be here in this camp with the snow on those sand dunes over there and the men having such a fun time. It's doing them good, don't you think?'

When Elsie didn't answer, Celia looked at her. Elsie's nose was wrinkled in distaste as she looked at the men enjoying themselves.

'I think it's appalling how they're encouraged to play games. This is supposed to be a prisoner-of-war camp, not a holiday camp,' she sneered. 'These men should be made to work. That would give them something to think about.'

'I heard that they were hoping to send them out to work on some of the farms,' Celia said, trying to recall where she had heard that information. 'With so many local men having enlisted and now being conscripted, the farmers are finding it difficult to get enough labourers.'

'Then what's stopping them?'

'I believe the men have to be paid a certain amount, by law.'

She couldn't recall what it was. 'I think it's an agreed amount for prisoners, or something.'

'What!' Elsie shook her head and glared at Otto, who Celia sensed was trying to keep from catching her eye. 'That's madness. I've never heard the like. Paying these men to work, during war time?'

Celia wasn't in the mood to argue with Elsie about this or anything else. 'I'm only repeating what I heard.'

She felt Elsie still and didn't dare look at her. 'There's a lot you hear, isn't there, Celia?'

Celia had no idea what Elsie was referring to. She tried her best to ignore her but just when she thought she was in control, her temper flared and she spun to face her tormentor. 'Actually, Elsie, I believe you're the one who's always listening at keyholes, trying to hear what's not meant for your ears. Not me.'

## TWENTY-THREE

# Phoebe

Cornwall

The sharp wind whipped across Phoebe's face as the horse and cart took her along the clifftop lane towards Jocasta Chambers' home. The sound of crashing waves somewhere below was loud already but it was dusk and misty, so she was unable to see much of any view. Although she had only left Archie that morning, Phoebe was aching all over and felt like she hadn't seen him in days. It had been torment to part from him at the train station in London, but now that she was in Cornwall Phoebe was determined to make the most of her time. She was going to relish the peace, take time to rest and enjoy as much of the fresh sea air as possible.

'This is you,' the driver said with a sideways nod of his head as he pulled on the reins to bring the horse to a halt. 'You need me to lift your bag down to you?'

'No, thank you, it's fine.' Phoebe climbed down carefully and picked up her bag from the cart. 'Thanks for the lift.' She took a few pennies from her change purse and reached up to place them in his hand.

'No problem, Missy. Mrs Chambers will be at home. Probably putting the babby to bed.'

'Right,' Phoebe said, wondering how he might know. 'Thank you.'

She watched him start to leave and turned. Opening the metal gate, she stood at the end of the short pathway and stared up at the cream-coloured terraced house. She shivered as a thick mist rolled in over the lane and hurriedly walked up the path to the front door. Taking hold of her coat collar, she turned it up so that it was slightly higher around her neck. Phoebe found the bell pull by the front door and grabbed hold of it. Then, remembering that the driver had mentioned a sleeping baby, she let go and knocked lightly on the wooden door, hoping Mrs Chambers would hear her.

Moments later she heard footsteps hurrying along wooden floorboards and the door opened to reveal a young woman, only a few years older than her, she supposed. Jocasta had a pretty, red-cheeked face. She was slightly plump and gave the overall impression when she smiled of being friendly. Phoebe instantly relaxed, relieved to be staying with someone who appeared to have a cheery disposition.

'You're here,' Jocasta said, stepping back and waving for Phoebe to enter the hallway. 'Quickly, come in out of the cold. I'm Jocasta Chambers,' she said, closing the door behind Phoebe and dragging a heavy green velvet curtain across the doorway. 'We need this kept closed to keep out the worst of the cold,' she explained. 'The winds can become particularly ferocious in the winters.' She looked Phoebe up and down. 'It's good to meet you, Phoebe.' Her expression changed to one of concern. 'I'm sorry, I'm getting ahead of myself. I should ask if you're happy with me addressing you by your Christian name, before I do it.'

Phoebe shook her head. 'I don't mind at all. In fact, I'm happy not to stand on ceremony here.' She sent a grateful thought to Geoffrey Sutherland for inviting her to this lovely home. 'I have enough of that at the hospital in France.'

'Yes, I can imagine.' Jocasta pointed to Phoebe's coat and hat. 'Leave your case near the door for now. You must be exhausted, and I think the first thing we need to do is to get you to take off that damp hat and coat and get you warmed up. The kitchen's the best place for that, if you're happy to sit in there. It's always the warmest room in the house.'

Phoebe felt much happier already. 'That sounds perfectly lovely,' she said. She followed Jocasta along the passageway and into a large kitchen with a range taking up half of one wall, a well-scrubbed pine table surrounded by chairs in the middle of the room, and a highchair next to one of the end chairs.

'Please, take a seat,' Jocasta said. 'I'll make us some tea. I've not long put the baby down in her crib.' She peered at Phoebe. 'I imagine you must be hungry.'

'I am rather,' she said, realising for the first time that she was.

'It's just a stew, I'm afraid. Nothing fancy. I hope that's all right for you. Beef, with lots of vegetables and potatoes.' She smiled as she lifted the pot onto the top of the range. A delicious aroma filled the room and Phoebe breathed it in. Her stomach grumbled in response. 'Gosh. Sorry about that. I appear to be even hungrier than I had thought.'

Jocasta giggled. 'I am a little, too. I didn't want you to eat alone, so I waited.' She breathed in the rich scent. 'It does smell rather good, doesn't it? One of my better efforts, I think.'

Phoebe didn't like to say that anything Jocasta presented to her now would taste better than the food at the hospital, but she was almost certain of it. 'I'm sure it's perfectly delicious.'

'My brother has given me strict instructions to take very good care of you.' Jocasta placed the lid back on the pot and turned to Phoebe.

'I'm sure he has. He's a very thoughtful and caring man.'

Jocasta smiled proudly. 'I'm glad. You know, I still find it strange to think of him as a proper doctor. I'm not sure why, because that's all he's ever wanted to be. Apart from a fisherman, but that was when he was a little boy.'

'He's an incredible surgeon,' Phoebe said. 'One of our best, so I'm told. He's not long been with the hospital but already everyone I know really likes him.' She smiled as Jocasta placed a mug of tea onto the table near her. 'Thank you.' She cupped the mug with her hands, relishing the heat. 'I hadn't realised how thirsty I was either.' She wished the tea wasn't so hot and that she could start drinking it immediately.

'And cold, I imagine,' Jocasta said, sitting opposite Phoebe with her own cup of tea. 'You have a little time before that cools enough for you to drink it and before the stew is piping hot. You could go upstairs and settle in, if you'd like.' She studied her for a moment. 'In fact, I should have really thought to offer to show you around first.'

'It's fine,' Phoebe said, not wishing her hostess to feel badly, especially when she had been so welcoming. 'I'm just happy to be inside this pretty, warm house.' She looked around the cosy kitchen with its pans hanging near the range, plates stacked neatly in a rack on a wall by the sink, and a small crystal vase with a single pink rose standing in it in the middle of the table.

'That's my last rose of the year,' Jocasta explained. 'I wanted to enjoy it for as long as possible, so cut it and brought it inside where I spend most of my time.'

'It's beautiful.' She looked around the room that felt like a comforting blanket somehow. 'This is such a welcoming room.'

Jocasta beamed at her. 'I'm so glad you think so.' She jumped up. 'I should offer you a biscuit while you wait for your supper to heat up.'

Phoebe was about to politely decline the offer when her stomach rumbled loudly once again. Both women laughed. 'I think I'd like one very much.'

'Good,' Jocasta giggled, getting up and fetching a tin from one of the two cupboards. Taking the lid off, she set it down on the table. 'There's really no need to stand on ceremony here.' She pushed the tin closer towards Phoebe. 'They're only plain. I baked them earlier today, so they're fresh.'

'Thank you,' Phoebe said, taking one, breaking it and popping a piece into her mouth. The sweet, vanilla flavour was delicious and she closed her eyes as she ate the rest. 'My, you're an incredible baker,' she said, even happier to have taken Doctor Sutherland up on his offer now that she had tasted some of Jocasta's baking.

'Do have another one.'

Phoebe shook her head and raised her hand in refusal. 'I'd love one, but don't wish to ruin my appetite. Thanks anyway. Maybe tomorrow.'

'I'm so happy you like them. I do too.' She took a sip of her tea and placed the cup back down on its blue-and-white saucer. 'I think I'm going to enjoy having you to stay very much, Phoebe.'

'I think so too. I'm so glad I wasn't too shy to take your brother up on his kind offer.'

They smiled at each other and Phoebe wondered if she had made a new friend. She hoped so.

---

In the end they didn't go upstairs until after Phoebe had helped Jocasta wash the supper dishes. Phoebe followed Jocasta up the stairs, trying to take in the paintings as she went.

'These are beautiful,' she said, stopping in front of one of a woman holding a baby, sitting at a table in front of a colourful flower border.

'My husband Ronnie painted those,' she said, a catch in her gentle voice. 'He loved to paint.' She stared at the painting for a few seconds before leading the way to the landing.

'Do this is your baby?'

'It's the baby he imagined us having,' Jocasta explained. 'Ronnie didn't live to see our baby.'

Phoebe didn't have a chance to hide her confusion before Jocasta noticed. 'I'm sorry, I don't understand.'

'Ronnie painted this picture, intending to update the baby's face after she was born. This is your bedroom here,' Jocasta said, changing the topic by pushing open a door to the left. 'It overlooks the cliffs.' She turned to Phoebe. 'I hope that's all right with you. I love the view, but my room is slightly larger and fits baby Bryony's cot in better. It also overlooks the garden and is a quieter room. Although we don't have many vehicles coming past the house, when they do, the wooden wheels on the carts can be rather noisy, as can the occasional motor vehicle that comes this way.'

'I'm happy anywhere,' Phoebe said honestly. She recalled the large shed that was their dormitory at the hospital in

France, with its uncomfortable camp beds and tiny amount of space for anything personal, and doubted that any room in this pretty house could be worse than what she had grown accustomed to, living there.

She followed Jocasta into the room, which had pretty floral wallpaper, a small double bed, a wash stand with bowl, ewer and towel hanging from a rail to the side of it, a bedside cabinet and double wardrobe. 'It's wonderful.'

Jocasta's free hand went to rest on her chest. 'Do you really think so?'

'Yes, I do. I'm going to be very happy staying here. Thank you so much for allowing me to come, I really do appreciate your kindness.'

Jocasta placed the lamp onto the deep windowsill. 'I'm so happy to hear you say so,' she said. 'It's been a long time since I've welcomed anyone into my home. I was concerned I might have forgotten how to entertain properly.'

Phoebe placed her bag onto the rug that was taking up most of the wooden floor. 'I can't wait until tomorrow morning when I can go exploring a bit and see what the area is like. I know I can hear the sea but I couldn't see anything really when I arrived, because it was too misty out there.'

'It's very dramatic, but beautiful,' Jocasta said, staring out of the window despite it being pitch black. 'I should close these for you.' She lifted the lamp and placed it on the bedside table, then drew the curtains. 'I'll leave you to settle in,' she said, walking over to the door. 'Please help yourself to anything from the kitchen whenever you need it. The bathroom is along the corridor at the back of the house. My bedroom door is the one opposite this one.'

'Thank you very much, Jocasta. I'm going to be very comfortable here.'

'I hope you are.' She looked at the fireplace. 'If you'd like to light a fire, please do. I can bring up some kindling and logs for you. I'm afraid we're low on coal thanks to the war, but we do have a store of chopped wood outside the back in the garden that my brother chopped for me on his last visit here. Or help yourself to water, or tea, or whatever you can find.'

'I'll be fine, thank you,' Phoebe said, wanting to reassure her. She had already been well cared for and all she really wanted to do was get into bed and unleash the emotion she had had to hold back since bidding farewell to Archie hours before.

'Then I'll say good night.' Jocasta reached the door and turned back. 'I'll try not to wake you. I imagine you'll need a lie-in on your first day.' She held the door handle. 'Come down whenever you're ready and I'll see you then.'

'Good night, Jocasta.'

Finally, she was alone. For a moment all Phoebe could think to do was sit on the bed and try to take in the pretty bedroom. Her mind whirred with all that had happened in the past fifteen hours. This time yesterday she was in France dealing with patients in pain, and constant arrivals of mud-soaked men. Now she was sitting here, the only sound being the noise of waves crashing against cliffs somewhere nearby. It was so different and so peaceful, and she knew she should be happy, but all she really wanted was to spend another five minutes with Archie, holding his hand and kissing him one last time.

She knew Archie was happy for her to be sent here for a rest, but Phoebe couldn't imagine being able to make the most of her time here while he wasn't with her. She had been scared that something would take him away from her and now it was her own injury that had separated them. She thought back to his reassurances that they would be together again and knew she could trust him. They would be together again. This was only a short holiday and maybe afterwards she could ask for a transfer to the hospital in Sussex where she could help take care of Archie during his stay.

# TWENTY-FOUR

## Celia

### 23 DECEMBER 1916

There was still snow on the ground the next morning and Celia thought it helped make the camp feel a little festive. She wished she could be with Phoebe over Christmas, but hopefully next year things might be different and they could spend the time together, supporting each other through their grief. She decided to write to her sister that evening and let her know that she was coping well. It wasn't the whole truth, but she wanted to do her best to make her sister feel better, especially at such a sentimental time, and being completely honest about how difficult she was finding being apart from Phoebe probably wasn't the best way to do that, Celia decided.

'Doctor Burton wants to see us,' Elsie snapped, poking her head around the ward door and pulling Celia out of her reverie.

Celia studied the other woman's face, her heart lurching as she tried to work out if Elsie had been telling tales on her and Otto. She supposed she must have done. Resigned to her fate, she left the other two nurses taking care of the patients and followed Elsie to the surgeon's office. He was a nice man, Celia mused as she walked behind Elsie, trying to think of something to say to the woman who held her future in her hands, but Doctor Burton was above all else a professional and he had always been clear about the high standards he expected from his staff.

They stopped at his office door and Celia closed her eyes and tried to calm herself as she and Elsie waited to be summoned inside.

'Ahh, Nurses Baker and Robertson.' He waved them in and they stood, hands clasped in front of their aprons, waiting for him to speak. 'You might be aware that some of the prisoners have been preparing a show to entertain themselves for Christmas. I'm assured it will only last around an hour and I would like all the patients in the hospital to be given the opportunity to attend.'

Celia could feel Elsie's distaste for the show and knew from Doctor Burton's expression that her colleague hadn't managed to hide it.

'Nurse Baker, I understand how some people feel that as prisoners they should not have access to sports, entertainment or anything light-hearted,' he said, his tone making it clear that he didn't share Elsie's opinion. 'However, I am of the belief that our work here is made easier when the patients are healthy and relatively happy.'

He stared at her pointedly for a moment and Celia wished she was facing Elsie to be able to see her expression. *Good*, Celia thought. *Finally someone is putting Elsie in her place.* The doctor turned his attention to her and Celia had to concentrate on keeping her emotions in check.

'I hope you do not feel the same way as your colleague appears to, Nurse Robertson.'

Before Celia had a chance to speak Elsie murmured something inaudible.

'What was that, Nurse Baker?'

Elsie moved her weight from one foot to the other. 'Er, only that you can be assured that Nurse Robertson and I have very different feelings when it comes to the prisoners, Doctor Burton.'

He frowned thoughtfully then looked from Elsie to Celia. 'I'm not certain I understand Nurse Baker's meaning. Would you care to explain what you think her meaning is, Nurse Robertson?'

Terrified that she was about to be found out, Celia struggled to remain calm. She knew her job and her reputation depended on her response. She took a deep breath. 'I believe Nurse Baker is referring to our different nursing styles,' she said, aware that it didn't quite answer his question but hoped that putting a different twist on her answer might be the best way to deflect him from delving further into their differences.

'I see,' he said, still frowning. She wasn't sure how he could. 'Well, regardless of that, I would like you both to ensure that all the patients who wish to attend the entertainment do so. Is that clear?'

'Perfectly, Doctor Burton,' Celia said, thinking how happy Otto would be to have time away from the ward.

'Yes, Doctor Burton.'

Celia could sense Elsie's gaze on the side of her face but didn't turn to look at her. She had no intention of giving the nasty woman the satisfaction of seeing how much she had unsettled her.

'Good. I believe the event begins at four-thirty tomorrow afternoon. I'll leave that with you, then.'

They began their return but halted a few feet from the ward

door when Elsie stepped in front of Celia, giving her no option but to stop.

Elsie glowered at her, a furious scowl on her face. 'You think you're clever, don't you?'

*What?*

'No, of course I don't,' Celia said. 'Why would you think I do?'

'I might not have told Doctor Burton about you just then, but I would hate you to think that I had forgotten what I said to you. I'll bring this out into the open, but not until I'm good and ready.'

Celia couldn't hide her shock at Elsie's aggression.

Elsie gave a satisfied smile. 'Yes, that's right. You should fear me. I'm not finished with you. Not by a long way.'

Celia flinched as Elsie's sour breath reached her nostrils. She was so stunned she couldn't think of a reply. Seconds later, Elsie turned her back and marched off past the ward, leaving Celia to wrestle with her fear about what exactly Elsie's plans were for her.

She took a deep breath to try and quell the nausea rising in her throat. Of all people, why did she have to have been seen by Elsie? The woman was mad and extremely unpleasant.

———————

That evening, still shaken by Elsie's nastiness, Celia sat down to write to her sister. She didn't dare share anything too detailed in her letter in case anyone else read it, but the feeling of closeness it gave her to write her sister's name and some of her thoughts might help calm her.

*Dearest Phoebe,*

*I hope you're coping as well as I know you can. Life here is filled with little difficulties, some bigger than others, but all of them making each day a bit of a struggle. Then again, the biggest struggle you and I have right now, as with many others, is with our grief. I know that our mother and father would be proud of what we are doing, and that helps me keep going, and reminds me that one day we will be together again and will be able to give each other a hug and sit and reminisce about our dearest family.*

*I tell myself that as tragic as Charlie's death might have been, and it was, that at least he is buried with our parents and not lost in some muddy field in France. It brings me little comfort, but that's better than nothing.*

*I miss you and look forward to the day that we can spend time together again and find some happiness for ourselves.*

*For now though, dearest Phoebe, I would like to wish you a peaceful and healthy Christmas and hope that 1917 brings an end to this war.*

*My sincerest affection, dearest sister,*
*Celia*

## TWENTY-FIVE

## Phoebe

24 DECEMBER 1916

Phoebe woke to the sound of birdsong and the smell of freshly baked bread. It was heavenly. She slowly opened her eyes, relishing the comfort of the bed and soft downy pillows. She saw from the light behind the curtains that the weather was fine. Good, she thought, there was nothing stopping her from going for a long walk. She stretched and rubbed her eyes, wondering what the time might be and was stunned to notice that it was after ten. She never slept that late.

She flung the covers back and got up.

The sound of happy burbling and Jocasta singing greeted her as she walked along the passage towards the kitchen. She was a little embarrassed to be arriving for breakfast so late, even though her hostess had told her to come down whenever it suited her.

'Good morning,' Phoebe said, walking into the warm kitchen. She looked at the cherubic face of the baby sitting in the highchair, hands mushing some concoction that looked like porridge onto the wooden tray.

Jocasta looked up from where she was washing up dishes

at the sink. 'Hello,' she said, wiping her hands on a towel. 'How did you sleep?' she asked.

'Extremely well, thank you. That has to be the most comfortable bed I've ever lain on.'

'I'm so pleased to hear you say so.'

'I don't recall the last time I slept for so many hours,' she said, embarrassed. 'I do apologise for rising this late.'

'Please don't worry about it. We agreed that there was no need to stand on ceremony, and I want you to make the most of not working while you're here. You need to rest and sleep, and hopefully eat well. It's what my brother prescribed to you!' She laughed. 'And I'm not joking when I say as much.'

Phoebe thought of Doctor Sutherland and could almost hear him saying such a thing.

'Take a seat and I'll make you some fried eggs and bacon, or I could make scrambled eggs, or boiled,' Jocasta said.

'Fried with bacon sounds heavenly.' Phoebe pulled out a chair and sat, smiling at the baby who was now staring at her intently. 'Hello, Bryony,' Phoebe said, unsure how exactly to address the baby. She realised how unused to them she was.

'She's transfixed by you,' Jocasta said, placing a rasher of bacon into a pan. 'She has her father's eyes, large and blue, unlike mine.'

Phoebe pictured Doctor Sutherland's hazel eyes and noticed that Jocasta's were almost the same colour but with flecks of gold in them. She wondered if she should ask about Jocasta's late husband and, recalling how patients often wanted to talk about lost friends, decided to take a chance.

'You must miss him very much,' she said.

Jocasta leaned against the worktop and crossed her arms. 'I do,' she said, her voice small. 'I sometimes try to pretend that he's still away fighting. Then, when I think of something

Bryony does and want to share it with him, that's when I remember that he's never coming home to us.' Her voice wavered. 'I can't bear that he'll never see our beautiful daughter growing up, getting married and hopefully having children of her own.' Her eyes met Phoebe's. 'He's missed out on so much already and it seems so unfair.'

Phoebe nodded. 'It does. I'm so very sorry.'

'As am I. We were so happy.' She swallowed. Turning back to the range, she picked up two eggs, cracked them on the side of the pan and dropped them in to cook before addressing Phoebe once more. 'He was the sweetest man.' Jocasta gave a sad smile. 'We were childhood sweethearts, did you know that?'

Phoebe shook her head. 'No. All your brother told me was that you were a widow.'

'That's right.' She flicked oil over the eggs with a spatula. 'I suspect Geoffrey offered for you to stay here to give me company as much as to find somewhere where you could relax for a couple of weeks. He's very thoughtful that way.'

'He's a lovely brother to have.'

'He is. He and Ronnie were best friends since they started school. I think he almost felt his loss as much as I did.'

'Did Doctor Sutherland live around here too?'

Jocasta poked the bacon with a fork and flipped it over to cook the other side. 'He lived here,' she said, surprising Phoebe. 'You're staying in his room.'

Phoebe didn't know why she was surprised and realised she must have shown it on her face when Jocasta added, 'He inherited this house from our father when he passed away two years ago. Ronnie and I rented a cottage on the other side of the village, but when he died and I found it difficult being there with all my memories of everything we had shared together, Geoffrey insisted I come live here with him. Then he was called away and I was happy to be living in my childhood home with Bryony where everything seemed familiar.'

'I'm pleased.' Phoebe thought of her parents' home and how pretty it had been before the bombing. The thought saddened her. 'I'm glad you have each other.'

'So am I. I feel very blessed.'

'You don't have any other siblings then?'

She shook her head. 'No. Sadly not.' Jocasta took a plate from the plate rack and placed the eggs and bacon onto it before serving it to Phoebe. 'I'll cut you some bread to go with that and we'll have a cup of tea. How about you? Do you have any siblings?'

Phoebe explained that she had a sister and about Charlie having been killed.

'That's terrible,' Jocasta said, buttering the thick piece of fresh bread. 'How about your parents? Are they still alive?'

'They were killed in the same Zeppelin bombing raid. Charlie was home on leave when it happened,' Phoebe explained, having to breathe deeply to calm herself. 'I feel guilty that I wasn't there with them.'

Jocasta shook her head. 'But then you would have also been killed, most likely.'

'I know, but I sometimes find the guilt that I survived, when they didn't, a little overwhelming.'

'I know what you mean,' Jocasta said, cupping her chin for a few seconds. 'I feel guilty that I'm here, enjoying watching Bryony grow and change each day, while my darling Ronnie is missing everything.' She sniffed and, pulling her handkerchief from her sleeve, blew her nose. 'Sorry. My sadness hits me like that sometimes.'

'Mine does too,' Phoebe soothed.

Neither spoke for a while, then Jocasta busied herself slicing bread and buttering it before cutting it into quarters and putting it on a side plate. She put the plate on the table near to Phoebe.

'Thank you.' Lifting a piece, she noticed it was still warm. Phoebe took a bite, relishing the soft doughiness. 'Mmm, this is perfection.'

Jocasta laughed. 'I've never had my bread called that before now.'

'That does surprise me.' Phoebe was happy to think that she had cheered Jocasta slightly. 'I don't think I realised quite how much I needed time doing normal things.'

'I'm please to help you in any way I can.'

'Thank you, and I want you to know that you can ask me for anything, any time you need it.'

'That's very kind of you,' Jocasta said, picking up a cloth and wiping the work-surface before making them both a cup of tea.

Phoebe watched as her new friend cleaned Bryony's face with a damp cloth and handed the baby a teething ring to play with.

'What do you plan to do this morning?' Jocasta asked, leaning back in her chair. 'It's a beautiful day, if bitterly cold, but at least you should be able to see for miles and enjoy the view. It's pretty spectacular, if I say so myself.'

'I thought I'd go for a walk along the cliff path, if there's one nearby.'

'There are many. I'll give you directions, though, so you know where you're going.'

Phoebe thought of Archie and felt the need to contact him. 'Is there a post box nearby anywhere?'

'There's one down the lane and if you turn right at the top

of the road and follow the road away from the sea for about three hundred yards, you'll come across the heart of the village. There's all the usual shops there – baker, butcher, greengrocer and a post office. A couple of other shops too. Naturally there's a pub. Actually there are two: The Nag's Head and The Penny Farthing. They're in the same old building, but one side is run by one brother and the other side by another. They can't stand each other and so the residents have had to choose sides if they want to drink in one of the locals.'

'That sounds rather complicated,' Phoebe said, amused. 'Which does Doctor Sutherland frequent when he's at home?'

Jocasta took a sip of her tea. 'Oh, he prefers the brother at The Penny Farthing. He's the older one, but a little less competitive than his younger brother. It's all rather silly, I think, and apparently their dislike of each other stems back to when they were at school and one cheated on sports day. Sad rather than silly, really.'

'It is. When you think how most of us would give anything just to have a loved one back, and they spend their time working against each other.'

'I would have thought that they might agree to disagree, if nothing else,' Jocasta said, passing what looked like some sort of rusk to baby Bryony.

Phoebe finished her breakfast. 'That was delicious, Jocasta. Thank you for everything.'

Jocasta grinned. 'You've only been here a few hours,' she said. 'Hopefully you'll feel the same way when it's time for you to leave us.' She sighed. 'I have a feeling I'm going to get used to having you here with me very quickly.'

Phoebe knew what she meant. 'I suspect I'll find it difficult to leave and have to sleep in my dormitory back in France.'

She clapped her hands together. 'I'm not thinking about that now, though. I'm going to have fun and hopefully spend a lot more time getting to know you and this little angel.'

Jocasta reached out and stroked her daughter's curly blonde hair. 'She is adorable, isn't she?'

'She is.' Sensing Jocasta might need some time to do her chores, Phoebe stood and went to carry her plate and cutlery to the sink to wash it.

'No you don't,' Jocasta said, reaching out and placing her hand on Phoebe's. 'You leave that there and go out and see what a beautiful area this is. You're on holiday, don't forget.'

She was itching to go but didn't like to be rude. 'Can't I first help you with any chores? I want to do my bit while I'm here.'

'No. It's enough that I have you for company. Now, go.'

Phoebe did as she was told and once she had freshened up and put on her coat, hat, scarf, gloves and grabbed her purse, she went back downstairs.

'I'm going for a walk to the cliffs,' she said before leaving. 'I'll pop back after that to write a letter and then take it to the village to post it.'

'That sounds like a good plan.' Jocasta smiled. 'Enjoy yourself and don't go too close to the cliff edge.'

Phoebe promised that she wouldn't and left, looking forward to her walk along the cliffs. She stood at the end of the short front path and breathed in the refreshingly cold sea air. It was still windy but less so than the previous day, she noticed with relief. And best of all, the sun was shining and she could see high cliffs rising to the east and a pretty golden beach about a mile to the west of her. She understood now why Geoffrey insisted she take him up on her offer to come here.

As she walked, she thought about Archie and wished he was there to experience this breath-taking place with her.

Maybe he lived somewhere similar to this. Did they have cliffs like these in Sandsend? If they did, then he was a lucky man to have experienced something this magnificent before.

She stopped and stared out over the sea as waves crashed against the cliffs far below. This was nature at its most magnificent. Why, she mused, were humans so intent on killing each other and causing destruction when they had places like this to go to and simply be? It didn't make any sense. Maybe one day she would be lucky enough to bring Archie here and walk with him hand in hand in the sunshine, marvelling at how lucky they were to have found each other. They were still at war though, she reminded herself, and there were probably months – even years maybe – until either of them might be free to do such a thing.

She arrived back at the cottage feeling invigorated and desperate to put her thoughts down on paper in a letter for Archie. Deciding first to check with Jocasta and see if there was anything she needed her to do, Phoebe walked down the passage and into the kitchen. Her friend was sewing and deep in thought. Jocasta jumped when she suddenly realised Phoebe was there.

'Oh, you're back. Did you have fun?'

Phoebe nodded. 'It's stunning scenery out there, isn't it?'

'I think so.' She cocked her head in the direction of the range. 'Why don't you make us both a cup of tea? I've been trying to darn these stockings for ages and I'm making a real mess of them.' She laughed. 'I've never been good at any needlework.'

'I'm not so good at it either,' Phoebe said, picking up the

kettle and shaking it slightly to gauge how much water was inside before holding it under the tap at the sink. At the mention of scenery, Phoebe's mind drifted to the show. It would be taking place today, she mused. She thought of Archie and how much fun they'd had together during the planning. He would be sad to miss the show, no doubt.

When they were sitting with their cups of tea Phoebe reminded Jocasta that she planned to walk into the village to the post office. Remembering that tomorrow would be Christmas Day, she decided to try and buy little gifts for Jocasta and Bryony. She had no idea if there was much choice of presents in the village but knew it was the thought that counted most where gifts were concerned. She would also look out for some tidbits to make their Christmas a little special. 'If you need me to do any shopping for you or to post any letters, do let me know.'

Jocasta smiled. 'We could do with a couple of sausages for our breakfast tomorrow and maybe some potatoes, if they have them at the greengrocers.'

'Of course.' She made her excuses then and went upstairs to pen a letter to Archie while everything was still fresh in her mind. She missed him so much already, despite it only being twenty-four hours since their parting.

*Dearest Archie,*

*I hope you're settled in well and aren't misbehaving too badly. Those poor nurses will have enough to keep them busy without you being mischievous. I only wish that I was one of them. I'm already missing you terribly and I've no idea how I'll bear not seeing you every day once my holiday is over and I return to work.*

*Enough wallowing though. I thought you might like to know a little about Pennwalloe. Oh, Archie, it's the most beautiful place. I've never been to Cornwall before but I'm certainly going to return and I'd love to introduce you to the area. I've yet to see the village but will be going there straight after I've finished writing this letter so that I can post it to you. There are cliff paths with the most incredible views down to the sea below. The wind is invigorating although it is rather cold, but then it is December. There's a pretty beach on the other side of the headland and I'm intending going there in the coming days.*

*I needn't have worried about coming to stay with Jocasta. I felt as if I'd known her for years within a few minutes of meeting her. She is friendly and terribly kind, although a little sad at times, which is understandable seeing that she lost her beloved husband Ronnie only last year. Her baby girl is about a year old and is the prettiest angel with blonde curly hair and big blue eyes. Her name is Bryony and she is bright as a button.*

*I've just seen the time and don't want to miss the post this afternoon, so I'll sign off now and send you all my love. I hope you have a peaceful and entertaining Christmas at the hospital. I only wish that we could have celebrated our first Christmas together in France and been able to entertain the patients there with the planned show. Never mind. We are where we are and we must make the best of it. Not that it's too difficult for me where I am but as I mentioned above, I do miss you, dreadfully.*

*Take care, dearest Archie,*

*Love, your friend,*

*Medina Glenn*

Phoebe read through her letter, then quickly penned one to her sister so she could post it at the same time, all the while remembering what Jocasta had told her about the nights drawing in at about four in the afternoon at this time of year.

*Dearest Celia,*

*I'm writing this thinking about you and hoping that your Christmas isn't too busy, but busy enough that you don't have too much time to think about everything. I hope you are keeping well and wanted to share that I am lucky enough to be staying in Cornwall with a new friend this Christmas. I wish you were here too and hope that one day I'll be able to introduce you to Jocasta and this beautiful part of the world.*

*I hope you're taking good care of yourself. I am doing my best and apart from missing Captain Archie Bailey, I'm doing all right. Yes, that's right, I am in love with a wonderful man who I met at the hospital in Étaples. He is an architect and funny and sweet, and I'm sure you will like him. Maybe we'll all be able to meet, if this war ever comes to an end. Either way, I hope it's not too long until I can introduce you to Archie and Jocasta.*

*I must hurry though because I want to get my bearings around this village before it gets dark and I need to post this letter to you and one to Archie before the evening draws in.*

*My love to you, dearest Celia.*

*Your loving sister,*

*Phoebe xx*

Satisfied that she had said all she needed to for the time being, Phoebe addressed two envelopes and, sealing her letters inside, slipped them into her coat pocket.

---

The walk along the quiet lane from Jocasta's home to the centre of the village took her less than ten minutes. There were the shops and pubs that Jocasta had told her about and a small village green that Phoebe thought must look very pretty in the summer when the flower borders were more than likely filled with colourful blooms.

Having bought the potatoes and sausages Jocasta had requested, she crossed the road and went to the post office and posted her letters to her sister and Archie, then bought several stamps, notepaper and envelopes so that she could write to them both again. At least now they would both know where she was staying, should they wish to contact her.

As she left the post office, she noticed a small shop with paper chains hanging across the window and went inside.

'Good afternoon, Miss,' the elderly lady behind the counter said with a smile on her face. 'Looking for something in particular?'

'Hello,' Phoebe said, looking all around her, hoping for inspiration 'I'm staying with a friend for a couple of weeks and was hoping to find a little Christmas gift for her and her baby girl.'

The woman seemed intrigued. She placed both hands on her hips and came out from behind her counter, staring thoughtfully at the display before making her way to a large cupboard. 'Would that be young Jocasta Chambers and baby Bryony, then?'

'Yes, that's right,' Phoebe said, excited that the woman knew who she intended buying the presents for. 'You know them?' As soon as Phoebe had asked the question, she realised what a stupid thing it was to say. This was a small village and no doubt everyone knew everyone else. 'Sorry, I suppose that goes without saying.'

The woman laughed. 'It does. We're a close-knit bunch here in Pennwalloe. In fact, I was wondering who the newcomer was who had been seen walking by the cliffs today.'

It was Phoebe's turn to laugh. 'Right, I see. Yes, I took a stroll up there. It's very beautiful.'

'Oh, it is that, dear.' The woman sighed. 'Let's find these presents for you.' Phoebe waited while she stood staring thoughtfully at the contents of the cupboard. It was mostly boxes but the woman probably knew what was in each one. Phoebe was tempted to have another look at the display but didn't like to interrupt the woman's train of thought.

'I'm Mrs Lanyon,' the lady said as she pulled out a box from the pile on one of the shelves and placed it on the counter. She then pulled out a flatter box and took that to the counter as well.

'I'm Phoebe Robertson. I'm pleased to meet you and to be here in this pretty place.'

'It is rather special. Good for lots of things,' Mrs Lanyon said, closing the cupboard and returning to her place behind the counter. 'For friends, beautiful scenery and for healing.'

'Healing?' Phoebe asked, taken aback. What on earth did the woman mean?

Mrs Lanyon took the lid from the first box and, turning it to Phoebe, indicated the teddy inside. It wasn't too big for the little girl to cuddle and Phoebe was delighted. 'It's perfect for her. Thank you.'

Mrs Lanyon gave her a self-satisfied nod and then, replacing the lid onto the box, moved it to one side and opened the other. This revealed a knitted hat-and-scarf set in cherry red. 'I thought this would suit young Jocasta's colouring and I've never seen her in anything this colour before. What do you think?'

Phoebe had no idea if her friend would wear the bright hat and scarf but thought it was the perfect colour for a Christmas present. 'I know it would suit her if she did,' Phoebe said. 'I'll take them both. Thank you very much.'

'I don't suppose you have anything in which to wrap them, do you?'

Phoebe hadn't thought of wrapping. She shook her head. 'No, I don't. Would you have something I could buy for the gifts and maybe a ribbon to tie around each of them?'

'I'll tell you what, as you're most likely my last customer of the day, I'll wrap them for you for an extra penny. How does that sound?'

Phoebe smiled at her. 'It sounds wonderful. Thank you.'

Recalling the postcard she was hoping to find for her friends, Phoebe asked Mrs Lanyon where she might purchase one.

'Are you looking for anything in particular?'

'Something with a photo of the village, or the cliffs, or beach? I want to give them an idea of what it's like here so they can imagine it.' She realised she ought to send one to Geoffrey Sutherland as well. 'In fact, I'll need two.'

Mrs Lanyon tapped the side of her mouth for a few seconds and gave Phoebe's request some thought. Then, raising her finger in the air triumphantly, she grinned. 'I was trying to recall where I might have put the ones I had in the shop before the war. We haven't had much cause for them recently and I usually put them away in the winter to keep them fresh looking. No one wants to buy a creased postcard. If you'll wait here, I'll fetch what I've got and you can see if any of them suit you.'

# TWENTY-SIX

## Celia

Half an hour before they were to accompany the patients to the show, Sister O'Brien and the doctor ushered a new prisoner into the hospital. He was shaking and seemed in a bad way with a blackened eye and swelling to the right side of his jaw. Celia wondered what might have happened to him.

'Please settle this officer in one of the beds, Nurse Robertson,' Sister O'Brien said.

'You'll remain in here until that swelling goes down,' Doctor Burton explained to the traumatised young man. 'I need to be certain your ribs have healed, too, before you go back into the dorm with the other men.'

Before he walked away, he took Celia's arm and led her from the soldier's bedside. 'He's been in a fight, as you can probably tell. I'm not sure why but I think he and one of the others are from the same town, so knew each other prior to the war.'

'Probably past differences coming to a head,' Sister suggested, coming over to them with a knowing frown on her face.

Celia hadn't seen many fights among the men, assuming that they were sticking together and trying to make the best of things rather than falling out over petty differences.

'Yes,' Celia agreed, returning to look after the young man, who seemed highly agitated. She glanced up at the doctor nervously.

'He's had something to calm him,' Doctor Burton said. 'And should begin to relax soon.'

She drew a screen around the bed and proceeded to wash and change the soldier, who seemed little more than a boy. He didn't speak but the frightened look in his dark-blue eyes upset her. Celia tried to soothe him with her words, aware that he didn't appear to understand her but hoping that her tone was in some way comforting to him. Seeing someone in this fearful state broke her heart and she had to concentrate on what she was doing so that her emotions didn't get the better of her. Eventually he was settled in bed and she folded the screen away.

'You'll be safe here,' she said, wanting him to relax and trust her, but when his fear didn't seem to subside she decided to speak to Otto and ask if maybe he could help.

'Do not worry,' Otto said. 'I will speak to him and reassure him that I will watch out for him while he sleeps.'

'Maybe don't say that bit,' Celia suggested. 'You'll be leaving to watch the show soon, and I wouldn't want him to wake and find that you're not there.'

Otto threw back his covers and carefully manoeuvred his damaged leg out of the bed, and followed with the other one. 'I shall not attend the show,' he said. 'I will remain with the boy.'

Celia stared at him. He was so kind. 'No, Otto,' she said. 'You need time away from the ward and you were really looking forward to the show. It's only for an hour, and I'll be staying here with him.'

Otto cocked his head towards the door, where Elsie had just arrived. 'I do not wish to spend time with that woman. I would rather miss the show than be with her for a minute. No, I am happy to remain here. I shall speak to the unteroffizier now before he sleeps. Hopefully I will be able to reassure him.'

'That's very kind,' Celia said gratefully. 'I hate to think of anyone being frightened.'

'I have experienced enough fear not to wish it on anyone else.'

She imagined he had. 'Thank you.'

Celia was aware of Elsie walking towards her, so turned away from Otto and waited to see what the other woman wanted.

'Why aren't your patients ready to leave?'

Celia looked at the pinched, scowling face. 'Because we have a new patient who Doctor Burton and Sister O'Brien have asked me to look after.'

'And him?' Elsie almost spat the words as she pointed in Otto's direction.

'Hauptmann Hoffman is very kindly speaking with the patient to try and reassure him. He will now be staying behind.'

'Of course he is,' Elsie sniggered. 'How convenient.'

Celia wanted to slap the woman's face but it wasn't the way to behave. Instead she ignored her snide comments. 'I'll help the patients into their coats so that they're ready to go with you.'

When Elsie and the patients had left, Celia gave a sigh of relief. She was finally alone with Otto, albeit also with the young unteroffizier, but he had begun to settle and she imagined he would soon be asleep. She had no intention of being careless, though, and didn't trust Elsie not to creep back to spy on them. She glanced at Otto and knew instinctively that he would think the same way.

Once the unteroffizier was sleeping and Otto was sitting in the chair next to his bed, Celia pulled up another chair and sat. 'Poor boy,' she said, looking over at the sleeping patient, the purple hues on his pale face revealing how hard he had been punched. 'How can someone pick on a boy like him?'

'There's no excuse,' Otto said. 'Tomorrow I will go and find out who was involved in this attack and speak with them. It is not acceptable. We should be looking out for one another in this place, not fighting. We are supposed to be disciplined men.'

He seemed sad and Celia wasn't surprised. Otto was a decent, honourable man and she could tell that this incident had upset him deeply. She wanted to tell him not to leave the ward in such bad weather, but knew he felt honour bound towards his fellow men and couldn't sit back and do nothing.

'I'm glad he has you to look out for him,' she said.

He stood and walked over to the boy's bed, standing next to her chair. Then she felt his hand take hers. Celia looked up at him to see him checking that the ward door was still closed, before he lifted her hand to his lips. 'One day we will be able to hold hands openly, *schatz*.'

'Yes, we will.' She sighed. 'And that day can't come soon enough for me.'

'And for me.'

# TWENTY-SEVEN

## Phoebe

Phoebe returned from the village and, before Jocasta spotted her, ran up to her room and hid the two presents in her wardrobe. She was delighted to have something for them both and couldn't believe her luck to have met someone as generous as Mrs Lanyon. Already this Christmas was turning out to be better than she had dared hope it might be.

'Oh, you are here,' Jocasta said, looking up from the bottom of the stairs when Phoebe left her bedroom a few minutes later. 'I thought I was imagining footsteps for a moment.'

Phoebe smiled and went down to join her, hanging her coat and hat on the hook by the door as she passed. 'Just back,' she said. 'I wanted to leave my bag and … er … some other things I found in my room so that they were out of the way.'

'That's kind of you.' Jocasta led the way to the kitchen. 'I've just finished feeding Bryony, which is why she's not yelling. She loves her supper time, that one. Ronnie would have been very proud of her healthy appetite.'

Phoebe thought how dreadfully sad it was that the young man wasn't here to see the ordinary daily comings and goings of his small family. How many other hundreds of thousands of men were missing out already, thanks to this dreadful war? How many widows were trying to keep going as best they could for their children? It was all too tragic.

'Do take a seat,' Jocasta said. 'I managed to buy us a couple of chops for our supper.' She turned to Phoebe to gauge her reaction.

'What a treat,' Phoebe said, delighted. 'I can't recall the last time I had a chop.' Her mouth salivated at the thought of the tasty meal that was to come.

'I thought you might be pleased. We're having carrots and boiled potatoes too. Maybe mashed if we have enough milk to spare.'

'I could have collected some for you from your local farmer if you'd asked me,' Phoebe said. 'In fact, while I'm here, please do give me any jobs you'd like me to do, especially ones like shopping that take time out of your day.'

'Thank you,' Jocasta said, continuing to peel some potatoes.

Phoebe stood and went to join her at the sink.

'No,' Jocasta said. 'You're a guest in this house. You should sit down and relax. I'm happy to do this.'

'No,' Phoebe said firmly with a smile. 'I like to think that I'm more than a guest now. As far as I'm concerned, we're friends. I hope you feel the same way as I do.'

Jocasta stopped peeling and smiled at her. 'I think of you as a friend, too.' She giggled. 'All right, there's another knife in that drawer,' she said, pointing to it. 'You can peel the carrots.'

Phoebe did as her friend suggested and as they stood side by side at the wooden worktop, she couldn't help feeling like she had come home somehow, as this was how she used to feel when helping her mother prepare for the festivities. She closed her eyes briefly to regain control over her emotions before she began to cry. Hopefully this would be how she could feel again, when she and Archie married and had a home, and if they were lucky, a family of their own. Maybe then she would feel whole again. She hoped so. She wondered how long it would take for Archie to receive her letter and if he would write straight back. Phoebe smiled to herself, certain that he would.

'What are you thinking?' Jocasta asked quietly.

Phoebe turned her head to look at her friend and smiled. 'How content I feel, being here with you and baby Bryony. It's a happy home here.' She hesitated, then, trusting her instinct to be honest, added, 'Despite all that's happened.'

She saw Jocasta still for a moment before continuing peeling her potatoes. 'You don't know how happy it makes me to hear you say so,' she said, her voice wavering slightly.

Phoebe relaxed and realised she had been holding her breath. 'It does? I wasn't sure if I should have said that.'

Jocasta finished peeling the potatoes and turned to Phoebe. 'Yes. Ronnie was always such a happy-go-lucky man. He always made the best of things, whereas I was always the one out of the two of us who worried about anything going wrong.'

Phoebe waited for her to finish, conflicted by her words, yet aware of how much she had lost when he had been killed.

'I know you're thinking that everything is not fine – far from it – but it is. I still have this house and Bryony, and now you.' She smiled and, wiping her hand roughly on a towel, placed it on Phoebe's arm. 'Thank you for coming to stay with us, Phoebe. I don't think you'll ever know quite how much I needed you to come into my life just when you did.'

Phoebe opened her arms and hugged Jocasta. 'I'm glad to

have been some comfort to you, and to have found a friend in you.'

'It seems that we've helped each other without even intending to,' Jocasta said thoughtfully. 'Do you think it was fate that brought you and my brother together?'

Phoebe had no idea. 'Maybe,' she said. 'Either way, I'm glad that we did bump into each other when we did.'

Jocasta gave her a searching look, but when Phoebe opened her mouth to ask what was on her mind, she stepped back, pulled open the cutlery drawer and took out two knives and forks. 'Why don't you lay the table for us and I'll put this lot on the range to cook.'

Phoebe did as she asked, realising that she needed to set Jocasta straight, in case she had any secret hopes for Phoebe and her brother.

'Geoffrey's a good man and I'm grateful to have a friend like him.'

Jocasta frowned for a second, then nodded. 'I see. Thank you for explaining.'

---

After supper they cleared the table and washed up and put away the supper paraphernalia. 'I thought we could go and sit in the living room tonight for a change. What do you think?'

Phoebe liked the idea. She loved sitting in the cosy kitchen but the wooden chairs were a little uncomfortable after a while, despite the seat cushions that were tied to them. She presumed they might have offered a little more comfort when they were new, but over the years the stuffing had been flattened and now they were little more than mere decoration.

She followed Jocasta down the passage into the pretty

room. There was another of Ronnie's paintings above the fireplace and this one was of the two of them.

'That's a beautiful painting,' Phoebe said, wishing she had been given the opportunity of meeting the man Jocasta had loved so deeply.

'He painted it from a photo of our wedding day,' Jocasta said. 'I don't know which I love best out of this one and the painting he did of me and the baby.' She went silent for a moment. 'I can't help wishing that he had painted one of the three of us.' She sighed sadly. 'I know he never met Bryony, but at least I could imagine that he did if there was a picture for me to look at with us together as a family.'

Phoebe stroked her friend's arm. 'It's so sad that he died when he did.'

'It is. I think I'm still in some shock, if I'm truthful. Having Bryony to look after, and with this war continuing, I've been able to pretend that he's fighting with his unit in France and not fully face what's happened.' She looked at Phoebe and shrugged. 'Do you think that's silly?'

'Of course I don't,' Phoebe replied, shocked that her friend should even think such a thing. 'You do whatever it takes to help you through this time in your life.'

Jocasta smiled. 'Thank you. And at least now I have you to speak to and share my thoughts with, if I need to.'

Phoebe was delighted to hear her say so. 'Yes, you do.' She looked around; there seemed to be something missing but she couldn't think what it might be.

'Sit down and make yourself comfortable,' Jocasta said. 'I'll pour us a sherry and light the fire; it'll soon warm up in here when that gets going.'

'You do the drinks,' Phoebe said. 'Leave the fire to me.'

As she walked over to the fireplace Phoebe noticed photos

of Geoffrey and several of two other people who she assumed by their clothes were possibly Geoffrey and Jocasta's parents. There was also one of a man she now knew to be Ronnie standing with his arm around Jocasta. She studied the photo. He had been a handsome man with a sweet, gentle face.

'He's very good-looking, don't you think?' Jocasta said, walking over and placing their sherries onto a small table set between the two armchairs.

Phoebe knelt in front of the fire and began setting down kindling wood, preparing to light it. 'Very much so.'

She lit the fire and when she was seated she raised her glass. 'I'd like to make a toast to you and Bryony,' she said.

'Whatever for?' Jocasta asked, raising her glass.

'For allowing me into your life, and...' It dawned on her what was missing.

'What is it?'

'There aren't any Christmas decorations,' Phoebe said, almost to herself. 'You're not putting up a tree, or even some holly on the mantelpiece or pictures?' *How sad*, she thought, wondering why Jocasta was ignoring the festivities and realising that maybe she should have kept her mouth closed and not mentioned it.

Jocasta looked stunned for a few seconds and Phoebe wondered what she had said.

'I'm sorry, I shouldn't have remarked on it.' She cringed to think that she might have upset her friend. How could she have been so thoughtless?

Jocasta shook her head. 'Not at all,' she said. 'I hadn't intended marking the occasion, that's all.'

'No?' Phoebe asked, hoping that she hadn't unintentionally been insensitive.

'I learnt of Ronnie's death last Christmas Eve,' Jocasta said eventually. Her voice was so quiet that Phoebe had to strain to hear her. 'A year ago today, in fact. I had written to him about the baby being born but I don't know if he ever received my letter.'

Phoebe grimaced, mortified at her carelessness. 'Oh, Jocasta, I'm so terribly sorry. I'm such a thoughtless fool. I shouldn't have said anything.'

'No, you're not.' Jocasta reached out and patted Phoebe's arm. 'You're sweet and kind. How were you supposed to know?'

She realised this was why Geoffrey was so adamant that she come to stay in Cornwall with Jocasta right away. He might not have been able to take leave to be with his sister to support her on this sad first anniversary, but he had done his best to ensure Jocasta wasn't alone. Phoebe had liked him before, but discovering the depth of his care for his sibling only went to make her fonder of him on a much deeper level.

'I am very sorry, though,' Phoebe said. 'Intentional or not, it was hurtful to you.'

Jocasta gave a tight smile. 'Please, it's fine. I've enjoyed you staying here. In fact, you being here has stopped my mind from dwelling on Ronnie too much, which can only be a good thing. Most of the time when I'm here alone, I battle to keep busy enough not to think about him for hours each day. Having you staying has given me more to do and someone to share chatter with. It's nice to be able to share the little nuggets of fun that Bryony gets up to with someone.'

'I'm glad.'

Phoebe watched her friend as she stared thoughtfully into the leaping flames in the fireplace. She was beginning to relax when Jocasta turned to her. 'It's a little late to find a tree,' she said. 'But I'm sure Bryony will enjoy a couple of decorations.'

She went quiet for a few seconds. 'It's Christmas, after all, and I really should mark it with some joy, shouldn't I? It's what Ronnie would have expected me to do.'

'Then that's what we'll do,' Phoebe said cheerfully. 'If you tell me where you store your decorations, then I can fetch them for you and when Bryony's asleep we can decorate this room, ready to show her on Christmas morning.'

Jocasta smiled. She seemed much happier, Phoebe thought, glad now that she had asked about the lack of a Christmas tree. 'You must be careful of your hand, though. My brother would be furious if I allowed you to do something that ruined his patching-up skills.'

'Yes, I must be careful, but I think I can fetch a box down from an attic, or wherever you store your things.'

'Well, if you're certain? I wish I'd thought to buy her a couple of little gifts to wrap up for her.' Jocasta sighed.

'I have something for her, so she will have a present,' Phoebe said, happy again to have managed to buy something when she was out.

Jocasta flung her arms around Phoebe's neck, surprising her with her exuberance. 'Thank you, Phoebe, that's incredibly thoughtful of you.'

Delighted to have been able to do something for her friend and to cheer her up, Phoebe added, 'The present can be from us both.'

'That's very generous.' Jocasta wiped a tear from her cheek and Phoebe realised she had made her cry.

'It's no more generous than you inviting me into your home when I don't have one of my own to go to for Christmas.' She rested her hand on Jocasta's and smiled. 'Please don't be upset. We're going to make this a wonderful Christmas. The festivities aren't all about Christmas trees and elaborate decorations and gifts under the tree. It's about being with people who mean something to you, and that's what I think we now are.'

'Yes, that's exactly right,' Jocasta said. 'I know I've only known you for a couple of days, but I already feel like you're the sister I never had.'

'Thank you,' Phoebe replied, aware that it was an enormous compliment. As she went to the attic to fetch Jocasta's decorations, she couldn't help thinking of her own sister and wondering how she was getting along in the camp. She hoped Celia was all right and that her Christmas wasn't too dull.

# TWENTY-EIGHT

## Celia

### LATE DECEMBER 1916

'Nurse! Come quickly!'

Celia glanced around her and, seeing that the other nurses were being kept busy by a new influx of prisoners, she quickly pushed the shards of broken glass she'd been sweeping so that they were out of the way and rested the broom handle against the wall above them.

'Coming, Doctor Burton,' she replied, rushing up to him to see what she could do to help. She concentrated on keeping her expression neutral, as she always did when going to new patients who had just arrived.

'Fetch me hot water, cloths and a couple of dressings, and hurry.'

Celia saw that the patient's face was mostly covered with a bloodied bandage and dreaded to think of the mess underneath, but knew from experience that her reaction mattered greatly and that the men, or at least those who could see her face, gauged a lot about their situation from her reaction. She fetched everything the doctor needed and was back at his side less than a minute later.

'Here you are, Doctor,' she said, placing everything he had asked for onto a nearby trolley.

'Good. Right, hold that bowl here while I remove this.' He took a pair of scissors and began carefully cutting away at the sodden bandage, then took tweezers and slowly lifted the mucky dressing from the soldier's face. 'What's your name, son?'

The man gave his name and it occurred to her that he was probably the same age as the doctor.

Celia soothed the man as he cried out, pleading with the doctor to stop what he was doing.

'We have to remove this,' Doctor Burton explained softly. 'You don't want an infection in the wound. I promise I'm going as gently and as quickly as I possibly can.'

Celia understood enough German to know the patient was complaining that he was in pain.

'You're in the best hands,' Celia said, calmly taking the soldier's hand in hers. 'You'll soon have a new dressing on and will feel much better.' She hoped she was right. Celia knew that some of the doctors expected the nurses to stand silently as they worked, but Doctor Burton didn't mind them trying to soothe the patients. Medical staff and prisoners might not speak the same language, but the tone of a voice went a long way to defuse panic.

As the wound was exposed, Celia saw that the man had pretty much lost one of his ears and had a deep cut across his cheek. She knew the doctors here did their best and some of the results were incredible as far as she was concerned, but she had no idea how anyone was going to fix this poor man's face.

The patient went to raise his hand to his face but Celia stopped him.

'Touching a wound with a dirty hand is the worst way to

go about it,' Doctor Burton said. 'I won't be much longer and then we can have a fresh dressing on this and get you into theatre to fix you up a bit. You'll feel much better after that.'

The soldier stared at the doctor, then at Celia with wide, fearful eyes.

Celia hated to see how petrified he was. She wasn't surprised, though. If it was still shocking for her to see these badly injured men after months of dealing with them, how frightening and painful must it be for them to actually be this badly wounded?

'Maybe if he hadn't tried to escape he wouldn't be in this mess,' the doctor mumbled. 'Silly sod tried to throw himself over the side of the boat, and when he was grabbed and pulled back his face was damaged.' He shook his head in frustration. 'Did he really think he could simply swim away?'

Celia doubted the poor chap was thinking clearly at all. She watched the doctor working in silence.

'I'm going to leave you in the capable hands of Nurse Robertson here,' the doctor said, turning to address Celia. 'Nurse, please clean this man up.' He took a few steps away from the bed and lowered his voice. 'Don't give him any fluids or food. I'm going to go and see if I can have him fitted into one of the theatres.'

'Yes, Doctor.'

She returned to the bed. 'I'm going to fetch some warm soapy water and then we can get you cleaned up. You'll feel much better when you're in a warm, dry bed.'

'Thank you,' he said through gritted teeth.

Celia suspected he either had no idea how badly damaged his face was, or that he was incredibly brave and wanted to be as positive as possible. 'Yes, and later you'll be able to have a hot meal and a nice cup of cocoa.'

He tried to smile and she wished she hadn't tried to cheer him up when he winced and tears ran down his cheek from the pain smiling had caused him. She picked up his discarded wet uniform and headed towards the laundry.

'I'll take those from you,' one of the other nurses said, reaching out and taking hold of the bundle in Celia's arms. 'Doctor Burton is calling for you.'

'He is?' Celia asked, surprised. 'Do you know where I'll find him?'

'Yes. You must have just missed him.' She groaned under the weight of the sodden material in her hands. 'He's in the ward with a patient he's wanting to operate on straight away. A facial wound, he said.'

Celia thanked the nurse and immediately rushed back to the ward to speak to the doctor.

'Yes, Doctor?

'I'd like you to prep the new patient and arrange for the orderlies to bring him to the theatre in twenty minutes, please. Accompany him, if you will.'

'Of course, Doctor.'

She waved an orderly over from the other side of the ward, then indicated that she needed two of them to carry the patient. She had no idea how long the surgery would take but the most important thing right then was to reassure the patient. He'd soon be under anaesthetic and wouldn't have any idea how long he would be unconscious.

---

Later that evening Celia had almost finished her shift when she decided to check on Otto and the newcomer from Christmas Eve.

'How's the young chap doing, do you think?' she asked Otto, glancing over at the soldier who had been in the fight.

'He will be fine,' Otto reassured her. 'I went to speak to the men involved and warned them that they would have to face me if they ever touched that young man again. I think there will no longer be any trouble from them.'

She was grateful to him for intervening and hoped he was right. Then again, Celia thought, as sweet as Otto was to her, his tall stature was imposing and she didn't like to think how that dear face of his might appear if his expression wasn't the one of love that he used when looking at her. She imagined he could be quite fierce when he needed to be.

'That cheers me up. Thank you.'

'It was my pleasure. I hate bullying of any kind and will not stand for it from my own countrymen.'

She thought of his fellow soldiers and some of the stories she had heard, aware that they could easily be propaganda and hoped that they were. Otto was a decent man and it was difficult to think of him as being the enemy. Even those pilots who had killed her parents and brother had been following orders, hadn't they?

When she was satisfied that the young patient was sleeping peacefully, she turned to leave and saw Sister watching her. When Celia went to ask if there was anything she wanted her to do, Sister gave her an approving nod.

'Well done, Nurse Robertson,' she said quietly as Celia reached her by the door. 'I'm told by the doctor that you were a great help to him today.'

'Thank you, Sister. I enjoyed helping in theatre.'

Sister walked over to check on the soldier. 'That poor boy will need his spirits kept up as much as possible. He's got a long road ahead of him before he'll be anywhere near recovered enough to leave.'

Celia left the ward saddened to think that such a young boy had already lost so much. She was grateful he didn't know it quite yet and hoped his body and mind would have a chance to rest and recover.

## TWENTY-NINE

## Phoebe

EARLY JANUARY 1917

Phoebe stood barefoot on the beach, relishing the damp sand under her foot. It was so cold it was becoming painful but she wanted to make the most of the sensation of the sand between her toes before putting her stockings and shoes back onto her feet. So she stayed where she was, staring out across the rolling waves, and took a long, slow, deep breath. Her stay with Jocasta had been relaxing so far and far more enjoyable than she had anticipated.

Phoebe was sad she would have to leave Cornwall soon. She was enjoying her time in the coastal village and wasn't looking forward to it ending, though Jocasta had invited her to return whenever she wanted.

She felt a drop of water land on her nose and held out her hand to see if it was starting to rain, or if maybe she had been splashed by one of the waves.

'Blast it,' she grumbled, realising that it was indeed raining, or soon would be. Phoebe turned her head to look at the sky behind her and saw that where earlier there had been bright-blue skies, now they were almost hidden from view by a bank of steel-grey cloud. She needed to return to Jocasta's house if she wasn't to be caught out in a deluge.

She hastily brushed away the worst of the sand from her right foot and decided to leave her stockings in her coat pocket and put on her shoes without her legs being covered. No one else was on the beach and she doubted that anyone she came across on her way back to the house would notice her bare legs. As soon as her second shoe was on she began running towards the lane. The soft sand made it hard going but she was soon on firmer ground.

Looking ahead up the hill that she was going to have to cover before reaching the edge of the village and Jocasta's home, she groaned. She was already slightly out of breath and this was going to finish her off, but the rain started to come down heavier then, giving her the impetus to get going again.

By the time Jocasta's house was in sight, Phoebe was desperate to stop and catch her breath but knew she needed to keep going. Alerted by a sudden movement ahead, she looked up and saw Jocasta waving frantically at her. She was pink-cheeked and as Phoebe drew up to the house, Jocasta rushed out to the gate, stepping from one foot to the other. Phoebe's heart raced. Something had happened, she knew it.

'Is something the matter?'

'Oh, bless you. No, nothing's wrong,' Jocasta said, fluttering her hands at Phoebe while glancing over her shoulder into the open doorway.

Relieved, Phoebe smiled. 'Then maybe we shouldn't be loitering outside in the cold.'

'Yes, but first I had to tell you...'

Phoebe waited for her to finish her sentence. 'Tell me what?' she asked, when Jocasta seemed to forget what she was about to say. 'Jocasta, my feet are freezing.' She indicated her bare legs. 'I've been walking on the wet sand. I need to go and wash my feet and warm up a bit.'

'Gosh, I'm so sorry.' She still didn't move though, Phoebe noticed. Instead Jocasta leaned forward and whispered in Phoebe's ear, 'You were far longer than I expected.'

Phoebe tried to work out what her friend was trying to tell her. 'You have a visitor. A very handsome one.'

Phoebe stared at her friend in confusion. 'Who?'

Phoebe noticed for the first time that her friend's face was pink from excitement rather than upset. 'Jocasta, tell me.'

'You'll have to see for yourself,' Jocasta whispered. 'In there.'

*Could it be Archie?*

She glanced at Jocasta, wondering why she hadn't told her friend about her and Archie, but it couldn't be him, surely. He was in Sussex. And no one apart from Geoffrey knew she was staying here. But who else could it be? She gasped. 'Archie's here?'

Jocasta nodded. 'How long has he been waiting for me?'

'He's only been here for about half an hour.' She gave Phoebe a conspiratorial smile. 'I've been happily questioning him.'

'I need to see him!' said Phoebe, desperate to get inside the house.

'Not until you've gone upstairs and put on some stockings. You can't see him in that state and I won't be responsible for you catching pneumonia. What would my brother say if I did that?' Jocasta stepped back and pulled Phoebe into the hall, closing the door behind them.

Frustrated, Phoebe unbuttoned her coat and took off her hat, staring at the living-room door. *Archie's in that room!* her brain screamed. 'Please, take these,' she said, handing her things to Jocasta to hang on a hook by the door, aware that she wouldn't worry about stockings if she was in her own home.

'Please tell him I'll only be a minute,' she said, running up the stairs to her room without waiting for an answer.

Two minutes later, her feet washed, hair brushed and a fresh pair of stockings on, Phoebe ran back down the stairs and went straight into the living room. He was alone and she was grateful to her friend for giving them some privacy.

Phoebe stopped at the living-room doorway and stared. There he was. Her Archie.

'I hoped you wouldn't mind me pitching up here uninvited,' he said, looking a little unsure of himself as he stood in front of the roaring fire, leaning on his walking stick.

'Archie,' she said, breathless from the shock of seeing him again and surprised that her heart didn't explode with love for him. 'You came to see me!'

Archie's mouth broke into a smile and, placing his cap under his arm on the side that was resting on the walking stick, he sighed. 'I would have been here sooner if I could,' he said, his voice husky.

She ran into his arms, nearly knocking him over. 'Sorry,' she said, wrapping her arms around his waist and kissing him hard on the mouth. 'I've missed you so much, Archie.'

His arm went around her back and held her tightly to him as he kissed her back. 'I've missed you too, my angel,' he whispered. 'So very much.'

They kissed again for a few minutes and Phoebe knew that she would have done anything he asked of her. She heard a gentle knock on the living-room door and felt him loosen his hold on her. She lowered her arms, hating to let go of him.

'We'd better take a seat,' Phoebe said, indicating for Archie to sit next to her on the small sofa.

He sat with a little difficulty, she noticed, and then, sliding his walking stick under his feet, took her hand in his and gave it a gentle squeeze. 'You look beautiful,' he whispered quickly. 'The sea air has done you good, I can tell.'

The door opened a crack. 'Do you mind if I join you?' Jocasta asked timidly.

'Not at all,' Phoebe said, wishing she could be left alone with Archie but knowing how few visitors Jocasta had and how exciting Archie's arrival must be for her. 'Please, come in.'

'I've brought us all some tea and a slice of carrot cake.' She carried in a tray and Archie went to stand. 'No. No, you stay where you are,' Jocasta said. 'I can manage this perfectly well.' She placed the tray on the table in front of one of the armchairs and sat. 'I've got used to carrying far more since having my baby,' she explained. 'Sometimes you can't leave a little one when you need to go into the next room to fetch something. Do we all want tea and cake?'

Phoebe smiled and nodded and looked at Archie to see if he was in agreement.

'Yes, please,' he said, then looked at Phoebe. 'I was saying to Mrs Chambers what a pretty home she has here.'

'Please do call me Jocasta.' She poured the cups of tea and served the thin slices of cake and handed out forks. 'It's jolly exciting having someone to entertain,' Jocasta said. 'It's been wonderful having Phoebe staying here with me.'

Phoebe smiled at her. 'You've thoroughly spoilt me,' she said. 'I've no idea how I'm going to cope, being back in France at the hospital with their food and those beds.' She laughed.

'I'm rather envious of you staying here,' Archie said. 'I've booked myself a room for two nights upstairs at a pub in the village.' He frowned. 'I must say, I found it rather confusing. There are two public houses but in one building.'

Jocasta and Phoebe laughed and Phoebe explained about the two estranged brothers.

'I see,' he said, still looking rather confused, Phoebe thought.

She realised what he had said about booking in to one of them and clutched his arm tightly with excitement. 'You're staying in the village? For two nights, did you say?'

He grinned at her. 'That's right. I've missed you so much and knew you were to return to Étaples on the third, so I thought I would come and see you.'

'You've been discharged from the hospital?' she asked, surprised. 'I had imagined you would be there for a couple of months.' She glanced at his bad leg, then back at him.

'Ah, not quite.'

Concerned about what he might have done, Phoebe's smile disappeared. 'Then you discharged yourself?'

'Pretty much. I told them I had a great-aunt who was expecting me to go and stay with her for a few days.'

Jocasta giggled and covered her mouth with one hand. 'Well done, you.'

Phoebe wasn't so sure. She hated the thought of him getting into trouble on her account. 'And the hospital was all right about you leaving?'

Archie gave Phoebe a gentle smile. 'They will be fine. Nothing is more important to me than spending time with you while I can. Who knows when we'll see each other again once you return to France? This leg is healing well now and I've a feeling I've not been damaged enough to remain in good old Blighty, so I'll probably be sent back to the Front at some point this year.'

'Don't say that,' she whispered, unable to bear the thought

of Archie being back in the trenches once again. 'I like to think of you over here, where you're safe.'

'I'll be here for some time yet. There's no need to worry about me unnecessarily.'

'I'm glad.' She realised they hadn't drunk their tea or eaten any cake yet. 'Let's make the most of this lovely treat.' As they ate and drank Jocasta began explaining how she had initially thought that Archie was her brother when he'd knocked. 'I gather you met him too,' she said to Archie.

'I did. He's a good doctor and I was grateful to him when he suggested that Phoebe come here for a bit of a break.' Phoebe saw him watch Jocasta as she cut a piece of her cake with the side of her fork and popped the piece into her mouth. 'I'm sorry that I wasn't your brother,' he said. 'You must have been very disappointed.'

'A little, but I'm intrigued to meet a friend of Phoebe's' Jocasta said. 'She's only ever spoken about her sister Celia, and even then said very little.'

Archie smiled and looked at Phoebe. 'You never spoke about me. Not once?'

She could see he was surprised but, thankfully, amused by Phoebe's omission.

'The, um, subject never came up.' Phoebe cringed inwardly at her clumsiness. She didn't want to offend Archie but was also desperately determined not to upset her friend, as the truth was that she had never spoken about him to Jocasta because she didn't want to speak about the man she was in love with, when Jocasta had lost the love of her life. She forced a jovial expression on her face. 'We mostly speak about baby Bryony, don't we, Jocasta?' Phoebe focused on eating her cake. 'This is delicious, by the way. Thank you.'

'It's fine, Phoebe,' Jocasta said, giving her a reassuring

smile before looking at Archie. 'I lost my husband just before Christmas 1915.'

Archie looked stricken. 'I'm so very sorry, I hadn't realised.' He glanced to his side at the photos on the table. 'I saw the photo of you two, but it never occurred to me that he … that…'

'Please don't concern yourself,' Jocasta said. 'I think one of the worst things about being a widow is that people never quite know what to say.' She looked at Phoebe. 'I presume you never mentioned the captain because you didn't want to upset me and remind me that Ronnie was no longer here with me.'

Phoebe nodded.

'You mustn't worry. If anything, seeing you so happy in this lovely man's company fills me with joy.'

'It does?' Phoebe was surprised and didn't understand how that could be.

'Yes.' Jocasta nodded. 'It reminds me that there is still happiness and romance in this terribly dark world and that one day my daughter will be grown and hopefully have a young man of her own. It gives me hope for the future, Phoebe.' She reached out and took Phoebe's hand in hers and gave it a squeeze before letting go.

Phoebe had to concentrate on not crying. 'I'm so relieved.'

Jocasta narrowed her eyes. 'I had suspected you had a young man,' she said, then smiling, added, 'but I had hoped, despite your protestations when you first arrived, that it might be Geoffrey.'

'I hope you're not too disappointed?'

Jocasta shrugged. 'A little. Then again, we've still become friends and hopefully you'll come back here to stay with me again at some point.'

'I'll make a point of doing so,' Phoebe promised.

Jocasta placed her plate onto the tray. 'I think I can hear my baby whimpering. She'll be hungry. I'll leave you two here to catch up.'

'Thank you,' Phoebe said. 'We'll tidy up these things and maybe if the rain stops we can go for a walk.' She smiled at Archie. 'Not too far. You mustn't put any strain on your leg, but we could go to the cliffs over there.' She pointed in the general direction.

'I'd like that,' he said. 'I know I'm intruding on you both. I hope you don't mind too much.'

Jocasta turned at the doorway. 'How can I mind? I've had the pleasure of Phoebe's company since she arrived. I think it's your turn now. So please don't worry about me.'

'Thanks, Jocasta,' Phoebe said.

'Yes, thank you for looking after my sweetheart so well.'

'It was my pleasure,' she said, leaving the room.

'We're alone again.' He smiled. 'Now I need to ask you something.'

## THIRTY

## Celia
------

C elia leaned against the doorway of the canteen, nursing a warm cup of tea as she stared out at the dismal view. At least the sun was shining, she thought, taking a sip. She wondered how Phoebe's Christmas had been and hoped that her sister was keeping well.

She was tired and wasn't sure if it was the constant attempt to keep up with her work or if she, like some of the prisoners, was finding it difficult spending most of her waking time behind barbed wire. Working in a prisoner-of-war camp wasn't something she had ever imagined herself doing and she wasn't sure how much longer she could bear being here. Celia knew it was only the thought of spending what little time she could in Otto's presence that helped keep her going.

They had been alerted to the prospect of more prisoners being brought to the camp in the next few days, but she had no idea how they would fit them in, as even the hospital wards were full. More of the men were succumbing to bronchitis and coughs, and Celia wasn't sure if it was simply because of the damp and cold of winter they were experiencing, or if the men's state of mind had something to do with their low immunity. They might have access to entertainment and a good standard of living for prisoners, but they were still prisoners. If she found it difficult at times to be working here, then how did they feel, being forced to live so far from their homelands and loved ones?

'Not on duty yet?' Elsie asked, coming up to join her in the canteen.

'I'm due to begin in ten minutes,' Celia replied. She wished Elsie would leave her alone, but she was aware that she needed to keep on the other woman's good side, if indeed she had one. 'How about you?'

'Just finished.' Elsie pinched the bridge of her nose. 'It's been an arduous shift this time.'

'Aren't they all?' Celia asked, barely able to contain her sarcasm.

'This one was particularly stressful.'

Celia sensed that Elsie wanted her to ask why, so did. 'Why, did something happen?'

Elsie sighed. 'That young unteroffizier died.'

'Pardon?' Celia had experienced many patients dying, but she had only seen the young soldier the previous day and although his facial wound was bad, it wasn't meant to be life-threatening, and the doctor hadn't mentioned any infection being present. 'But how? What happened?'

'We don't know for certain, but the doctor suspects his heart gave out under the stress of what he's gone through,' Elsie explained, sounding, Celia noticed, more upset than was usual. 'It was truly shocking, Celia. I hate to admit it, but my reaction to seeing him die wasn't as professional as I would have liked. I almost made a show of myself with one of the other nurses, which isn't like me.'

Celia struggled to imagine Elsie having any feelings for anyone other than herself. She had never seen her seem upset, or even happy before now, other than when she'd spoken of her brother.

'I'm sorry to hear that.'

'What, that I made a show of myself?' There was the antagonistic side of Elsie that Celia recognised so well.

'No,' Celia said pointedly. 'That the poor chap died.'

'I see.' Elsie stood and, leaving her plate and mug, stared blankly at Celia. 'I'm going to go back to my quarters. I'll leave you to take my crockery, if that's all right?'

Celia nodded. 'Yes.' She watched Elsie leave, shoulders hunched. She knew she should feel more compassion for the woman, but all Celia felt at that moment was relief that she could finish her meal in peace without everything she said or did being scrutinised.

'What's up with 'er, then?' one of the orderlies asked from further into the room where he was eating his breakfast.

'One of her patients died unexpectedly,' Celia said. 'She's a little upset.'

'Not like 'er to feel anything for one of these blokes.'

He looked confused and Celia wasn't surprised. 'I was thinking the same thing,' she replied, then regretted her own honesty. 'I shouldn't say such things, that was mean.'

'About anyone else it might be, but not 'er. I wouldn't feel too badly, she wouldn't feel a thing for you.'

Another of the nurses sighed. 'Some of them take you that way, don't they?'

Celia sighed. Somewhere in Germany was a mother who had yet to hear the news that her young son had died. It broke Celia's heart and she realised why she was feeling so down. It wasn't the weather or working behind bars – it was the

204

proximity to death and the loss that never seemed to be far away these days. She wondered when life would brighten again. It couldn't come soon enough, as far as she was concerned.

Her appetite lost, Celia carried her and Elsie's plates and mugs over to the end of the counter where they left the dirty crockery.

She began walking to the ward, wishing that she didn't have to go there straight away and could instead take some time to come to terms with the news Elsie had just imparted.

'Poor boy,' she said, shaking her head and willing herself not to cry.

One of the British guards heard her speaking to herself and gave her a knowing look. All of them at the hospital understood the pain of losing a patient, especially when it wasn't expected.

She arrived at the ward and, after taking a steadying breath, walked in. Her eyes automatically went to the unteroffizier's bed where a new patient now lay sleeping. How could she feel so much loss for a man she had barely known? It didn't make much sense, but then neither did this relentless war, she mused as she reported to Sister's desk.

'Ahh, Nurse Robertson,' she said, looking up from where she had been writing her notes. 'I'm afraid we've had rather a night of it here.'

'I heard, Sister. Such sad news.'

'Indeed.' Sister shook her head slowly. 'An unexpected loss, too.'

Celia wanted to ask if they knew exactly what had happened, but knew that Sister didn't appreciate nosiness.

'I want you to help pack up his belongings, what little there were of them, and take them to the office for processing.'

'Yes, Sister,' Celia said, aware how unfeeling Sister might sound to someone passing. She knew now, though, that Sister felt just as deeply as she and Elsie for the men under her care, and presumed she had learnt to deal with her emotions over her many years of being a nurse.

As soon as Celia had taken the unteroffizier's meagre belongings to Matron's office she returned to the ward and decided to go and meet the new patient who had taken his bed, as he was now awake.

*Another young one*, Celia thought. He looked about twenty, just a few years younger than her.

'Good morning ...' she peered forward to look at his records for his name and rank, '... Lieutenant.'

'Good morning, Nurse...?'

'Robertson,' she replied, forcing a smile. His English was good and he seemed sweet. 'You must have arrived early this morning or during the night, I suppose?'

'At about two this morning,' he said. 'So far I'm very satisfied with the accommodation.'

She presumed he was joking but he didn't smile at first. Then, when he did, his entire face seemed to light up.

Celia smiled. 'I'm pleased you're happy,' she said, enjoying their banter.

She noticed the soldier's eyes widen with surprise and followed his line of vision, to see Otto grinning at him.

'Otto Hoffman!'

Celia's mood lifted to see the two men so happy to see one another. She couldn't understand what they were saying because they spoke too quickly in German, but it was clear that they were old acquaintances.

She set about her work, leaving them to catch up, and later

when Doctor Burton was examining the lieutenant behind a screen, Celia went to Otto to ask more about the newcomer.

'You obviously know each other well.' She watched his smile widen.

'We have known each other since he was in kindergarten with my younger brother,' he said with a far-off look on his face. 'He and I used to fight in the playground until we discovered that each of us was better than all the other boys in the class at climbing trees. It was our love of climbing that brought our friendship.'

'His English is excellent, just like yours.'

He smiled. 'He tells me that he went to university for a year in England, as I did. Although opposite universities.' He gave an amused chuckle.

'Opposite?' She didn't understand what he meant.

'I was at Oxford and he at Cambridge.' He laughed. 'Typical of us to apply to different places.'

'Well, I'm glad you have a familiar face around you here now.'

He stopped laughing and looked up at her, love shining from his eyes. 'I already had a familiar face. One that no one else could ever replace in importance to me.'

Her heart full, she smiled. 'I feel the same way,' she whispered without moving her lips. Celia sensed she was being watched and straightened Otto's blanket, smoothing it down at the side. 'I ought to be getting on with my duties.'

'Yes. We don't want you getting into trouble.'

If getting into trouble didn't involve her being sent away from Otto, then she wouldn't mind one bit, but she would never risk that, Celia thought as she walked away from his bed.

# THIRTY-ONE

# Phoebe

'What question?' Phoebe asked, not daring to imagine it might be the one she hoped to hear above all others.

Archie gave her a thoughtful frown. 'I wanted this to be perfect but it's raining outside and I can't kneel properly yet, so I hope you'll not mind me doing this differently to how I've been imagining it.'

She could barely find the words to reply. 'I don't care how you do it,' she said honestly.

'That's a relief.' He took her right hand in his and, raising it to his lips, kissed the back of it. Then he looked her in the eye, smiled and cleared his throat.

He was nervous, she realised. 'I love you, Archie,' she whispered.

'I love you, too.' He took a deep breath and exhaled sharply. 'Phoebe Robertson, will you do me the honour of becoming my wife?'

'Yes.'

He drew her into his arms and kissed her. 'You didn't even think about that before answering.'

'I didn't need to!' She laughed, holding him tightly.

'You've made me the happiest man alive.'

Phoebe kissed him again. 'I'd love us to be able to marry straight away,' she said, wishing she never had to leave his side ever again.

'As do I, my angel. Unfortunately we don't have enough time, before I return to the hospital and you to France, to register a notice of marriage and wait the necessary number of days before marrying.'

'No, I suppose not,' she said, telling herself that being married to Archie wouldn't make him any safer. She pushed away the thought. Nothing was going to happen to him. She had to believe he would be fine and stop fretting that he would be killed, like her parents and brother had been.

He kissed her. 'There is something we can do, though.'

Excited to know what he might have in mind, Phoebe forced a smile. 'Really? What?'

'Will you meet me first thing in the morning so we can at least buy you a ring?' he asked, smiling at her.

'Yes, of course.'

'Maybe Jocasta will know of a jeweller in the village or a town nearby where we could buy one.'

'I'll ask her tonight,' Phoebe said, 'and tell you when I meet you in the morning.' Hearing Jocasta's footsteps upstairs in her bedroom, Phoebe felt the need to spend time alone with Archie. She glanced out of the window and was cheered to see it had stopped raining. 'Will your leg be all right if we take a walk?'

'It will be fine,' he said, smiling.

'Good. Let me go and tell Jocasta that we're popping out for a while.'

'I'll wait here for you,' he said. 'But first there's just one thing I need to do.'

Phoebe glanced at him and had opened her mouth to speak, when he took hold of her arm, pulled her close and kissed her.

Phoebe closed her eyes and relished the feeling of being held by him.

'Are you happy for me to go now?' she teased a few moments later, loving how much he wanted her.

'Only if you're back here in less than a minute. I don't think I'll be able to cope with being away from you for any longer.'

Phoebe laughed. 'You can start counting,' she said before running from the room.

---

As they walked slowly from the house towards the cliff path, Phoebe relished every moment of her hand being in his as she walked alongside the man she loved above all others, whom she would soon be married to.

'What are you thinking?' he asked quietly, smiling down at her.

Phoebe rested her free hand over her heart. 'Just that I can't ever imagine being happier than I am right at this moment.'

He pulled her to a stop. 'A newly married friend of mine once told me that when you meet the right woman, you just know it. I never believed him until I opened my eyes and saw you, that first time at the hospital. At first, I noticed your eyes and then your soothing voice as you tried to reassure me, and I knew then that I wanted to spend the rest of my life with you.'

Phoebe couldn't speak. 'You knew then?'

He raised his eyebrows and narrowed his eyes. 'You mean it took you longer than that?'

She nudged him. 'It did, but not much longer.' Phoebe thought back to seeing Archie for the first time and how handsome she had thought him, once she had cleaned him up and changed him into fresh clothes.

'I recall coming round and seeing a pretty nurse leaning over me tying my pyjama bottoms, and it dawned on me that you must have seen me naked.'

Phoebe recalled his reaction, and laughed. 'You seemed very angry with me.'

'That was mortification, my darling, not anger.' He winced. 'Anyway, what did you think of me?' he asked, as if sensing where her mind had drifted off to.

'I thought you were incredibly handsome,' she admitted. 'And you are.'

'That's very kind of you to say so, but then, as my fiancée, I presume you would probably approve of the way I look.'

'Fiancée,' she said to herself. 'I've never been a fiancée before.'

'That's a relief!' He laughed. 'If you had been, then you'd more than likely be married to some other lucky man and bringing up his brood of children somewhere.'

'Children,' she said. 'We've never discussed children before.' Phoebe realised she desperately wanted to know what her husband-to-be thought about children. 'How many would you hope to have?'

She looked up at him, waiting for him to answer as he stared out over the sea thoughtfully. 'I don't know. Two, maybe? Six?'

She saw his lips draw back into a cheeky smile and knew

he was teasing. 'Six?' She had never imagined having so many children and was glad he was joking.

'Why? How about you?' He gazed down at her.

'Three? Maybe four at the most, but I don't think I could cope with more than that.' She also didn't want to spend most of her marriage being pregnant.

'We'll have as many as you wish,' he said, kissing to the top of her head affectionately. 'I would love to have at least one child and know that you and I will live on forever through them.'

Phoebe thought it such a sad thing to say. She didn't want to think about their mortality when they would have to part in two short days' time.

'We will,' she said, wanting to reassure him. Maybe he was anxious about her returning to France and being closer to danger, she mused. Or it could be that Archie was preparing himself to return to the Front in the next couple of months. He knew only too well how it felt to be injured. 'Come along,' she said, wanting to change the topic of conversation. They needed to enjoy every moment they had together. 'I want to take you to see the most perfect view I've ever seen.'

'It'll have to be pretty impressive to beat Sandsend,' he said, giving her a wink.

She thought of the place he had grown up in and loved so much. 'Will we live there when we're married?'

'Sandsend?'

'Yes. Your home in Yorkshire.'

'I'd love to return there to make a home with you and bring up our children, if that's what you're happy doing.'

He had a look of hope in his eyes and Phoebe knew that he could have told her he wished to move to anywhere in the world, and she would have gone with him without a moment's hesitation. 'I can't wait to see it for the first time,' she said honestly.

He bent and kissed her again, cupping her cheek with his hand. 'You are perfect, do you know that?'

She pulled a face. 'I'm not sure my sister would agree with you,' she said, 'but I'm happy you think so.'

They reached the top of the cliff and stood on the damp grass a safe distance from the edge. 'Well?' Phoebe said, waving an arm in an arc to encompass the sea, with its white horses far below them. 'What do you think?'

He gazed at the view and, slipping an arm around her waist, held her close to his side against the windy weather. 'I have to agree, it is impressive.'

'Better than Sandsend?' she teased.

He must have heard the smile in her voice and looked down, grinning at her. 'They're two very different places,' he said. 'But this comes a close second, in my opinion.'

'Maybe we can come here on our holidays each year, then?'

He nodded. 'I like that idea very much.'

She noticed him wince and realised his leg must be giving him pain. It hadn't been that long ago that Archie struggled to stand, and now she had him standing on the edge of a cliff on a freezing January afternoon. *What was I thinking?* She should know better.

'We should go back,' she said, aware that Jocasta's home was closer to them than the public house where he had booked to stay.

'I'm all right, if you're concerned about my leg.'

She gave his hand a gentle squeeze. 'I'm sure you're fine,' she fibbed. 'But it is rather cold out here, with no protection from this sharp wind, and I think we should probably go back and warm up for a while before you have to return to your room at The Penny Farthing.'

He looked down at her thoughtfully before smiling. 'You're right. Let's make our way back.'

They walked in silence and Phoebe was trying to commit every second to memory: the touch of his hand over hers, the sound of his footsteps, his smile, his kiss.

The following morning she woke too early to walk to meet him, so lay in bed until she knew Jocasta would be up and making breakfast, and then washed, dressed and went downstairs to join her.

Jocasta looked up from where she was stirring porridge for their breakfast. 'Good morning.' She gave Phoebe a cheery grin. 'I was going to ask how you felt today but I can imagine it's deliriously happy.' Phoebe went to make them some tea but Jocasta shook her head and pointed for her to sit down. 'I want to hear everything.'

Without meaning to, Phoebe blurted out her news. 'Archie asked me to marry him.'

Jocasta dropped the wooden spoon into the pan and spun round. 'Marry him?' She looked stunned, then smiled. 'And I'm guessing by the look on your face that you said yes?'

'I did.' Phoebe had lain awake most of the night, not sure if it was because of the excitement of being engaged to the man she loved, or because they had spent the day together and she still had two more days to look forward to. 'I know we've not known each other for very long, but…'

Jocasta spooned the porridge into two large bowls for them and a smaller amount for Bryony. 'These are unusual times, though,' Jocasta said, confirming what Phoebe also thought.

Phoebe blushed. They were.

'What?'

'I've seen him naked,' Phoebe explained. 'I had to wash him when he arrived at the hospital.'

Jocasta's eyebrows shot up and she stared at Phoebe for a moment. 'Well, then.' She laughed. 'Sorry, I'm not certain what to say to that comment.'

'I shouldn't have said it.' Phoebe wished she had thought before speaking but her mind was on Archie today and little else, it seemed.

Jocasta placed the bowls on the table. 'It's fine. It must be enlightening in more ways than I can imagine, having to nurse these men.'

Phoebe nodded. 'I have to admit I've had many shocked moments since starting my training. I thought that the things I saw and had to do at the hospital in England were surprising, but the hospital in Étaples is something else entirely. I doubt there's much that could shock me now.'

'I can imagine.'

They stared at each other for a few seconds before Jocasta grimaced. 'I always thought I might want to be a nurse, but now I'm not so sure I'd have been any good at it.'

'I didn't think I had it in me to nurse either, but now I find that I love it. I'll miss it when I'm married.'

'I suppose you will. Now eat,' Jocasta said, handing Phoebe a spoon. 'I can tell there's more.'

Once her friend was seated, Phoebe continued. 'Archie wants us to be married as soon as possible, but first he wants to buy me an engagement ring.'

'I could see how much he loved you, just by the way he

looked at you when I walked into the room yesterday.' She stroked Bryony's cheek and smiled. 'I sense that he's a very kind, decent man. I like him very much.'

'I'm glad you think so,' Phoebe said, a happy warmth washing through her that had nothing to do with the mouthful of porridge she had just eaten.

'When I met and liked you so much, I was excited to think that one day we might become sisters-in-law.'

'But I explained about Geoffrey and me…'

Jocasta shook her head and smiled. 'You did. I was just being fanciful, I know that.'

Phoebe noticed something in her friend's eyes. She was troubled, Phoebe realised. 'What's the matter?'

'What do you mean?' Jocasta asked, busying herself feeding Bryony.

Phoebe sensed she was hiding something. 'What is it? Please tell me.'

Jocasta shrugged. 'It's just that I suspect Geoffrey might have feelings for you – perhaps that's partly why he offered for you to come and stay here.'

Phoebe gasped. 'Do you really think so?' she asked, needing time to come to terms with the thought that she might have hurt Geoffrey, albeit unintentionally.

'Please, don't be upset,' Jocasta said. 'You don't know him well and it's not your fault if you didn't suspect this to be the case. Knowing you now, I can understand his fondness for you,' Jocasta said. 'Whether it be as a friend or otherwise. I'm very fond of you myself.'

'As I am of you,' Phoebe said gratefully.

'Anyway. Enough of Geoffrey. We're supposed to be discussing your engagement with that very handsome man. I'm glad you found each other.' Jocasta skimmed a little of the porridge from Bryony's bowl and blew on it before feeding it to the toddler.

'Me, too.' It made more difference to her that Jocasta liked him than Phoebe had imagined it might. 'We were wondering if you knew of a jeweller near here.'

Jocasta spooned another small amount as she considered Phoebe's question. 'There's only one in the village,' she said thoughtfully. 'But he is trustworthy. Where are you meeting Archie?'

'Outside the public house where he's rented a room.'

'Then the jeweller's will be easy enough to find. There's a lane almost directly opposite where Archie will be waiting for you, and the shop has a small bay window and is at the start of that lane. You won't be able to miss it. Go inside and mention my name. I haven't been in there apart from once, but we have met up a few times at local events in the past.'

Phoebe's excitement for her day ahead grew. 'Thank you. I'll do that.'

'I can't wait to see it,' Jocasta said as Bryony began grumbling and pointing to the spoonful of porridge. 'Oops, there you go, sweetie.' She pointed at Phoebe's bowl. 'Now it's your turn to eat,' she teased. 'And I'm not letting you leave until every morsel has vanished.'

Phoebe took a mouthful of the cooked oats. She had no idea how Jocasta made them so tasty, but they were delicious.

---

After eating and helping Jocasta clear up, it was almost nine o'clock, so Phoebe put on her hat and coat and walked to the village.

He was waiting outside for her, smiling broadly when he spotted her. 'Are you ready to go shopping?'

'Yes,' she admitted, barely able to conceal her excitement that in a few minutes she would be wearing an engagement ring. 'Jocasta said there's one jeweller and he should be along this way,' she said, recalling her friend's directions. Spotting the small bay window by the corner of a lane, she pointed. 'Look, there it is.'

'I just know we're going to find the perfect ring in here,' he said, pushing open the door and holding it for her to enter.

They soon discovered there wasn't much choice, but the selection of rings they did have was enough for Phoebe to immediately spot one that called out to her. She waited to see if Archie reacted to the same piece, wanting him to like it as much as her.

He studied the rings. 'Are there any that you like?'

'Yes,' she said.

'Which ones?' he asked, looking delighted.

'I want to see which one you like best,' she said. 'This ring should mean as much to you as it does to me.'

He grimaced. 'This is the time we discover if we share the same taste in jewellery. I'll have to cross my fingers that we do.'

## THIRTY-TWO

# Phoebe

'I can't wait until we can be married,' Archie said as they sat in a small tea room facing each other across a table.

Phoebe was studying her hand, thinking how much better it looked with her beautiful diamond and sapphire engagement ring on her finger.

'I'm sorry we couldn't find one with larger gemstones.'

Phoebe worried that Archie might not realise how much she loved her ring. 'It's the most exquisite ring I've ever seen and I wouldn't change it for the world.' She looked down at it once more. It was sparkly and even if it had been made of tin instead of gold, she would have loved it simply because of Archie having bought it for her and the sentiment behind it.

'I never want to take it off,' she said, aware that once she was back in France she would have little choice. 'I wish we could marry right away, but I'm glad I'll be able to return to France for a little while, if only to feel like I'm finishing what I started there and end my time as a VAD at the hospital properly.' She thought of her close friends. 'And I want to say a proper goodbye to Hetty and Aggie face-to-face. And to

Geoffrey Sutherland,' she added. 'He's been so kind to me, letting me come here in the first place.'

Archie reached out and took her left hand in his, kissing the ring, and then, turning her hand over gently, drew back her fingers to look at her cut. 'I've only ever met him a couple of times, when he examined my wounds,' Archie said. 'I can't say I know him but he seemed pleasant enough. He must like you, to arrange for you to come here, and I can't blame the man if he has feelings for you. After all, I do, don't I?'

'Geoffrey has other options,' she said, not wishing to say anything more about Hetty and Geoffrey.

He shook his head. 'I'm pleased. We all need someone to love, don't you think?'

'We do.'

'I'm glad you love me, Phoebe,' he said. 'I'd hate to be the one having to see you with another man.'

Phoebe placed her hand on his cheek. 'That, my darling, will never happen. You are the only man I will ever love.'

Archie's smile vanished. 'Don't say that.'

She was confused. Surely he would want her to only love him?

Archie took both her hands in his and kissed the back of them in turn. 'It's not that I want you to love anyone other than me, but if anything did happen to me, I wouldn't want you to spend the rest of your life alone.'

She didn't want to think about such horrible things. 'Please, Archie. Let's not discuss this. I want to be happy and enjoy being engaged with you.'

He sighed. 'I know, my darling. I want to do the same thing, but now that this has come up, I feel it's the right time for me to share my feelings about it with you.' He gazed down at her hands thoughtfully before looking her in the eyes again.

'We don't ever have to mention it again, but it's important to me to know that you aren't alone. If the worst ever did happen to me, I would want you to find someone to love, who loves you back.' He narrowed his eyes and grinned. 'I wouldn't want you to love him as much as you do me, of course.'

She could see he was trying to make light of their conversation and smiled back, wanting to reassure him that she wasn't offended. 'I understand.' She did, and hoped that he would never mention the prospect of not being there for her again. The thought was too horrendous to contemplate, even if only hypothetically.

He turned her right hand over and opened her fingers gently with his thumb. 'It's healing well.'

'It is. The rest here has done me more good than I ever imagined it might.' She pursed her lips at him. 'You coming here was the perfect tonic.'

She saw him smile and knew she had said the right thing. For such a handsome and often cheeky man, there was a part of Archie that she sensed lacked confidence.

'I think maybe I should meet your family before we get married.' She also hoped he could meet Celia.

'I would love you to meet them. I know Mrs Dunwoody will be in Sandsend but my brother is with his unit and my sister is with her family in London. Hopefully we'll have a chance for you to meet them before too long.' He sighed. 'As a gentleman, I should have liked to be able to ask your father for his permission before proposing to you.'

Phoebe waited for the waitress to place the pot of tea that they had ordered onto their table. 'I'm sure he would have enjoyed that,' she said, trying to picture her father meeting Archie. 'I know he would have taken to you. Then again, I can't imagine anyone ever not.'

'I like to think that your parents would approve of me.'

'They would have, I'm certain of it. Do you think your parents would have liked me?'

He nodded. 'Definitely.'

'Shall I be mother?' she asked, indicating the jug of milk and the tea pot and smiling at him.

'Yes, and I'll sit here and make the most of watching my wife-to-be pouring us both a perfect cup of tea.'

---

That evening Jocasta invited Archie to the house for supper.

'What time are you leaving in the morning, Archie?' Jocasta asked. 'Will it be early, like our dear Phoebe?' She looked at Phoebe with a miserable expression on her sweet face.

'Yes,' he replied.

'We decided to catch the train back to London together,' Phoebe explained. 'Then I'll make my way from Victoria on one of the returning ambulance trains back to France, and Archie will take another train to Sussex.'

'I'm going to miss you both,' Jocasta said. 'Especially you, Phoebe. You've been a joy to have around these past ten days.'

Phoebe's heart ached to hear her friend's sad voice. 'And I'm going to miss you and Bryony terribly.'

As soon as supper was over, Jocasta suggested Phoebe and Archie make themselves comfortable in the living room. 'I'm going to have an early night,' she said, making a point of yawning to emphasise her words. 'Will I see you tomorrow, Archie?'

'You will,' he said. 'I've hired a horse and cart to collect me from The Penny Farthing and bring me here for Phoebe, so I'll see you and little Bryony then.'

'I am pleased.' She led the way from the kitchen, stopping in the hallway outside the living-room door. 'I'll say good night, then.'

'Good night, Jocasta,' Phoebe said, giving her friend a kiss on her cheek.

'Good night,' Archie said. 'Thank you for supper.'

'It was my pleasure,' Jocasta said, her voice slightly wobbly. Without another word she took hold of the banister and began walking upstairs to her room.

Once settled inside the living room, Phoebe gazed up at the portrait of Ronnie and Jocasta, unable to help thinking how fleeting life could be. She shivered and lit a small fire before settling down to snuggle up to Archie. 'It's going be strange being back in France again, especially as you won't be there.'

'I suppose it will.' He kissed her forehead. 'I'm not looking forward to returning to the hospital. They'll probably court martial me for leaving without permission.'

Phoebe gasped in horror and sat up. 'You don't really think that, do you?'

'No,' he said. 'At least, I hope they won't. Mind you, I wouldn't mind being able to return to being an architect. I miss it very much.'

'I imagine you do.' She looked up at him, wishing they could make the night last for much longer. 'I love you so much, Archie,' she whispered, her voice trailing off as his lips met hers in a passionate kiss.

'I want to make love to you so much,' he murmured, his voice husky. 'I wish we could have been married by now.'

So did she. Phoebe melted into him, wishing she was the sort of girl who didn't have such strong principles.

'It would be wrong of us to take advantage of Jocasta's hospitality, and I could never ask you to come to my rooms.'

'I know,' she whispered, pulling him into another kiss.

Phoebe knew she should be shocked to hear him even mention them becoming intimate, but instead she resented that there was no decent way they could. If it was summer, they might have been able to find a private place outside, but it was the middle of winter and that wasn't an option.

'We'll just have to make the most of kissing each other, then,' she said, lying back and holding onto Archie, making him smile as he lowered himself over her and began kissing her again.

---

Their parting came only too soon, and Phoebe wondered if she felt more emotional to be leaving him at the station because she had been unable to sleep the previous night. Or maybe it was simply because she had no idea when she would be with Archie again.

'I'm going to miss you so much,' she said, clinging onto him, aware that she had mere seconds to get on board the waiting train. 'How am I going to cope without seeing you each day?'

His arms wrapped even tighter around her waist. 'Because, my darling, we know that once this war is over, we will be married and living in Sandsend, happily bringing up our babies. We have the rest of our lives to enjoy, you must never forget that.'

Unable to hold in a sob, Phoebe kissed him. 'Promise me you're right, Archie.' He had no way of knowing what their future held, she knew that only too well, but needed him to promise her nonetheless.

'I promise you, my darling girl.' He took her face in his

hands and kissed her. 'Always trust that I will do all I can to be with you again. I came to Cornwall when you didn't expect me to, didn't I?'

Phoebe nodded. 'You did.'

'And I will find you wherever you are. I love you, Phoebe Robertson, and I will do my best to give you the future I've promised you.' He kissed her hard on the mouth. 'You do believe me, don't you?'

'I do, Archie,' she sniffed as he lightly wiped away her tears with his fingers.

The whistle rang out and Phoebe tensed.

'You must go now, my darling,' Archie said, leading her to the train and holding her hand as she stepped on board. He closed the door and she pulled down the window and leaned out to take his hands once more. 'We will see each other again. But until then, take good care of yourself, Phoebe. You are very precious to me.'

'As you are to me, darling Archie.'

The train began to move slowly away, and for a few seconds Archie managed to keep up, but then she felt his hand slip from hers as the train picked up speed, and although she wiped away her tears, more replaced them. She waved at his blurred figure for as long as she could before sitting down heavily on the seat and giving in to her sobs.

# THIRTY-THREE

## Celia

### FEBRUARY 1917

C elia could sense the anticipation in the hospital and also in the entire camp. She was relieved it was almost time to finish her shift, as her back ached more than it usually did and her limbs felt heavy and her head fuzzy. She had been feeling worse than usual for the past couple of weeks and now sensed that her body was struggling. Almost half the nursing staff were confined to quarters and unwell with colds and a lot of them with measles, but she wasn't surprised. The long hours, stressful days and cold, damp weather didn't help, and when there were so many of them sharing quarters and the food wasn't as nourishing as most of them were used to, she was actually surprised more staff hadn't succumbed to sickness.

She just didn't want to be one of them. If only she could take a couple of days to go home and sleep.

'You know that senior officer who died the other day?' said Bill, one of the orderlies she knew, as he stopped her in the corridor on her way to collect dressings.

Celia recalled the doctor mentioning how sad he'd been

when one of the first prisoners to have arrived at the camp had died suddenly. She didn't know him well but had seen him around and knew he was respected by the guards as well as the prisoners.

'Yes?'

'I heard that the commander has given permission for some of the prisoners to accompany the man's coffin as it's taken from here up the hill to the parish church,' Bill told her.

'He has?' Celia was astonished. 'Isn't he worried that they might run away?'

Bill shrugged. 'Where are they going to run to?'

He had a point.

'Anyway, they've done it before, haven't they?'

Celia recalled someone mentioning something once, but spending most of her time in the hospital, she knew she missed out on a lot of what went on outside. 'It must have been before I came here.'

'Last time it was a young sailor, back in 'fifteen. They say that quite a few locals lined the roads to get a good look at the goings on, but there's more.'

Celia waited. 'Go on then,' she said when he didn't elaborate. 'What else have you discovered?' She had to admit, she was intrigued.

He looked one way then the other before lowering his voice. 'You know there were mumblings last year about soldiers being sent out to help the farmers?'

'Yes.' It hadn't gone ahead, she recalled, because the War Office were insisting that the farmers paid the prisoners more than they were willing to.

'Well, I heard that it's been decided to send most of the soldiers to the mainland to a camp, and they're sending them out to work on farms when they get there.'

Celia was horrified. 'You mean they're sending them to England?' She knew it was a stupid question, but the idea of Otto potentially being sent away when she had expected him to remain in the camp and near her until the end of the war, had shocked her.

Bill looked at her as if she was dim. 'That's what I said, didn't I?'

Not wishing to antagonise him further, she urged him to continue. This chap loved a gossip and seemed to enjoy being the one to impart news first, before anyone else discovered it.

'They'll be going very soon.'

Celia felt sick at the thought. 'How soon?'

'Any day now, I imagine. The paperwork's been done and they'll be shipping the buggers off as quick as they can.'

'What about the camp? Do you think they'll close it?'

'I doubt it,' he said, frowning. 'There's still some of the lads too ill to work. I imagine they'll be kept here. But they won't need as many of you lot working here from now on, will they?'

'Thanks for letting me know,' she said, aware he was relishing the opportunity to gloat. Bill had never kept to himself how distasteful he thought it was having female staff working at the camp.

She decided to speak to Otto as soon as she could, and as she made her way to the ward it occurred to her that if he was well enough now to be one of those sent away, then she should offer her services as one of the nursing staff to go with them. Maybe it would mean she could also leave Elsie behind, as Elsie surely wouldn't want to accompany the POWs. The thought cheered her.

She finally managed to have a few minutes alone with Otto later during her shift and told him everything that she had learnt.

'I have heard from my superior that I will be one of the men leaving,' he admitted. 'I was waiting for a time when we had some privacy to let you know.'

Even though she had suspected he would be going, it still shocked her for some reason. *It really is happening*, she mused.

'I've decided to put in for a transfer and offer to travel with you all. They're bound to need extra staff at the camp, and that way I'll be able to stay near to you. I might not be able to spend much time with you, though,' she said, the thought only occurring to her as she spoke. 'But at least I'd know where you are, and that's the most important thing.' She was terrified of losing contact with Otto and not knowing how to track him down.

'Then I will pray that you are able to accompany us to England.' He lowered his hand from the side of his bed and found hers, giving it a gentle squeeze. 'We will find a way through this, Celia. I know we will.'

She wished she had his confidence but, not wishing to concern him, smiled. 'I know we will too,' she said. 'We just have to keep plodding along until this is all over.' *Whenever that will be*, she thought miserably.

## THIRTY-FOUR

## Phoebe

Stationary (Base) Hospital in Étaples, France

'Here you go, Private,' Phoebe said, slipping her arm around the young soldier's back and lifting him so that he was in a more comfortable position to drink the tea she had waiting on the trolley next to his bed. 'You'll feel better after a warm drink.'

The soldier was shivering violently, either through cold or shock, she wasn't sure which. Phoebe grabbed a spare blanket and wrapped it around his shoulders, draping another one over his body. 'You'll soon warm up,' she said, hoping she was right.

'Don't worry about me, Nurse,' he said, taking the tea from her in his trembling hands and drinking a mouthful. 'Ooh, tha's good. Thanks.'

'I'm afraid we don't have much sugar but there's a little in there for you.'

'This is better than anything I've tasted for weeks,' he said, taking another drink from the cup and swallowing. 'It's just good to be inside somewhere right now.' He gave a nod in the direction of his feet, still encased in his boots, resting on the rubber matting she had been told to place under them so the sheets weren't soiled by the mud. 'I'm scared to take them off, in case me ruddy feet come with them.'

Phoebe knew he wasn't joking; she had seen for herself how badly some soldiers succumbed to trench foot. 'Sister will be here soon to let me know what she wants me to do. At least you've got a bed.'

'I'm grateful for that,' he said, a glint in his eyes. 'I never thought I'd be so happy to have a bed to lie on.'

'We aim to please,' she said, trying to sound chirpier than she felt. New patients had streamed into the hospital almost constantly over the past few days, and they were in serious danger of running out of beds again, despite another two wards being built recently.

She left him to drink his tea and went to serve mugs to the rest of the ward. As Phoebe worked, she wondered what her sister was doing at that moment and if she was well and happy in Jersey. She hadn't heard from Celia for a while. Maybe her sister was still cross with her about Archie? She hoped not. It wasn't like Celia to hold onto something that annoyed her. Maybe her sister's last letter had gone astray somewhere.

Phoebe heard shouting but didn't take any notice once she saw that Sister and Doctor Parslow were with an hysterical newcomer. She hated hearing men scream in fear, it was worse than anything else she had dealt with during her time at the hospital, and this man was clearly very distressed.

'Nurse Robertson!' Phoebe recognised the urgency in Sister's voice and immediately pushed the trolley to one side so that it wasn't in anyone's way, before hurrying to where

Sister and Doctor Parslow were helping an orderly restrain the patient.

'Run ahead and find Doctor Sutherland and warn him we're sending a patient to him right away.'

Phoebe left the ward as quickly as she could and ran in the direction of the theatre wards where she supposed Doctor Sutherland was working. She raced into the scrub room and, not seeing the doctor or any qualified nurse, pulled back the canvas flap and went to step into the theatre.

Doctor Sutherland glanced up. 'Get out!'

Phoebe stepped back, stunned by his tone. She had never heard Geoffrey use such aggression towards anyone.

'What do you think you're doing?' one of the nurses asked, keeping her distance from Phoebe as they stepped out of theatre. 'You're not allowed in there.'

'But it's an emergency,' Phoebe explained.

'Most of them are,' the nurse said, her voice tired. She lifted the flap to return to assist the surgeon.

Concerned about what would happen to the patient in the ward if he didn't get the immediate attention Sister had sent her here for, Phoebe stepped forward and raised her hand. 'Wait. Please.'

'What is it?'

She explained what had happened in the ward. 'I'm not sure what's wrong but he's being brought here now. Sister told me to run ahead to warn the surgeon so he can be ready to receive him.'

'Wait here.'

Phoebe watched the nurse go back into the theatre and heard Doctor Sutherland's raised voice. He had always seemed so calm and polite when she had spoken to him before, and his kindness to his sister seemed to have come from another man entirely. Phoebe waited anxiously, aware that the patient would be brought in at any moment.

Shortly afterwards two orderlies carried in an unconscious patient and for the first time Phoebe understood the urgency. He was bleeding profusely, so much so that she wasn't sure where the blood was coming from. Aware that they didn't have long, she called out to Doctor Sutherland.

'I'm sorry, Doctor,' she shouted. 'I know you're busy but I think this man might bleed to death if he's not seen immediately.'

Seconds later the door flap was flung backwards and Doctor Sutherland marched out, pulling off his gloves. He threw them into an almost-full metal bin to the right side of the door and grabbed another pair, immediately pushing his hands into them.

'Nurse Robertson, go and assist the theatre nurse. She'll need help finishing the dressing.'

Phoebe did as he asked, keeping her focus on helping the nurse who was bandaging the patient. They were soon finished and she moved back to give the orderlies room to take him away, and was about to leave when the next orderlies brought in the patient from her ward.

'You may as well stay,' Doctor Sutherland said. 'I'm going to need both of you to help.'

Phoebe widened her eyes in fright. This was the first time she had been allowed inside a theatre, let alone been asked to help.

'Just follow my lead,' the nurse said quietly as the doctor cut away the patient's clothing and began working on him.

Phoebe had to concentrate on breathing calmly. This was far more intense than anything she had done before, but as time wore on she realised she quite enjoyed being part of the operating team. She supposed it could be the adrenaline rush she felt as the three of them worked to save the man's life.

After quite a few scary moments Doctor Sutherland seemed to have managed to slow and then stop the bleeding. 'Go and call the orderlies to take him into recovery,' he ordered. As Phoebe went to leave, he added, 'Oh, and Nurse Robertson?'

'Yes, Doctor?'

'You did well. Good show.'

She didn't know whether to thank him or carry out his order, and decided that a quick thank-you wouldn't take any time. 'Thank you. I enjoyed it,' she said.

She ran out of the theatre before he could say anything further, and found that rather than feeling tired by what she had just experienced, she felt a strange sort of exhilaration.

She returned to the ward and checked on the trembling private that she had given the tea to earlier. Satisfied that he was now as comfortable as he could be, Phoebe made her excuses and left again, desperate to find somewhere quiet to read the letter she had received from Archie in that morning's post.

Phoebe pushed her right hand into her skirt pocket and touched the envelope with his untidy handwriting on it. She was still sad not to have been able to marry him at the beginning of the year, but it couldn't be helped. She knew they were lucky to have been able to spend those few precious days together and become engaged, and she hoped they would have the chance to arrange their wedding soon.

She walked to the end of the row of tents where new wards had been set up and, finding a solitary bench, sat down and read his letter.

*My sweet Phoebe …*

She stopped reading and closed her eyes, trying to summon the sound of his voice saying her name.

*... I know I shouldn't be writing to you at the hospital but I have to hope that Matron takes pity on me and allows this letter to reach you. I don't have much time to write but needed to let you know that I am being sent back to the Front tomorrow.*

Phoebe cried out and covered her mouth with her hand. 'No, Archie.' Surely he wasn't fit enough to be sent back to his unit yet? She hurriedly read on to find out more.

*This news isn't totally unexpected, so please don't worry about how I'm feeling about going back there. You may recall me mentioning that I could be in rather a lot of trouble for leaving the hospital. What I didn't like to add was that my commander thought, probably rightly, that if I had the strength to 'wander across the country to see my sweetheart', then I was 'well enough to join my unit'. After being examined by one of the doctors here at the hospital, I was given two months' reprieve to allow me to have physio on my bad leg.*

*I am walking almost perfectly now, so I'm told, and my time lounging around the auxiliary hospital has come to an end. Please don't worry about me, my darling girl, I'm a seasoned soldier now and know to keep my head well down and not take any chances. I have too much to lose to be careless.*

*Who knows, I might even end up being sent your way to give you even more work to do. Please take very good care of yourself and hopefully one day soon we will be with each other again and finally have our turn at being married.*

*My deepest love, as always,*

*Your Archie x*

Phoebe stared at the piece of paper in her hands. Noticing the ink on one of the words blurring, she tried to work out why. Then it occurred to her that she was crying. She wiped her eyes with the backs of her fingers and, kissing the bottom of the letter, folded it and placed it back in its envelope before slipping it into her pocket.

Archie was being sent back to the Front. She had been naïve to believe he was safe from danger. She couldn't regret their wonderful two days together in the New Year but would have given them up to know he was forever safe. 'Oh, Archie.'

'Talking to yourself?' a deep voice asked, making her jump.

Phoebe leapt to her feet and turned to see who had spoken. 'How long have you been there?' she asked, as the man stepped forward from the shadows and she saw that it was Geoffrey.

'I've just arrived.' He frowned and peered into her face. 'You're crying. What's the matter? Was it me snapping at you earlier?'

He looked horrified to be the cause of her upset and Phoebe hated to think that he believed his actions had provoked her tears. 'No. It wasn't you.'

'Is there something I can do for you, Phoebe?'

She shook her head, wishing it hadn't been Geoffrey who had found her crying. 'No,' she said, wiping her damp cheeks again.

'Has somebody done something to upset you?'

'I was reading a letter from my fiancé,' she said, feeling a bit embarrassed. 'I thought Jocasta might have mentioned something to you.'

'Ahh, Captain Bailey,' Geoffrey said quietly. 'Jocasta happened to mention him in one of her letters. I hope you don't mind. I gather he came to visit you quite unexpectedly and stayed in the village for a couple of days.' He smiled, although Phoebe felt it was forced. She could see he was feeling as awkward as her now.

'I see.'

'I seem to recall Captain Bailey was a patient here a while back.'

'I know it's not allowed,' she said, ashamed to have been caught out, especially by someone she respected so well.

'Don't worry on my account,' he said. 'I'm aware these things happen. They're bound to, when you have people working and living in such close quarters, and especially during such a surreal time.' He rested a hand on her shoulder. 'Am I wrong in presuming it was a troubling letter?'

Phoebe looked at his hand and then up into his eyes and, seeing the concern on his face, took hold of her emotions. 'It was.'

'Is it anything I may be able to help you with?'

She shook her head. 'Thank you.' He was her friend and he and his sister had been extremely kind to her, despite not knowing her at all well. 'But no, there's nothing you can do to help. I'm grateful to you for offering, though.'

'There's no need for your gratitude, Phoebe. Your friendship has made an enormous difference to my sister's life.'

'It has?'

'Yes. Since your stay at the house she seems to have come alive again. It's something I had never expected might happen, despite my hopes that the day would eventually come when Jocasta saw some joy in her life again. If anyone should feel gratitude, then it's me.'

She was surprised by his words but delighted that she had inadvertently helped such a dear friend. Two dear friends.

'Jocasta is a kind and thoughtful woman, and no one should ever have to suffer as she has done.'

He sighed and motioned for her to take a seat. Once Phoebe was seated, Geoffrey sat next to her on the bench and, crossing one leg over the other, rested his hands on his knee. 'I agree. Unfortunately, though, there are no doubt hundreds of thousands of young wives who have found themselves in the same unenviable position as Jocasta.' He sighed heavily. 'And if this war doesn't end sometime soon, then I fear there will be hundreds of thousands more.'

Phoebe shuddered.

'You're cold,' Geoffrey said. 'You need to go back inside. We don't want you coming down with a chill, especially when so many other nurses are in the sick bay.'

He was right, but she wasn't ready to return to the dorm yet. To do so would mean having to speak to people, however kindly they might be. The only other place was the canteen, but again she would end up having to speak to someone.

'I'll sit here for another few minutes yet,' she said. 'But only a couple. I promise.'

He stood and stared down at her. 'You make sure you do. I would hate to have to write and tell Jocasta that I hadn't been looking out for you. She'd never forgive me if you fell unwell here at the hospital.'

Phoebe smiled, recalling Jocasta saying almost the same thing to her about Geoffrey expecting her to look out for her. 'I'll go inside very soon. I just need a little more time to think.' *And cry*, she thought, but didn't say that bit aloud.

# THIRTY-FIVE

## Celia

### APRIL 1917

Frith Hill Prisoner-of-War Camp, Camberley, Surrey

The camp in Surrey was much bigger than Les Blanches Banques in Jersey, but that wasn't surprising, as she had expected things to be significantly different. She stood at the entrance gates, having just posted a letter to Phoebe letting her know she was no longer in Jersey and a little about the camp where she was now working.

She had been surprised by how much happier Otto was, now that he left the camp each day to go and work with two other men on a nearby farm. When he had first been given his work assignment, she had warned him to be careful of his leg, worried about him.

'Celia, I enjoy being away from these barbed-wire fences and guards for hours each day, so I don't worry much about my leg.' He had smiled softly at her when she had started to argue and promised to be careful, just to keep her happy. 'I can pretend that my life has some normality in it again.'

'But you said you were a doctor before the war,' she teased. 'This work is nothing like what you were used to doing.'

'I agree, but digging and planting a field is more normal to me than sitting around in a chair each day. I feel alive for the first time since I was captured.'

It cheered her to see his pale pallor being replaced by a golden tan and his blonde hair lightened by being outside in the sun. He was stronger and smiled much more often, despite still being held in a camp so far from his family in Austria. The only downside for her was that as Otto was no longer a patient at the hospital, she saw him far less than she used to. Now she had to rely on unexpected encounters, or times when she was able to be in the right area when he was delivered back to the camp each evening, or when he managed to find her in the grounds when she was going about her work.

'How was it at the farm today?' she asked when he stepped out from behind one of the wards as she passed the rear corner on her way to the stock room for supplies.

His hand grazed hers lightly and Celia felt the familiar sensations coursing through her body that she experienced every time Otto's skin came in contact with hers. She looked down at their connected hands and wished she could take his properly in hers. Her eyes travelled up past his muscular, tanned forearms to where he had rolled up his sleeves above his elbows. The collar of his shirt was worn and grimy from a day's work in the fields, but he looked happier than she could recall him ever being.

'You've had a good day, I can see that much.'

'It feels good to do work,' he said. 'I am now becoming used to the manual labour and my body does not hurt nearly as much as it did when I first began.'

'I'm pleased. You look…' Her heart raced as she stared at

him and without meaning to, Celia sighed. She had never experienced wanting a man before meeting Otto. Now, though, her yearning for him was almost painful.

'How do I look?' he asked, his voice husky.

'Perfect,' she whispered. Unable to help herself, she glanced around and, happy to see there was no one nearby, took his hand and pulled him closer to the building.

His mouth dropped open in surprise. Then, looking quickly from side to side, he smiled, took her in his arms and kissed her.

She breathed in his musky scent, not caring that she might get dust on her pristine uniform, and ran her hands up his arms, relishing the feel of his muscles as she lost herself in his kiss. Hearing voices somewhere nearby, they jumped apart.

'That was wrong of me,' Otto said, looking angry with himself.

'Why?'

'You know why, Celia,' he whispered. 'I am being selfish. How can there be a future for us?' He gritted his teeth. 'However much we might wish for there to be.'

'Don't say that!'

'Hush, someone will hear you.' He pressed two of his fingers against her lips.

She took his wrist in her hand and pulled it down. 'Then don't say such things.'

Celia sensed his conflicting emotions. 'I know why you said what you did, and I understand.' She sighed. 'I feel the same way too sometimes, but when you're near me, like this, I can't bear to think that we won't have a chance to be together. We have to at least try, don't you think?'

Otto took her face in his hands and stared into her eyes briefly before lowering his lips onto hers. 'I am sorry. You are right. I mustn't be frightened for us. We will try to make this work.'

'Do you promise?' she asked, wishing that she had the strength to let him go. Holding onto Otto like she was doing would probably end in one or both of them ruining their lives, and for what? For a pipe dream.

'I do.' Male laughter sounded closer than before and Otto tensed. 'I must not be found here with you,' he said, turning and hurrying away without a backward glance.

Celia took a calming breath and checked her hair was neat and her veil straight. She smoothed down her skirt and, satisfied that she was presentable, continued on her way to the supply room, her legs shaky from the illicit kiss she had just enjoyed.

'Where have you been?' Elsie asked when Celia arrived.

She stifled a groan to see her nemesis standing waiting to be served. Was she never to get away from the dreadful woman? The only negative part about being at the new camp was that Elsie had chosen to transfer there with her and most of the other nurses. It took all of Celia's willpower not to show her disdain for the woman, who made sure to keep her in a permanent sense of unease. *Life would be so much better here if Elsie Baker had chosen to stay behind in Jersey*, Celia thought miserably.

'I wasn't aware you were waiting for me,' Celia said scornfully.

Elsie looked Celia up and down slowly. It was as if she could sense Celia and Otto had been kissing, Celia thought, feeling uncomfortable under the other nurse's scrutiny.

'Is something the matter, Elsie?'

Elsie didn't answer straight away and Celia suspected she

was taking her time to unnerve her. It was working, but Celia had no intention of letting Elsie know that.

'I'm not sure.' Elsie studied Celia's face. 'You look different somehow.'

'I do?' Celia asked, feeling anger rising in her at the blatant attempt to bully her. 'In what way?'

'I'm not sure.' Elsie suddenly gave Celia a broad smile. 'Don't worry though, I'll work it out soon enough.'

*Not if I have anything to do with it, you won't,* Celia thought angrily.

# THIRTY-SIX

# Phoebe

'Missing presumed dead?' Phoebe stared at the telegram in her shaking fingers, unable to believe she had just read those words about her beloved Archie. 'He can't be.'

She felt an arm go round her shoulders. 'I'm terribly sorry, Phoebe.'

She heard Hetty's voice, sounding as if they were both underwater. 'He ... he can't be. We were to be married.'

Fear of the pain she knew was coming coursed through Phoebe. Was this the period of shock before Archie's loss hit her? She stared at the typed words before her. How had his brother known where to send this she wondered.

'What else does it say?' Hetty asked, her voice gentle as her hand reached out and took hold of the telegram. The paper stopped shaking and she began to read. 'Sorry to inform Archie pronounced missing presumed dead. Wanted to let you know as soon as possible. Please send address for further information. Sincerely, Louis Bailey (Brother).'

Phoebe cried out, immediately covering her mouth with one hand.

'Oh, Phoebe,' Hetty said, pulling her into a tight hug. 'I don't know what to say.' After a few seconds she loosened her hold and, taking Phoebe by the shoulders, held her away from her and stared into her eyes.

Phoebe stared back, unable to think what to do or say next.

'Look,' Hetty tapped the telegram, now scrunched in Phoebe's right hand, her face brightening slightly. 'It only says he's presumed dead.' Her mouth gave a tight smile. 'It doesn't say confirmed, does it?'

Phoebe mulled over Hetty's words. She was right. 'It doesn't,' she agreed, hope slowly seeping into her crushed heart. 'Do you … do you think there's still a chance, then, that he might be alive?' Her hope washed away when there was an unmistakable split second of doubt in her friend's eyes before Hetty nodded.

'I do,' Hetty said.

Phoebe was grateful to her friend for trying to comfort her, but she hadn't mistaken that doubt and reasoned that the army wouldn't return Archie's effects to his family if they didn't believe he was dead. Her legs gave way and she slumped onto her bed.

'He's gone.'

'No. You must stay positive,' Hetty argued. 'Until you know for certain.'

Phoebe turned and looked at Hetty. 'I don't know what to do.'

'About what?'

'I don't know what to do next,' Phoebe whispered, opening her hand and smoothing out the telegram against her leg. 'Or what I'll do without him.'

Hetty's hand rested on Phoebe's and gave it a light squeeze.

'What you do is break everything down into small jobs. The first thing to do is reply to his brother's telegram.'

Hetty was right. Phoebe was grateful for her guidance. 'Thank you, I'll do that right now.' She went to stand and realised she had no idea what to say. 'And tell him what?'

'Um … let me think. Well, you could thank him for letting you know and then ask if you could meet him.'

'Meet him?' Phoebe stared at her friend in horror. 'Why would I want to do that?'

Hetty gave her a gentle smile. 'Because you'll be given compassionate leave for a few days, at least. I think you need that time away from all the noise around here.'

She had a point, Phoebe decided, almost convinced but not quite.

'Ask if you can meet him and then arrange to do so. It might help you to find out more about Archie. You know, like what his family is like, that sort of thing. It …' she hesitated, '… I just thought it might help you come to terms with what's happened if you can picture more about his personal life. But it's only a thought.'

Phoebe stared at her friend, trying to process her suggestions. Hetty was right, she decided. She had to do something and it might help her cope if she met his family and learnt more about Archie's past and those he loved the most. 'I will do that.'

A sudden rush of terror swept through her body as grief slammed into her. Phoebe opened her mouth to cry out, but although in her mind she was screaming, no sound came.

What was she going to do without Archie in her life? How could she even contemplate a life without him? What about the home they were planning to have? What about their babies that would now never be born?

She wasn't aware that Hetty had moved away from her until Aggie was kneeling in front of her camp bed, gripping onto Phoebe's wrists. Seeing Aggie's pain-etched face snapped whatever was holding back Phoebe's cries, and suddenly all the pain and anguish trapped inside her erupted. It was the strangest sound, one she didn't recognise as hers. Like a terrified animal.

Phoebe felt herself being tugged forward into Aggie's grasp. Her friend's arms went around her back and held her so tightly, Phoebe wondered if she might stop breathing. She wished she could.

The following day Phoebe was packing her bags to leave with a group of soldiers being sent back to England. She would turn up on Jocasta's doorstep unannounced. Her friend had offered for her to return whenever she wanted, and Phoebe was certain Jocasta would welcome her now, no matter what.

She heard the door open and close and footsteps coming closer to her, and looked up to see Aggie with something in her hand. Another telegram.

Phoebe gasped. Was it from Archie's brother, letting her know the War Office had made a mistake? Maybe Archie was safe and well. Without waiting for Aggie to hand her the telegram, Phoebe snatched it from her friend's fingers and ripped it open, scanning the words.

It was from Archie's brother, but did not enclose the message she had desperately hoped to see.

Aggie gave Phoebe a questioning look.

'Archie's brother Louis has sent their address and invited me to go and stay with them for a few days.'

'I'm pleased.' Aggie smiled, relief on her pretty face.

'But I haven't contacted them yet,' Phoebe said, confused. 'I was planning to do so once I was at Jocasta's home.' She shook her head. 'I don't understand.' Aggie looked a little less sure of herself, Phoebe noticed. 'Tell me.'

'Hetty and I spoke and thought that as you were in no condition to contact anyone, we would send your reply to Louis Bailey ourselves.' She frowned. 'Was that wrong of us?'

Phoebe would have liked to wait until she was ready to contact Louis, but knew her friends had her best interests at heart. 'It's perfectly fine,' she said, attempting to smile and not sure if she quite managed it.

'I'm so relieved to hear you say so. Hetty wasn't sure whether it was the right thing to do. I must admit, I was the one who persuaded her we should do it, and I would have hated to upset you, especially now.'

It was sweet of Aggie to want to take charge, Phoebe thought, and comforting to know that they were both trying to care for her. 'You mustn't worry about me.'

Aggie gave her a questioning look. 'But what about Jocasta? I presume that's where you were planning to go and stay?'

'It was,' Phoebe said, re-reading the telegram. 'But I hadn't asked her so she won't have done anything to prepare for my arrival.' She wondered what it would be like to visit the Bailey family. 'Would you mind replying to this for me and letting them know I'm on my way and should be with them by …' she gave her new journey some thought, '… I suppose, tomorrow afternoon?'

'Yes, happily.' Aggie went to leave but Phoebe called after her. 'Would you also write to my sister, Celia?' She rummaged around in her belongings and found her sister's letter that she had only received the previous day.

'Of course. What would you like me to say?'

Phoebe thought quickly. 'Simply let her know about Archie

and that I'm going to Sandsend for a few days. I'll write to her when I'm back, or if there's any news.'

'No problem at all,' Aggie said, taking the letter and pushing it into her pocket. 'I'll write to her immediately.'

'Thank you.'

Phoebe watched her friend hurry out of the room, looking hugely relieved. She wasn't ready to meet Archie's family yet, but maybe going there immediately without giving herself too much time to think was the best thing for it. At least this way they could process the news together and maybe, she thought hopefully, she might be able to give them some of the comfort she needed so much herself at that moment.

As she bent to place her neatly folded nightdress into the open case, a fresh wave of tears overwhelmed her. Phoebe sat heavily onto her bed and sobbed. What was she thinking? How could she expect to contain her emotions while staying with Archie's family?

Phoebe took a few minutes to regain control. She wiped her eyes and blew her nose. She must go, she decided. She would find a B&B before going to their home and book a room there. At least then she would have the privacy to allow her tears for Archie to flow.

Feeling a little calmer, Phoebe washed her face with cool water. It wouldn't do to have a puffy face, especially as her travel companions were men who had been injured at the Front. Phoebe had helped care for enough of them to know that she must attempt to put on a brave face.

'You ready, love?' Dennis, one of the orderlies, asked as he poked his head around the door.

'Yes, almost.' She closed and fastened her valise. Then putting on her coat and hat, she lifted it and grabbed her handbag before walking to the door.

'Let me take that from you,' he said, taking the valise from her hand without waiting for a reply. He seemed a nice man and she wondered if one of her friends had told him why she had been granted leave.

'Thank you,' Phoebe said, following him along the walk boards to where several motor ambulances were parked, their engines running noisily as soldiers and nurses clambered up temporary wooden steps to board. Her step faltered; she wasn't ready for this.

Dennis seemed to sense she was no longer following him and turned to her. 'Come along, now. Let's be 'avin' yer. There's no time ter waste if you lot are ter catch the train.'

Not wishing to be the cause of any delay, Phoebe forced herself to resume walking. She reached the back of the vehicle where Dennis was waiting and took his hand when he offered it to help keep her steady as she climbed up the roughly hewn steps. Once seated, he placed her bag at her feet.

'You take care now, Nurse Robertson.'

'I will, Dennis,' she said. 'Thanks for your help.'

## THIRTY-SEVEN

## Celia

---

'There you are, Celia,' Martha Kelly, the nurse with whom Celia now shared quarters, said, running up after her near the ward where Celia was headed.

Celia didn't miss the urgency in her new friend's voice. 'Whatever's the matter?'

Martha pushed her hand into her apron pocket and withdrew a letter. 'I thought you'd want to read it straight away,' she said, thrusting the envelope towards Celia.

'Probably from my sister, Phoebe,' she said, excited to hear from her.

'I just thought, as you'd only just left for your shift, maybe you should read it now rather than later.'

Celia understood her roommate's logic. She would have done the same if the roles were reversed. Who knew what news they might receive at any minute during this terrible war? 'Thank you,' she said, taking the letter. Not recognising the writing, she frowned thoughtfully. She held up the envelope and smiled. 'Actually, I've no idea who this is from.'

'Stop studying the envelope and read it to find out!' Martha giggled.

Celia opened it and read.

*Dear Nurse Robertson*

*You won't know me but I am a friend of your sister, Phoebe. She is well but has received some worrying news and wanted me to write and let you know that her fiancé, Captain Archie Bailey, has been reported as missing, presumed dead. She has been invited to his home by his brother and has now left France and is on her way to England.*

*She asked me to let you know and said that she will write to you as soon as she has news.*

*With kind regards,*

*Agatha Phipps*

Celia sighed. 'Poor Phoebe,' she said, her heart welling with emotion for her sister as she explained the situation to Martha. 'I do hope she's all right.' She looked down at the letter again. 'If only I knew where they lived. I could have gone to be with her.'

Why didn't Phoebe think to let her know where she would be going, Celia wondered. She would have loved to be able to help her through such a frightening time.

'Maybe she didn't like to bother you,' Martha said thoughtfully. 'Or she could want to do this alone. Either way, you can only be there if she asks you to be.'

Celia agreed. Martha made perfect sense but she wished she could do something to help her sister. Celia thanked Martha and began walking to the ward, her mind filled with thoughts of her sister. *How terrible Phoebe must be feeling right now*, Celia thought. To have gone through the loss of their parents and brother, and now to lose the man she loved was cruel beyond words.

'Poor Phoebe,' she murmured again as she arrived at the ward door and opened it, ready to step inside.

'Did you say something, Nurse Robertson?' Sister Crowley asked, looking perplexed when Celia shook her head. 'Well, never mind. Matron would like to see you, so you must report to her office right away.'

'What does she want?' Celia asked, forgetting who she was talking to.

'Nurse Robertson,' Sister Crowley snapped, 'it is not for you to query why Matron does anything. Now, go.'

Celia felt suitably chastised and left the ward to make her way to Matron's office. What could she want from her though, Celia wondered. Had she done something to warrant a telling off? Her stomach twisted as she recalled her heavenly kiss with Otto. Maybe someone had reported her after all. She hoped not. That was all she needed right now.

She arrived at the office, knocked on the door and was called inside. Celia stepped in and saw Elsie already standing there. Had Elsie told on her? Celia clenched her teeth to stop herself saying anything.

'Ah, there you are, Nurse Robertson.'

'Sorry, Matron, I've only just heard that you were wanting to speak to me.'

'Never mind all that.' She looked down at some notes on a notepad and then up again. 'I've called you both in here today to let you know that it's already been noticed that you both work to a superior level compared to most of your contemporaries. We have also received reports from your previous camp with recommendations that you both be promoted.'

Celia was astonished. Pride coursed through her to think that her hard work and diligence had been noticed and reported on. Her mother and father would have been so proud, she thought, wishing they were still alive to hear this exciting news.

Elsie gave a little gasp and grinned happily at Celia for a second before resuming her serious stance in front of Matron's desk.

Matron looked from one to the other of them, her expression dark. 'However, I hear that there is some tension between the pair of you, for some reason.'

Celia's mood dipped and she saw Elsie's smile vanish.

'I would have thought my nursing staff far too busy caring for patients to have time for silly squabbles.'

Celia bit back a reply. If only Elsie was a bit more open to people changing their minds about others. Celia knew now that her initial dislike of all Germans was unfair. These patients were mostly decent men who would rather be doing the jobs they had worked hard at before the war, than having to kill men purely because they were on the opposite side in the war.

'Regardless of your issues, which I expect you to contain and find some resolution for, I'm afraid there is currently only one vacancy and it falls to me to decide who the worthy appointee will be. I won't be doing it today.' Celia relaxed slightly. She needed time to think about what this would mean to her. More money? Certainly, but also more responsibility. She decided she didn't mind that prospect at all and could handle the senior role.

'I thought you both should know that I will be assessing your work ethic and performances over the coming days and once my decision has been made, I shall inform you both separately.'

Celia realised that Matron had finished when the older woman picked up her fountain pen, unscrewed the lid and began writing. She didn't like to presume that it was time to leave but also wasn't sure what to do next.

Matron seemed to notice they were still there and looked at Celia and then Elsie above her glasses. 'Off you go then, Nurses. I'll call for you when the time is right.'

As they walked out, Celia hung back and let Elsie go first, groaning inwardly as a thought struck her. If she was awarded the promotion instead of Elsie, there was going to be hell to pay.

# THIRTY-EIGHT

# Phoebe

### Sandsend

By the time Phoebe arrived in the little town of Sandsend she had been travelling over twenty-four hours and was exhausted. She asked about places to stay at the train station and when given a few options, chose the nearest one. She registered with the landlady and was relieved when she walked into her bedroom and saw that although it was small and at the back of the house, it was clean and the bed was much comfier than the camp bed she was used to sleeping in.

Phoebe sat on the bed and thought of Jocasta and how much she would have preferred to now be in her friend's sunny, welcoming home. She pictured sitting at Jocasta's table with a mug of cocoa in her hands as she and her friend chatted about their days. But she wasn't there, she was here in Sandsend.

Phoebe unbuttoned her coat. She needed to freshen up and have an hour's sleep before going to meet with Archie's brother, Louis. She pulled the curtains closed and lay on the bed, closing her eyes.

---

The next thing she knew, it was almost dusk.

She sat up with a start, furious with herself for sleeping for so long. Phoebe pulled back the curtains and opened the window to let in some fresh air. She was relieved to see that the weather had cleared up and the rain had stopped. She hoped it wasn't too late to call in at the Baileys' house, but thought it preferable to go straight away rather than the next morning, as she had mentioned in her telegram that she would arrive at some point that day.

Having asked her landlady directions to the lane where Archie's home was, ten minutes later she was standing in front of the door, trying to muster the courage to walk up to it and knock.

The door opened and the sight of the man standing before her made her catch her breath. Phoebe had to concentrate on not letting her legs give way. People thought she and Celia were similar in looks, but this man was the image of Archie.

'Miss Robertson?' he asked, walking out to greet her.

Phoebe was unable to speak and, try as she might, she could not force her legs to move. She noticed a look of concern on his handsome face, but before he could say anything further an older woman stepped past him and put an arm around Phoebe's waist.

'Can't you see, Master Louis, you've given this young lady a shock?'

'What? Oh, right. Sorry about that. I forget it's a surprise for people when they first meet one of us. Archie and me, that is.'

He stepped back to give the woman and Phoebe space to walk into the house.

'I'm Mrs Dunwoody. You sit right here, my dear.' Phoebe felt a seat behind her legs and the pressure of hands on her shoulders, and sat as instructed. 'There, that's the ticket. You take it easy while I fetch some tea for you.'

She heard the woman walk away and speak to someone in the hallway. 'Poor lamb obviously had no idea you and Master Archie were twins. Go in and speak to her. I'll fetch some sweet tea and something for her to eat. She looks washed out, poor soul.'

Phoebe struggled to gather herself, still unable to believe what she had just seen.

The man she now knew to be Louis stepped in front of her and sat on the chair facing hers. 'I'm sorry for upsetting you, Miss Robertson,' he said, looking distraught.

'Please don't apologise,' Phoebe said. 'Truly. It was a momentary shock, nothing more.'

'I think you're being generous. I had presumed my brother might have mentioned that we were twins.'

Phoebe grimaced. 'He did.' She studied the face in front of her. It was the face of the most precious man she had ever loved. 'For some reason, though, I didn't expect you to look exactly like him, and it threw me for a moment.'

He began to make pleasantries and as Phoebe watched him speaking she realised his mannerisms were slightly different, his voice slightly lighter. Although his features matched Archie's, they clearly had their differences, albeit subtle ones that weren't initially obvious, and more in their character than in their appearance.

'It was good of you to come all this way,' he said. 'It's much easier to speak face-to-face than via letter. I had considered waiting until my leave ended and I was back in France, but thought you might request compassionate leave. I'm glad you did. I'm glad we didn't have to wait to meet.'

She saw the unmistakable sorrow in his eyes. How selfish she was being. She might be in love with Archie and hoping to marry him and spend the rest of her life with him, but hadn't this man been close to Archie while in their mother's womb? *How much pain must he be in right now?* she wondered, realising she needed to acknowledge his loss.

'As am I.' She looked down at her hands for a moment, trying to form the right words to convey her thoughts. 'Mr Bailey...'

'Louis, please.'

'Thank you. And you must call me Phoebe.' She took a steadying breath. 'It's very kind of you to invite me here. I, too, am glad to be able to meet you and find out more about Archie.' Her voice caught as she said his name and Phoebe realised she had a long way to go before she even began to feel relatively normal again. If she ever did. He was waiting for her to continue. 'Mostly, though, I want you to know how very sorry I am.'

'What for?

'Archie going missing is heartbreaking for me, but I can only imagine how it must feel for you to know your brother is unaccounted for.'

'Thank you, Phoebe. That's kind of you.' He smiled. 'You're right when you say it is difficult for me, and for Mrs Dunwoody. She's known and cared for us for many years.' He looked as if he was struggling to contain his emotions for a moment. 'We might be men now but she's cared for us in some capacity ever since we were babies, and she was devastated when I told her about my brother. But please don't think that I feel your sorrow is any less for you not knowing Archie as long as I have. A fiancée's feelings for her partner are passionate and deeply felt, and I can only imagine how heartbroken you must be right now.'

'I haven't given up hope he'll come home,' she said a little too brusquely. 'Sorry. I didn't mean to snap. I'm a little overtired.'

Mrs Dunwoody walked back into the room carrying a tray weighed down by a tea set, plates and a large fruit cake that made Phoebe's mouth water.

Louis got to his feet and took the tray from the older woman and waited while Mrs Dunwoody pulled a table over towards their seats. Then he placed the tray down on it. 'There are only cups and plates for two here.'

Mrs Dunwoody frowned. 'Yes, of course there are.'

'I want you to join us,' he insisted, glancing at Phoebe. 'Miss Robertson, er, Phoebe, won't mind you doing so, I'm sure.'

'I'd be happy if you stayed,' Phoebe said, wanting to get to know this woman who cared so much for the man she loved.

'Thank you, dear.'

Phoebe watched while the woman retrieved another cup then poured three cups of tea and cut their slices of cake. When they were eating, Louis said, 'Mrs Dunwoody, Phoebe was saying how she hasn't given up on Archie.'

'Neither have we,' Mrs Dunwoody said, giving Phoebe a nod. 'He's a resourceful young fellow and it'll take a lot for him not to come home, especially when he has a lady such as yourself waiting to marry him.'

Phoebe felt much better to be in the company of others who loved Archie so much. 'This is delicious cake,' she said. 'I hadn't realised how hungry I was before now.'

'I'm not surprised,' the housekeeper said. 'Coming all the way from France like you have. Was it too terrible, the crossing and all that?'

Phoebe told them about coming over in the ambulance train and how there had been a couple of delays and how she had overslept at the B&B.

'You could always stay here,' Louis suggested.

Phoebe thanked him for his kind offer but didn't think it was the right thing for her to do. 'The place where I've taken a room is very clean and I'm sure it'll suit me well.'

As they finished their last mouthfuls of the delicious cake, Louis placed his plate and fork onto the tray and picked up his cup and saucer before sitting back in his chair. 'They returned his personal effects, and I've taken out letters from me and Mrs Dunwoody to Archie, but I thought you might like to keep the ones you sent to him?'

Phoebe was touched by his thoughtfulness. 'That's very kind of you. I'd love to have them. I can always return them to him if…' She took a deep breath and raised her chin defiantly. She was not going to let herself think the worst. 'No, I will return them when he comes back to us.'

'Quite right.' He smiled. 'They're in his small study. I'll bring them through to you before you leave. I didn't think it was right to have them on display here, in case it upset you seeing them.'

'I find that any reference to Archie, or thought about him, is rather upsetting at the moment.' She swallowed the lump in her throat and sat up a little straighter. 'But it's something I'll have to deal with.'

'Quite.' Louis looked at her. 'Archie mentioned in his last letter to me that he had proposed and you'd accepted,' he said, smiling. 'He didn't mention when you were planning to marry but…' He seemed to regret his words and Phoebe wanted to reassure him that she wasn't going to cry because of them.

'We were hoping to be married on his next leave, if possible.' She closed her eyes, feeling tears threatening to make an appearance and not wishing them to. 'But plans change. That is something I've learnt in my time at the hospital in Étaples.'

'They certainly do,' Mrs Dunwoody said, finishing her tea and pointing to the tea pot. 'More tea, anyone?'

Phoebe shook her head. 'No, thank you.' She felt a wave of tiredness come over her. 'I should be going. I'm a little weary from the journey and don't wish to take up too much of your time.' She stood.

Louis and Mrs Dunwoody got to their feet. 'You will come back to visit us again tomorrow though, won't you?' Mrs Dunwoody asked. 'It's been lovely meeting you, but your visit has been too brief to show you photos of young Archie.'

'Or tell you much about him and our family, and I'm sure he would want you to know,' Louis said. 'He was always so proud of coming from Sandsend.'

'He was,' Mrs Dunwoody agreed. 'Always telling folk how splendid this place was.' She smiled. 'And it is. Maybe you could come here mid-morning tomorrow and Master Louis could take you for a walk around the village. Would you like that?'

Phoebe sensed that the housekeeper was used to organising the men in the family. 'Yes, I would. Very much. Thank you.'

'That's good news,' Louis said, brightening slightly. 'I'll find some photos for you and look forward to giving you a tour of the place.'

'I'll look forward to it, too.'

'I'll just fetch those letters for you.'

As Phoebe walked back to the B&B, she felt relieved that Louis and Mrs Dunwoody were even nicer than she had dared hope.

*What a perfect life Archie enjoyed here before the war took him away from Sandsend*, she mused. She would have loved being a part of it, and she still would be a part of his future. She had to believe it, if she wasn't going to completely fall apart.

## THIRTY-NINE

## Celia

'Take the other end of this sheet,' Elsie said, throwing it in Celia's direction without waiting for her to answer.

Celia took a corner in each hand and waited for Elsie to do the same with the opposite end. They didn't usually have to fold the sheets but for some reason they had been tasked with doing so today. Or Elsie had, Celia mused. She had been instructed to ask one of her colleagues to go with her to the laundry and help her, and for some reason had chosen Celia, much to Celia's annoyance. She had no idea why Elsie kept her so near whenever she had the chance and sensed it was to keep an eye on her or to keep her in a constant state of flux.

'What did you think of Matron's announcement yesterday, then?'

*So that's why she's brought me here,* Celia thought. 'It's a wonderful opportunity for one of us.'

Elsie didn't say anything further but concentrated on the folding of the sheet. When it was done, she took it from Celia and placed it on the worktop next to her before grabbing the next one.

'Would you accept the promotion if it was offered to you?' Elsie asked.

*What sort of question is that?* 'I would,' Celia replied, aware that she had given the wrong answer as soon as Elsie stopped folding to glare at her. *Damn*, Celia thought, *why didn't I think before answering?*

She stared back at Elsie, waiting for a nasty comment to come her way, and as the silence between them lengthened Celia was unable to stand it any longer. 'And you? Would you accept if it was offered to you?'

Elsie shrugged. 'I'm not sure. I'd have to think about it.'

Celia could tell Elsie was lying. A sense of unease swept over her. Why couldn't Elsie have chosen to work elsewhere? Life would be so much easier without this woman constantly trailing her and commenting on her every movement.

'What's the matter?' Elsie asked.

Celia guessed she knew exactly what was wrong but had no intention of giving her the satisfaction of confirming her thoughts. 'Nothing. Why?'

Disappointment on her face, Elsie shrugged. 'You looked unhappy there for a moment, that's all.'

'No,' Celia lied. 'I'm fine. Probably a little tired, maybe. I could do with a holiday.'

'Couldn't we all.'

---

Celia hadn't seen Otto for a couple of days but it would be far too dangerous for her to go looking for him. He would have to come across her naturally at some point, and she hoped it would happen soon. She had been kept busy in the hospital and she imagined he was working long hours on the farm. It cheered her to know he loved what he was doing, and those months in the hospital seemed like a distant memory now he was tanned and getting stronger and healthier.

She was on her way to take a note from Matron to the Camp Commander when she saw a group of prisoners talking. One had his back to her but she recognised Otto's blonde hair and her stomach flipped over. Not daring to acknowledge him, she kept walking and hoped he might spot her. She sent him all her love and wondered if he would sense her thoughts as she passed.

Having delivered the message, Celia reached the front door on her way out of the building, hoping to catch Otto's eye, but when she stepped outside into the bright sunlight he wasn't there. Her heart contracted painfully. She had missed her opportunity. Miserable, she kept walking, hoping her disappointment wasn't too obvious on her face.

She neared one of the large sheds that housed a ward and as she passed an alleyway between two buildings, she heard a 'Psst.' It was Otto; she just knew it. Not wishing to alert anyone by acting suspiciously, Celia stopped, pressed a finger thoughtfully to her lip and acted as if she had forgotten something. Then, turning to retrace the couple of steps she had made past the alleyway, she went back and sidestepped into the shady recess.

'Otto,' she whispered, her heart pounding as she went to him without a second's deliberation.

He opened his arms and Celia stepped into them, pleasure coursing through her as they closed around her and held her tightly against his hard body. 'Celia, my love.'

She slipped her arms around his back and held him. 'You did see me,' she whispered, breathing in his warm skin and looking up into his bright-blue eyes. 'I should have known you would.'

He lowered his head and their lips met in a kiss. 'I sense when you are around,' he murmured. 'I always know when you are near to me and when you are not.' He let go of her and rested his right hand over his heart. 'I hold you here.'

She swallowed her emotion, not wishing to waste a second of this stolen time with him by crying. 'I love you so much.'

'As I love you.'

He held her to him and kissed her. Celia met his passion, unable to help herself. This was all she wanted out of life. Time with Otto. The freedom of being with the man she loved.

Celia heard a discreet cough behind her and felt Otto's arms drop from around her. She looked into his face and saw horror as he took a step back from her.

Celia spun round to see who had discovered them.

'Elsie.' Her voice was flat as she saw the look of triumph on her colleague's pinched face.

'I think we need to talk, Celia,' Elsie said. 'Don't you?'

Otto stepped forward. 'Please. This is not Nurse Robertson's fault. It is mine alone.'

Elsie narrowed her eyes as she moved closer to them. 'I wouldn't be too quick to share that information,' she said, keeping her voice low. 'You would be shot if it was discovered that you lured a Red Cross Nurse down an alleyway to force yourself upon her.'

Celia gasped. 'You know perfectly well that's not what happened.'

Elsie raised an eyebrow. 'Maybe, but I wonder how many other people will believe him over me?'

Celia couldn't believe what she was hearing. Otto began to speak but, taking his hand briefly in hers, she shook her head.

'No, Otto. You need to leave this with me.' Then it came to her what this was all about. She glared at Elsie. 'You're going to use this as leverage to persuade me not to accept the role of Sister, aren't you?'

Elsie clapped her hands lightly together. 'Clever girl.'

Celia shrugged. She would rather have been the one to get it and suspected that out of the two of them, her record was better and she might have been given it, but Otto was more important to her than any job. If it meant keeping him safe, then she was happy for Elsie to get it, despite dreading Elsie being her superior.

'Fine. I'll tell Matron I'm not interested. Satisfied?' Celia went to turn to Otto, relieved to have resolved the matter.

'Not so fast, Celia,' Elsie said, almost spitting her name. 'I haven't quite finished.'

Tensing, Celia shook her head. 'Isn't that enough?'

'No.'

It was a simple word but the dread of what Elsie was about to spring on her seemed to fill it. 'Go on then.'

'You will tell Matron that you don't wish to be considered for the promotion because you wish to leave the camp.'

Celia heard Otto's sharp intake of breath. She was damned if she was going to let this bully get the better of her. Clenching her jaw, she tried to quell her rising temper but, unable to manage it, shook her head. 'No, I won't be doing that. And, what's more,' she said, feeling stronger in her determination, 'you can't make me.'

Elsie laughed. 'I think the three of us know that isn't true.' She jutted her chin in Otto's direction. 'It's up to you. Either you leave, or he gets the firing squad.'

'They would not shoot me for kissing Celia,' he said confidently.

'Maybe not,' Elsie said. 'But they might it they thought you had tried to rape her.'

Celia's mouth dropped open. 'But that's completely untrue.' She thought of her darling, sweet Otto. 'He would never do such a thing, it's preposterous.' Celia stepped closer to Elsie, wishing she hadn't when the woman's foul breath reached her nostrils as she laughed. Determined not to let Elsie get the better of her, Celia folded her arms across her chest in defiance. 'I'll tell them you're lying.'

Elsie frowned. 'And I would argue that you were such a sweet innocent that the thought of anyone learning that he had defiled you was terrifying to you, and that you were lying to cover up what he had done, in an effort to save your reputation.'

Celia swallowed. She was lost for words. She didn't think she could hate anyone as much as she hated Elsie right at that moment. 'You would stoop that low?'

'I will if you don't go to Matron this afternoon and give notice to leave.'

'But where will I go?'

'That's of no consequence to me.' She eyed Otto up and down. 'I'm sure Oberleutnant Hoffman will soon forget all about you.' She turned to leave. 'You have two minutes to say your goodbyes before I go to Matron myself.'

Celia stared after the woman, stunned to think that anyone could be so wicked. Otto's hand rested on her shoulder and he slowly turned her to face him. 'I will tell them it is all a lie,' he said softly, his hands cupping her face before kissing her lightly on the lips.

Celia wished it could be that simple. 'No,' she argued. 'They will take her word over yours and we both know that. I can't let you be punished for something you haven't done.'

He took hold of her arms. 'Celia, I can't let you leave here. Not like this.'

She had to think, and quickly. They had no choice but to make a plan. 'Otto,' she said, digging deep for the resolve to cope with what she now needed to do. 'She meant what she said about only having two minutes. I will give my notice. I can't risk anything happening to you.'

'No.'

'I've made up my mind.'

'How will I know where to find you when this is all over?'

She thought quickly. She had no family home anymore and needed an address for him as a contact. 'Before the war I considered applying for work at King's College Hospital in London. I will apply there now.'

'But what if you do not get work there?' His healthy, strong demeanour seemed to have lessened in the last few minutes.

She needed to be strong for them both. 'They're desperate for nurses,' she said, hoping she was right. 'I will tell Matron that the reason for my move is something to do with my family, though I'm not quite sure what yet. I'll ask her to give me a reference and mention that she had considered me for promotion to Sister. That will help.'

'Celia.' He shook his head miserably, looking lost.

She reached up and rested her hand against his cheek. 'Darling Otto. We will be together, never lose faith in that happening. I will stay there until the war is over and then I will try to find you.'

He pulled her into his arms and kissed her. Celia felt all his love and desperation in their final kiss as her heart broke in two.

# FORTY

# Phoebe

Phoebe was much happier on her return to the cottage the following morning than she had been the previous day. It had been pleasant meeting Louis and Mrs Dunwoody and to learn that they were kindly people. She supposed she shouldn't have expected anything less from the two people closest to her beloved Archie. She was looking forward to getting to know them better now that she had enjoyed a good night's sleep and was more herself.

She spotted Louis's face at the window as she neared the property and the split-second thought that it was Archie threw her slightly. Then, moments later, he was standing at the front door welcoming her with a wave.

'It's good to see you again,' he said, walking down the small pathway to open the garden gate for her.

'Thank you,' Phoebe said, passing him. 'It's nice to be back here again.'

He seemed happy to hear her say so and closed the gate, accompanying her into the house and indicating she should follow him down the passageway towards the back of the house. 'I thought you might like to see Archie's office.' His step faltered and he turned to her. 'Only if you're happy to, of course. We can always sit in the living room, or it might even be warm enough to sit in a sheltered part of the garden, if you prefer.'

Phoebe knew it was going to be difficult to go into the room where Archie had spent so much time doing what he loved, but it was something she needed to make herself do.

'I would very much like to see Archie's study, if you don't mind. I've pictured him working in there many times and it will be nice to be able to imagine the room as it actually is rather than how I presume it to be.'

Louis smiled at her reaction then led her a few steps further before stopping briefly outside a door. 'It's in here.'

She walked into the room and stopped to take in everything around her. Two walls were lined with built-in bookcases filled with hundreds of books.

Louis followed her gaze to the books and smiled. 'Archie always had a notebook on him to draw something.' He stilled. 'In fact, one was returned with his … with his effects. I haven't had the courage to look inside it yet, but I'm happy for you to do so, should you wish?'

Could she trust herself not to break down if she did look at Archie's work? She wasn't sure. Not wishing to make a spectacle of herself, Phoebe was about to thank him for his offer and decline, but then it occurred to her that he might have drawn a scene from the hospital in France, or something else she could relate to.

'If you don't mind,' she said, determined to be strong, 'I'd like that very much.'

Phoebe took a deep breath. She needed to keep moving and not give in to the melancholy that was threatening to consume her. Seeing a photo of Archie and Louis standing either side of a couple she presumed must be their parents, with the young woman holding a small child, she leaned forward to have a better look.

'Those were such happy times.' Louis studied the photo. 'I have a similar one in my room of us all together.'

'I imagine you treasure that photo.'

He nodded. 'I do.'

They stood in silence for a moment. Phoebe saw the sadness in Louis's posture and knew she needed to distract him. She looked to see what else there was in the room as she struggled for something to say and noticed another table, although this one was higher than the desk and the top was set at an angle.

'What is that?' Phoebe asked, intrigued.

'That's his drafting table,' Louis explained. 'It's where Archie sketched his designs.'

Phoebe saw that it was facing the window. 'I suppose it's here for the best light, although I would be distracted by that pretty view.' She looked out at the flower-filled, walled-in garden and wondered who was keeping it in such perfect neatness.

'I would too,' Louis agreed. 'Archie said that when he was stuck with a design it helped him to look out at the flowers and birds in the garden and clear his mind, allowing his subconscious to flow, and then he usually had an idea what to do next.'

Phoebe stared at the view and tried to picture Archie standing in the same spot doing the same thing. The thought brought him a little closer to her.

She felt a gentle touch on her shoulder and glanced up for a second, thinking it was Archie. Phoebe reached up and rested her hand on his, remembering she was standing with Louis and not Archie when she felt him tense. She snatched her hand away.

'I … I'm so sorry,' she spluttered, turning quickly to face him. 'I forgot myself for a moment.'

Louis shook his head slowly, an expression of understanding on his handsome face. 'Please don't concern yourself. I also forget he's not here.' He indicated the two worn leather chairs each side of the fire. 'Shall we sit? I've asked Mrs Dunwoody to bring us in some tea. I hope that's all right?'

'Yes, thank you.' Phoebe sat in one of the chairs, grateful to him for his understanding.

Louis sat and stared momentarily into the fire. Then looking at Phoebe, he sighed. 'I've been caught a few times, just like you.'

She couldn't understand how. 'In what way?'

'When I've passed a mirror. It's given me a jolt when I thought I saw Archie, then realised that it was my reflection.' His gaze dropped and Phoebe could see the muscle working in the side of his jaw. He cleared his throat and when he looked into her eyes once more, she saw they were filled with unshed tears. 'I miss him so much, Phoebe. Having you here has helped enormously.'

'How so?' she asked, glad to have been a comfort to him at such a terrible time, but unsure what she had done to warrant the compliment.

'Seeing your love for him makes me happy that he experienced such closeness with someone like you.'

Someone like her? She tried to imagine what he meant by his comment. 'I'm not sure I understand'

He shook his head, embarrassed. 'I mean, a beautiful woman. Someone with something about her.' He grimaced.

'That isn't right either. Let me think.' He thought for a moment. 'My brother was never interested in women who didn't have an independent thought in their head. As soon as I met you, I understood why he fell for you.' His face reddened and Phoebe was thrown for a moment. 'What I mean to say is, he was always fascinated by women who wanted more from life than simply to be a wife and mother.'

'But surely that is what most women want,' she replied, unsure whether it sounded anything at all like the Archie she knew.

'No, I mean...' He sighed, clearly frustrated with himself. 'Don't get me wrong, Archie always wanted a family, but he would never be the sort of man who would expect his wife to live her life solely through him and his hobbies. He would have encouraged you to continue doing what you loved. For example, if you loved to travel, he would have enjoyed planning trips with you. If you loved painting, or, um, writing, my brother would have supported you in your endeavours.

'He will come back,' Louis assured her quietly. 'I can't allow myself to think otherwise yet. If ever.'

Phoebe rubbed her hands together. 'I feel the same way as you. Archie must come home. I can't contemplate a future without him in it.'

'Neither can I,' Louis said, looking over at Archie's desk.

They were pulled from their thoughts by Mrs Dunwoody's knock on the door.

'I'll go and fetch that notebook for you, Phoebe,' he said. 'You pour our tea, I shan't be long.'

Phoebe watched him go, turning to smile at the housekeeper. 'Thank you,' she said. 'You're not joining us today?'

The woman shook her head. 'No.' She glanced at the door

and, keeping her voice low, added, 'He needs someone other than me to reminisce with. He's struggled terribly since dear Archie went missing. We all have, but with them two being twins...'

'Yes, I believe you're right. I'm happy to spend time talking about Archie with him during my stay in Sandsend.'

'Here it is,' Louis said, returning to the room and holding out to her a book with a grey cover. 'You take that with you today. You can let me have it back any time.'

'Thank you,' Phoebe said, holding the book and running an index finger lightly across where Archie had written his name, before slipping it into her handbag. 'I'll take very special care of it.'

'I'm sure you will.'

After they had finished their tea, Louis suggested they go for a walk. 'Archie wouldn't forgive me if I didn't show you around this beautiful place.'

'I'm looking forward to seeing every part of it,' she said, pushing away her regret that she wasn't being shown Archie's home village by him.

———

As they walked along the seafront past homes and hotels, Phoebe thought how wonderful it must be to live by the water all year round. As they walked, several people spoke to Louis, saying how good it was to see him again and commiserating about Archie. He introduced Phoebe to them and she enjoyed being known as 'Archie's fiancée'.

'What a beautiful place in which to grow up,' she said when two little boys and a girl of about seven ran by laughing and shrieking.

'It was. We were very lucky. Archie loved sailing our father's small boat with him and going fishing,' Louis said, pointing to the slipway where they must have begun their journey.

Phoebe listened to all of Louis's stories and tried to commit them to memory. She wanted to be able to tell Archie all the things she had discovered about his childhood and how precious she thought his closeness to his twin brother was.

Back at the house after their long walk, they went to the living room and sat down to continue chatting. After a lunch of cold meats, boiled potatoes and salad, Phoebe wasn't sure if it was the sea air or exhaustion from the emotion of the last few days, but she found it a struggle to keep her eyes open.

She dreamt of Archie leading her onto the beach at Sandsend and opened her eyes to see Archie's sweet face peering down at her. She sighed to see his familiar features and threw her arms around his neck, pulling him down to her. He didn't initially respond to her kiss and she presumed she had taken him by surprise, but then his hands took hold of her wrists gently and lowered her arms.

'Phoebe, it's me, Louis.'

For a moment her brain struggled to understand.

'Louis?' she whispered, horrified by what she had done.

She pushed him away and stumbled to her feet, unsure where to go. Picking up her bag, she ran out to the hallway, relieved when the shocked housekeeper moved out of her way.

'Phoebe!' Louis shouted.

Phoebe couldn't face him or Mrs Dunwoody. She grabbed her coat and hat and, without wasting time, put them on and hurried out of the house, hearing their voices behind her as she ran down the pathway and along the lane. How could she have mistaken Louis for her darling Archie?

Phoebe began to cry and had to slow to a walk as her sobbing increased. She stopped, unable to go any further, and leaned against a wall, trying to make sense of what had just happened.

'Are you all right, miss?' an elderly man asked, crossing the road to check on her.

'I…' She opened her bag and withdrew a handkerchief. Wiping her eyes and blowing her nose, Phoebe struggled to gather herself. 'I'm fine, thank you.'

'You don't look fine to me, if you don't mind me saying.' His lined face studied hers. 'I can offer you a cup of tea, if you'd like to come to meet my missus.' He pointed to a nearby cottage. 'She would be very happy to make one for you.'

'That's very kind of you,' Phoebe said gratefully. 'But I have a train to catch and I really should be running along.'

'If you like. You take care of yourself, miss.' He gave her a look of such sadness that it almost set her tears off again.

'Thank you for being so kind, though. I do appreciate it.' She gave him a smile and continued on her way. As soon as she was back at the B&B she gave notice to her landlady that she would be leaving immediately, then ran up to her room to pack. She couldn't face Louis again. Not now. All she wanted to do was put as much distance between them as she possibly could.

It took no time at all to pack her few belongings into her valise. She closed and fastened the top, then stopped. The vision of Louis's stunned face as she had pulled him down to kiss him made her want to cry again. The poor man. What had she done? She sat down heavily on the bed, struggling to make sense of it all.

'Oh, Archie.'

# FORTY-ONE

## Celia

### AUGUST 1918

King's College Hospital, London

I t was another stifling day in London, and Celia longed for time on the coast with a sea breeze like the one she recalled only too well from the summer months living in Jersey. That time seemed so distant now, as did being in Surrey. A more dangerous strain of the mild flu they had seen in patients in the spring seemed to be returning with force, and doctors at the hospital were praying that the Spanish Lady – or Flanders Grippe, as it was often called – was waning, and Celia hoped the virus hadn't reached the camp where Otto was probably still being held.

How had it been over a year since she had last seen Otto, Celia wondered as she waited for the doctor to begin his rounds. Sixteen months, to be precise, she worked out miserably. She wished she could write to him but the risk of being discovered was far too great. It was difficult enough that Elsie still worked there and Celia knew the woman well enough to trust that she meant every threat she had voiced. If only there was some way she could make contact with him, just to discover if he was keeping well and being cared for as he should be.

Instead of their time apart getting easier, she found that it became much harder to bear. Thank heavens her job kept her so busy.

She prayed each night that the war would soon come to an end and that Phoebe would hear news of her Archie, but it had been so long that Celia doubted he could still be alive. Thankfully, Phoebe seemed to be coping as well as she could in France and like her, appeared to be happiest when keeping busy.

As soon as her shift ended she changed, deciding, as she did most sunny days, to take a walk to Ruskin Park. She liked the fact that this large, green space with its pond and beautiful planted areas had been named in honour of the famous artist. Celia was grateful to the powers that be for creating such an oasis where she could enjoy spending time contemplating life in the shade of one of the trees, or listening to music when a band played rousing tunes from the bandstand.

As she entered the park, Celia saw the familiar sight of recruits from the First Surrey Rifles training. She had been told that they were based nearby at Flodden Road in Camberwell and supposed the park made the perfect training ground in the busy city. She stopped to watch for a few seconds, imagining Otto training before he had been sent to the Front. He must have been very handsome in his uniform. She pushed away the thought, not wishing to see him as an enemy officer. He was simply her Otto and to think of him in any other way filled her with unease.

She found a place to sit and despite the dappled shade of the trees, the stillness of the air exhausted her. She closed her eyes and listened to the birdsong, breathing in the warm air and unable to miss the hint of roses in the flower border nearby. Celia could almost forget there was a war on when she sat peacefully in the park this way. *At least there are fewer Zeppelin attacks now,* she thought, wishing her parents had survived.

The thought of her parents made her wonder where she might end up living after the war ended. She could of course stay at the hospital and live in nurses' quarters, but how long would she want to do that? No, Celia thought, she needed her own home, not just a room she had to share with another nurse. She still longed to be together properly with Otto but couldn't help the nagging feeling that she was being unrealistic. Would she, a British girl, ever be accepted in Austria or Germany? And would he be able to live in England? When this war ended – she was determined to remain positive that it would – how long would it be until each nation forgave the other for the casualties they had inflicted over the war years?

The band struck up and Celia jumped. She had been so deep in thought that she hadn't noticed them setting up their instruments. More and more people arrived to watch, clapping after each song finished. They were the songs everyone had come to know well: 'It's a Long Way to Tipperary', 'Keep the Home Fires Burning' and 'When Tommy Comes Marching Home'. Whereas most people seemed to enjoy them, Celia decided that she would be glad when she didn't hear them played most days.

She wasn't sure if she was even truly living anymore. Getting up each day to nurse patients in the hospital or spend time walking or sitting here in the park felt more like merely existing. She needed a future to look forward to. They all did.

She pictured Phoebe waiting endlessly for news of Archie and wished she could see her sister, if only for an hour or so, to give her a hug and reassure her that everything would be all right.

But would it?

# FORTY-TWO

# Phoebe

P hoebe stared at Louis's crumpled letter in her hand.

*Dear Phoebe,*

*I trust you are keeping well. I have wanted to write to you many times over the past sixteen months but didn't know what to say. I understand that you might have been embarrassed by what happened but please know that there is no reason to be. There have been many times over the years when Archie and I have been mistaken for one another and so it is hardly surprising that you did the same thing when I surprised you like I did.*

*I hope that enough time has passed since the last time we met that you will now be able to think of me as your friend. I want you to know that you have my friendship always and hope that you will, if not now then at some point in the future, feel able to turn to me for help should you ever need it. If you do not feel that is possible then I ask you to try and find it in your heart to contact Mrs Dunwoody at this address should you ever need to. She still keeps the house ready for Archie's return and sorts any post that has been received and I know that she would wish to see you again and maybe speak to you about Archie and answer any questions you might have about him.*

*I am returning to my unit today after ten days' leave and I felt compelled to contact you before I go to let you know how much I would value your friendship. To be able to share stories of my brother with you – someone who loved Archie as much as I did – would mean so much to me. You are all that my brother wanted in a wife and I hope that we can move on from any awkwardness and become the friends he would have wished us to be.*

*Wishing you all good health.*

*Until we meet again,*

*Your friend,*

*Louis*

She scanned his words once again. Louis was right, they should be friends. Didn't she want to know all that there was about her darling fiancé?

Phoebe decided she would give her reply to Louis some thought, but she would write to him. It was unfair of her to let him go back to fight still worried about what had happened between them.

---

Phoebe was on her way to the laundry room when she saw Geoffrey Sutherland coming towards her along the boardwalk. He wasn't smiling.

Geoffrey was staring at her as he neared and Phoebe pushed her hand into her pocket to ensure the letter was well hidden. He glanced down at her hand and Phoebe realised she needed to distract him in case he asked what she was concealing.

Seeing another nurse nearby, Phoebe made a point of addressing him by his professional name. 'Hello, Doctor Sutherland,' she said when he stopped in front of her.

'Nurse Robertson.' He smiled at the passing nurse before turning his focus back to Phoebe. 'I was hoping to speak to you,' he said, lowering his voice.

'You were?'

'Yes. Do you mind if we talk for a moment?'

Phoebe nodded, aware that to refuse would seem rude. 'What about? Is something the matter?'

He took her lightly by the arm and led her away from the walkway to stand by a tree. 'That's what's troubling me.'

He wasn't making any sense. 'Sorry?'

He sighed. 'Phoebe, I'm concerned about you.'

She wished he wasn't. Now he was going to ask her questions that she wasn't sure she could answer honestly. 'You are?'

He frowned. 'Are you all right?'

'What do you mean? Of course I am.'

'Phoebe, I thought you trusted me.'

'I do, Geoffrey,' she insisted, aware her cheeks were reddening and revealing her lie.

'I thought we were friends.'

She looked into his eyes and guilt coursed through her. Geoffrey was her friend. Hadn't he been there whenever she had needed him? If she couldn't trust Geoffrey, then who could she trust?

'Phoebe? Please speak to me. I know you're suffering and I understand why.'

*Do you?* she wondered.

'I can't ignore that you've lost weight, far more than is healthy for anyone, let alone a busy nurse.' He took her gently by the shoulders. 'I understand if you can't speak about Archie. But I feel the time has come when I can't ignore what's happening to you and not step in to do something.'

She stared at him, frightened to imagine what he might be about to say. 'Geoffrey, please. I ... I promise I'll try to do better.'

'Oh, sweet girl,' he said, looking distraught. 'I don't want promises from you. I want you to leave here and go to stay with Jocasta. You need time away from all these reminders of Archie.' He stared at her silently for a few seconds. 'You must see him each time you walk in the ward where he used to be. Don't you?'

'I do,' she admitted, barely able to contain her relief. He didn't suspect anything. 'Geoffrey, you are the sweetest man,' Phoebe said, taking a steadying breath. 'I don't know what I would have done without you and Jocasta this past year.'

'Does that mean you'll do as I ask? My sister is worried and said that despite her writing and offering for you to go and stay with her in Cornwall, you never have.'

'I didn't like to take advantage of her kindness,' Phoebe admitted. 'Jocasta has enough to deal with, bringing up Bryony by herself.'

'Nonsense. She has me supporting her and you are always welcome to stay with her. Surely you know that?'

She thought about what he said and nodded. 'I suppose I do.'

'Phoebe, the time has come when you need someone else to take charge.' His expression softened. 'Please tell me you'll at least consider my suggestion?'

Phoebe realised that apart from Archie's immediate return, all she really wanted was to go home to England and be with her friend Jocasta once more. 'I'll do more than that, Geoffrey,' she said. 'I thought that coming back here after he went missing would keep me busy and be the best thing for me, but I think you're right that all I'm doing is tormenting myself, being in the same place where Archie spent those months.'

'Dear girl.' The look of sympathy on his face made Phoebe want to cry.

Determined not to, she continued, 'I'm going to leave here as soon as I possibly can and go to Jocasta.'

He sighed loudly and stunned her by pulling her into his arms and giving her a bear hug. 'I'm so relieved. So utterly relieved.'

She rested her head against his chest and tried to imagine that the strong arms around her belonged to Archie. Phoebe only managed to fool herself for a few seconds. Geoffrey was not as tall or as broad as Archie. She gently moved away and his arms fell from around her.

'I have to ask Matron's permission, though. We're busier than ever at the moment, so she may decline the request.'

'I will speak to Matron on your behalf.'

'Oh, no!' She tried to quell her panic. 'I would hate for her to think I put you up to it.'

'She won't. I'll tell her I've noticed your weight loss and that I'm concerned that you're here, around so much illness. She will understand where I'm coming from and won't dare take it out on you. She's a good woman, if a little fierce at times.' He stared at her silently before continuing. 'In all honesty, I'm sure she's concerned about you, too. She'll probably be relieved you wish to go somewhere and recover from everything that's happened.'

'Thank you, Geoffrey,' she said, smiling. 'I appreciate everything you've done for me.'

'It's my pleasure,' he said. 'I'm very fond of you, Phoebe.

You were the first friend I made here and I haven't forgotten how you put me at my ease.'

'I did?' She wasn't sure how she had done that, but was glad to know that she had helped make his arrival better in some way.

'Yes. I also haven't forgotten how you helped Jocasta find her way back to being happier. That, to me, is worth everything.'

'I'm glad to have had the opportunity.'

He looked down at her pocket. 'Now, I don't know what you have in your pocket or why you seemed lost in thought when I bumped into you, but I'll not keep you a moment longer.'

'Geoffrey, wait.'

He turned back to her. 'Yes, Phoebe? What is it?'

'There's something I want to share with you.' He stood silently as she explained what had happened between her and Louis. 'I thought for a moment he was Archie, but I was mistaken. Then I stupidly ran away because I was so embarrassed and made everything so much worse between us.'

'But he's written to you now?'

'He has. He understands and wants us to be friends.'

She saw Geoffrey's face relax into a smile. 'I'm glad.'

'You are?'

He took her hands in his. 'Of course I am. You're a dear, dear friend, Phoebe, and I want you to be happy. I've seen how heartbroken you've been about Archie.' He pulled her into another hug. 'I want you to know that you can always confide in me or come to me for anything.'

'Thank you, Geoffrey. You've been so kind to me.'

'Don't. It's what friends do.' He kissed the top of her

head. 'I hope you're going to write to Louis Bailey. I have a feeling he needs you as much as you need him now. Talk to him, tell him about his brother and how happy you were together. Tell him about Archie's time in the hospital with you. He'll want to hear everything you're willing to share with him.'

Geoffrey was right. And for once it felt good to know that she had the power to help someone else. 'I will write to him. Thank you.'

'Good.' He released her from the hug. 'Now, you run along and carry on with whatever you were doing and I'll speak to Matron the first chance I get today.' He smiled. 'And once I've done that I'll write to my sister. She's going to be very happy to learn you'll be returning to Pennwalloe.'

'That's very kind of you.' She leaned forward and kissed his cheek without thinking, horrified when two nurses appeared from one of the nearby buildings and stared at them in surprise.

Phoebe leapt back as if she had been stung.

'What's the matter?' He looked around him and spotting the nurses, sighed. 'Ignore them. They have enough to be getting on with and won't think about what they've just seen for very long.'

Phoebe doubted he was right. After all, what did he know about how the nurses and VADs gossiped when one of their own became too close to one of the surgeons? 'I'd better be on my way before anyone else comes along and thinks there's more between us than there actually is.'

'Yes, all right. I'll catch up with you once I've spoken to Matron.' He stared at her thoughtfully. 'If you decide you wish to return to work and need me to put in a good word for you, either here or elsewhere, please don't hesitate to ask me.'

'I won't,' she said, grateful for another generous offer from him. 'Thank you, Geoffrey.'

As Phoebe made her way back to the dorm she thought about her impending return to Cornwall.

It would be strange being back there again, she thought, especially as she and Archie had made such wonderful memories together there. She thought of his proposal and of them buying her engagement ring. Her head swam. She was grateful to Geoffrey for stepping in and insisting she leave the hospital. She was weaker than she had realised and if she didn't do something to build herself up again, she was in danger of falling ill. Staying in France was no longer an option for her.

# FORTY-THREE

## Celia

---

Celia's need to see her sister increased so much that she decided it was time she did something about it. But what? She wrote to Phoebe, asking if she had any plans to return to England and, if so, maybe they could meet up in London for a few days. She was delighted to receive a reply just a few days later.

*Dearest Celia,*

*As chance would have it, your letter reached me two days before I leave France for good. I've found things difficult since Archie was reported missing and although I still hold out hope of his return to me, I have struggled more with each passing month to keep my thoughts positive.*

*Geoffrey, Doctor Sutherland, is my friend here and is the brother of Jocasta Chambers who you might recall I went to spend time with in Cornwall in December of 1916. He spoke to me last week and told me of his concerns for me and insisted I allow him to make arrangements for me to leave the hospital and go to stay with his sister once again in Cornwall. I know you will be reading this and worrying but please don't fret. I have to admit to having lost weight, but I am healthy other than that.*

*I will write to Jocasta and ask if it wouldn't be too much of an imposition if you also come to stay for a short time. I'm sure she won't mind. Jocasta is a dear friend and I have often spoken to her about you, sharing anecdotes of our childhood with Charlie. I'm sure she will be delighted to finally meet you.*

*I shall write and let you know what she says as soon as I hear from her and we can then make further plans.*

*Until then, my love to you as ever,*

*Your sister,*

*Phoebe xx*

Celia clutched her sister's letter to her chest. The thought of spending time with Phoebe and finally meeting her friend Jocasta was exciting. More than anything, she wanted to confide in her sister about Otto, as she didn't dare risk writing down her thoughts and feelings for the man who she loved so much.

Both of them were separated from the men that they loved and both had spent their time working tirelessly looking after soldiers, witnessing things they couldn't have imagined four years earlier. Yes, a reunion was long overdue.

She wrote back to Phoebe immediately, telling her she would love nothing more than to meet Jocasta and be able to give Phoebe a hug and catch up with her about everything they had both been through since they had last met. Celia promised to request leave as soon as possible to come and visit her.

The letter sent, Celia made her way to Matron's office. She

hadn't had any time off in months, but then neither had the other nurses been given much time away from the hospital. Too many injured soldiers and full wards had kept all of them busy and she had been glad of it, until now. Now, she needed to see her sister and see for herself how Phoebe was coping.

## FORTY-FOUR

## Phoebe

EARLY SEPTEMBER 1918

### Cornwall

Phoebe stopped by the garden gate and breathed in the fresh spring air as she turned to take in the view. As it hit the back of her throat, she closed her eyes. It felt good to be back, despite the circumstances.

And she was going to see her sister again. Finally. It had been a long four years since Celia had left to work in Jersey, but Phoebe knew that they were as close now as they had always been. They were sisters.

'You're here!' Jocasta shouted from behind her, her voice taking Phoebe by surprise.

Phoebe turned to her friend and returned Jocasta's beaming smile. 'It's wonderful to be back in Pennwalloe.'

Jocasta opened the gate and waved for Phoebe to join her. Phoebe willingly stepped forward and into her friend's welcoming arms.

'I've missed you so much,' Jocasta soothed. 'I was excited to receive your letter and Geoffrey's arrived the following morning.' She frowned and, taking Phoebe by her upper arms, held her at arms' length and looked her up and down. 'The first thing we're going to do is help you get well again.'

'I am well.'

Jocasta gave her a sympathetic frown. 'I'm sure you are,' she said, taking Phoebe's valise in one hand before taking hold of her friend's hand with the other and leading her inside.

---

'It's a lot warmer this time around,' Phoebe said once they were sitting outside in the walled garden nursing cups of sweet tea. 'I didn't come out here then.' She looked around at the array of roses, lavender and fuchsias brightening up the well-kept borders. 'It's so pretty out here.'

'Thank you,' Jocasta said. 'When life seemed too difficult, sometimes I forced myself to come out here and deadhead the roses, hoe the flowerbeds, or plant seeds. I'm certain this little garden saved my life.' She stared into space and then gasped. 'Oh Phoebe, I shouldn't talk that way, not when you're going through so much.'

'Don't be silly. If you can't be open with me, then I've failed you as a friend.'

Jocasta reached across the small metal table and gave Phoebe's hand a light squeeze. 'Thank you. And I hope you feel as comfortable telling me whatever you wish.' She gave Phoebe a pointed stare. 'And I mean anything at all. Do you hear me?'

'Yes, of course,' Phoebe fibbed. After all, she had no qualms being open about Archie and her feelings for him, and how lost she felt without him. She watched Jocasta telling her more about the garden and wished she could share what happened with Louis and the real reason behind the depths of her torment. Phoebe sighed deeply.

Jocasta must have heard because she turned to face Phoebe, frowning. 'I'm sorry. Here I am, wittering on about my flowers, and you must be exhausted after travelling all the way here from France. I'm so selfish.'

Phoebe laughed. 'You're not at all, and don't let me ever hear you say otherwise. I am a little tired, but I'm more excited. I can't tell you how grateful I am to you for letting me come back and stay here with you and Bryony. And for generously letting me invite Celia to come here, too.'

Jocasta pulled a face. 'Nonsense. It's a joy having you here and I can't wait to meet your sister. We're going to have such fun together.' Bryony cried and Jocasta stood. 'I'll go and fetch the little one while you sit out here and drink your tea. I'll see you inside whenever you're ready.'

'Thank you.'

Phoebe watched her go, hearing Jocasta's gentle soothing coming from an upstairs window shortly afterwards.

She thought of Archie, and how strange it was that the last time she was here, he was too. Her heart ached for him. She longed to hold him in her arms and breathe in the scent of his skin. 'Oh, Archie, where are you?'

Phoebe thought she heard the doorbell ring as she took a sip of her tea, but it could have been at one of the houses either side of Jocasta's, so she sat back in her chair and watched a robin sitting on a branch of the heavily laden apple tree. *How wonderful must it be to be a bird,* she thought, longing for freedom from the ties that kept her in such a low mood. *To fly away the instant something frightened you.*

'Look who's here!' Jocasta joyfully called from behind Phoebe. She turned in her chair and saw shock register on

Celia's face for a split second before it vanished. Had she changed that much, Phoebe wondered. She supposed she must have done, to someone who hadn't seen her for so long.

Phoebe rose to her feet and, pushing any concerns away, smiled at Celia before they met in the middle of the lawn and hugged each other tightly.

'It's so good to see you again,' Phoebe said, resting her head on her sister's shoulder. 'I've missed you so much.'

'I feel like I'm in a dream,' Celia murmured. 'I can't believe I'm here with you.'

'I'm going to leave the two of you to talk,' Jocasta said, returning to the French doors. 'Bryony needs feeding and then I'll take her for a stroll. Take as long as you like and please help yourself to anything in the kitchen.'

Phoebe watched her go over Celia's shoulder and let her arms drop from around her sister. She took a step back to take a good look at her, as Celia did the same.

'You've lost too much weight,' Celia said in her usual matter-of-fact way. Her expression softened. 'Though I already sense that Jocasta will nurture you and make sure you're well looked after.'

Phoebe knew this was Celia's way of letting her know she liked Jocasta.

'Most definitely,' Phoebe said, indicating the table and chairs. 'Why don't you make yourself comfortable and I'll make us a fresh pot of tea. Then we can talk to our hearts' content.'

'I am a bit parched,' Celia said, her hand going to her throat. 'Thanks.'

Phoebe took a few minutes to gather herself while she made the tea and placed some of Jocasta's delicious shortbread biscuits on a plate. She had been expecting her sister to be shocked by her appearance, but she hadn't imagined that Celia would look as drawn and worn out as she did. Not wishing to waste time that could be spent with Celia, Phoebe carried the drinks and biscuits outside to the garden.

'Here we are,' she said, setting everything down onto the table. 'You have to try one of those,' she said, pushing the plate of biscuits towards her sister. 'Jocasta is the best baker in the world.'

Celia laughed and Phoebe was relieved to see something of the sister she recognised in her happy face. 'The best?'

'Tell me she isn't when you've tasted them. I bet you won't.'

Phoebe poured the tea and made small talk about the garden, both sisters sharing anecdotes about their journeys to Cornwall. Knowing they only had three days together, and some of that time would be spent with Jocasta, Phoebe decided to address the elephant in the room while it was just her and Celia. 'I know you were shocked to see me this way,' Phoebe said. 'But I hadn't expected you to look quite so … um…' She struggled to think how to put it politely.

'Dreadful?'

'No, I'm the one that looks that way,' she said, attempting a smile but failing. 'Troubled, maybe. It must be busy working at King's College.'

'It is rather hectic there at the moment, with all that's going on.' She took a bite of one of the biscuits and sighed after swallowing. 'It's not work though, Phoebe. Work is what has kept me going. Not having the time or energy to lie awake at night thinking has helped me get through a difficult two years.'

'I know. I'm sorry we haven't been able to meet up since the funeral.' She thought how much she had needed her sister then, but hadn't wanted to burden her with her own troubles, when surely Celia must have had enough of her own grief to struggle through.

Celia looked downwards. 'I'm so sorry I haven't been around.'

The last thing Phoebe wanted was for her sister to feel any guilt. 'It works both ways, Celia. Life hasn't been exactly normal for any of us over the past couple of years,' she said, determined to reassure her. 'Anyway, I've been busy working, as have you, and I don't know about you, but it helped me when I was at my lowest to have something to focus on other than myself.' She thought back to that mind-numbing time. 'I still sometimes think I've imagined losing all three of them,' she admitted. 'I think it was the shock of losing Mum, Dad and Charlie all at once.'

Celia took Phoebe's hands in hers and gave them a gentle squeeze. 'Nonetheless, we should have been together to help each other through our loss.'

Phoebe agreed. 'It couldn't be helped.' She smiled, wanting their reunion to be about happy things, not their shared heartache.

'That's not really what I meant.' Celia let go of her hands and withdrew them, staring at her in a strange way.

Concerned, Phoebe leaned forward slightly. 'What do you mean?' she asked, anxious to hear.

Celia took a moment, staring down at her hands before clasping them together. 'I've got something to tell you, but I'm not sure how you're going to react.'

'You're my sister and I love you,' Phoebe said, sure nothing could ever change that fact.

'Maybe you should listen to what I've got to tell you before saying anything further.' Celia took a deep breath and, staring at the apple tree, began to speak.

Phoebe listened in stunned silence as her sister told her about falling in love with a German soldier.

*A German soldier?*

'I don't understand,' Phoebe said, struggling to remind herself that this was her beloved sister, and how brave Celia was, sharing something this shocking.

'When he was sent to the camp in Surrey with the other inmates from the Jersey camp, I volunteered to transfer there as one of the nurses,' Celia said. 'They needed fewer of us in Jersey and more in Surrey, so it made perfect sense to my superiors.'

*And she could remain close to him,* Phoebe thought.

'But I don't understand how you could even be attracted to someone like that.'

Celia stared at her silently before shrugging one shoulder. 'If you had been the one sitting here now, saying the same thing to me, I would probably react the same way you have.' She took a deep breath. 'At first I was confused by my attraction to him. I couldn't understand how I could betray British soldiers like Charlie and his friends by falling for someone like Otto.'

'Otto?'

'Yes, that's his name.'

'But you seem to have come to terms with that now, if you're telling me you've fallen for him.' Phoebe winced at the sound of accusation in her voice and immediately felt guilty. Celia couldn't help who she fell for, any more than she could. 'Sorry, I didn't mean it to come out that way.'

Celia stared down at her cup. 'I know you're shocked and most likely disgusted with me, and I can understand why.' She looked Phoebe in the eye once more. 'But then I tell myself that if Otto and I had met and fallen in love at any other time in history, no one would care.' She clenched her fists together and raised them, closing her eyes tightly. 'Why did we have to meet now, during this blasted war?'

Phoebe could see how her sister had struggled and was still trying to cope. 'This war can't last forever, though, can it?' she reasoned, trying her best to reassure Celia. 'You need to press on until it's all over. I'm certain that if you've managed to do it for this long, then you can keep going for a bit longer.' It was what she constantly had to tell herself when missing Archie became too much.

'Thanks, Phoebe. I know I don't have any right to ask you to understand,' Celia said miserably. 'Not after I was cross with you when you told me that you were falling for a patient. At least he was British.'

'I was cross with you for a while,' Phoebe admitted. 'But with all that's happened, I believe we need to grab happiness when we can.' She rested a hand on Celia's and felt her sister's hand trembling under hers. 'We both know only too well how life can change in an instant, and we've learnt the hard way that life is too short. I'm not going to sit here and tell you what you should or shouldn't do where your love is concerned, Celia. You're all the family I have left, and I'd rather accept something I don't understand than lose you.'

'I'm so grateful to hear that,' Celia whispered. She looked past Phoebe towards the house, and Phoebe knew her sister was thinking of Jocasta and the loss of her husband. 'I'm not sure everyone could get past me loving an enemy soldier.'

Phoebe knew she was right.

Celia took a deep breath and pointed at the plate of biscuits. 'I think it's about time I tried one of these.' She took a bite. 'You were right about Jocasta's baking,' Celia said after finishing her biscuit. She rested her hands on her lap. 'Now, while we're bearing our souls to each other, I want you to tell me why you're so thin. And no excuses, because I will be able to tell if you're keeping something from me.'

Phoebe winced.

'We've been through so much together and I can't imagine there's anything you could do that would stop me loving you, Phoebe. Now, take a deep breath and tell me before Jocasta comes back to join us.'

'I don't know what to say,' Phoebe said later, having told her sister about losing Archie and then the embarrassing mix-up with Louis. 'So many people manage their grief better than me, and I feel weak, not being able to pull myself together.'

'But others haven't lost their parents and brother as well as the man they hoped to have a future with, have they?' When Phoebe didn't reply, Celia added, 'We, like millions of other people, have been through so much over the last four years. I think that if we can't be kind to ourselves, then there's something very wrong in this world.'

Phoebe knew her sister was right. 'Thanks, Celia.'

'Now, unless you have anything else you'd like to speak to me about…?' Celia narrowed her eyes and grinned. 'No? Good. Neither do I. Shall we focus on more cheerful things?'

Phoebe liked that idea. 'Like what?'

'When are you going to show me around this beautiful place? I'll be back in London in three days, and I need to make the most of this fresh sea air while I can.'

'Why don't we start right now?' Phoebe suggested. 'After I've washed these dishes and shown you to my room. We're sharing; I hope that's all right.'

'Perfect. We can talk for as long as we want without disturbing the rest of the household.'

Phoebe laughed. 'Just like when we were children and smuggled food into the bedroom to eat when everyone else was asleep.'

Celia shrieked with laughter. 'Only we had always eaten all the treats we had pinched from Mother's pantry by seven o'clock.'

'They were good times, weren't they?' Phoebe asked wistfully.

'The best.'

Phoebe looked into her sister's tired eyes. 'Maybe the best is yet to come for us,' she suggested, hoping she was right.

# FORTY-FIVE

## Celia

'I want you to think of this house as your home from home,' Jocasta said later as the three of them sat in the living room while the sun slowly set outside. 'And I know my brother Geoffrey would want the same thing.'

Celia thanked her. 'It's very kind of you both,' she said, taking in the pretty room. 'Is that your husband?' she asked, admiring the unusual painting of the smiling couple hanging above the unlit fire.

'Yes,' Jocasta said wistfully. 'Ronnie was a wonderful painter. There are others around the house too.' She smiled proudly. 'You might have noticed the one of me and the baby on your way up to your room?'

She had. 'I wondered if it had been done by the same artist.'

'My brother wasn't sure if I should have them hanging where I could see them all the time, but although it upsets me sometimes when I'm reminded of how much Ronnie is missing out on, they also bring me comfort.' She glanced in the direction of the window. 'He loved it here,' she said with a sigh.

'You live in a beautiful part of the country,' Celia said. 'Phoebe took me for a walk earlier.'

'Thank you. It's very different to London.' Jocasta smiled shyly. 'I don't know the last time I went there. It must have been when I was about fifteen and my parents took Geoffrey and me to visit friends. Gosh, that was so long ago now.'

Celia didn't know how old Jocasta was but surmised that she couldn't be more than twenty-five or twenty-six. Celia wondered if she seemed older because of all that she had suffered. 'I think that if I lived here I wouldn't be in a rush to go anywhere else either.'

She turned to Phoebe and noticed how relaxed her sister was in this house. It was a relief to know Phoebe had a home to go to and someone as kind as Jocasta to look after her. She sat and watched Jocasta and Phoebe chatting about the events of the months they hadn't seen each other, and how much Bryony had grown and all the things she had learnt to do or say. Phoebe appeared to be happy enough but Celia hadn't missed the haunted look in her sister's eyes. That business with Louis hadn't shocked her, but she knew how deeply her sister loved Archie and could tell the guilt was eating Phoebe up inside. Celia hoped she had said enough to reassure Phoebe that she had nothing to blame herself for, but doubted her words had made much of a difference.

If only Archie would return. Phoebe had always been a strong woman – both of them were, she mused – but there was something about her sister that now seemed broken inside, and it frightened her.

Celia wondered if she should try to take Jocasta to one side and share her concerns, but she knew that if Phoebe thought she had betrayed her, then she would never trust Celia with anything ever again, and she couldn't risk that happening.

She was going to have to trust that with Jocasta's friendship, her sister would have the strength to find her way back to full health.

———————

The following days and nights went by far too quickly and on their last morning, as she sat at the kitchen table with Phoebe, Jocasta and her adorable little girl who chatted away to them all constantly, Celia wished that she had asked for more time off work.

'There's your breakfast,' Jocasta said, putting down a plate with a scrambled egg on a toasted slice of her freshly baked bread. 'I wish I had more to give you, but I could only buy four eggs.'

'One each is fine,' Celia reassured her. 'Especially when it's cooked so perfectly.'

'That's very kind of you to say.' Jocasta gave Phoebe hers and then sat to eat her own. 'It's been wonderful getting to know you, Celia,' she said. 'I do hope you come here again before too long. I'd love you to see Cornwall in the different seasons, as it changes so much with each one.'

Celia loved the idea. 'Thank you, I'd love to come back.' She smiled at Bryony. 'It will be nice to see how much this little lady has learnt by then. She's so clever.'

'How she ever learns anything when she rarely stops talking, I don't know,' Jocasta laughed, ruffling Bryony's hair. 'Thank heavens she enjoys her food, it's the only time she's quiet.'

'I'll come with you to the station,' Phoebe said. 'I'm sure old Josh won't mind having me for company on the way back again.'

Celia was delighted. 'Thank you. I don't mind admitting, it's going to be hard saying goodbye to you again.'

She saw tears well in her sister's eyes. 'These few days have gone by in a blur,' Phoebe said, her voice strangled. 'I'm glad we've had a chance to talk properly.'

'So am I. And when I come back this way, or when you come to London, we can talk more.'

'I'd like that,' Phoebe said.

'You'd better get on,' Jocasta teased. 'Old Josh is going to be coming down the lane in ten minutes and won't think anything of not stopping if he doesn't see you ready and waiting for him.'

---

As Celia waved goodbye to her sister from the entrance to the train station, she couldn't shake the thought that she would have to make a plan to return as soon as she had the chance. However much Phoebe wanted her to believe she was fine, Celia knew that she was far more troubled than she was letting on.

## FORTY-SIX

## Phoebe

### NOVEMBER 1918

S eptember morphed into October and then November, and
the war finally came to an end.

She and Jocasta had celebrated the occasion by attending a
street party in the village and a special service in the local
church. It was wonderful to hear church bells ringing once
again and there was a palpable sense of relief that no more
young men would be killed.

Phoebe sat in her room on Armistice Day before Jocasta
woke and stared out of her window at the peaceful garden. She
knew she should be happy but she could only think of the
tombstone that Archie didn't have. She needed somewhere to
go and direct her grief – an engraved headstone, maybe, under
a shady oak tree where she could go to be alone with her
thoughts and perhaps tell him about her day and how she was
still missing him so desperately.

Today was filled with so much joy and intense relief but
also – for those, like her, who had lost family members or the
man they'd imagined building a life with – heartbreak and
deep, deep sorrow.

Was this why she felt more bereft than she had been for the past few months? Was it because she was losing her last vestiges of hope that Archie could still be alive? She sighed heavily and lay back against the wall, too exhausted in her misery to cry.

Phoebe heard the familiar sound of movement on the floorboards coming from Jocasta's room and knew that her friend was up. She forced a smile on her face and opened her bedroom door at the same time as Jocasta opened hers.

'Good morning,' Jocasta said, smiling. 'Did you manage to sleep at all last night?'

'Yes, thank you.' It wasn't true, but she couldn't bear to cause her friend any more worry that she already had. 'And how is this little one this morning?' She gave Bryony a genuine smile when the little girl wriggled in her mother's arms and held hers outstretched for Phoebe to hold up.

'Go on with Auntie Phoebe then,' Jocasta said, pretending to be put out as she handed the toddler to Phoebe.

Phoebe kissed the little girl's pudgy hand and, holding her tightly, followed Jocasta downstairs. When they reached the kitchen, Phoebe lifted Bryony into her wooden highchair and strapped her in. 'Shall I make the tea?'

'Yes, please,' Jocasta said. 'What would you like for breakfast this morning?'

Phoebe wanted to say 'Nothing' but knew that wasn't an option and would only put Jocasta's senses on high alert. 'I'm not sure. What are you thinking of having?'

They both knew that the only choice was porridge or an egg from one of the neighbour's chickens.

'I thought a fried egg on toast for me this morning,' Jocasta replied, lifting the frying pan down from its large hook over the range. 'How about you?'

'I'll have the same, thanks.'

'You're seeming brighter recently,' Jocasta said a few minutes later as she handed Phoebe her plate of food. 'I'm relieved.'

Phoebe pushed away the guilt that immediately rose within her. It was far easier to pretend to be happier so that Jocasta left her alone and didn't ask probing questions.

'Have you got anything planned for today?' Phoebe asked, before forcing herself to eat her last mouthful.

Jocasta wiped Bryony's mouth with a cloth and cut a piece of her toast as she gave the question some thought. 'I do have to go into the village for a few bits,' she said before frowning. 'Would you like to come with me?'

'Thank you, but not this morning. Another time, maybe.'

The mention of going at some other time seemed to please Jocasta. 'Then if you're happy to be left here on your own, I'll take Bryony to visit Mrs Lanyon in the toyshop. I thought I could buy her a little gift to celebrate our freedom. Then I'll do some food shopping. Is there anything you'd like me to pick up for you?'

Phoebe shook her head. 'No thank you. I can't think of anything I need.'

---

Phoebe waved to Jocasta as she pushed Bryony in her pram down the garden path. Finally she was alone. She closed the door and leaned against it for a few seconds. Then, compelled to go for a walk, she put on her coat, not bothering with her hat or handbag. She only wanted to walk up to the headland and doubted she would see anyone else there at this time of day.

She stepped outside and took in a deep breath of the fresh sea air before leaving the garden and crossing the road. Thoughts of walking hand in hand with Archie along the same route made her sad. She missed him terribly. His arms around her, his perfect smile and the way he kissed her.

Phoebe stared out across the sea. It looked so tempting. All it would take was one step over the edge and she wouldn't be tormented any longer, wouldn't need to force herself to smile, when all she wanted to do was curl up in a ball on her bed and sob. No more worrying about upsetting others by being honest about her true feelings.

Unable to cope with her guilt, she began walking forward, a stronger sense that she was doing the right thing with each step. She had nothing to live for, not really. She knew in her heart that Archie was dead. They all did. It was simply that no one wanted to admit it, least of all her.

'Phoebe! Phoebe, stop!'

She realised Jocasta was calling her. Phoebe didn't turn. She hated to hurt her friend in this way, but at least Jocasta still had Bryony to love and care for. What did she have apart from regret and guilt?

'Phoebe!' Jocasta's scream shocked her with its primal tone. Phoebe turned to see her friend running towards her, Bryony in her arms. 'Phoebe, stop. Please.'

Phoebe stilled.

'I only met Archie that one time he came to stay in the village, but I do know that he would never wish for you to throw away your life over his loss.' She stood well back from the edge of the cliff and reached out her hand for Phoebe to take. 'Please, take my hand. You're standing too close to the edge and we've had landslides here recently. I'd hate for you to fall.'

Phoebe hesitated. Was Jocasta right? Would Archie be angry with her for jumping? She pictured his handsome face, almost black hair and kind eyes, and knew her friend was right. Phoebe turned and went to reach out to Jocasta. As their fingers touched, the ground beneath her feet slid downwards.

Jocasta screamed and stepped forward, holding Phoebe's fingers with the tips of her own. Phoebe knew instantly that she didn't want to die and she needed to move if she was to have any chance of not falling. She grabbed Jocasta's wrist with her other hand and fell forward, her chest and shoulders on the grassy verge that still remained stable.

Jocasta cried out and fell backwards, digging her heels into the earth, one hand still wrapped tightly around Bryony's body. The little girl was howling in fear. Horrified to think she had caused her friend and her daughter such stress, Phoebe concentrated on clawing her way forward, Jocasta clinging onto her.

For what seemed like hours but was probably merely seconds, Phoebe crawled forward enough for her toes to connect with the grassy soil. The women knelt and then scrambled to their feet, hurrying away from the cliff edge.

'You silly, stupid girl,' Jocasta snapped. 'If I hadn't come when I did, you would have been killed.'

Phoebe couldn't speak. Jocasta was right. She had been seconds away from perishing and almost put her best friend and her darling baby in danger of following her. She burst into tears and slumped on the grass as her legs gave way. 'I'm so, so sorry, Jocasta,' she sobbed, beginning to tremble and then shake violently.

Phoebe was vaguely aware of Jocasta sitting next to her, trying to comfort the toddler while allowing Phoebe to sob out her grief. Her guilt at putting her friend in such danger terrified her. 'I … I'm so sorry,' she said again through gulping sobs. 'I can't believe I was so selfish. I could have killed you,' she said as her crying increased once again. 'Both of you.'

Jocasta rested a hand on Phoebe's back and stroked her gently. 'Hush now. I followed you up here, remember?'

'How did you know where I'd be?' She blew her nose and wiped her damp eyes with the backs of her fingers.

Jocasta pressed her lips together and then shrugged. 'Because I came here not long after Ronnie was killed, with every intention of doing exactly what you came here to do.'

Phoebe gasped. 'You did?' Without thinking, she immediately glanced at Bryony.

'Yes.'

'What stopped you?'

'Leo Illey. He was out walking. I hadn't realised. I thought he was still in bed asleep, but luckily for me, he saw me from a distance and ran up to me, grabbing me around the waist and pulling me away from the edge. He was furious with me,' she said, staring out across the sea, clearly remembering the scene well. 'He took me home, like I'm going to do with you now, poured me a cup of tea and gave me a telling-off that I'll never forget.'

Phoebe didn't want to be lectured.

'Don't worry, I have no intention of doing the same with you,' Jocasta said. 'You had changed your mind when you turned to come away from the edge. I hadn't got that far yet; I was still determined to end my life.'

Phoebe stared at her friend, a hundred thoughts whirring around her mind. 'Do you regret what you did?'

Jocasta nodded. 'Very much so. It was selfish and cowardly of me.' She tilted her head to the side. 'You'll find happiness again, Phoebe, I promise you. Your life will be different to the one you had imagined, but no less worthwhile.'

'Do you really believe that?' Phoebe asked, desperate for her friend to say that she did. She couldn't bear having to carry the weight of Archie's loss forever.

'I truly do.' Jocasta sighed. 'I'm talking from experience. I've not met another man to measure up to my Ronnie, but then I've not been looking and I do have my beautiful Bryony. Right now, she is all I need.'

Phoebe reached out and ran her hand lightly over the toddler's soft curls. 'I wish I had Archie's baby.'

'I know,' Jocasta said quietly.

Phoebe blew her nose again, determined to try and overcome her emotions, at least for a short while. 'Shall we go back to the house now and make that tea?' What other choice was there, Phoebe mused, shaken by what had happened.

'Good idea,' said Jocasta.

# FORTY-SEVEN

## Celia

### EARLY DECEMBER 1918

### King's College Hospital, London

Celia waited for Sister to finish giving her orders for the day and thought that it was times like these that made her consider giving up nursing. She was tired of waiting to be told what to do, then spending the rest of the day never seeming to catch up on all her duties. The emotional strain of dealing with other people's pain and heartache after four years of war had drained her.

She wished she could leave now, but even if she hadn't promised Otto that she would be at King's College until he found her, she knew her conscience wouldn't allow her to walk away when the hospital needed all the nurses they had, now that this terrible flu was running rampant through more of the country.

Hadn't everyone suffered enough? Wasn't it bad enough that 'the war to end all wars' had killed millions? She groaned internally, unsure if she had the capacity to keep going for much longer.

Sister's talk over, Celia got on with her work and soon it was lunchtime, when she did the same thing as always – checked if Phoebe or Otto had written to her. She knew she was expecting too much to hope that Otto might have been able to write to her, but Phoebe owed her a letter and Celia was becoming impatient to hear her sister's news. It was unlike Phoebe not to write each week and she was becoming a little concerned that something might be wrong.

*Stop being paranoid,* she told herself. Celia supposed she was bound to be a bit anxious. She tended to be that way when she was overtired, and having spent most of her waking hours the past few weeks coping with more and more patients struggling to breathe and with many of them succumbing to the flu virus, she wasn't surprised that her nerves were on edge.

She asked Charlie, who looked after the nursing staff's post, whether she had received anything today, expecting him to say that she hadn't.

'Yeah, just the one,' he said, holding out a small brown envelope to her.

She stared at it without taking the envelope from his hand.

'Look love, are you takin' it or shall I put it back in with the others?'

'No, I want it,' she said, snatching it from his fingers. 'Thanks, Charlie.'

She hurried to the staff room to read it, unable to recognise the unusual writing. Who on earth could it be from?

As soon as she was in the staff room Celia sat on the nearest chair and ripped open the envelope. Scanning to the bottom of the page, she saw who it was from and gasped. Then, starting from the beginning, her heart pounding with shock and delight, she began to read.

Celia,

A friend offered to affix a stamp and post this letter for me and I hope it reaches you. Where to begin? I am still in the camp in Surrey and until recently have been working at the farm. Since the outbreak of this terrible virus I have been allowed to use my professional knowledge to help care for some of the other prisoners. Sister Baker is happy with my work and I am grateful to have been allowed to do what I know best and be of help to those in need.

I am hoping you are still in London nursing and that you are safe. Please know that I am healthy and strong.

There is talk of plans to repatriate us to Germany and from there I will return to my family home where I hope to set up a medical practice once more. I had hoped to visit you to thank you for all that you did for me at the camp in Jersey and here in Surrey but, unfortunately, I am told that I will not be given permission to visit acquaintances in England before we are sent away. I have to hope that once a little time has passed we will be able to correspond and maybe meet.

I will keep this letter brief as I have no certainty that it will reach you. Mostly I wanted to contact you to find out how you are and to let you know that I haven't forgotten you, Nurse Robertson.

Until we meet again,

Your friend,

Otto

Disappointment washed through Celia at Otto's loveless words. Did he no longer feel anything for her? Was she the only one missing him so terribly? She wished Phoebe was nearby so she could ask her for her thoughts. She stared out of the window for a few seconds and then read the letter once more.

Silly goose! Of course Otto still loved her. He was simply

being careful with his words. At least he had managed to let her know he was well and tell her what he was doing, and that he would be sent away at some point. That was a lot of information. As she re-read the words she realised his love for her shone through with his actions in writing to her at all. Even if he was unable to tell her he loved her or display his fondness for her.

'Thank you, my darling,' she whispered, lifting the letter and kissing his signature before folding it carefully and re-inserting it into the envelope. Darling Otto had been thinking of her all this time and he did want them to be together again as soon as they could.

---

After a quick bite to eat, Celia returned to the ward where a fresh intake of patients had been admitted. One was clearly an ex-soldier, as she recognised the injuries to his face and his heavily bandaged hand as being typical of war wounds. Although they had many patients still receiving ongoing treatment, it was unusual for a soldier to be admitted. He seemed a little out of place in the hospital now.

He was asleep, so she picked up the clipboard at the end of his bed to read his notes, almost dropping the board when she read the name.

*Captain Archie Bailey.* She stared at the name, then looked up at his face. He was badly bruised. Why she was looking at his face, she had no idea. It wasn't as if she had ever met Phoebe's Archie. Could this be him? She re-read the name to double-check that she hadn't made a mistake.

Hanging the clipboard back on the end of the bed, she walked up to stand by his upper body. He stirred. She needed to ask, make sure she hadn't been mistaken. The last thing she wanted to do was give her sister false hope.

Celia waited for him to open his eyes. He looked up at her and a range of emotions crossed his face, from astonishment, to delight, to disappointment.

'You're not Phoebe. Are you?'

That was all she needed to know. Almost overwhelmed with delight, Celia smiled at him. 'I'm her sister, Celia,' she said, more calmly than she felt. 'And you must be Archie.'

His eyebrows rose. 'How did you guess?'

'Nothing too clever, I read your name from your notes.' She pointed to the end of the bed.

'Ahh.'

'Phoebe is going to be the happiest woman on earth when she discovers you're alive and here.'

'You'll tell her for me?'

'I'll send her a telegram immediately,' she confirmed, thrilled to be able to do something so monumental for her sister. 'Is there anyone else you'd like me to contact for you?'

He thought for a moment and as she looked at his handsome face with dark-brown eyes and almost black hair, she couldn't help thinking how she and her sister had fallen for men who looked so completely different to each other.

'I think the War Office will send a telegram to my brother, Louis. They have my home address for him and Mrs Dunwoody, my housekeeper, will let Louis know. He'll tell my sister. We don't have anyone else.' He smiled again. 'Apart from Phoebe.'

'I'll go and sort out that telegram to her now,' she said, impatient to get going. 'You rest and I'll come back and check on you a little later.'

'Nurse?'

'Yes?'

'Please tell her I'm here but that she's not to come.'

Celia frowned, confused. 'But she'll want to be here.'

He shook his head miserably. 'No. I don't want her to see me like this.'

She looked at his damaged face and heavily bandaged hand. 'She won't be shocked in any way,' Celia said, certain her sister had dealt with far more terrible injuries during her years working as a VAD.

'It's not that,' he said, looking down at his right hand. 'This thing is badly damaged. I'm an architect and can't see how I can continue working without being able to use this.' His eyes met hers again and Celia saw the torment in them. 'I've no idea how I'll provide for her. How can I marry Phoebe if I can't look after her in the manner she deserves?'

Celia had heard this argument from many men over the years and although some of them had unfortunately been right to think that way, most loved ones didn't care and were only too relieved to be reunited with them again. 'My sister will love you, no matter what,' she insisted. 'I know that as clearly as I'm standing here.'

'No. I can't be with someone because they feel sorry for me.'

Celia could see he was adamant. 'Fine,' she said, having no intention of carrying out his instructions. She was going to let her sister have the opportunity of deciding her future for herself. 'I'll check up on you later,' she repeated before leaving the ward.

## FORTY-EIGHT

# Phoebe

P hoebe needed to promise Jocasta a handful of times that she would not harm herself before her silently believed that she could be trusted to be left alone.

It sounds odd but after the excitement and celebrations of Armistice Day, I think it dawned on me that Archie really would not be coming home,' Phoebe said apologetically.

'But he still might.'

Phoebe heard the doubt in her friend's voice. 'It's kind of you to say so, but I think we both know that the chances of that happening now are low.' She wanted to change the subject. She was fed up with focusing on herself and her stupidity that nearly cost her friend's life. 'I can't believe I've been here almost a year now and that it will soon be Christmas, can you?'

Jocasta shook her head. 'No. Another Christmas, but this time the country is at peace. With all that's happened, we still have a lot to be thankful for, don't you think?'

Phoebe did. 'I'm so ashamed about what I did, Jocasta. Truly.'

Jocasta took Phoebe's hand in hers. 'Don't be. I've been

where you were then, and it's a dark place. I'm just relieved I found you in time to stop you. Let's forget about it now and concentrate on our futures, shall we?'

Phoebe wasn't sure she wanted to think about her future just yet, but nodded. If Jocasta could keep going, then the very least she could do was to try to do the same.

'I thought I'd take a walk into the village,' Phoebe said, needing to get out of the house and take some exercise. 'May I fetch anything for you while I'm out?'

'Would you like me to come with you?'

Phoebe saw the uncertainty in her friend's face. 'No. You stay here with Bryony where it's warm. I promise you I'll be fine. I have no intention of repeating my silliness, so there's no need to worry about me. I really do wish to take a walk into the village.'

'Then I'll give you a small list of items that I need to restock the cupboard. If you don't mind watching Bryony for a moment, I'll go and fetch it.'

Bryony gave a frustrated yell.

Phoebe looked to see the cause and saw that one of the building blocks she was playing with was out of her reach. 'You fetch your list,' she told Jocasta. 'I'll help this little one.'

Phoebe bent down to retrieve a green building block from under the coffee table that they had pushed to the side so that Bryony could play. She placed it in Bryony's outstretched hands and ruffled her wavy hair. 'There you go.' She watched the little girl play and wondered what she might be when she grew up. 'You could build houses, with all the practice you've had stacking those,' she smiled. 'Or maybe even...' The thought stuck in her head. She had been going to suggest that maybe Bryony could design houses. Be an architect. She swallowed the lump at the back of her throat. Dear Archie. She hated to think of all the things he would now never do, like getting married and having a family. It was all too cruel.

'Right, then,' Jocasta said, entering the room and interrupting her thoughts. She handed Phoebe the basket and a list. 'You'll find my ration book and my purse in there as well.'

Phoebe lifted the purse from the basket and handed it to Jocasta. 'I'll pay for this.' She raised her hand to stop Jocasta arguing. 'I need a few things for myself, and I'm sure it's my turn to pay for the food.'

'No, it isn't.' Jocasta scowled at her.

'It is. I have my wages from when I was working, and as you and Geoffrey won't allow me to give you anything for my keep, the very least I can do is help with the food I'm eating and a few other small bits and pieces.' She frowned. 'I'm not buying those things if you don't let me pay for them,' she said, waving the list in her hand.

'Fine. If you insist.'

Phoebe stood. 'I'll see you both later, then.'

She left the room and moments later was walking down the lane towards the village. There was a fresh breeze and she heard someone cough behind her. Recalling stories about the feared three-day fever that many of the soldiers seemed to have brought back with them from France, Phoebe hurried on a little, wanting to distance herself from the person behind her in case they had it. She had read news reports that some people who had seemed perfectly healthy at breakfast time were dead before supper. The thought frightened her.

How odd to be scared of an illness so soon after attempting to take her own life. Her actions didn't make much sense, but then nothing seemed to anymore. She thought back to Celia's last letter, telling her that her work at King's College Hospital was keeping her busy and for Phoebe not to consider travelling to London, or anywhere else on crowded transport, if she could possibly help it.

Phoebe felt the familiar clenching of her heart and pushed herself to walk a little faster.

---

Returning from the shop, she breathed in the salty air and attempted to focus on a robin that she spotted perched on a camellia bush growing next to the front wall of a cottage she was nearing.

She reached the end of the lane and turned left to walk the final hundred or so yards, seeing a man stopping with his hand on the garden gate at Jocasta's. He was wearing a hat and when he removed it and raked his fingers through his hair, she thought it was Archie. Stunned, she stared at him. Was her tormented mind playing tricks on her again?

'Archie?' she whispered, unable to give volume to her voice. She began to run towards the house, desperate to reach him. He knocked on the front door as she pulled back the low metal gate, just as Jocasta opened the front door and cried out.

'Archie?' Jocasta's face drained of colour and Phoebe saw her clutch at the doorframe.

Phoebe's heart plummeted as she saw him up close. She knew this wasn't the man she loved. 'Louis,' she said quietly as she walked up the pathway to join them.

He turned to her. 'Hello, Phoebe.'

She looked into his sad eyes and felt guilty. 'Louis.'

Jocasta looked as if she was about to pass out.

'It's not Archie, Jocasta,' Phoebe whispered, putting her arm around her friend's shoulders.

'I'm Louis,' he said gently. 'Archie's twin brother.'

'Let's go inside,' Phoebe said, leading her friend into the house without waiting for her to answer.

'Why are you here? Has something happened?' Phoebe noticed how pale and exhausted he looked.

'Phoebe?' Jocasta said, holding something out towards her. 'This telegram came for you a little earlier. Maybe it has something to do with your visit?' she said, glancing at Louis before ushering him into the living room.

'Aren't you going to open it?' Jocasta whispered, waving for Phoebe to follow her to the kitchen.

'Do you mind if I leave you to make the tea alone?' Phoebe said, wanting to know why Louis had rushed to see her.

'Of course not.'

She left her friend busying herself with the kettle and hurried to join Louis, ripping open the telegram as she entered the room.

'It's from Celia,' she said, one hand resting on her chest as she read her sister's words. Phoebe could hardly believe her eyes:

*Phoebe Stop Come immediately Stop Archie alive at King's College Hosp Stop Very sick but alive Stop Love Celia*

'Oh my God, Louis!'

'That's what I came here to tell you! I received notice from the War Office.'

Phoebe nodded and let out a sob before going to Louis and taking him in her arms, both crying on each other's shoulders.

'What's happened?' Jocasta asked.

'Phoebe has had an enormous shock.'

'A good one,' Phoebe said to Jocasta when her friend misunderstood and covered her mouth with her hand. 'Archie's alive, Jocasta. That telegram was from my sister and Louis came to tell me he'd received word as well.'

'I'm so happy for you both,' Jocasta said, bursting into tears. 'I'm sorry, I don't know why I'm crying.'

'Because you're happy!' Phoebe said, still unable to completely take in the news she had just heard.

Louis swallowed and then, clearing his throat, wiped one eye with his fingers. 'I can't believe how lucky we are to have him back, Phoebe.'

'Neither can I,' she whispered. Phoebe cried out and jumped to her feet. 'We must go to him immediately.' Before either of them argued, Phoebe ran out of the room and up the stairs.

She needed to think. If Archie was in London then she needed to pack spare clothes to wear. She would stay with him for as long as it took for him to recover, as she had no intention of returning to Cornwall without him. Or leaving him ever again.

She grabbed her valise, and after hurriedly packing a spare skirt, top, underclothes and stockings, Phoebe took her wash bag and rammed it in on top. She was about to close the bag when she realised she had forgotten Archie's notebook. She had no idea if he still had the one he carried back to France with him and didn't want him to be without one. Relieved she hadn't forgotten it, Phoebe quickly opened her bedside drawer and took it out, pushing it down one side of her valise before running back downstairs to join the others.

'Come along, Louis we must go.'

'I know for a fact that you have at least an hour before the next train going in that direction leaves the station,' Jocasta said calmly. 'So there's no need to race out of here. Drink your tea, you'll be glad of it in a few hours' time.' She looked at Louis. 'I hope you don't mind me saying so, but you look exhausted. Would you eat a sandwich if I made one for you?'

He thought for a moment and then nodded. 'I would. Thank you.' He caught Phoebe's eye. 'Mrs Chambers is right,' he said. 'We may as well wait here instead of out in the cold on a station platform.'

'I suppose that does make sense,' Phoebe said, wishing the train was due to leave earlier. The journey was going to be long and arduous, she knew that much already, having travelled on that journey with Archie once before.

'I'll make it now.' Jocasta stroked Phoebe's shoulder, staring at her thoughtfully.

'What's wrong?' Phoebe saw her friend battling with herself, trying to make up her mind about something. 'Tell me.'

Jocasta looked away and groaned before looking Phoebe in the eye once more. 'I know you're desperate to see Archie. Of course you are. But I'm concerned about you going into a hospital in London.'

Phoebe frowned. 'It's where he is, Jocasta.' She began to suspect why her friend was concerned. 'You're worried about this flu virus, aren't you?'

Jocasta nodded. 'I am, and I know that if it was my darling Ronnie in that hospital bed I'd also be rushing to him, but I'm frightened you'll be exposing yourself to this dreadful sickness.'

Phoebe rested a hand on her friend's shoulder. 'I understand your fears and would probably be warning you off if you were the one about to go to London, but I'd rather take the risk of being infected and at least seeing Archie again, than ...' she hesitated, unable for a moment to put her fears into words, 'than risk the chance of him succumbing to an infection or something else. We don't know what his injuries are, but I've worked with enough patients to know that it's sometimes the ones you don't expect to die who do.'

Jocasta gave her a sad smile. 'I understand, but I had to say something.'

'I know you did, and I appreciate you caring about me. Truly, I do.'

Jocasta sniffed. 'Right then, I'd better make those sandwiches.'

Phoebe watched her friend leave the room and wished she wasn't leaving Jocasta so unexpectedly. Hearing about Archie must have shaken Jocasta and probably made her think of Ronnie, and the knowledge that this could never happen to her.

'I can't believe he's alive,' she said, shaking her head. 'My darling Archie is alive and I'm going to see him.'

'We both are,' Louis said.

She needed to know more about Archie's situation. 'Do we know how badly injured he is?'

'He's in a bad way, I believe, but that's all I know.'

'You'll need to wrap up warm,' Jocasta shouted from the kitchen.

'We are,' Phoebe replied, desperate to get going.

Jocasta returned and handed Louis the sandwiches, tied in greaseproof paper held together with string. 'Promise you'll send me a telegram as soon as you've seen him,' she said, taking hold of Phoebe's shoulders.

'I will.'

'And remember you can both come back here any time and for as long as you wish.'

'I know. Thank you,' Phoebe said, unable to help the tears she felt running down her cheeks.

Jocasta wiped them away with her thumbs, then kissed Phoebe's cheek and pulled her tight. 'I'm going to miss you so much. But my tears are happy tears. I'm so happy one of us is getting our happy ending.'

Phoebe hoped Jocasta was right. Surely fate wouldn't be so cruel as to bring him back to her, only to snatch him away again?

'Come along,' Louis said, catching Phoebe's eye. 'We'd better get going, otherwise the pair of you will upset each other.'

As they walked to the station, Phoebe replayed Jocasta's words over in her head. She had got her Archie back, and whatever state he was in, she would love him just as much as she did before he was injured. What she was frightened about was how *he* would react to whatever injuries he had sustained.

'He'll be fine,' Louis said, sensing her thoughts. 'Whatever's happened to my brother, you and I love him more than enough to ensure that he can cope with it.'

Phoebe only hoped Louis was right.

## FORTY-NINE

## Celia
---

Celia rubbed her eyes and leaned against the worktop on which the new medical equipment was stacked. She had thought working at the camps in Jersey and Surrey was exhausting, but nothing was as bad as working through this flu epidemic.

Maybe some of her weariness was due to sadness that after all the death and horror of the war, peace had finally come, and along with it came this cruel virus. She didn't think she would ever not be haunted by the rasping sounds of victims fighting to breathe.

At least she had finally heard from Otto. It comforted her to know he was still in England. For now. She needed to find a way to get to him before he was repatriated.

She placed her hands on her lower back, arching it, trying to ease some of the ache that she seemed to feel all the time now.

Celia thought of her telegram to Phoebe and conflicting emotions battled in her heart. On the one hand, it was a joy to be able to share with her sister that Phoebe's beloved Archie was alive and right here in her hospital. On the other, she knew she was opening her sister up to the threat of catching the flu virus and had also gone against Archie's wishes by not telling Phoebe to stay away. But Celia knew that if things were the other way round, she would want her sister to do exactly as she had done.

*Phoebe's trained,* she reminded herself. *She understands the need for intense hygiene and knows better than most how to protect herself from catching anything.* 'As much as any of us can,' she murmured.

'Talking to yourself, Nurse?' a cheeky young trainee asked.

'Did you want me for something?' Celia asked, embarrassed to have been caught acting oddly.

'You have a visitor,' the pretty young girl said. 'She said she's your sister. She's with a man who says he's the brother of one of our patients, an Archie Bailey? I've put them in the waiting room down the corridor from his ward.'

Celia's heart leapt. Phoebe was here. She wasn't surprised her sister hadn't wasted any time coming all the way from Cornwall.

'Thank you for telling me. I'll go to them now.'

Celia had to force herself not to run. Her mind raced as she hurried along the corridors, stopping at the door to take a breath before going in to face her sister.

She opened the door and Phoebe looked up. Celia opened her mouth to speak then saw the man's face. No wonder her sister had mistaken him for Archie. 'You must be Captain Bailey's brother,' she said, pulling herself together.

'This is Louis,' Phoebe said. 'He came to Cornwall to let me know Archie was here and was with me when your telegram arrived.'

Celia looked from Phoebe to Louis. 'It's good to meet you,

Louis,' Celia said. 'Come with me,' she said after hugging Phoebe. 'I'll take you straight to him.'

She caught Louis's eye. 'Thank you,' he said, giving her an appreciative smile.

'I'm happy to help,' she said, hoping that Phoebe could persuade Archie that all was not lost and that he did in fact have a future.

# FIFTY

## Phoebe

'I've dreamt of this moment for so long and now I feel like I'm not really here,' Phoebe said, aware she probably sounded a little mad.

Celia rubbed her back lightly as she led the way to the ward. 'It's probably the shock of everything,' she said. 'He's this way.'

'How is he?'

Celia reached the ward door and stopped. 'He's recovering,' she said quietly. Phoebe felt her sister's hand rest on hers. 'He's struggling to come to terms with his injuries, though. He did tell me to insist that you don't come here.'

'Why would he do that?' Phoebe asked, stung to think that Archie wouldn't want her with him.

'He's still in shock, I think. I'm relying on you to help him through the next few days. I know you will.' Celia looked past Phoebe's right shoulder and addressed Louis. 'Between the two of you, I'm sure you'll be just the tonic he needs.'

What did her sister mean, Archie was struggling? Phoebe thought of patients she had helped nurse in France and how some of them wanted to end it all when they discovered their injuries were life-changing. Her stomach churned. Just what had happened to Archie?

'Where is he?' she demanded, not caring that her voice was slightly raised.

Celia shot her a worried look. 'We're nearly there now.'

Phoebe followed her sister into the ward and to a corner bed, unable to make out Archie's face for a moment. Once she was standing next to him she stared at his sleeping form, her heart aching as she fought not to take him tightly in her arms. She still didn't know where he had been all this time, but wanted to let him tell her when he was ready. Right now she needed him to know that she loved him and still wanted to marry him more than anything.

Celia pulled over two chairs and set them down by Archie's bedside. 'He's still slightly sedated so he's sleeping a lot. He should wake soon.' She gave Phoebe a sympathetic smile. 'He's very weak and still in shock, so don't press him on anything he doesn't wish to discuss.' Celia gave Phoebe's right shoulder a gentle squeeze. 'I'll leave you both to it but I'll only be over there, so let me know if you need me for anything.'

'Thanks, Celia,' Louis said.

Phoebe glanced at him and saw he was waiting for her to sit before taking the seat next to her. She pulled her chair closer to Archie's bed and gently stroked his right cheek before taking his hand in hers and sitting down.

Phoebe couldn't believe their skin was touching once again. The thought made her throat constrict with tears. 'I never imagined I'd be lucky enough to be holding his hand again, Louis,' she whispered.

'I know.' Louis's eyes widened. 'Look, I think he's about to come round.'

Phoebe reached out and rested her right hand lightly against Archie's cheek. She could feel his cheekbone through his thin skin and noticed for the first time how hollow his eyes had become. Wherever he had been, they hadn't fed him well. Poor Archie.

She held her breath as his eyelids twitched and then slowly opened. Archie looked from her to Louis, blinking several times as if he couldn't believe what he was seeing.

'We're here, my darling,' Phoebe whispered. 'Phoebe and your brother Louis. We've come to take you home, when you're well enough.'

He stared at her silently, and Phoebe wasn't sure whether he was trying to think what to say, and if maybe she should speak, but then she felt the dampness of a tear against her hand.

'Oh, my precious love,' she whispered, leaning forward and moving her hand so that she could kiss away his tears. She rested her cheek against his and whispered in his ear: 'I love you so much. I'm so happy you've come back to me. To us.'

'Phoebe.' His voice quaked and lacked strength, but hearing him saying her name was more than she had ever dared imagine happening.

Phoebe sat back. 'Is there anything I can fetch you?'

He shook his head slowly. 'No. Just sit here with me. Let me look at you. I need to know I'm not imagining this is happening.'

'You're not, Archie,' Louis said. 'We're here, and I can't tell you how good it is to see you again.'

Phoebe ached when Archie's gaze moved from her face. It was selfish, she knew, but she couldn't help herself. She wiped away another stray tear from Archie's cheek with her thumb.

'Louis, you're safe,' Archie said. 'I hoped you were.'

'Yes, only minor scratches for me, thankfully,' Louis said. 'And you? I see you have a bandaged right hand.'

Phoebe felt Archie's left hand tense in hers and she knew instinctively that something had happened that had devastated him. 'What is it, Archie?'

'Oh, Archie,' Louis groaned.

Archie gave a shuddering sigh and gave Louis a nod before his eyes moved in Phoebe's direction. 'My brother has guessed, I can tell.'

'What?' she asked, not wishing to know anything that might be too difficult for Archie to cope with.

He raised his heavily bandaged hand slightly. 'Sniper caught me. Shot my thumb clean off and damaged the nerves in my hand. No more designing houses for me, thanks to him.'

*His beloved job*, Phoebe thought, her heart aching for him. 'Is there anything the doctors can do?'

He sighed heavily. 'I gather not. One suggested I practise drawing with my left hand, and of course I will try to do that, but I don't see how I'll ever manage to work my left hand well enough.'

'I'm so sorry Archie,' she said, aware how much being an architect meant to him. Phoebe couldn't miss his sadness and knew better than to try and persuade him that it was early days yet, and that together they would search for some way to help him. Archie needed to be left to come to terms with this change in his life. He was strong and she trusted that he would overcome his loss eventually.

'We're here for you,' Louis said. 'Whatever you need. I'd give you my right hand if I thought it possible, you do know that, don't you?'

Archie gave Louis and then Phoebe a searching look and she

had to concentrate on remaining calm. She had no intention of ever letting the man she loved know of her indiscretion. It was a pointless and potentially harmful thing to share, and she was certain that Louis wanted to forget it as much as she did. Phoebe raised Archie's good hand and kissed the back of it, hoping to distract him from any hint of guilt that might show on her face.

Archie nodded. 'I do.' He smiled at his brother and then at Phoebe. 'I don't believe I thought to mention that my twin brother was identical, did I?'

'You didn't,' she said in mock annoyance.

'It must have been a shock to see him, then?'

'Hmm, you could say that,' Louis joked. 'She wasn't impressed that I wasn't you. I don't think she's forgiven me yet.'

'There's nothing to forgive,' she said, wanting to put an end to any speculation Louis might harbour that she was still upset about mistaking him for Archie. 'Archie's here and he's safe, and that's all I care about.'

Louis gave her a nod. 'Me, too.'

Archie smiled, unshed tears in his eyes. 'He looks a darn sight better than I do right now.'

Phoebe shrugged. 'We'll soon have you back to your old self again, Archie,' she promised. 'As soon as you're allowed to go home we'll go back. And if Mrs Dunwoody allows me to cook, I'll help her feed you up again.'

'But if I can't work again, how will I support us?' Archie asked, his eyes downcast. 'I can't expect you to marry me now, my darling.'

She put her fingers under his chin and forced him to look at her. 'Now you listen to me, Archie Bailey. You asked me to marry you and I accepted. I have no intention of marrying anyone else, so unless you want the guilt of a spinster on your conscience, you will marry me like you promised to do.'

Louis laughed. 'That's telling you, Archie. I like this fiancée of yours.'

'But how will I support us?' Archie repeated, becoming distraught.

'You can stop talking like that, for a start.' Phoebe scowled at him. 'I love you and you love me and that is all that matters.'

He didn't look convinced.

Louis stood. 'Maybe we should discuss this another day when both of you aren't quite so tired.'

'I think that's probably a good idea.'

Archie didn't speak but stared glumly at his bandaged hand.

'We should think about finding somewhere to stay,' Phoebe suggested as the thought occurred to her.

'Can't you stay with Cora?' Archie asked. He smiled at Phoebe. 'She's our sister.'

'She would have been the first person I asked,' Louis answered, 'but I thought it unwise when we've spent so much time in the hospital. I'd hate for us to inadvertently take influenza into her home.'

Phoebe recalled that their sister had three small children. 'That does make sense. Maybe Celia will be able to suggest somewhere to us.'

'Good idea.' Archie lifted her hand to his mouth and kissed it.

'I'm going to look for a doctor to speak to,' Louis said. 'I want an estimate as to when they think you'll be fit enough to travel home. And what treatment you're going to need when you get there. I won't be long.'

Phoebe didn't take her eyes off Archie as Louis walked

away. 'I love you so much, Archie,' she said, honestly thinking herself incapable of loving anyone more than she loved him now. 'But I don't want you to feel cornered. We'll do as Louis suggests and leave this for another day. Right now I just want to enjoy being here with you.'

'I still can't believe you're here by my bed,' he said quietly. 'The whole time I was captured, it was thinking of being with you again that kept me going.'

'I wondered what had happened to you. Captured, you say?'

'I was. I escaped along with two other blokes.' His eyes lowered. 'We thought we were lucky at the time, but it turns out that if we hadn't escaped when we did, we might have got home earlier.' His voice cracked with emotion. 'And all three of us could have made it rather than just me.'

'Why? What happened?' Phoebe asked, grateful that he was here at all.

'We were fired at as we escaped, and the two others were shot. One died instantly and the other of his wounds a few days later. I was recaptured eventually but was ill with an infection, and it took a while for them to figure out who I was so they could send me back.'

She stroked his cheek. 'You're here now.'

'I am, and I can't help feeling guilty for still having my life when theirs ended.'

'Well then, you'll have to enjoy your life as much as you can, Archie. For them as well as for yourself.' She hoped he would think about what she had said, but didn't want to press the point too much. 'I do love you, Archie.'

# FIFTY-ONE

# Celia

After giving Phoebe and Louis a couple of suggestions for cheap hotels where they might stay for a few nights, Celia left them and returned to her rooms, exhausted from emotion and being on her feet all day.

The following afternoon Celia arrived at the hospital for her shift and discovered that Archie wasn't the one causing concern anymore.

'What do you mean, my sister's been admitted?' she gasped, instinctively knowing that her worst nightmare was happening. Why had she not done as Archie insisted and persuaded Phoebe to remain in Cornwall?

'I'm sorry, Nurse Robertson,' the nurse said. 'Miss Robertson seemed fine first thing today, then collapsed at Captain Bailey's bedside when she was visiting him this afternoon.'

'Which ward is she in now?'

Without waiting to find out her own orders for her shift, Celia rushed to the next floor up to go to the ward where her sister had been admitted.

She neared the door of the ward and spotted Louis pacing outside in the corridor. 'What are you doing up here?' she snapped. 'You must leave. Now.'

'I need to know she's going to be all right,' he said, a wildness about his eyes.

Celia went to argue with him, then thought better of it. 'You can't know that, not yet,' she said quietly, staring at him as his eyes locked with hers. 'I know what happened between you.'

His mouth opened in dismay. 'What are you talking about?'

'She told me, about the kiss.'

'Why would she do that?' he looked horrified.

'Because we're very close and she felt guilty,' she explained. 'Phoebe needed to share it with someone, and apart from you I haven't, nor will I ever, share it with another soul.'

'Thank you.' He closed his eyes briefly. 'It was a moment of madness and I hate myself for confusing her like I did.'

'You're going to have to find a way to forgive yourself,' Celia said, resting her hand on his arm. 'For both your sakes, and Archie's.'

'I know.'

'Right now my biggest concern is my sister,' Celia soothed. 'I need to do my best to ensure she recovers from this dreadful virus. You being here will only put you and, in turn, Archie at risk. I think he has more than enough to contend with, don't you think?' Celia asked, not wishing to be unkind but aware that if her sister had been admitted, then she would be fighting for her life. She couldn't let Phoebe die, especially not when she had only just been reunited with Archie.

Louis lowered his head and covered his face with his hands. 'He can't come back to us, only to lose her to this. Archie would give up if he lost Phoebe now.' Louis lifted his gaze and settled it on Celia.

She struggled to think how to respond. 'Listen, you really must go. I promise I'll keep you and Archie informed about her progress and I will do everything in my power to make sure she's fine. But I need to go to her now. You go back to your brother. Wash your hands before you go through and wear one of these masks. I can't have you taking anything back into a ward of sick men.'

She took two masks from the container by the door and handed one to him, tying her own behind her head. 'Go, Louis. Now.'

He nodded. 'Thank you,' he said, looking desolate. She closed her eyes to steady herself. Then, pushing open the ward door, she walked in and scanned the room, finding her sister almost immediately when one of the doctors pulled back a screen and left her bedside.

'How's she doing, Doctor?'

He shook his head slowly. 'It's not looking good, I'm afraid.'

Celia swallowed the lump in her throat. *Damn it*. No virus was going to take away her only remaining relative, not if she had anything to do with it.

---

Over the following three days Celia only left her sister's bedside to return to her room to shower, change and catch several hours' sleep. Mostly she slept in a chair by her sister's bed, determined not to leave her side until she was recovered.

'Come on, Phoebe,' she whispered to her sister for the hundredth time. 'You've got to fight this. Archie's downstairs and he needs you now more than ever.'

Sister came in and threatened to have her forcibly removed

from the hospital if she didn't leave willingly, but Celia told her that was not going to happen. So what if she lost her job, she decided. Her sister's life was worth more to her than anything else.

Finally on the fourth day, after falling asleep on the chair next to her sister's bed, Celia was woken by Phoebe's hand twitching as she held it. She immediately sat upright and stared at her, aware that if she didn't get a decent night's rest soon, then she ran the risk of falling ill herself.

The blue pallor had vanished and although her sister had a long way to go until Celia could cheerfully say that she had colour in her cheeks, she knew that Phoebe had pulled through the worst of it. She was going to be all right.

## FIFTY-TWO

## Phoebe

Phoebe struggled to wake and as she opened her eyes she saw her sister sitting next to her bed, wearing a white mask over her nose and mouth. Celia had tears running down her cheeks and it took a moment for Phoebe to work out why.

'I collapsed,' she murmured. Her stomach clenched in fear. 'I have the flu?' She felt the pressure of her sister's hands over hers.

'You have,' Celia said, clearing her throat. 'But you're going to be fine now.'

Phoebe remembered she had been visiting Archie when everything went black. 'Archie?' She hardly dared ask, but needed to know immediately if he was well or not.

'He's exactly as you left him four days ago,' Celia assured her. 'He's been panic-stricken since you collapsed, though, and desperate for constant updates about your well-being. He's going to be enormously relieved to hear you're on the mend.'

Phoebe took the deepest breath she could manage. 'You've been here nursing me all the time, haven't you?' She didn't know why she was asking the question. Phoebe knew Celia

344

would refuse to leave her unless she had no choice, and would have done exactly the same thing if it was her sister lying in this bed.

'Of course I have. I couldn't let anyone else care for you, not when I knew I have so much experience of this damned virus.'

Phoebe tried to swallow and groaned, realising that her throat felt like sandpaper had been used against it. 'Thirsty.'

Celia poured her half a glass of water and helped her sit up slightly to drink it.

'Slowly,' she insisted, removing the glass from Phoebe's lips when she was tempted to drink too fast and ended up coughing.

'You always were bossy,' Phoebe said when she had finished and Celia had wiped her mouth. Then she settled her back against her pillow once more.

'It's for your own good.'

Phoebe knew her sister was trying to be amusing and was grateful, but most of all she was relieved to hear that Archie hadn't caught the virus. With the state of his health, she wasn't sure he had enough strength to survive, and she couldn't bear to be without him now that she had found him again.

'When will I be able to see Archie safely?'

Celia gave her question some thought. 'Probably in a week or two. It's up to the doctor. You're both going to have to be patient.'

'If it keeps him from catching this, I'll wait as long as necessary.'

Two weeks later Phoebe was discharged from the hospital. She couldn't wait to be reunited with Archie again. She arrived at the door to his ward and saw he was watching out for her, waiting. He caught her eye and they smiled at each other. He had begun to put on a little weight but not as much as he needed. Then again, she suspected he had been fretting about her and unable to eat as much as he should have been. His eyes didn't appear to be quite as hollow as she remembered but he was still pale.

'You're finally here,' he said, reaching out to take her hand. 'I've been so worried about you, my darling.'

Phoebe leaned forward and kissed him, relishing the pressure of his lips on hers once again. 'I'm fine now, Archie,' she soothed. 'And I don't care what you say, I'm never leaving you again.'

'Apart from the necessary.' He laughed. 'Louis has booked you a room at the hotel and the doctor said I can be discharged in the next few days.'

'Hello, there.'

Phoebe heard Louis's voice and turned to smile at him. 'Hello. I hope he's been behaving while I was away.'

Louis frowned and looked at his brother thoughtfully before smiling at her and shaking his head. 'Not really. But he was fretting about you, so I'll allow him to misbehave just this once.' He grinned at Archie. 'Have you told her yet?'

'Told me what?' she asked, intrigued.

Archie raised his eyebrows. 'Louis and I have been planning something.'

'You have?' What had they been up to, she wondered.

Archie nodded, a twinkle in his dark eyes that she was happy to see. He truly was getting better.

'Tell me.'

'Louis kindly applied for a special marriage licence for us,' Archie explained. 'If you're still happy to marry me, that is?'

'You know the answer perfectly well.' She looked up at Louis. 'When is it for?'

'Friday.'

'This Friday?' She gazed at Archie in surprise, thrilled to think that in three days' time she would be his wife. 'But I have nothing prepared.'

'Your sister has bought you a dress and some shoes. Louis found me a suit and we're being married in the hospital chapel by the chaplain as a special favour.'

She gasped. Was this really happening? 'Special favour to whom?'

'Me,' Louis said. 'We were at college together. I persuaded him that it was the decent thing to do if you were going to travel to Sandsend the following day and live in the same house as Archie.'

'You did that?' She caught the happiness in Archie's face and smiled. 'Good. I'm glad.'

Archie gave her hand a gentle squeeze. 'I'm so relieved. I wasn't sure if you were hoping for a big church wedding.'

Phoebe shook her head. 'Who would I have invited? Apart from Jocasta and your sister and her husband, but it's too far for Jocasta and not the best idea for your sister, as we know. I'll have everyone else who's most important to me there.'

She heard Louis clear his throat and glanced at him, noticing him struggling with his emotions. 'Are you all right?'

He took a deep breath. 'I think all this worry about Archie and then you has exhausted me. I'm not usually this emotional.'

'I think we're all struggling a bit,' Archie said kindly.

'I certainly am,' Phoebe agreed.

Louis made an excuse to leave them in peace and Phoebe pulled up a chair and sat down. 'Why did you really change your mind? I thought you were adamant that we shouldn't marry, but now you've arranged a wedding?'

'You know me too well.' Archie smiled. 'Nearly losing you was like a slap in the face and made me see how ridiculous I was being about my hand.'

'You have every right to be upset about that.'

He shook his head. 'Not when it was put into the context of a life without you,' he argued, raising his bandaged hand and resting it momentarily on her cheek. 'I love you with all my heart. I don't care what I do as a job. I know we'll work this out together somehow. I wanted us to be married as soon as possible so that we could begin our married life in Sandsend, just in time for our first Christmas together.'

Phoebe loved that idea. 'The perfect Christmas present,' she said, leaning forward and kissing him.

## FIFTY-THREE

# Celia

## MID-DECEMBER 1918

The range of emotions Celia had experienced watching her sister marry the love of her life both thrilled and drained her. She couldn't take her mind off Otto, yearning to see him again even for a few minutes. It had been so long since she had held his hand, or kissed him. Not that they had kissed often, when there had always been someone – either guard or prisoner – around.

Phoebe looked happier than Celia could ever remember her being. She and Archie were clearly besotted with each other and Louis seemed as happy to see them both reunited as she had been. It was strange to think that she now had a brother-in-law, but a relief to know that her sister had a husband to love her. She suspected Phoebe would benefit from having someone to care for, now that she was no longer working.

Celia left them together and walked away, needing a little time to herself to gather her thoughts. She sighed and sat on a bench near one of the flower borders in the nearby park.

She hadn't been alone for very long when Louis walked over to her. 'I hope you don't mind me joining you?'

She didn't like to appear rude, so smiled and motioned for him to take a seat next to her. 'It's a little cold out here, but it helps to clear my head.'

'Mine too,' he said, sitting down. 'I was intending to join you for a walk and went to follow you, but lost you for a bit.' He peered at her. 'Please do say if you'd rather be alone. I really would understand.'

She shook her head. 'It's fine, truly.' When he smiled, she added, 'It must be wonderful for you to see your brother happy, after thinking you'd lost him.'

'It is. He's a good chap, Archie.' He rubbed his hands together, presumably to warm them slightly in the cold. 'He loves your sister very much.'

Celia nodded. 'I can see that. I'm so relieved Phoebe has him back. So many others aren't in such a lucky position.'

Louis didn't speak for a moment and it occurred to Celia that she might have hit a nerve. 'I'm sorry.'

'What for?' He seemed genuinely surprised.

'I, er, don't know you well enough to know whether you've lost a special someone.'

He shook his head. 'No, not now my brother's come back to us. I'm one of the lucky ones.' He narrowed his eyes and studied her for a moment. 'You?'

Celia shrugged. 'I haven't lost anyone other than my parents and brother to the war, if that's what you mean.'

'But you have lost someone. I can see a sadness in your eyes. You can talk to me about it, if you need someone to share your burden with, you know.'

'Thank you,' she said, grateful to him for his kindness. 'But that's not necessary.' She liked Louis and could see how kind he was, but worried that it was far too soon to start admitting to a British soldier that she had fallen in love with an enemy officer.

'I'll leave you to it then,' he said, rising and giving her a slight nod before walking away.

She really couldn't be happier for Phoebe that she had found happiness, and with a man as adoring as Archie, too, but seeing her sister so in love made what she was missing with Otto even more painful. When would they have a chance to be together? They had assumed their time would come after the war had ended, but still he was being held in that camp.

She stood and walked back the way she'd come. By the time she reached the hospital entrance, Celia felt a little calmer. She had to trust that she and Otto would find their way to be together somehow. She just needed to keep working and wait for their time to come.

———

The following morning Celia waited for the doctor to complete his rounds before going to Archie's ward, finding that he was in the midst of being discharged.

'I'm so pleased,' she said, seeing him buttoning the suit jacket that he had worn for his wedding the day before. Celia laughed. 'You didn't waste any time dressing, I notice.'

He smoothed down his hair and exhaled sharply. 'I've had enough of hospitals. I'm impatient to head home with my darling wife.' He took Celia's hand in his for a moment. 'I know Phoebe is your sister, but even so, I wanted to thank you for all you've done for her, and for me. I don't know how I would have coped if...'

Celia didn't want him upsetting himself by focusing on something that hadn't happened. 'Let's not think about it.

Phoebe is well, you're healing more each day. By tomorrow morning you'll be starting your new life back in Sandsend.'

He smiled and nodded. 'We will. I hope she likes it there.'

'She wouldn't be going back with you if she didn't,' Celia teased, aware that her sister would live anywhere with Archie, she loved him so much. 'Now, if you have everything you need, I'll accompany you down to meet your wife and brother.'

Celia saw her sister's eager expression as she stood clasping her handbag in both hands next to Louis as they waited for Archie's arrival in the reception area of the hospital. She and Archie descended the last couple of steps and Phoebe's right hand flew to her chest and rested there as she beamed at him before running forward to join him.

'I can't believe you're downstairs already.' Phoebe kissed him lightly on his smiling mouth and Celia felt emotion wash over her to see the couple so much in love. 'He was dressed before the doctor had left the ward,' Celia joked.

Phoebe reached out and put her arm around Celia, pulling her into a hug. Celia hated saying goodbye to her sister. They had spent so much time apart in the last few years, and here they were again, preparing to part. At least they still had each other. She slipped her arms around Phoebe's waist and held her sister close.

'I'm going to miss you so much,' she admitted. 'But I know you two are going to be very happy together.'

'Thank you for everything, Celia.'

'Don't be silly. You would have done the same for me.'

'I would.'

Celia could feel her throat constricting with emotion. She needed to see her sister away from the hospital before she made a fool of herself and cried.

'You two ...' she sent an apologetic smile in Louis's

direction, '… sorry, you three had better leave. You don't want to miss your train.' She had no idea what time their train was due to leave, but it was the perfect reason to use to persuade them to hurry along.

'You must come and stay, the first opportunity you get.' Archie smiled.

Celia had no intention of disturbing the first couple of months of their married life. 'Maybe not the first chance.' She laughed. 'But I'll definitely come and see you soon.'

She watched the three of them leave, wondering what might happen to Louis. He had seemed happier today, she thought. Celia wondered if he could possibly have met someone, considering he had been at the hospital so much of the time while in London. *Oh well*, she mused, *as long as he's happy.*

## FIFTY-FOUR

## Phoebe

'What do you mean, you're not coming back with us to Sandsend?' Archie asked as they waited on the platform for their train to arrive.

'It's your honeymoon,' Louis argued, giving a shrug. 'What sort of man imposes himself on his brother and new sister-in-law?'

Phoebe was grateful to Louis for his consideration. 'Where will you go?'

'I had planned to look for work somewhere new, but haven't decided where that might be yet.'

She sensed he was keeping something to himself and was happy to leave him with his plans.

'But where will you go if not with us?'

Phoebe wished that Archie would stop pressing his brother but knew it wasn't for her to question anything that happened between them.

'Cornwall.'

Phoebe glanced at Archie, surprised. 'Cornwall?' She was starting to sense that she might have missed something important. She tilted her head to one side. 'Whereabouts exactly?'

Louis grinned at her. 'There's this little village called Pennwalloe. I thought I might pop in to see a mutual friend of ours and tell her all about your wedding.'

Phoebe gasped, delighted to think that he might have feelings for Jocasta. They would make a wonderful couple. Both were kind and thoughtful.

'It's fine,' he said, smiling at her.

'What is?' Archie looked confused. 'I'm clearly missing something here.'

Louis handed Archie two train tickets for him and Phoebe. 'When I went to Cornwall to tell Phoebe about you being found, I met Jocasta Chambers.' He turned his attention to Phoebe. 'We've been corresponding ever since.'

'You have?' She who excited for Jocasta but slightly concerned that Louis might not understand the depth of Jocasta's grief.

'Don't worry,' he said. 'I'm aware how much she misses her husband. I'll take good care not to overstep any boundaries.'

'I know you will,' Phoebe said, reassured. 'Was she surprised when you first wrote to her?'

'Before we left her house, when you were upstairs packing, she asked me to keep in touch and let her know how things were with Archie, and how you were coping. Our friendship grew from there.'

'You're developing feelings for Phoebe's friend?' Archie asked, catching up with the conversation.

Louis grinned. 'She's a caring lady and we could both do with a friend.'

Phoebe beamed at Louis, thrilled for him. 'She is the best

friend I could have asked for, and I know she thought you very handsome.'

He looked delighted. 'She said that?'

'She was terribly welcoming to me when I went to Cornwall in the New Year so unexpectedly,' Archie interjected.

Phoebe nodded. 'She was.' She gazed at Archie and kissed him. 'She has very good taste.'

'I'm glad you think so,' Archie said, slipping his arm around her waist and pulling her to his side. 'Then I wish you both all the luck in the world, Louis.'

'Here's our train,' Phoebe said. They were only going to be sharing the carriage with Louis for the first few stops, then she presumed he would part ways with them to make his way west while they continued northwards. 'I have such a good feeling about all of us,' she said, sensing that everything was working out exactly as it should do.

'So do I, Mrs Bailey,' Archie agreed, opening the train door and taking her hand to help her inside.

## FIFTY-FIVE

## Celia

I t had been a week since Celia had bid farewell to her sister and Archie, when she received a letter from Phoebe who rapturously extolled both Archie and Sandsend's virtues. Clearly Phoebe was blissfully happy in her marriage and Celia felt much lighter to know that she no longer had to worry about her. She was the only family left to her, and with Phoebe happily ensconced in her new home, any responsibility that weighed on her shoulders had now seemed to vanish.

Celia was beginning to feel a little lost and unsure what to do or where to go next.

There was a knock on her bedroom door. 'Letter for you, Celia.'

Thanking the trainee nurse, she took the letter and went to sit on her bed to read it. She looked at the envelope and vaguely recognised the writing. Opening it, she took out the slip of paper and saw that it was from Elsie. Celia's mood dipped and she felt the familiar irritation when thinking about the woman who had been so vile to her and Otto. Her instinct was to scrunch up the sheet of paper and burn it, but something stopped her. Maybe there was news of Otto? She couldn't risk missing something important.

She began to read.

*Celia,*

*I hope my letter finds you well. I am smiling and imagining your reaction seeing this but want you to know that I write to you in apology. I am truly sorry for my unforgivable actions.*

Celia groaned. What could have happened to change her ex-colleague's feelings? Celia took a deep breath and read on, unable to rid herself of her suspicion that this letter held an ulterior motive.

*I deserve any ill will you hold towards me. The reason for my feelings changing are simply that I had the good fortune to work with Doctor Hoffman (yes, that is how I now think of him) these past few months in the isolation hospital in the camp. I had no idea he was a doctor, not that his profession should make a jot of difference, and I admit that getting to know him better has brought about a respect for him that I hadn't imagined possible before. In fact, I have found myself reconsidering my feelings towards the prisoners. Prior to this I thought of them as 'The Enemy'. Nothing more, nothing less. All they deserved from me, I believed, was my contempt and, as you well know, that is all they received.*

*I am now ashamed to think of my behaviour and wish to make what amends I possibly can. It is for this reason that I am writing to you. I should not be sharing this information but hope that in doing so you will believe the depth of my regret.*

*The prisoners are being repatriated to Germany. Some have already left but Doctor Hoffman will be one of a group stopping at Victoria Station in two days' time. They will be at Platform 6 at*

*noon and will have a waiting time of approximately thirty minutes*
*before their next train is due. Should you wish to see him, I will not*
*stand in your way.*

Celia gasped. Two days? She glanced at the date and saw
that was tomorrow. Thank heavens the letter hadn't been
delayed. She could barely believe that she would see her
beloved Otto again, and so soon.

Without a second's delay Celia left her room and rushed to
Matron's office to request the day off. 'I have an urgent family
issue to which I must attend,' she said, reasoning that Otto
would hopefully one day be her family and that her request
wasn't too far-fetched. 'I'm sorry for the lateness in my request,
but I was hoping you would be able to give me permission to
take a day's leave earlier than I had imagined.'

'How early?' Matron didn't look up from making her notes.
'Tomorrow.'

Matron glanced up and then considered her words before
nodding. 'Yes. You've worked tirelessly over these past
months, Nurse Robertson, and like most of my nurses, have
time owing to you. Take tomorrow and I hope that whatever
you are dealing with, it works out for the best.'

She thanked Matron and returned to her room to finish
reading Elsie's letter.

*The men will only be allowed to disembark to be led immediately to*
*their next train on Platform 3 leaving for Dover. I shall be travelling*
*with them as far as that and will then go my own way. If I do see*
*you, I should like to apologise in person.*

*If I do not, then I hope you find it within you to forgive my*
*previous actions.*

*Yours faithfully,*

*Elsie Baker (Miss)*

---

Celia was waiting at Platform 6 two hours earlier than she needed to be. She knew it was probably ridiculous but found comfort knowing she would be ready and waiting when Otto's train arrived. She hoped to be able to see him when he got off the train and follow discreetly to Platform 3 where she would also board. She had no idea what she would do after that but would decide when the time was right.

Several porters stopped to ask her if she needed any assistance. She thanked them and said that she was waiting for a friend to arrive and had got the time wrong. She pushed her hand into her coat pocket and felt the smoothness of her train ticket to Dover.

Her heart raced as she watched the train slow to a halt. *Otto is on that train.* She took a steadying breath, hoping he would see her and that she didn't lose him between this train and the next. The doors opened and passengers rushed to be on their way, but although she waited, Celia didn't see a group of men she thought might be the POWs. She certainly hadn't seen Otto anywhere.

Then, when the platform was fairly clear, two doors in a rear carriage opened and several guards, two nurses, one of whom she realised was Elsie, and approximately fifteen to twenty men stepped off the train and began walking in pairs along the platform.

Elsie saw her and glanced over her shoulder, as if to tell Celia to look behind her. Celia acknowledged her subtle message with a nod. She held her breath as she scanned each man, looking for Otto.

Then she saw him.

She stared at him, willing him to sense her presence, and seconds later he did. His step faltered and the man behind him gave him a light push, and smiling, Otto began walking again.

She saw him mouth her name and she mouthed *I love you* in reply.

As he passed her she whispered, 'Meet me on the train.'

He looked stunned to hear what she had said but kept walking. She waited until they were off the platform to follow at a safe distance. Then keeping watch, she made sure she sat in the next carriage to theirs, facing the rear of the train, so that she had the best view of the lavatory door between his carriage and the one she was occupying. She had to trust that Otto would ask to use the bathroom at some point, giving her the opportunity to meet him.

Celia could think of no other way to spend some time with him. She trusted Elsie to keep to her word and help Otto not to be followed by one of the guards. It was all rather wishy-washy but there was little else Celia could hope for.

She was grateful the train was fairly empty and that she was in a carriage alone. She kept the carriage door slightly ajar in order to hear the door opening further down, and about an hour into the journey she heard the door in Otto's cabin open and waited to see who came out.

'Otto,' she whispered, her heart racing as he looked around him and then, not seeing her, went to the lavatory and closed the door. Aware they had little time to waste, Celia immediately made her way to the same lavatory and knocked once before opening the door and stepping inside, immediately closing the door behind her and locking it.

'*Meine Liebste.*'

She leaned against the door, staring at him, unable to believe they were finally together. 'Otto.'

With one step he took her in his arms and held her against him, his lips finding hers. Celia's thoughts and worries vanished as his kiss sent sensations coursing through her body. She heard him groan and clung onto him, not wishing the moment to end but aware that it had to.

'*Meine Engel*,' he whispered. 'I could not believe my eyes when I saw you waiting. And now you are here.' He kissed her again. His mouth then moved to kiss her mouth, her eyes, her neck. 'I cannot bear to leave you again.'

'I know.' Celia realised she needed to be strong for both of them. 'I had to come.'

'But how did you know?'

She stared into his bright-blue eyes and, taking her hands from around his waist, placed them either side of his face, remembering that she needed to take in every inch of it, to savour it until she was able to stare into his beautiful eyes once more. 'Elsie wrote and told me.'

'Elsie?' He frowned in confusion. 'Ah, Sister Baker. She is a strange woman. I do not understand her.'

'Neither do I,' Celia admitted. 'We don't have time to waste talking about her, except to say she wrote and told me she was sorry for everything she did and wanted to make up for it.'

'That is surprising, but good.'

'It is.' She kissed him again, wishing they could have more than stolen moments together. 'We need to make a plan. They might wonder where you've got to and come looking for you.'

His face was etched with pain and she saw that he was as unwilling to part from her as she from him.

'I will remain at King's College Hospital for as long as it takes for us to make plans.'

'Yes. I shall write to you there once I know where I will be. Or when I am at my family home. Then we find a way to reunite.'

Celia smiled, aware it wasn't reaching her eyes but desperate to do her best, for she wanted his last look of her to be one where she was smiling. 'It won't be long now, Otto,' she insisted, hoping she was right. 'We've done the difficult bit and you survived.'

'We both survived,' he whispered, taking her face in his hands and kissing her longingly. 'I love you with all my heart, Celia.'

Someone banged heavily on the door and Celia shrieked in fright, relieved when Otto covered her mouth to stifle the sound. 'Oi, what you doin' in there?'

'I will be one minute longer,' Otto said, not taking his eyes from hers. 'I must wash my hands.'

'No dawdling. You've been too long already.'

'Yes, Officer. One moment more.' Turning back to Celia, he whispered, 'I will go out first. Then you follow when he accompanies me back to the carriage.'

'I love you,' she whispered as he pulled her to him and gave her a last passionate kiss.

The officer banged on the door impatiently. 'I am coming now,' Otto shouted, his impatience with the man barely concealed.

He gave her a smile. 'I will write to you as soon as I can.'

Panicked that he was leaving but aware he had no choice, Celia wanted something to hold onto. 'Where will we meet up?'

He frowned thoughtfully before smiling. 'Switzerland. We will reunite in Lucerne.'

'Perfect,' she said, standing on tiptoes to kiss him one last time as he reached for the door handle.

'Until we meet again in Lucerne.'

'It won't be long to wait now,' he assured her as he opened the door and walked out to join the grumbling guard, closing the door quietly behind him.

Celia leaned against the door and touched her lips where his had been moments before. 'Yes, Otto,' she murmured. 'Not long now.'

# Acknowledgments

My thanks first and foremost must go to my wonderfully supportive editor, Publishing Director Charlotte Ledger and to her brilliant team at One More Chapter. Their encouragement and belief in me and my books helps give me the confidence to write these stories.

To my fabulous sister-in-law, Sabine Troy for her friendship over the past three decades and for her help translating Otto's words into German. Any mistakes are mine alone.

Thanks also to editors, Simon Fox and Dushi Horti for their suggestions and edits for this book.

As usual I'd like to thank my husband Rob, children, James and Saskia for their continued support and for making me laugh each day.

To my wonderful author friends and to the brilliant blogger/reviewer community for all your support and encouragement, I couldn't do this without you.

And finally, to you dear reader, for choosing to read *The Poppy Sisters*. I hope you enjoy getting to know Phoebe and Celia as much as I loved writing about them.

Dear Reader,

Thank you for choosing to read *The Poppy Sisters*, I hope you enjoyed getting to know sisters, Phoebe and Celia and spending time in their lives.

As with all my books, I love setting them at least partly in Jersey, in the Channel Islands where I live. In *The Poppy Sisters*, Otto is captured and sent to Les Blanches Banques, a prisoner of war camp on the island housing almost 2,000 German prisoners of war from 1915-1917. The camp no longer exists but if you go down to St Ouen's bay and look across the road from Le Braye café car park towards the base of the sand dunes you might see the footprint of some of the huts covering approximately 300 square yards along the road. There are the concrete bases for some of the buildings including, I believe, the latrines and concrete stones for the cookhouse base.

There were around forty huts each housing thirty men. It seems that the men were well treated and catered for and even had electric lighting. There was also electric fencing around the camp but that didn't stop escape attempts with the prisoners tunnelling out. Several prisoners escaped this way but being imprisoned on an island they had little chance of finding a way off it. As far as I'm aware all the escapees were caught and returned to the prison camp. The last prisoner left the camp in 1919. One of those prisoners, a senior NCO returned to Jersey during the Second World War as a Commandant during the Occupation. Apparently he didn't seem to hold his previous detention on the island against the locals, which must have been a relief.

I like my books to be as true to life as possible but needed to use a bit of artistic licence in parts of the book. One of these times was having Celia as a nurse at Les Blanches Banques camp. In the book she was sent to nurse sick prisoners in the camp hospital. There was a hospital although women were prohibited from being anywhere near the camp and I don't know for certain if nurses were actually allowed to work at the hospital.

When a prisoner died the camp the commander did agree that his body could be taken on a carriage from St Peter's Barracks to the parish church with a number of his colleagues allowed to form a cortege. It must have seemed very strange to locals a lot of whom lined the route to watch these prisoners of war walking past in a final mark of respect. This actually happened in August 1915 when a young sailor died. In this book the same thing happens but it was in January 1917.

Artistic licence has also been used when naming the Cornish village where Jocasta lives. I have given my imaginary village on the south west peninsular the name Pennwalloe. You won't find it on any map but it's an amalgamation of various villages on the Lizard Peninsular and my imagination.

Otto could have been sent to a POW camp in Surrey and would have been put out to work on local farms when he was well enough. There were many POW camps in Britain, however, although the one used in my book is based on a camp in the same area, the real Frith Hill Prisoner-of-War Camp in Surrey was actually a tented camp that originally had German civilians housed in it. It moved several times and then re-opened in 1916. Most POWs there were brought from the camp at Eastcot in Northampsonshire to build a light railway connecting Pirbright Camp to Blackdown and Deepcut. This was completed in March 1917 and closed. By March 1918 there were two camps, one for German prisoners and another for Austrians and other nationalities.

I have loved writing this book and returning to the First World War once again. I hope you enjoyed getting to know Phoebe and Celia, and if you wish to keep up to date with new books and other writing news please feel free to subscribe to my monthly newsletter here: https://deborahcarr.org/newsletter/

Thank you again for choosing to read *The Poppy Sisters*.

Best wishes,
Deborah

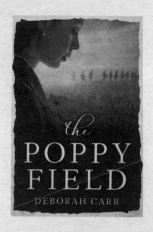

**Don't miss *The Poppy Field*, another epic historical novel by Deborah Carr...**

Young nurse Gemma is struggling with the traumas she has witnessed through her job. Needing to escape from it all, Gemma agrees to help renovate a rundown farmhouse in Doullens, France, a town near the Somme. There, in a boarded-up cupboard, wrapped in old newspapers, is a tin that reveals the secret letters and heartache of Alice Le Breton, a young volunteer nurse who worked in a casualty clearing station near the front line.

Set in the present day and during the horrifying years of the war, both women discover deep down the strength and courage to carry on in even the most difficult of times. Through Alice's words and her unfailing love for her sweetheart at the front, Gemma learns to truly live again.

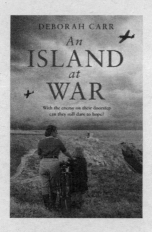

### June 1940

While her little sister Rosie is sent to the UK to keep her safe from the invading German army, Estelle Le Maistre is left behind on Jersey to help her grandmother run the family farm. When the Germans occupy the island, everything changes and Estelle and the islanders must face the reality of life under Nazi rule.

Interspersed with diary entries from Rosie back on the mainland, the novel is also inspired by real life stories from the author's own family who were both on the island during the occupation and in London during the Blitz and is a true testament to the courage and bravery of the islanders.

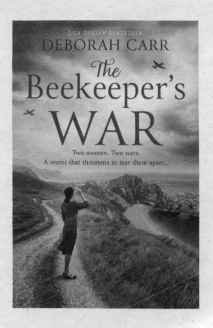

**1916**

At the onset of war, Nurse Pru le Cuirot left her home in Jersey
to care for injured soldiers at Ashbury Manor, Dorset. She
wanted to do her bit but she never expected to meet American
pilot, Jack Garland, so unlike any man she has ever met.

**1940**

Another lifetime, but another war and Pru's daughter Emma
comes to Ashbury Manor. As Jersey falls to the Germans,
Emma is fearful for her mother back home. And when she
meets the mysterious beekeeper who lives in the grounds of
the manor she finds herself caught up in a web of lies. As past
and present collide, will the secrets of her mother's life finally
be resolved?

YOUR NUMBER ONE STOP

# ONE MORE CHAPTER

FOR PAGETURNING BOOKS

One More Chapter is an
award-winning global
division of HarperCollins.

Sign up to our newsletter to get our
latest eBook deals and stay up to date
with our weekly Book Club!
<u>Subscribe here.</u>

Meet the team at
<u>www.onemorechapter.com</u>

Follow us!
@OneMoreChapter_
@OneMoreChapter
@<u>onemorechapterhc</u>

Do you write unputdownable fiction?
We love to hear from new voices.
Find out how to submit your novel at
<u>www.onemorechapter.com/submissions</u>